The Path to Phillips Cay

The Path to Phillips Cay

Francis Nash

First published in 2021 by whitefox

Copyright © Francis Nash 2021

ISBN 9781913532529

Also available in paperback, ebook and audiobook
ISBNs 9781913532536, 9781913532543, 9781913532697

Typeset by seagulls.net
Cover design by Arneaux
Project management by whitefox
Copy edited by Monica Byles

Printed and bound in Great Britain by CPI Group (UK) Ltd,
Croydon, CR0 4YY

To
Peggy Nash (1925–2017)
who created her own world built on love.

The old ways will not die
and the new cannot be born;
we are in an interregnum
when a great diversity of
morbid symptoms will emerge.

Antonio Gramsci 1930

'What was that? Where am I?'

Lianne's hand jerked back as it touched the glass surface just above her. Breathing fast, she lay still, eyes closed.

*It's okay, calm down ... What did he call it? 'Quiet and cosy',
wasn't it?* 'More like quiet and claustrophobic,' she mumbled, slowly stretching out across the bed which filled the matchbox-shaped room.

Picking up the remote control beside her, she pointed it at the screen embedded in the ceiling. Flicking through several channels, she came to a road map, in the centre of which a blue dot was slowly moving from right to left.

*He said 'south' but we've gone west – why in God's name has
he done that?*

Resting back, she closed her eyes again. *Still spinning
that coin, Grady, with 'need-to-know' on one side and 'no-
surprise' on the other? Elizabeth got it right on the voyage – 'a
man who confuses control with protection'. I wonder how she
and Methuen are doing on Phillips? Why didn't we stay there?
Wasn't he as frightened as me of heading north – even before
The Incident?*

She aimed the controller at one of four wall-mounted monitors at the end of the bed. Selecting *Internal*, she watched as the screen filled with multiple views. Enlarging one labelled UPPER DECK DRIVING CABIN, she stared at a man dressed in a cowhide jacket and jeans, bent over a corner desk with a steering wheel folded up beside him.

*He's not changed out of those woodsman's clothes since he
bought them in Bismarck on the day we arrived.*

She zoomed in on the man's bearded face and straggly hair.

Where's the well-groomed businessman I've known for the past thirty years – a man who always kept a sharp crease in his trousers? 'Will the real Nick O'Grady please reveal himself?' she muttered loudly.

'You're awake,' the man said a little wearily, his face filling the screen. 'Come and join me – the sun's just coming up.'

'Why didn't you come to bed? What's the point of a self-drive if you spend the whole night next to the steering wheel?' she yelled at the monitor as she slid back the metre-high door of the bedroom and swung her feet into the adjoining stairwell.

Crawling up the uncarpeted stairs and raising the hatch door, Lianne felt the same tingle of excitement she had experienced three weeks earlier when he had first shown her around the vehicle. Back then, she had barely registered the absence of windows or doors, just the sheer size of the upper space. In contrast to the cramped lower deck, the low-ceilinged bedroom and the narrow stairwell, upstairs she had been able to stand upright in a well-equipped kitchen, small lounge and bathroom, while at the far end of the space, two black leather seats faced an array of electronics and monitors. *More like the cockpit of a plane than the driving cabin of a road vehicle*, she recalled thinking.

'Coffee?' he asked cheerfully, swivelling around to face her.

Lianne smiled gratefully, settling into the other seat and looking over at the monitors surrounding him.

'Have you had those up all night?' she asked, nodding at the images of five airborne objects.

'Pretty much,' he replied, walking through to the kitchen. 'They can detect the slightest movement on the ground, even at night. "Better than an eagle with the sun behind it" is the manufacturer's claim.'

'Why didn't you test them out in Bismarck – we were there long enough?'

'You're joking,' he snorted, pouring water into a percolator. 'The curfew and other restrictions on the ground applied just as much to anything in the air. The mayor and his buddies were under strict orders from this new government to prevent any filming of refugees flooding in from The Incident out west. That's why they shoved them all down to Sibley Park at the edge of the city, where the world's press couldn't see a superstate in distress.'

Is that how he copes with it all – categorising every last detail and then fitting it into Methuen's global model to reduce its emotional impact on him? Wish I could do that ... 'So is this the American Superstate finally adapting to Methuen's Time of Less?'

Nick put down the cups he'd taken from the cupboard and stared back at her. 'You would never have asked me that type of question before The Incident,' he said with faint amusement.

And you would never have noticed my comment, she thought.

'Like everywhere else, we've been transitioning into this Segmented World for decades. It's just that The Incident has given this country a window on what things may be like in the future – unless we start cooperating a whole lot more.'

She felt an urge to reply but stopped herself as the image of a drone approaching the vehicle caused Nick to rush over and grab the joystick on his desk. As he steered the object back onto the roof, she looked over at the front camera screen, which showed an empty road disappearing into the distance with flat farmland on either side.

After several minutes with Nick preoccupied with landing the remainder of his small squadron, Lianne spotted the image of a tractor, its cabin door open, frozen in the act of ploughing. She was imagining the panic of the driver, frantically rushing away from his work, when the flashing blue dot on the navigation screen turned red and a calm voice in the cabin instructed them to fasten their safety belts. She gripped her seat as the vehicle swung abruptly over to the opposite carriageway to avoid a line of abandoned cars and the personal possessions of their owners, strewn across the highway.

Lianne glanced at Nick, who had ignored the request to buckle up, still focused on returning the drones to the RV. *Always busy, planning for the future – never looking back. But this is different. You had no plan for this outcome.*

'I wish we'd stayed in Phillips Cay,' she blurted out.

Nick tapped at the terminal in front of him and turned towards her. 'I thought you didn't like the place.'

'I didn't before, but it would have been different with the Pryces there – they've been our closest friends for almost twenty-five years and—'

'But you know that doesn't fit the plan,' he said firmly. 'Phillips is Methuen and Elizabeth's business now – we have other things to do.'

'Correction: you have other things to do – not me,' she said, sipping from the cup he'd placed beside her.

Nick rubbed the side of his face. 'How was I to know what was going to happen after we left Phillips?'

'You could have made it easier though, Nick–'

'How do you mean?' he said, picking at his beard.

'By controlling your *need-to-know* obsession when you're anxious,' she snapped back.

He hunched his shoulders and then sighed a little, as she continued.

'After we left Phillips, I asked you, "Where are we going?" and all you said was, "North to the small yard in Southport, Maine." And that was it – until a week after The Incident. Even then, with the chaos all around us, I had to seek you out to ask why the *Allied Clipper* was being loaded for a new voyage. Remember your reply?'

Nick shook his head, his face drawn, his shoulders slumped.

'"West to New York and then on to Lincoln, Nebraska" were your precise words. As if I could make sense of that. West through McFall Land – isn't that what the press are calling the area our rebellious senator has carved out for himself? And then on into what has become a radiation belt, down through the centre of the continent!'

He leant forward to speak but she raised her hand. 'I know, I know – it's not permanent, but look at the damage it's caused,' she said, pointing to the monitor in front of her. 'When I asked why we were heading in that direction, you gave me some bullshit about "needing to ensure the Allied Answers' New York and Lincoln offices had been closed down properly".'

'That wasn't *bullshit*,' Nick retorted and then added in a softer voice, as if he were talking to himself, 'there were other things I had to take care of.' Looking up at her, he said, 'I did offer you the option to go along the coast to Rockwell, where your mother had relocated. That far east you would have been even safer from any of McFall's gangs.'

'Unlike my family home in Vermont, trashed by those misfits,' she wailed, adding quietly, 'Maybe I should have gone.'

'But you *didn't*, and I was really happy you chose not to – after all, as I said at the time, we've always done everything together.'

Lianne fell back in her seat and sighed. 'Lucky you made that rare admission of affection, Grady, because my decision to go with you was severely tested in the days that followed.'

'You're talking about the bread van, right – after the *Clipper* dropped us off near Portland?' he said, daring a chuckle.

She glared back at him, wiping the smile off his face. '"We're going *incognito* to New York", you said, and then they slammed the door and left us in the dark for six hours.'

'We smelt of dough for days after,' he replied, with another tentative laugh.

She sat up, arms folded, not responding to his attempt to lighten the mood. 'The next little surprise came after that meeting in your mothballed New York office. First, you panicking when you found that one of your precious AVIII communication devices had gone missing, then that government helicopter suddenly appearing on the roof of the building and whisking us off to Chicago. And even after that, landing at O'Hare – well outside McFall Land – being driven to Union Station in a car with dark tinted windows and shown into a compartment in which the blinds remained down all the way to Lincoln.'

'We couldn't take any chances – there were McFall supporters everywhere. You know only too well, he hates me – and everything to do with Allied – about as much as he hates this new government. Remember that Lincoln isn't only CENCOM's HQ and central control for all FSA communications and intelligence operations, it's also the location of Allied Answers' main research base for Comms and AI – at least, until recently. Anyone travelling to Lincoln was regarded then, as now, a legitimate target for McFall's hitmen.'

'So why go there at all? You'd already started to relocate your staff from the research centre before the troubles flared up with McFall. Anyone could have closed the place down.'

'Yeah, but as I said, there were other things going on. These are tough times, Lianne; the unspoken bottom line on all sides is "either you're with us or against us". The alienation between governments and global companies like Allied was bad enough before The Incident, now we have McFall taking advantage of the disruption and increasing the level of distrust everywhere, for everyone. I had to show my face and express my support for the new administration.'

'But they wanted more than that, didn't they?' Lianne said sceptically. 'They'd built that new CENCOM HQ right next door to the Allied campus and insisted on an underground tunnel linking the two complexes. I remember you once describing it as a "polite coup d'état".'

'Except, after The Incident, it didn't stay *polite*. CENCOM closing ALL-SAT – Allied's back-up satellite-tracking station, just outside the city – with no consultation.'

'Why did they do that?' Lianne protested. 'They knew you were relying on it while you fixed the problem with the dirigible-based network.'

'They were levering me,' he snorted.

'I thought they were meant to be friends,' she said.

'The only friends I have in this new administration are in CENHQ in Minneapolis – pupils of my father, who moved over from Washington when the FSA constitution came into being. But don't get me wrong, most of the CENCOM people are okay—'

'So why shut down ALL-SAT? What did they want – this AVIII communication technology?'

Nick sat back and sighed deeply. 'They'd certainly like that, though they were going to get some of it through the frame agreement I had with the old administration. What they were actually angling for was something far more precious: access to the coding for our new artificial general intelligence module – you must have heard me talking about AGI?'

'And they would do all that just to get their hands on a bit of software?'

'It's not just a *bit of software*, Lianne. This is a major breakthrough. They were gagging for information – referring to it in terms of its "national security importance". That's why, even before they opened their new office, I'd moved my main AI and Comms people out of Lincoln. By the time CENCOM was fully installed, there were only a few Allied Associates remaining, while the rest were contractors partly employed to give the impression that the place was busy.'

'So you had to go in person to Lincoln to appease CENCOM?'

'Pretty much. In the meetings, I handed over the buildings and a whole lot of kit. I also gave them assurances of my "loyal support for the new government" – you can imagine the kind of guff I had to spew out. I gave them a little more on the AVIII technology but nothing at all on AGI.'

'Your charm worked too well though, didn't it?' she said with a cynical laugh.

'You mean, them using the emergency powers to second me—'

'And turning me into the wife of a colonel! That drove me stir-crazy – being confined to the officers' quarters, with everyone curious about this middle-aged, crop-haired woman who sat in the conservatory all day, writing. And then there was you, prohibited from entering the main CENCOM buildings for security reasons – what was all that about?'

Nick shook his head in acknowledgement but remained silent.

'It certainly stopped me making any objection when you bounced your next little surprise on me.'

'Pulling you out of that CENCOM evening reception at the end of May and driving you to a parking lot north of the city at midnight,' he retorted.

'I knew you were up to something days before when I saw suitcases being packed by that young adjutant. I'd always assumed he was a spy—?'

'No, he was CENHQ, sent over to look after me by the Defense Department in Minneapolis,' Nick said.

'But you said nothing at all about your plan until we reached that hideous industrial estate and parked in front of what looked like some great lump of rusting metal.'

Nick smirked at the description as Lianne carried on talking.

'You told me to wait in the car, but my curiosity was aroused – that's why I went over and checked it out. It was clearly some kind of oversized recreational vehicle with two sets of double wheels, a pair of massive chrome exhaust pipes and, oddly, instead of a windscreen, windows and doors, just their outlines – moulded in the same dull red-grey metal. I stood there a fair few minutes staring at it, and then because of all those death threats McFall's people had made against you, I started worrying as to where you might be. That's when I walked round to the rear and there you were, strolling down the ramp, with an intense light behind you, looking like an alien coming out of a spacecraft!'

'Except I was still in my tuxedo and bow tie,' he chipped in, genially.

'Remember what you said to me?' she asked, raising her eyebrows.

'That you'd "always wanted an RV"?'

'Mmm. You were so proud of your acquisition, telling me how you'd *borrowed* it from CENCOM and how it was one of two hundred battle buses they were fitting out for the Middle East. You went on and on like some military salesman, describing the lead lining, the bullet-proof composite material and the washing machine-sized object in the lower deck – that you later informed me was a mini-reactor. What lingered in my head though, as we dragged the luggage on board, was that word "borrowed". And then when the vehicle moved off on its own, a more troubling question: Where in the hell are we going?'

'Well, I told you that for sure,' Nick interjected, a little indignantly. 'I said we were off to Allied's local office in Bismarck.'

'Need-to-know Nick – you were *still* doing it,' she said, waving her finger at him. 'You knew already you had no intention of *staying* there—'

'Nor did you want to – you objected to that place almost as much as living in Lincoln.'

'Still no excuse for not giving me the full picture. If you'd only told me what was going on, it would have avoided the argument we had last night when I found myself being led to an underground lock-up, and once again all our luggage being loaded into the RV.'

'Challenging times, my dear, challenging times. We needed to move fast – CENCOM people were everywhere, looking for me. I told you when we left last night that we were going to a place that will be entirely safe.'

'"Entirely safe"?' she fired back. Pointing to her ear, she said, 'I recorded your exact words on my teleplant last night, which were:

"We'll be going south for a while, and then *eventually* to a place that's entirely safe." How does driving west into the radiation belt for seven hours square with "south" and "entirely safe", Nick?'

'Well, south is where we're heading right now, and have been since we took Highway 47 an hour ago ...'

As he spoke, the vehicle veered to the left onto a bumpy side road.

Lianne sat up and stared at the navigation screen. 'Why did we turn off?'

Nick pointed to an image from the front camera, which showed a gravel drive leading into a small wood. 'It's getting light. I want to find somewhere to park out of sight before people wake up. According to a database I downloaded in Bismarck, we should be able to refill the water tank here and even pick up some gas.'

'Gas? Why does this thing need that? I thought you said it ran on nuclear and was good for ten years?'

'There's a small internal combustion engine in the lower deck. The exhaust it produces makes the vehicle indistinguishable from what many people still drive around here. It was all part of my plan to avoid attention and get away from CENCOM.'

'Just because you've taken some unauthorised leave and *borrowed* one of their precious vehicles?'

'It's more than that, as I've explained.'

'That makes no sense, Nick. You know zilch about computer source coding. What's CENCOM going to do – hold you hostage until Allied deliver the AGI software? There's got to be more to it than that?'

She fell silent as the front camera showed them entering a circular courtyard with a single-storey house, a general store and, under a concrete canopy, a gas pump.

As the vehicle slowed, it tilted sharply, causing them to grab the sides of their seats.

'Nothing to worry about,' he said, enlarging the rear camera image, 'we've just dislodged an old drain cover. I don't think it'll upset anyone – this place looks deserted. Let's get kitted up and have a look around.'

Down on the lower deck, he helped her into a bodysuit taken from a cabinet signed DECONTAMINATION UNIT. She pulled back as he handed her a full-face mask.

'It's up to you,' he said nonchalantly, 'but one speck of plutonium, caesium or strontium in your lungs and all that longevity treatment you've had will have been a waste of money.'

Outside, still adjusting her mask, Lianne heard through her teleplant Nick give a joyful yell as liquid gushed from the fuel nozzle in his hand.

'Can you get those canisters over here?' she heard him holler. 'We'll fill the lot – could come in handy if we need something to appease any locals as we head south.'

But she ignored his request, having noticed the door to the general store standing slightly ajar.

Inside, she found a room lit by a single flickering fluorescent strip and shelves still packed high with goods.

'Hello there?' she called, but hearing no reply, walked over to the main counter, where an old-style cash till lay open and empty.

About to leave, she looked up in surprise as she heard the voice of a well-known newscaster coming through a door further back. Pushing it open, she walked into a well-lit, T-shaped lounge with a broken window at the far end through which the wind howled. As she turned the corner at the end of the room, she jumped back in surprise at the sight of two people sitting on a sofa, facing a TV on which the early morning news was being broadcast.

'Oh gee, I'm *so* sorry, I didn't realise anyone was here,' she spluttered. But as she drew level with the couple, she screamed out as she saw the one nearest to her, an old man, sitting rigidly upright, smears of blood congealed around his eye sockets, his hand clasping that of an elderly woman who, like him, stared lifelessly at the screen.

Nervously, Lianne scanned around for other bodies but finding none, walked briskly back into the store, closing the empty till on her way past.

Out in the courtyard, she marched over to Nick, who was still engrossed in filling containers. 'Did you know how serious the radiation risk would be before we left Bismarck?' she asked calmly through her teleplant.

As he straightened up, she added, 'How much radiation are we absorbing at present?'

'Not enough to cause us any permanent damage,' he said, rolling back a large black drum. 'The Russians believe that a small amount can even be quite good for you,' he said light-heartedly.

'I suspect this has gone way above that brain-enhancing level, Nick, or why did we have all those injections in Bismarck before we left?'

'Inside there we're okay,' he replied, pointing to the vehicle.

'And outside?'

He cleared his throat. 'Probably not a good idea to be outdoors too long – we're in a bad patch here. It'll get better as we travel south, according to the fallout maps.'

'Ah, the maps,' she responded with mock reverence. 'My guess is that this little route you designed, takes us through the most intensely radiated areas to avoid any CENCOM patrols. Am I right, professor?'

'As ever, you put two and two together and make it sound a lot more fun than four,' he said jokingly, putting the pump back into its housing. 'You're quite safe. Remember, I'm living in the same atmosphere as you, and as you know only too well, I value myself more than anyone else on this planet.'

'Well ...' she remarked, tilting her head back in the direction of the store, '... it's just that I don't want to end up like the poor bastards in there.'

Nick turned abruptly in her direction. 'Shot or what?'

'Died of causes that around here are probably regarded as quite normal these days ... It's just that the birds have made a bit of a mess of one of them.'

'Phew! Well, that's a relief,' he grunted, walking back towards the van.

'A relief, Nick?' she bawled back, shaking her head.

Not reacting to her concern, he waved at a collection of filled containers beside them. 'Help me with these?' he called to her.

Walking towards him, Lianne stopped as a succession of high-pitched bleeps sounded in her head and she saw Nick gaze skyward.

'Could be a CENCOM reconnaissance drone. We need to get these inside quick!' he said.

As they hurried towards the vehicle, both with a can in each hand, he gestured with his chin towards a mass of black clouds over the mountains to the west. 'Surveillance drones won't be the only thing that might cause problems for us today – that storm's going to stir up the dust.'

After removing their suits, showering and returning to their seats in the driving cabin, Nick enlarged an image of a small airborne object. 'Just as I thought – CENCOM drone on a scouting mission.'

'So nothing to worry about?' Lianne said, running her fingers through her wet hair.

'Well, I wouldn't say that exactly ...' he replied. 'It may not have spotted the van under the canopy here, but its sensors could have picked up the hydrocarbons from the pump or even detected the drain cover we disturbed as we drove in.'

'You mean it'll be back?'

'Probably, but not immediately with that storm approaching. We need to disappear, and I think I've found the perfect place.'

He punched a few keys on the panel in front of him and, as Lianne watched on the front camera, the vehicle moved slowly down a rough track towards a towering red-painted barn.

'Look at that,' Nick said, nodding at a side camera display showing a pair of rotating wind turbines. 'Power but no people – ironic, huh?'

'No animals either,' she rejoined, pointing to a line of empty stables. 'Someone's taken them but left their owners.'

The vehicle pulled up in front of a pair of wooden doors on which two yellow posters had been pasted, bearing black triangles and the words CAUTION! RADIATION SEVERE HAZARD.

Nick looked over at the external Geiger counter on one of the screens. 'It's about 1.5 millisieverts per hour – that's not a problem.'

'Then why the posters?' she snapped back.

'To keep people away – it's all locked up,' he replied, zooming in on the doors. 'Probably farm equipment or some-thing valuable in there. Wait here – there's no point in both of us suiting up.'

Lianne watched on the camera as Nick set off towards the barn doors, carrying a set of cutters, which he then used to remove two heavy-duty locks. As he pulled the doors open, she could see a dirt floor ahead of him surrounded by a wall of hay bales extending up to a heavily timbered roof.

Several minutes later, he emerged from the barn and gave her a jubilant double thumbs up. Just as he did, a flash of lightning illuminated his face, followed by a roaring downpour. Running inside, he pushed the doors back to their full extent and then pointed a remote control at the vehicle, which started to gradually move towards him.

As the RV entered the barn, Lianne watched helplessly as it ploughed into the wall of bales, causing an alarm to sound in the cabin and a reading of 101 millisieverts to appear on the screen in front of her. Unable to communicate with Nick through the protective layers of the vehicle, she stared anxiously at the stair-well until the upper hatch door opened and he appeared, stripped down to his T-shirt and underpants, grinning broadly.

As he took his seat alongside her, she pointed to the hay bales displayed on the front camera and then at the counter. 'I wouldn't describe that as a perfect landing. What were you doing?'

'I had to get the whole vehicle in ...'

His voice trailed off as she saw him staring at the radiation reading on the screen. 'Probably dust thrown into the air by the storm,' he said, switching off the engine and walking through to the kitchen.

'But, Nick, the levels only started to rise once the vehicle was inside,' Lianne pleaded.

'Forget it – we're safe now. I pulled a couple of metal bars over the door so no one can get in.'

'How long are we here for?'

'Sunset is around nine-thirty, so we have about fifteen hours.'

'Can we communicate with anyone? Like Methuen and Elizabeth on Phillips?'

'I would have to raise an aerial and that might alert CENCOM.'

Lianne swivelled around to face him. 'And what are they going to do? From what you've said, they need *you* more than you need *them*,' she scoffed.

'Take us back to Lincoln and confine me to barracks ...' he replied, and with a slight sneer added, '... and subject you to endless coffee mornings until I give them whatever they want.'

'Yes, that is rather an unpleasant thought,' she said with a smirk.

'There are things going on in CENCOM that I don't understand,' Nick added in a more anxious tone.

'Besides them trying to extort information from you – what else?'

'Something I haven't mentioned before. My secondment and then our confinement to the officers' compound in Lincoln were ordered by CENHQ. They were worried about possible McFall sympathisers in CENCOM.'

'So that's who we're *really* hiding from?'

'Don't worry, we're away from it now,' he replied, smiling at her reassuringly.

Lianne stood up, stretched and walked into the kitchen. 'Breakfast then, Milord?' she said, taking out plates from a cupboard.

He looked at her in surprise. 'That'll be a first – you making breakfast for *me*.' And as he moved towards the stairwell, he added, 'While you're doing that then, I'll prepare something in the bedroom that I guarantee will easily distract you for the rest of the day.'

'Ha!' she shouted back, pressing the knob to open the door of the microwave. 'That'll also be another first!'

Five minutes later, crouched on the stairs, Lianne passed a tray of food through to Nick, who was sitting up on the bed, checking outdoor images on the monitors in front of him.

'Our outriders all on duty?' she said, crawling across him and then lying back.

'Umm ... they'll be our eyes and ears while we immerse ourselves in this,' he replied, looking up at the screen in the ceiling.

'*Immerse?*' Lianne exclaimed. 'You know I don't do that.'

'Yeah, I know you don't like immersing in the SWVRP ...' He stopped himself as he saw her frown. 'Oh, come on, Lianne, quit fooling around – the Segmented World Virtual Reality Program ...' he said in a sing-song voice.

'I know, I know,' she said impatiently.

'You must have used VR for your writing at some stage?' he fired back, taking two pairs of black glasses from a drawer in the wall.

'That's precisely why I don't "indulge". I get all I need to know about the *Segmented World* from listening to you and Methuen – I don't want all this VR messing around with my imagination.'

Nick sighed deeply and shook his head. 'Look, we're stuck in this vehicle for at least the next two days. I'm not asking you to *participate* in virtual space, just be an *observer*. I have here ...' he said, using the remote to move the cursor on the ceiling screen, '... a beta module that my special research group gave me before we moved them out of Lincoln. They're turning the Exemplars into Embodiers for the people on the Phillips Cay Project.'

'Exemplars? Embodiers?'

'Good God, woman, where've you been for the past fifteen years?'

'Being normal – building my writing career,' she fired back.

'Not having an Exemplar is, these days, abnormal – and in the future not upgrading it to an Embodier will leave you even more disadvantaged.'

'Rubbish! All this VR stuff is just escapism.'

'That's not true and you know it. When we launched the SWVRP in the 2030s it started everyone thinking about the future a lot more. I remember you using it to experience the manifestos of the different political parties. And there's lots more to come – these new virtual representations are about to transform actual human relations.'

'Human relations – that's going a bit far, isn't it?' she said, inspecting the glasses.

Nick pointed the remote back at the screen. 'I've just had a brilliant idea for getting you into all this. There's a file here starring your beloved god-daughter as she undergoes her first immersion.'

'Bliss!' Lianne said, her face lighting up.

'Yes, plus a few other characters, but she's the main one. I'll set it to run on her "Thought Mode".'

'What's that?'

Nick brought up a dashboard on the ceiling screen. 'I have to explain this first. We have a specialist IA – *intelligent assistant* – that puts all this together. We call it The Storymaker.'

'What do you mean, "puts it all together"?'

'Edits and narrates the data to produce what we see and hear.'

'Where does all this personal information come from?' she asked warily.

'Up to the end of '48, it was sourced from historical records, interviews and the questionnaires everyone had to fill in to access

VR programs like the SWVRP. Oh, and since '46, also from any Memory Monitor recordings – you know that device we had in the apartment in London.'

'And after '48?'

'Everything changed for those who had installed the new exo-cortex version of the AA-Plant—'

'I *do* know what that is,' Lianne cut in tetchily. 'It's always been too invasive for me – that's why I stuck with the ear plug option I had with my first teleplant in the '30s.'

'What you may not have read in the guidelines is that the new AVIII device I gave you last year records all actions, words and, if you had the exo-cortex AA, thoughts—'

'You mean *actual* thoughts?'

'Yes. Prior to the exo-implant, all thoughts had to be scripted for these VR reconstructions; after that, a continuous record of the user's thoughts became available. It saves all this data, via the Allied Answers network of dirigibles, into what we call Hub Tool Boxes. The whole set-up is still in the testing phase but when it's ready, people will be able to play back the entirety of their post-'48 lives.'

'You mean, all their sleeping, eating and ...?' Lianne paused, and shaking her head said, 'Uh, most of that's going to be incredibly dull, isn't it?'

'Yes, but that's where The Storymaker comes in. It selects significant events and makes them into what it calls *scenes*. It then adds narration as required, once you've immersed via your teleplant and these glasses. The whole thing is still in the developmental stage so some of the scenes are a bit raw—'

'So let me get this right: we'll be standing in virtual space, watching what people did and said while also getting commentary from this IA narrator?'

'And as I mentioned, we can also run the scene in Thought Mode – not just hearing what people said, but also what they were thinking,' Nick chipped in.

'But that must be unbearable – having everyone's thoughts and feelings flooding into one's head all at the same time?'

'No, no. Before we begin a scene, we can select from the dashboard which person's virtual perspective we will experience, or if you wish, what is called a General View – from no particular viewpoint. Where the scene involves only one contributing character, you can increase the level of the Thought Mode with hardly any Storymaker narration.'

'You mean a sort of first-person perspective?'

'Exactly, although personally I find the General View, with the reconstruction based on everyone's input, the most balanced account of events.'

'Ugh, it makes my flesh creep to even think that people would allow their lives to be captured to such an extent.'

Nick looked at her in surprise. 'You're fitted with Allied's latest AA ear plug, aren't you?'

'I suppose so, if that's what the upgrade was last year ... uh, just a minute, are you telling me this thing has been recording everything I do?'

'It doesn't matter—'

'What do you mean it doesn't matter! What about all that privacy protocol stuff you've been harping on about in Allied for years? I presume everyone appearing in these "scenes" gave permission for you to view them?'

Nick held his hands out to calm her. 'These are only test files that the team wanted me to check before they're sent out for contributors to finally approve – it's no big deal.'

'I take that as a "no" then to my question regarding privacy?'

'Look, why not watch the first few scenes? They're all pre-'49. Everyone involved in making them realised they would eventually be widely viewed.'

'But they've not actually signed off on them – have they?'

Nick gave a deep sigh and turned to her. 'So what do you want to do – sleep for fifteen hours or immerse?'

Lianne inspected the glasses, refusing Nick's offer of help as she tucked them behind her ears. 'I wouldn't do this were it not for the weird situation I find myself in right now,' she said grumpily and then, wagging her finger at him, added, 'Don't you dare tell Bliss I did this – she may be suspicious of you but she still trusts me.'

Nick lay back on the pillow, adjusting his frames. 'Okay, as this is new to you let me tell you what's going to happen. First, you'll see a 3D screenshot of a scene with a title, date and location. Decide where you want to stand and then confirm it by pressing this button on the remote. Once you're in position, press the top of your frames to immerse.'

'So I have to stay in one place?'

'Once you've installed yourself, you will automatically move as the Exemplar moves to a new location in the scene. You can also change position while in a particular location, but I would rather you didn't do that because it uses too much processing power. If you want to move, wait until there's a new section in a scene, then use the snapshot to reposition yourself.'

'Got it,' Lianne said a little impatiently, taking the remote and pressing the button Nick had pointed to.

'Virtually Real … Soft Rush Estate, Sandy Hollow, Hampshire, UK; morning, 25 July 2045,' she read out. 'Oh … and is that Bliss in bed? I'll stand by the wardrobe. Now … I need to press these … Oh, Nick, what's that noise?' she said, sitting up.

'Lie back, lie back. The editing is still a little crude in places,' he said reassuringly. 'You'll observe Bliss receiving the latest version of the SWVRP and then shortly afterwards as she immerses, you'll enter into what amounts to a virtual world within a virtual world …'

AA-Com File: Virtually Real

Soft Rush Estate, Sandy Hollow, Hampshire, UK
Morning, 25 July 2045

Virtual Scene snapshot: A young girl lies on a bed. The room is in semi-darkness and filled with the sound of waves crashing on a cobble beach and a squabble of gulls cawing, loudly.

Wait for it … Ah yes, there it is – one of my favourite wake-up smells: seaweed blended with the faintest whiff of candy floss!

'Good morning.'

Bliss stretched her neck as the voice from her teleplant continued. 'The weather report is about to begin on your preferred station. Shall I tune you in?'

'Sure,' she replied, opening her eyes before closing them tight as barbs of light streamed in through the shuttered doors at the end of the room. As she lay back, a more eager but no less annoying voice began to talk in her head.

'It's a gorgeously warm day already. The temperature right now is a comfortable twenty-three degrees, but by mid-afternoon, it will have sizzled up to a toasty thirty-eight, so don't forget your anti-tan shower before you go out. As for humidity, just relax; it will stay around a comfortable thirty to forty per cent. And now for some news. Today will see the much-awaited launch of the government's free support-medication plan. The "little grey pills" as they have been—'

'Turn it off, please,' Bliss said, closing her eyes. *Who are they trying to fool with all this happy-go-lucky drivel? Just because we happen to live on a little island off Europe that has so far* escaped the worst excesses of this overheated world doesn't mean we should make light of it.

'Would you like me to open the shutters?'

'That would be good,' Bliss said, rotating her head from side to side to switch off the voice coming from her teleplant. Still rubbing her eyes, she strolled out onto the balcony.

'Ouch!' she squealed, hopping back onto the carpet and slipping on a pair of flat shoes.

Venturing forward again, she cautiously tapped the hot metal railings until she was able to rest on them and view the garden and the woods beyond.

So many memories. The meadow lawn where I used to have secret tea parties with my imaginary friends – back in the days when the grass grew tall. And beyond that, the lily-covered lake that Dad built in the '30s, which is now part of our water management plan.

She lifted her head and followed the line of the bridge, zigzagging over the water to the sunken end of the main drive, deep in the garden.

I must have been six or seven that day I escaped from under the beady eye of Mrs Rawlins. It was a shock though, finding that the main drive ended in a great amphitheatre of wooden stakes, topped by a tall laurel hedge. I felt trapped, that was until I spotted three gates in the circular barricade. 'Just like Alice in Wonderland', as I described it recently to Ramona, I was uncertain which to take. The one to my left, across the zigzag bridge, was the safest and quickest, for sure, but Mrs Rawlins would almost certainly have seen me then. The gate to my right led to steep steps curving up to the raised vegetable plot that runs around one side of the garden, two or three metres above where I stood. That way offered the reward of a well-stocked fruit cage at that time of year, and the possibility of being able to sneak back into the house unnoticed.

So why, when I was so young, did I choose the third gate in front of me – shaded by overhanging trees and covered in brambles? I guess it was all those years of peeking through these railings at the fifty-acre wood and wondering why my father disappeared so regularly into that mass of greenery. I was as determined then, as I am now, to get to the bottom of things.

It wasn't easy though. At that time, there was only a narrow bridge made from two wobbly telegraph poles, not to mention the nettles and brambles – fine for Dad wearing trousers, but not for me in my cotton frock; I remember every sting and prickle. But I struggled through the undergrowth until I came to a clearing in the woods, where I saw two buildings. The nearest looked shabby and uninviting. Only later would I discover that this was his writing shed – a place which over time would become my regular retreat, playing on the floor while he worked. Just then though, what really grabbed me was the other building, where I could hear music playing. And, as I crept inside, I saw to my surprise, my father dancing. Only during future visits would I also notice the running ramp on which he performed and the banks of computers recording his every movement.

Sweeping me up in his arms that day, he laughed loudly as he carried me back to the house, where he made light of Mrs Rawlins' concerns and sat with me on this very balcony drinking lemonade and telling me about the virtual world he was creating.

'Happy days,' she said with a sigh, and then turned towards the sound of someone coming up the stairs.

'Mornin'! Breakfast for the birthday girl,' called an elderly woman, struggling with a large tray.

'Oh, Mrs Rawlins, that's so sweet of you – thank you, thank you!' Bliss said as the family housekeeper placed the tray on the bedside table and handed over a card.

'None of that now. I've been getting you out of bed for most of those sixteen years, young lady!'

Bliss plonked herself in the chair beside her bed and smiled at the woman. 'I've always thought of you as part of the family,' she said.

The woman waved away the comment with an uncertain laugh. 'You 'ave your eggs and that funny salsa stuff you like, and I'll bring up the packages and cards that 'ave been arrivin' here over the past few days. I've never seen so many presents for one person.'

Bliss poured hot water onto the herbs in the teacup and felt something rub against her leg. 'Pushy! Come on, baby, sit on my lap,' she crooned invitingly, as a large Persian cat leapt onto the table.

'Get down, Pushkin!' Mrs Rawlins hollered, reappearing at the top of the stairs, her arms full of parcels.

'Goodness, I see what you mean!' Bliss laughed, as she took several of the packages.

'This isn't all of them, mind – there are more deliveries due later,' the housekeeper said.

'Shall we open them together?' Bliss asked.

'I'll 'ave to go in a minute, but … Oh, go on then – I've been wonderin' what's in some of them.'

'What do we have here?' Bliss exclaimed, and spotting a label read out loud, '"To my adorable sister, from your loving brother Martin." Hah! That's a joke. I bet Beth wrote that for him.'

Peeling off the wrapping, she handed the paper and string to Mrs Rawlins, who folded it neatly and placed it on the floor beside her.

'"The Definitive Guide to the Segmented World Virtual Reality Program, Version 12",' she read. 'Only Martin would buy me an interactive electronic reference book for my sixteenth birthday,' Bliss said, dropping the weighty volume on the floor.

'This one's from the United States – came special delivery yesterday,' Mrs Rawlins said a little excitedly, handing Bliss a padded envelope.

'You open it,' Bliss giggled.

Mrs Rawlins carefully eased open the flap of the envelope before extracting a thin document. '"Welcome to the AstroPlane",' she read. 'Looks like one of those old-fashioned air tickets. Is that right?'

Taking it from her, Bliss laughed cheerily. 'Great! It's from Auntie Lianne and Uncle Nick. Oh . . .' Her face fell as she scrutinised the slip of paper more closely.

'Anything wrong, dear?' Mrs Rawlins asked.

'Well, it's a bit odd. Lianne's like a second mother to me and even Uncle Nick's been quite friendly over the past few years. I've stayed with them every summer in New York for at least a month since I was thirteen – but this is only for a week in September.'

'There's somethin' else in 'ere,' Mrs Rawlins said, retrieving a small brochure from the envelope. 'Lady Caroline's ... Oh, and there's somethin' written on the cover: "Uncle Nick is on board",' she read. 'What's that mean, Bliss?'

'Uh, nothing. It's just an idea about what I might do after art college. Could you pass me that big box over there, please? I can't begin to imagine what's in it.'

Bliss pulled back the wrapping paper, handing it to Mrs Rawlins, who by now had begun to make separate piles of paper, envelopes, string and ribbon. From the box, Bliss drew out a set of oil paints and smiled gleefully at Mrs Rawlins. 'These are like hens' teeth at college – where on earth did Jack find them? My elder brother's amazing at getting hold of stuff.'

'Maybe open one of your cards next?' Mrs Rawlins suggested, handing her the largest envelope.

'Wow!' Bliss exclaimed as a folded sheet of paper exploded into a metre-square photo, showing six girls in eye-catching outfits, each with a personalised message handwritten in a speech bubble.

Mrs Rawlins reached in a pocket for her glasses and scanned the words printed in large letters across the top of the card: The Coven Rules Okay. 'What's it mean, Bliss?'

'That's what I call my friends from college – you know, the ones I went on holiday with last year?'

'Oh, that lot ... You almost killed yourself bungee-jumpin', didn't you?' Mrs Rawlins said disapprovingly, but then saw Bliss scanning the picture more closely. 'Somethin' wrong?'

'No, it's just that Ramona's missing.'

'Who's that?'

'She's not at college. She's our new virtual member – joined in January but goes to school in Nebraska. I would have thought they'd include her—'

'Just a minute,' Mrs Rawlins interrupted and began rummaging through the unopened parcels beside her. 'There's another small package from the US 'ere – maybe it's from her?'

Bliss took the parcel, and ignoring Mrs Rawlins' careful unwrapping technique, tore off strips of paper to reveal a black leatherette box containing a small jewelled bracelet.

'She must think an awful lot of you,' Mrs Rawlins said, rolling the scraps of paper into a ball.

'Yes, I think she does, and I like her too. She's funny without going over the top, like the others often do. We've agreed to meet up next year.'

'Look, there's a card here from your mother with something inside.'

Bliss studied the handwritten words:

Dearest Bliss, Happy Birthday.
Here are your first keys to freedom. Mum xxx

Snorting with displeasure, she said, 'A key pass for using the self-driving car contract – boring!'

'If it means fewer rows in the 'olidays between you and your mother over transport down to 'er clinic in Bentham, then it's a good idea, isn't it?' Mrs Rawlins retorted.

Bliss made no response, her attention having now turned to a small rectangular object lying on the floor. As she removed the wrapping paper, she cried out in delight, 'I know what this is! I saw Martin's when he got one on *his* sixteenth.' She slid back the lid of the box and took out a set of tortoiseshell-framed glasses.

'What's that then?' Mrs Rawlins asked, taking the box and trying to close it.

'It's from my father, giving me access to the SWVRP – you know, the Segmented World Virtual Reality Program: that thing he created years ago?'

'I *do* know about that,' Mrs Rawlins scowled. 'My Tommy saved up and got membership last Christmas. His wife can't get 'im off it now.'

Searching through the pile of presents on the floor, Bliss picked up the guide she had discarded earlier. 'This book's out of date. I bet Dad didn't tell Martin he was giving me access to Version 13. My bro's going to be seriously jealous when he hears about this,' she sniggered.

'And why's that?'

'Everyone's talking about it – it's a "quantum change in realism" apparently.'

'A what?'

'Oh sorry, Mrs Rawlins, I'm getting carried away. Tell me, will any of the family be here today? It's just that I'm probably not meant to use these without someone being in the house,' she said, holding up the glasses.

'Your father left for the States last week as you know, and your mother went to attend 'is stepfather's funeral yesterday. From the schedule 'angin' in the kitchen, Jack and Martin are comin' with their families next week, while Grandad Morgan and your step-grandmother will be 'ere in August. If you want someone who knows all about this, I could ask my Tommy?'

Bliss smiled weakly at the woman. 'I don't think they'd let him into the hamlet. Didn't you say he hadn't taken any of that infection medication the government gave out last year?'

'Too busy on that virtual program to do anything, so 'is wife says. Don't worry, I'll be in and out all day, 'cept for a few 'ours this afternoon. I've got some shoppin' to do for Tommy's wife – you know, she's expectin' again,' the woman said, shaking her head. 'All unplanned, so no government support.'

'It's all right, I'll take it slowly,' Bliss answered, gently patting the woman's hand. 'Ah, there's Pushy – Pushkin, Pushkin, come here, boy!'

'I'll leave you to it then, and if you don't mind, I'll take these for my recyclin' fund – you know, "It all adds up",' Mrs Rawlins warbled, mimicking a widely broadcast government jingle.

The door closed behind her, and Bliss opened the instruction manual from Martin. She was about to address her teleplant when she noticed a sheet of paper tucked inside. Pulling it out, she found a scribbled note.

Dear Sis,
Dad said he's giving you access to the SWVRP.
Be careful!
I know you won't read this manual before trying it out and the instructions that come with the glasses are crap, so as an act of brotherly love, I've written out these simple guidelines. Please follow them.

Typical Martin – rational and ordered, always seeing the problem rather than the opportunity. She sat back to read out the instructions. 'Okay, so let's see: "One, make sure that you're not disturbed." Well, that's no problem because there's nobody here! "Two, sit down in the most comfortable chair and relax." Is he going to tell me how to breathe next?'

She walked over to a fan-shaped chair in the shady part of the balcony and continued reading. 'Next: "Activate your teleplant – you should know how to do that. Ha!" It's on. "Put on the glasses and press the top of the frames and wait for your new life to begin ..." New life? More like get a life, brother—'

'Woah, woah – what's happening? Everything's moving too fast … This can't be right? Maybe I need to adjust the specs, pull them tighter? No, it's not that. Reset the teleplant – maybe the AA-Com connection's out of sync or something … Ah, wait a minute, that's better. Oh, my heart's thumping, and I'm … I'm … actually … panting …'

'Hello, Bliss,' she heard a soft, uninflected male voice say in her teleplant.

'Who's that?'

'I am E-manual, your assistant, here to help you get the full benefit of Version 13 of the Segmented World Virtual Reality Program. I am currently downloading your profile to confirm your authorisation to enter the SWVRP. While we are waiting, I am happy to answer any questions you may have, although I should point out that my interactive vocalisation is rather limited at present.'

'When I first pressed the top of these glasses all I saw were flashing lights, but now I can't see a damn thing – it's pitch-black. How long will it be before I can enter the program?'

'If all goes well, you will shortly have your first immersion … just a second, just a second. Good, your authorisation has come through. Now I want you to close your eyes and touch the top of the frames again,' the assistant requested calmly.

'That's better, I can see around me now … Hang on, is this virtual space? It looks just like my bedroom. There's my easel, and over there is my flute … and here's Pushkin.' Bliss laughed and leant towards the cat. 'Pushy, Pushy, come here … Oh, wait a minute … he's bigger than before—?'

'You are in virtual space and you do not need to move except for your head when you want to take a different view,' E-manual advised patiently. 'Imagine that you are picking up the cat and it will happen. The same is true of moving around. If you imagine the movement, then you will move—'

'You mean, I don't have to work out on any of those awful running ramps that everyone installed in their homes a few years ago?'

'You're in Version 13, which has many new features. The first you must master is moving in virtual space without physically moving your body. Try to imagine that you're walking onto the balcony and looking out. You will be surprised at how quickly your brain adapts.'

'I'm walking, I'm walking ... but who's that ahead of me—?'

'I will explain that in a moment ... No, no, you reached out for the balcony rail – just *imagine* reaching out.'

'Got it, got it. The garden is so lifelike.'

'Can you spot any differences?'

Bliss scanned the view that she had been musing over only an hour before. Nothing seemed different at first – the same meadow and lake and the woods beyond. Only when she looked over to the right did she spot something unusual.

'The vegetable garden's more planted out than I've seen it before and there are people I don't recognise working on the plots ... And what's that big white box in the drive? A vehicle of some sort. Oh, now there's a big difference – the scaffolding around the coach house has gone and there's even a climber over the doorway. So what year are we in here?'

'Before I answer that, return your virtual self to where you are sitting.'

Bliss jiggled in the chair and then rested her head back.

'I have set the program for the year 2050. It's a world not dissimilar from the one you already know.'

'You're easing me into V13?'

'I'm not quite sure what you mean by "easing me in".'

'Sorry, I need to be in listening mode – please go on.'

'I understand that request. Let us talk about the different settings in the SWVRP. There are a number of scenarios in this Version, ranging from Segmented Lite, or SL for short – with global cooperation

widespread and therefore limited segmentation of global activities –
to Segmented Full, or SF, with greatly reduced cooperation and widespread segmentation. I suggest you stay in Segmented Lite until you
become fully familiar with residing in your—'

'Oh, what's that? It's Pushy again, but he feels different.'

'Ah, that is a confusion. In future, I advise you to have no
sentient beings in the room that might disturb you while you are
immersed. Let us move on to the most important development in
V13: your Exemplar.'

'Oh yes, I've heard about that.'

'It is your representation in virtual space. That was what you
saw ahead of you, a few minutes ago. For anyone spotting you on
the balcony, what they saw was not you, but your virtual representation in 2050—'

'When I'm twenty-one!' Bliss interrupted excitedly, and without waiting for the assistant's instruction, pressed the top of the
frames and walked her other self over to the wardrobe mirror.

'Hey! Who decided to cut my hair like that?' Turning her head,
she then added more positively, 'That spot on my cheek has gone
at least … And, oh, I have a bust at last!'

'Please come back into real space now. I need to outline some
limitations of your virtual self before you proceed any further.'

'Sorry, go on,' Bliss said, resting her head back.

'I set the date only five years in advance to minimise what some
people have called "virtual shock". You would understand this if
I'd set the time to, say, 2075, when you'd be forty-six. Then you
would have noticed differences not only in appearance and stat-
ure, but also in your pace, balance, sight and hearing. All these
things are incorporated into your older Exemplar representations.'

'Why d'you call it an Exemplar? It's just a virtual avatar, isn't it?'

'I understand your question. All individuals inhabiting the
virtual space of SWVRP have been assigned positive personas.'

'You mean everyone is nice?'

There was another slight pause, before E-manual replied. 'I'm not qualified to answer that question, but here is an extract from a recent interview with one of the SWVRP lead developers which may help.'

A slick American voice came through on Bliss's teleplant.

'The purpose of the SWVRP has changed from Methuen Pryce's initial design of fourteen years ago, which originally placed people as observers in the program in order to familiarise themselves with living in a Segmented World. Depending on the setting of that scenario, the physical landscape, political, economic and social conditions evolved over time, but individuals remained unchanged, acting only as outside observers. As rival products came along, aimed purely at entertainment, Allied Answers began to introduce new features to keep market share and continue our mission of preparing people for the world ahead. The innovation that secured our lead position was moving the user from observer to participant through the creation of a virtual self. Using data from their psychological profile, we gave this virtual self a persona that is the positive expression of each user's true self – hence, Exemplar.'

'This sounds more like *virtuous* than *virtual* space?'

'I am unable to respond to your remark.'

'Sorry, sorry … it doesn't matter. Please go on.'

'Thank you, I will continue. In a few minutes, you will be free to enter the world of SL2050. As *you* will be virtually present, your Exemplar will be in "active mode". In this state you can choose whether you – through your Exemplar – or the Exemplar by itself, interacts with the surroundings. You can also change her character if you wish. You could, for instance, provide your Exemplar with a more aggressive persona, although that will then be adopted by your passive Exemplar—'

'Passive?'

'When you're not logged in, your Exemplar still exists but only in a reactive state. It has no desires and takes no initiative. It is purely a visual phenomenon until an *active* Exemplar approaches it, when it will respond to questions in a manner dependent on how much you have changed it from the standard model. When you log in after such an encounter, you will be updated on the interactions it has had, and the things it has learnt. If you program your Exemplar to be more aggressive, there is a risk that it will have a narrower range of positive interactions. Even when you are present in active mode, you may still be ignored if your virtual persona has not fitted in with the community it inhabits. You only have one life in the SWVRP so you need to manage it carefully.'

'Let me get this right – out there is another world not so different from this one, inhabited by my positive doppelgänger?'

'I need to check the word "doppelgänger" – just a second ... Yes, I see what you mean. I'm not sufficiently programmed to discuss this with you in detail. Your Exemplar has similar limitations. Its primary function is to answer questions about the future you have entered. It currently has limited capacity to engage in discussions about the past or present.'

'Okay, I understand. Can I immerse again?'

'Before you do that, you must decide how you will address your Exemplar. Many users employ the default word Exemplar, but if you want something else, I can input it for you now.'

'Bliss the Good; Good Bliss; Bliss the Nice ...? I don't know – what about BlissX?'

'That is a common approach – adapting the active user's name.'

'Oh, I didn't want it to be *common*.'

'I'm sorry, I didn't—'

'Doesn't matter, BlissX it is. Now tell me, how has it been possible to recreate these surroundings in such minute detail?'

'Here is an extract from a speech on that topic given by an Allied Answers executive last year.'

'Just as in the last century, we mapped roads and buildings for satellite navigation, so in the late 2030s, we began to record many other aspects of the planet for virtual reality programs such as the SWVRP. In Allied Answers AI, we recognised from the outset that a task of this magnitude could only be undertaken by engaging the help of our users. To do that, we created spectacle frames with the dual purpose of displaying the virtual world of the SWVRP and, in another mode, recording it. Along with the new specs have come portable atomic-storage devices with free download points in most cities. We provide financial rewards for high-quality recorded data and a personal recognition system that allow the Exemplars of exceptional contributors to display rings of increasing levels of status from bronze to platinum. We already have the architecture of most major towns and cities recorded and expect over the next ten years to have captured much of the populated countryside in the US and Europe.'

'I hope you found that helpful. I don't think I am breaking any rules of confidentiality if I inform you that your brother Martin's Exemplar was recently allowed to display a platinum ring for the work his user had done in recording areas of southern England.'

'Oh, surprise, surprise,' Bliss groaned.

'Why are you surprised?'

'Sorry, it's a turn of phrase,' she said apologetically. 'So when I enter the virtual space of this house, you're saying that Martin has already recorded every corner?'

'Yes. You're extremely fortunate – his work must be of the highest quality.'

'Can I go ahead and enter the space now?'

'Please wait a little longer. I have further information to pass on to you. Even though the basic architecture has been recorded, you can personalise the surroundings – the garden, the house, this room, the bed, even your cat – with your own memories and interpretation. It will deepen *your* experience and also that of others whom you allow to incorporate your virtual world into theirs—'

'Can I change things that I think the program has predicted wrongly?'

'I understand your question. For details not solely connected with yourself, you would need to go through a notification procedure to gain agreement from all parties involved. May I explain how this is done?'

'No, my question was just about this twenty-one-year-old who's representing me in virtual space. Is she married? Does she have kids? What's her job?'

'I understand. You can change whatever you like in your Exemplar, but as I said before, you need to be careful not to make BlissX too unusual. This is the standard advice.'

'I can't wait to go back in!' she said, rubbing her hands in excitement.

'I have two remaining points. The first is that your immersion time is limited to one hour. After that you may not re-enter for six hours.'

'And why's that?'

'The information on this is covered under Section Eight of the Exemplar Ethical Code for Adolescent Safeguarding, subsection: Duration of Immersion. All this is available on your teleplant.'

'Okay, okay. What's the other point?'

'It's about your teleplant. While you are in virtual space it will divert to me. If someone tries to contact you, I will explain to the caller that you are immersing. If they insist on talking to you, I will break into your session and ask you what you want to do. Is that clear?'

'Clear,' Bliss replied crisply.

'After fifty minutes of immersion, you will hear a series of buzzes in your ear. This will give you and your Exemplar time to find your way back to this room and avoid abruptly terminating any virtual interactions you are experiencing. This is covered under the section called Etiquette. You are now ready to begin your first full immersion.'

Bliss fidgeted around and then touched the top of the frames.

'Oh, how amazing! Let's go outside,' she said aloud and watched in surprise as her virtual self moved towards the balcony. This disassociation quickly ended as she found herself standing in front of the railings, staring at the people working in the vegetable garden.

'Happy birthday, Bliss,' a warm motherly voice called out behind her.

Turning round, Bliss saw a cylinder-shaped object hovering just off the floor. 'What is this?'

'This is Mildred,' a mellow-sounding version of her own voice said in her head. 'She's a housebot who was purchased in 2046 and upgraded in 2048 and 2049.'

'And, err … who are you?' Bliss asked.

'I am BlissX, your Exemplar.'

'Oh yes, of course, you're also here.' Bliss laughed aloud. 'You said "housebot". Has it replaced Mrs Rawlins?'

'No, it supplements her.'

Looking at the metal object below, Bliss asked with slight amusement, 'Hello, Mildred. Who are those people over there in the garden?'

In a Hampshire dialect matching that of Mrs Rawlins, the device hovered up to the level of the railings. 'They are part of the Food Alliance Group that manages the grounds for your mother and father. They keep us regularly supplied with vegetables and fruit. There's even a little left over for me to do some bartering.'

'Mildred, I want to roam around a bit. Is it safe to walk through the hamlet right now?'

The housebot lowered itself to the floor and moved back a little. 'It is now 08.04 'ours. You should be able to move freely until 09.30. After that, they open the night gates at either end of

Sandy Hollow – you will then need to be more careful because of the through traffic.'

The housebot began adjusting the AC and closing the shutters, so Bliss imagined herself walking back into the bedroom. She moved around the bedside chair and thought, *I must get this thing dressed.* Instantly, she saw her Exemplar – once again, slightly ahead of her – open the wardrobe and pull out some clothes. Then with no mental prompting, she found herself putting on shoes and brushing back her hair in front of the mirror.

'No, not like that, like this,' she interjected, imagining herself combing her hair into her usual style. For a few minutes, Bliss experienced a sense of intimacy as her virtual self obeyed the instruction from her true self.

She then thought, *I want to go downstairs and then outside to look around the hamlet.* Again, without delay, she moved off towards the staircase, now without having to consciously imagine herself walking. At the bottom of the stairs she decided to stop, and for a moment there was another brief disassociation between herself and her Exemplar.

Looking down into the large familiar room, Bliss could see the usual piles of books on the floor, walls covered with paintings and odd pieces of sculpture sitting in equally odd places. Moving through the entrance hall and opening the front door, she cautiously stared outside although the only obvious difference she could immediately see was the bright orange tiled roof of the newly converted coach house.

Stepping onto the gravel path alongside the cottage, she found herself walking effortlessly with no need for imagining or any further blurring of selves. Halting at the steps leading up to the road, she espied someone on the far side pavement carrying a woven basket.

That's Mrs Heddown. Don't suppose I'll get much out of her. 'BlissX, tell me what you know about Mrs Heddown,' she whispered.

'Resident of 3 Sandy Hollow, teacher, retired 2035, in financial distress since reduction of payments from the Teacher's Pension Fund by two-thirds in 2037. Bronze Ring Holder.'

As Bliss walked to the top of the steps, the woman waved at her and crossed the road.

'Hello, Bliss, how are you? I've not seen you and your Exemplar before – what do you call her?'

Goodness me, she's so friendly! I don't think I've even seen her smile until now. 'Oh hello, Mrs Heddown. This is the first time I've had access to the SWVRP and been able to venture out with my Exemplar. I call her BlissX.'

'How exciting for you! I'll never forget my first immersion – I felt as free as when I first owned a car, but ten times better,' she said gaily. 'Your father generously gave everyone in the hamlet access to Version 6, back in '41. I didn't take it up straight away, of course, but then I heard so many people talking about it in the shop that I had to have a go. Your mother kindly came over and helped me get used to it. My life has changed since then and these days I hardly leave the hamlet. As soon as I'm notified that someone is in active mode, as I was a few minutes ago with you, I go into the program to meet them. I mostly stick to a maximum of five years into the future – I'm getting too old to go any further. As it's your first time I'll give you a tip – don't stray beyond the hamlet until you can fully coordinate with your Exemplar. I participate a lot in those virtual podcasts ... Life outside is less good these days, particularly if you are in the Fully Segmented scenario.'

'Thank you. I'll certainly take your advice. What are you carrying there?' Bliss asked.

'We are going to do an exchange of eggs for root vegetables with your Mildred. She manages everything for your mother these days. What about you – where are you off to?'

'I'm just orientating myself at present. Where would you recommend I go?'

'For a first-timer, I suggest you avoid going into the shop and the pub for now as there are too many people to deal with. Try the night gates: the securobots will be there, preparing to open the road. They're a lovely bunch. I have a chat with them every morning, though I must say I can't wait for the gates to come down in the evening. Once I see them across the road, I know that the electrification around the hamlet has been turned on and we're all safe. Anyway, I must go – busy busy. Toodle-oo!'

* * *

Virtual Scene snapshot: BlissX stands in the small entrance hall to Soft Rush with Mildred, the housebot, hovering in front of her.

'Welcome back. Did you enjoy your stroll around Sandy Hollow?' Mildred asked as BlissX closed the door.

'I met Mrs Heddown,' Bliss replied. 'Does she have a small-holding or something?'

'After her pension was reduced, the community kept her spirits up. They helped her convert her garden into a chicken run so she had eggs and fresh meat to trade. Of course, we have the Food Alliance Group now, but she still carries on. Friendly, isn't she?'

BlissX climbed the stairs up to her room and returned virtually to the bedside chair. Leaning her head against the backrest, Bliss recalled her first foray into the virtual world of 2050. At the gate near the pub she had remained silent as BlissX had initiated a conversation with the securobots, but then it had started to rain. *Even the unpredictability of the British weather has been simulated. The people in the pub – or maybe their passive Exemplars – were friendly, waving at me – or was it at BlissX? – and then laughing as I initiated a dash back to the house to avoid the shower—*

Her musings were interrupted by the soft voice of E-manual.

'Bliss, I'm sorry for cutting in but I have your father online. He'd like a quick chat. You'll need to come back into real space to take the call.'

'Hi, Pappa, what time is it there?' Bliss asked, rising from the chair and flexing her shoulders.

'Very early, but I wanted to wish you a happy birthday before I got busy. I heard from your VR assistant that you've had your first immersion. How was it?'

Bliss continued her stretching exercises. 'I thought you were all mad when you ranted and raved about the SWVRP, but I was wrong – it's worth all the fuss!'

'How did you get on with your Exemplar?'

'A bit strange at first because my body wasn't quite in tune with it – I call her BlissX by the way. Gradually though, I melded with its movements ... or did it meld with mine? I'm not sure.'

'That's good going after only one session. It took me weeks to get used to it – even though it was my invention. It reminded me of my first attempts at windsurfing – remember how I kept falling off?' Methuen laughed loudly.

'The conversation with BlissX was better than I've managed with any other device, especially when we chatted about the Segmented World.'

'And how did the experience make you feel?'

'Blissful!' she shouted out joyfully, lifting her head and matching the volume of his earlier laugh. 'The whole thing is quite addictive. I can't wait to go back in.'

'That's why we impose limits on the amount of immersion – even for adults. Some of the rival programs allow continuous residence, meaning that people stay virtual for days on end without eating or socialising. So what did you and ... BlissX get up to?'

'At the gate, near the pub, I let her chat to the securobots using her default programming. She's very polite, Pappa – way more so than me. They were only carrying out mechanical duties but she wanted to know everything they were up to. Some of her questions seemed a little pointless because the bots were even less articulate than my VR assistant, but afterwards I realised that she'd extracted all sorts of gossip from them. You know the sort of thing: which residents have already gone out or come in through the gate this morning? At what time? What were they carrying? And then they started offering all sorts of titbits about small things that happened overnight – like a deer getting tangled up in the fencing at the bottom of the fifty-acre wood. Just chit-chat really, but amazingly realistic.'

'I found V13 fascinating but also a little frightening,' Methuen reflected thoughtfully.

'How so?'

'We gave the securobots a high sociability setting to foster community spirit—'

'By gossiping …?'

'Precisely, but with very little moral or social judgement program-ming. They'd give away every last detail if asked – as BlissX was clearly aware. But all they're really au fait with are the comings and goings around the gate, so their subject matter is pretty harmless. In contrast, a bot like the Soft Rush housekeeper, who's involved in our private affairs, needs numerous lines of additional coding to limit her topics of conversation while at the same time keeping her socially agreeable. Did you meet anyone other than securobots?' he asked.

'Mrs Heddown.'

'And how was that?'

'Great! She's always seemed like the most unsociable person in Sandy Hollow – in the past she wouldn't come out of her house unless there was a serious road accident, a freak weather or some-thing like that. But now, my goodness, she's transformed – at least in the world of SL2050.'

'And not just in the virtual world, according to your mother, if you bump into her in real-time, you'll be surprised at quite how cheery she's become.'

'Well, that's good. I had visions of her living in squalor in the real world, lying on a mattress, lost in space. Anyway, where are you calling me from, Pappa?'

'The Allied Campus in Lincoln, Nebraska.'

'Why did you need to go over in person?'

'Well, you know I have this advisory role on the Allied AI executive for overseeing the development of the SWVRP? We've got some pretty critical decisions to make over the next couple of days, so Nick insisted we did it face to face.'

'I heard Mum's at Grandpa's funeral today. How is Granny Pryce?'

'She's not too good, I'm afraid.'

'Oh, that's so sad.'

'Look, this is only a quick call, Bliss, to see if we can link up early evening your time for a longer chat. We've not talked properly in ages.'

'That would be brilliant, Dad. I'll set everything up on the terrace – it should have cooled down by then.'

'Cooled down? Lucky you. Winter and summer seemed to have got all mixed up here – it's freezing.'

* * *

Virtual Scene snapshot: On the garden terrace of Soft Rush, Bliss lies stretched out on a wooden recliner, just as the final rays of light glint through the trees of the fifty-acre wood. Behind her, Mrs Rawlins is wiping down the surface of a table.

'Waiting for your father?' the housekeeper enquired in a deadpan voice.

'Yes, he's about to call me from the States,' Bliss replied turning around, only to see the woman standing behind her, frowning with her mouth tightly shut. 'Is there something wrong, Mrs Rawlins?'

'Perhaps you might ask 'im, Bliss, about my job? My Tommy's just told me that 'e met someone on this virtual reality thing who said that in the future I've been replaced 'ere by some robot. If that's what's goin' to 'appen, I'd rather be told now than at the last moment. Money's tight and this work's important to me, you know.'

Bliss turned around and laughed. 'Mrs Rawlins, I wouldn't worry about that, it's just a program!' But then, seeing the woman unmoved by her words of assurance, she added, 'Don't worry, I'll ask him.'

'Given your father's so 'igh up in all this VR business, I would have thought 'e might 'ave taken care of that by now,' Mrs Rawlins grumbled, shuffling back into the house.

'No problem, I'll talk to him about it,' Bliss shouted out, as she pulled over a monitor attached to a telescopic arm and switched it on.

Mrs Rawlins returned with a tray. 'I've brought you something cold to drink – it's goin' to stay warm tonight.' The woman peered at the screen, which was now displaying an office desk with the Allied Answers logo on the wall behind. 'Looks like you're goin' to be busy. Your father's a good man. I'm sure 'e'd have done the right thing – even if I'd not said a word.'

Yes, he is a good man – more than people realise, Bliss thought, just as the screen went blank and then came back, displaying her father grinning broadly through his heavy beard.

'Hi, Bliss, was that Mrs Rawlins I saw, disappearing into the house there?'

'Yes, Pappa, and you need to tell her what plans you have for her in the future. She knows about the housebot idea.'

Methuen closed his eyes for a moment. 'Well, we're not going to fire her if that's what she's worried about. We need to team her up with the sort of device you met in the SL2050 simulation—'

'You mean Mildred?'

'What Mrs Rawlins needs to understand is that whether it's ... Mildred ... or some other android device, nothing remotely competes with her general ability to look after us all. But equally, she must also understand that running something like the Soft Rush Estate these days requires a set of skills that she simply doesn't have—'

'Such as?'

'Well, the domestic accounts for one. The accountbot that recently came with the new commodity credit system needs to interact with whoever's running the finances of the whole estate – including the house. Can you just imagine Mrs Rawlins having to instruct it? At present the bot calls Mum or me, usually in the evenings when we'd rather be relaxing. A specialist housebot can take care of all that – paying tradespeople, for example. Unfortunately, living sustainably at the level we do at present just does not equate with living simply. Anyway, tell Mrs Rawlins her job is safe, but don't be too specific. I'll deal with it when I get back. Let's talk about V13. I want to hear more of your impressions.'

'I still can't quite get my head around the fact that I can live in two worlds now. I wonder if that means I'll pay less attention to the real one?'

'Well, you could turn it round the other way, Bliss. Allied mainly uses the VR space to envisage different business outcomes. Take this meeting in Nebraska – we all got together in our different locations beforehand in the SWVRP and held a pre-meeting online, to jointly experience different possible futures for Allied AI—'

'So why travel there?'

'That pre-meeting in SWVRP-space allowed us to define the critical issues as well as all the options. That then freed us up to focus, today, on our choices and any points of disagreement. You can only solve those by a face-to-face get-together like this. There's also tomorrow when Nick will join us to discuss what he described to me, as a "new path for the future". And no, I have no idea what that's going to be,' Methuen said, laughing aloud. 'All the corporate heads from Comms, Livings and Health will also be patching in. It's going to be something big.'

'One thing that surprises me, Dad, after immersing in the SWVRP, is why Allied, let alone you and Nick, are still involved in all of this? You always said the main goal was to show people how to live sustainably in a Segmented World, but that was way back in the 2030s. Do people still need this type of virtual guidance? Most accept that what you called the Segmented World is now here in buckets?'

Her father sat back with his hands behind his head and gave a deep sigh. 'This world is not static, Bliss, as the discussions here today have underlined—'

'So will you adjust the SWVRP to help people cope in the challenging times ahead?'

Methuen shuffled uneasily in his seat, his face solemn. 'It's always done that and always will, but ... it's something Allied is going to be less involved with in the future.'

Bliss's head jolted back and then staring at her father, she said, 'You're pulling out?'

Methuen squirmed at the question and then put his finger to his lips. 'This is all very hush-hush right now. The SWVRP employs over one hundred thousand people worldwide and generates a sizeable income stream, but we're moving into a global situation where Allied needs to focus on other stuff, and that I guess is the big topic Nick is going to talk about tomorrow.'

'But you can't just drop the SWVRP. Think about people like Mrs Heddown – it's what helps her get through the days.'

'No, no ... we're not abandoning it as such. The plan is to find a partner for fifty-one per cent of the business to take over operating responsibilities, while leaving development of the SWVRP program with us, in Allied AI. The monies Allied receives from the deal will then be directed towards developing new products such as enhancement of the Exemplar and, I understand, a special tele-plant for a new AA-Com system. Having said all that, Allied also won't, necessarily, be selling to the highest bidder.'

'Doesn't sound like Uncle Nick?' Bliss said, instantly regretting her remark as she saw her father's disapproving frown.

'There are pages and pages of conditions in the sales document dealing with the platform's operational requirements that a successful bidder will need to meet in order to qualify their bid,' he said.

'Such as?'

'Well ... understanding those social responsibilities you mentioned and, of course, maintaining a neutral political stance.'

'But this thing's always been political—'

'But not *party* political,' he cut in. 'Allied have always stuck to my original aim of using the SWVRP to communicate to everyone the ideas and practices of living sustainably with no political slant.'

'That's not exactly what Uncle Nick did when he got involved in Sam Harding's Unity Party in the early 2030s.'

Methuen shrugged. 'In the '30s Nick went political, while I went virtual to get our message over. We'd realised that change had to come through influencing ordinary folks' attitudes as much as getting their leaders to act. Nick thought Harding was the man to deliver it. "Obama's integrity combined with JFK's effectiveness for getting things done" was how he described him.'

'He was a Republican, Dad!'

'But over and above that, he was also a statesman who cared about his country and its people—'

'But look at the mess after Sam Harding died. I remember Mum making a big issue about Nick not supporting Harding's son when he moved over to the Democrats in '37. And she was right, Tom Harding has become the driving force for creating this new Coalition Party that, today, controls everything in the US. If Nick had followed him, he could now be working alongside the man who talks of nothing else but sustainability and global cooperation ... and just happens to be the newly elected president of this coalition government. Instead, he stayed with that scumbag McFall. How did Auntie Lianne describe McFall the other day? "Emperor of a land called Himself", wasn't it?'

Bliss saw her father sigh heavily and his shoulders sag. 'At times Nick's political choices surprise me every bit as much as they do you. I hear that McFall's wanting now to change the name of the Unity Party to something more in line with his latest slogan of "Back to the Old Values" – or whatever twaddle he's currently pushing. You can fool a lot of the people a lot of the time – when they're feeling lost.'

'He's a nasty white supremacist, Dad, who's tearing the US apart. I can't understand why Uncle Nick has anything to do with him!'

Methuen scratched his head and then held his hands over his mouth, a private signal they shared when one of them wanted to end a conversation.

Bliss sat back as her father relaxed and smiled warmly at her. 'So how's college?'

'Oh, you know, same old flaky stuff. I need to move on.'

'What were you thinking of?'

'Something radical,' she shot back.

Methuen leant forward, his eyes widening.

'Lady Caroline's.'

'What – that finishing school in Herefordshire? Why would you want to go there? It's nothing more than a repository for the kids of the super-rich.'

'That's why I want to go – to get to know these people you're so critical of.'

'Wait a minute,' Methuen said, wagging his finger, 'if you're referring to the Attitudinal INs in my book, then please do remember that that argument only applies to those who are *misusing* their wealth.'

Bliss shook her head. 'I agree with what Mum said a few days ago: "We've allowed a technologically enhanced class of human being to emerge." "Closed barrels", she called them. It's just so wrong. We need to reverse it.'

'It's not so straightforward as mere inequality, Bliss. As I said, you need to distinguish between people who acquire and maintain their wealth fairly and squarely and those who do not. That distinction has always been at the heart of identifying the ones I labelled as OST in the Attitudinal studies.'

'From what I hear, most people who send their kids to Lady Caroline's fall into that group.'

Methuen's face tightened sharply. 'And how would you know that?'

'From people I speak to.'

'Well, what do you intend to do about it – become some sort of evangelist?' he fired back.

'In your own words, Dad, I want to "make them aware". Get them to realise that they have just as much a part to play in defending our civilised values as anyone else. And that starts by recognising that the ability to take, needs to be matched by an equal determination to give back.'

Methuen remained silent, resting his chin on his thumbs.

'I've spent the whole of my life listening to you sounding off about OST mentality and now I want to do something about it,' she continued.

'I don't see how you can do that, Bliss. They're not passive clones – like your Exemplar – and besides, why do you think they'd even offer you a place at the school?'

'I may have screwed up my early education, Father dear, but I'm achieving straight As now and will come with excellent references.'

'Umm, I don't think academic achievement is going to be the deciding factor for admission to Lady Caroline's! If it were, many of its students would never have had a snowflake's chance of getting in—'

'I am also the daughter of Methuen Pryce and god-daughter of Nick O'Grady. That will count for something, I'm sure.'

'I'm not sure Nick would be willing to go along with that, and in any case, who's going to pay for it? We may be comfortably off, but we're not in the same league as people who send their kids to Lady Caroline's – not by any stretch of the imagination.'

'Well, I have a surprise for you, Dad. Not only are Mum and Lianne on board with the plan, but from something Lianne sent me this morning, shows that Nick is also supportive of my idea.'

'Is that so?' Methuen said slowly, sitting back and scratching his head.

'Auntie Lianne and Mum have already discussed it. The O'Gradys will provide the funding and if I qualify at the end of my third year, they'll also fund an IT course for me.'

'IT? Computers?' he exclaimed.

'Come on, Dad – Intervention Treatment? You know – one of these new cognitive programmes. Everyone with squillions is getting onto them.'

'I do, Bliss, and I'll tell you now that I am emphatically opposed to all this tampering with our brains. It's flying far too close to the sun.'

'Well, it's not for you or Mum, that's for certain. Only people under thirty can receive the Treatment.'

Her father scribbled something on a notepad. 'I'm not happy about this,' he said. 'The thought of my lovely daughter being re-engineered—'

'Pappa, I'm not going to be re-engineered – just a little ... enhanced,' she added cheekily.

Methuen rubbed his forehead. 'As for your mission to convert the kids of the wealthy ... without wishing to dampen your ardour, just keep an eye out for the significant minority who actually put their wealth to good use. Take your Uncle Nick, for example—'

'Uh, as much as I love Lianne, the jury's out on *him*, or at least until he unhooks himself from McFall.'

'Babies and bathwater, Bliss. If you discount everyone who's made a bad choice, then you also exclude all the good things they have done in the past or may do in the future.'

'Or the evil,' she fired back.

Her father blinked for a moment and then frowned. 'Anyway, what are your plans for seeing them this summer?' he asked.

'I don't know – I thought you might be able to tell me? Lianne's got something arranged but only for a week in September.'

'Oh, that does sound odd. Another thing to ask him about tomorrow.'

'Dad, if you do, please don't upset my plans over Lady Caroline's.'

'Only if you promise to consider a few alternatives. Can't say I'm very happy with this Lady Caroline idea,' he said, and then turned as someone called his name. 'I must go. I've got a pre-lunch meeting with some of the Allied guys. Speak soon. Love you!'

'Love you too, Pappa Bear.'

* * *

Virtual Scene snapshot: Mrs Rawlins is coming through the inside door to the garden terrace, where Bliss is still sprawled on the recliner – but with the telescopic arm and monitor pushed to one side.

'You were on that thing for 'ours after you spoke to your father this evening,' Mrs Rawlins protested mildly. 'Must 'ave been something important?'

'Nothing much, Mrs Rawlins – just checking in on a few of my college friends.'

'I won't disturb you then. I'll switch on the security alarm before I leave, like your mother always insists on – though I don't really see why it's necessary,' the woman mumbled as she started watering the plants around the terrace.

'Oh, I spoke to my father,' Bliss called out, 'and he confirmed there are no plans at all to replace you with any kind of mechanical device. It'd be like replacing Martin with a robot – though maybe that's not a good analogy,' she said to herself with a snigger.

'Oh, thank you, Bliss – that's such a load off my mind. I love workin' up 'ere. I said to my Tommy, "I don't need any virtual world when I 'ave Soft Rush and Sandy Hollow to go to every day.'"

Mrs Rawlins scuttled off and Bliss leant across to switch off the monitor. Slumping back onto the recliner she stared out into the night. *Why are you wasting your time with those idiot girls?* she thought. *It used to be great going a bit wild, but I'm getting bored with all this idle natter about boys and holidays and, worst of all, today's main topic: facial rejuvenation. When I did actually manage to get a few words in about using VR to convert the super-rich kids, what did they say? 'We're stuck in this world, Bliss – so let's just enjoy it.' And then came the real humdinger that showed they hadn't understood a word of what I'd said: 'There are always people with more money than the rest of us – we just have to get on with them.' The only interesting thing they had to say on the subject of VR was about a girl they knew who'd got through to some illegal site and was obsessed with one of the avatars who did unspeakable things to her. God help us if this new technology simply gets used for self-indulgent stuff like that. The only person who interested me at all wasn't even physically there. It's a pity we never see her face, but those are the rules in the Nebraska Nunnery.*

Bliss laughed out loud as she recalled the nickname the others had come up with for Ramona's school.

She didn't have a lot to say, which I could understand from a newbie, except for that one weird outburst when the other girls dismissed all involvement in the SWVRP. I distinctly heard her say, 'Oh, the joy of ignorance …' Strangely enough, no one else seemed to hear it – they just carried on wittering. Makes me realise how much Ramona and I actually have in common: we're no longer girlies.

Bliss took a sip from the drink Mrs Rawlins had left and lay back on the recliner.

It'd be great if she becomes a new friend, because Rasputin – or whatever his name was – is definitely no longer on my mailing list. *The only reminder I've got left of my little Russian fling is the name of my pussycat. I only got together with the guy because he and his mates agreed with me that the super-rich needed a kick up the backside. The only problem was their solution – just a bit too extreme!*

As this last thought crossed her mind, Bliss sat up straight. *Hang on a mo' – what if he's working for his homeland and our little liaison happened to leak out? It could totally scupper my plans to get into Lady Caroline's. Maybe I'll call Ramona and ask what she reckons?*

Inside the red-painted barn;
Hardin, Montana, NCSA, FSA
08.00 hours, 15 June 2050

'So what do you think?' Nick asked as he turned towards Lianne, who lay with her arms outstretched, still wearing the VR specs.

'Where do I start? I was there, but not there. Bliss sat in the chair, opening her presents and talking with the housekeeper, but as soon as she immersed, the scene blanked and then came back with Bliss or rather Bliss represented by her Exemplar, moving around. Except that in my head I heard the real Bliss talking as well as her Exemplar. How was that even possible?'

'The Storymaker has access to the SWVRP and since we have everything archived—'

'Does Bliss know you can access her Exemplar?' Lianne interjected, taking off the specs.

'During this test phase, I allowed the team to have access to everything.' He looked up and scrolled through the file. 'I see Methuen has viewed this scene and verified his record—'

'But not Bliss?'

'She will – just as soon as she settles down on Phillips and communications there come back on stream. So, did it bring back any memories for you?'

Lianne sneered. 'What, 2045 – how could it not? Your darkest moment – realising what your pal McFall was really up to—'

'And you coming to my rescue ...'

'Not that you saw it like that at the time. I seem to remember you were angry with me at first, for not immediately sharing with you what I had on McFall.'

Nick slumped back on the pillow. 'It's strange watching it now. I have mixed feelings about '45. It was also a time of great opportunity and growth for me in some ways. The political side may have gone belly-up, but that was the year I got the go-ahead from the Allied board to convert Phillips Cay into a fully sustainable community.'

'And that was the big surprise you dropped on Methuen and the rest of your Executive on that second day in Nebraska. At least it's not just *me* who suffers from your congenital need-to-know, Grady.'

'It was a very tough time but you were there for me,' he said, touching her hand.

Lianne turned on her side to face him. 'I didn't see you there in that virtual world with Bliss.'

'Of course not. As soon as you immerse, all you perceive is what is programmed. I don't exist there and nor do you. You only experience what's on the file.'

'What's in the other scenes?' she asked, lying back and staring up at the ceiling.

Nick scrolled through a list on the ceiling screen. 'Pre-'49, the most complete ones are of Elizabeth and Methuen's early life, covering the transition into The Time of Less,' he said, enlarging the file icons. 'There are quite a few of me but I've not reviewed many of them yet. After '49, there's nearly complete coverage, based on the combined feed from all our AA-Plants. The Storymaker seems to have made a lot of scenes of the journey down to Phillips on the *Clipper*, involving us as well as Elizabeth and Methuen.'

'Nothing else from Bliss?'

'No more virtual reconstructions with her on her own – there was something wrong with her teleplant, I seem to recall.'

'Have you viewed all the scenes?'

He emitted a short derisive laugh and then said, 'When would I have found time to do that?'

'Okay then, let's look at a few from Elizabeth and Methuen's past. Maybe it'll help me understand some of the terminology that came up in the last one.'

'Yeah, that's a good idea,' he said, moving the cursor to the top of the list. 'Hmm … this one's from 2012.'

'Same request as before, Grady,' she said, picking up her glasses. 'Not a word to anyone that we did this. Bliss would never forgive me.'

He nodded in agreement and then sat up to view the monitors at the end of the bed. 'Before we do that I just want to run a quick check outside.'

Lianne heaved herself up on her elbows, viewing a display of the gas station, general store and the barn.

Another image flashed up. 'This one is from the drone positioned on the treetops looking west,' he said. 'You can see the mountains in the distance – where the bad weather usually comes from.'

The camera zoomed in on a thin spiral of smoke rising vertically into the air. 'That's Billings, fifty miles away – nothing between us and there. I've also put a drone on the barn roof, pointing east towards the highway, to keep a watch for any visitors.'

He lay back and pointed the remote at the screen on the ceiling. 'This is Methuen as a kid – he can't be much older than Bliss was in the last scene. I've flicked through some of it. Even *then* he had a clear idea which way the world was heading.'

AA-Com File: 'Fuck the IOCs!'

St Stephen's Church, Nottingham, UK
Early evening, 10 February 2012

Virtual Scene snapshot: A tall wiry figure wearing a dark blue duffle coat and shouldering a school satchel walks along a snow-covered path towards the arched doorway of a small church.

I'll freeze to death if I stay out here much longer, Methuen thought. Lifting the metal latch and pushing hard, he grunted triumphantly as the old oak door creaked open. *Boy, it's dark in here ... And what the heck is that smell?*

Following his nose, he spotted a small oil heater in the central aisle. After warming his hands, he slid along the nearest pew to a stone pillar, where he lowered his head as if in prayer.

Now, what was that new phrase I woke up with this morning? Oh yes: 'The Segmented World'. It's right – I know it's right. Come on, look for the logic behind it.

* * *

Virtual Scene snapshot: Fifteen minutes have passed. Methuen is rummaging frantically through the satchel beside him.

Pulling out a mobile phone, he switched off the shrill tone that had butchered the silence he had been enjoying. As he slipped the phone back into his bag, he noticed a text from his elder brother, instructing him to call home immediately.

'Oh, for cryin' out loud! I'm seventeen years old – just leave me alone,' he howled, but as he buried the offending object in the bottom of his satchel, his hand brushed against the hard edge of the invitation card. *This is why I've travelled across the city on this bloody awful night and am sat here, waiting for that theatre to open over the road. It'd better be good.*

Stuffing the card in a side pocket of his coat, he tried to return to his stream of thought about the Segmented World, but a memory broke through of his mother angrily waving the card at him as he returned home from school.

'What's this, Methuen?' she asked suspiciously.

'I've asked you so many times, Mother – please don't open my mail.'

'So how do you explain *this*?' she fired back, pointing to a slip of paper attached to the card on which someone had written in a stylish hand: You will find this stimulating. 'Who's sending you stuff like this?'

'I don't know, Mother.' *And what business is it of yours if I did?*

'Until you tell me something about the writer of this note, you are not to attend this event. Do I make myself clear?'

Oh, I understood all right – her and my brothers always ordering me around and snooping into my personal affairs. The next day, I went straight to Mr Demming. He'd become more than my personal tutor and maths teacher by then, although his initial response was disappointing, as he delivered the same lecture my mother had given me the day before about meeting strangers on the Internet.

'Yes, sir, but I wondered whether you could throw any light on the three gold characters in the top right-hand corner – NOY?'

It worked. He wasn't normally someone lost for words, but on this occasion he went quiet as he studied the card.

'I see ... how fascinating ... Leave it with me, Pryce; I'll make a few enquiries.'

I didn't have long to wait. I was running between classes the very next day when I saw him standing by the staffroom door, holding the card up and waving me over. He seemed excited for some reason, completely oblivious to the pandemonium around him.

'I called Trent Theatre. No one knew what the letters meant, but I can see no reason why someone from the Lower Sixth should not attend this event – the place is quite respectable.'

He then gave a short, uncharacteristic titter that I can hear, even now.

'My only slight reservation comes from the title they gave for the talk: "Fuck the Amazon". I don't think you should raise your hopes as to the quality of either the content or the contributors, Pryce.'

What's that? Oh crikey, it's the church bell striking the hour. I'll be late for the talk.

Rushing out of the church and charging across the icy road towards a Victorian red-brick building, Methuen felt in his satchel for the invitation card. Unable to locate it, he stopped outside the theatre and tipped the contents of his bag onto the steps. As he raked through papers, pens and the remains of that day's lunch, the theatre door opened and a large portly man in a black uniform appeared above him. At first, all Methuen saw was his grandad – invoking happy memories of summer holidays spent at his engineering works in Derby.

'You 'ere for tonight's performance or that talk upstairs?' the man enquired brusquely.

Do I look like I'm here to attend a play, dressed like this? Methuen thought, but with shades of his kindly grandfather still lingering in his head, he mumbled apologetically, 'I'm … err, trying to find the invitation card.'

'Invitation card?' The man stepped back, looking shocked. 'You'd best come in and sort this out – you're blocking the entrance 'ere.'

Methuen entered a warm, brightly lit interior and for a split second imagined lying down on the sumptuous carpet beneath his feet. Not that anyone would have noticed: the foyer was empty except for a couple walking towards the bar, while the commissionaire had headed off towards a dark passageway.

Untoggling his duffle coat, Methuen felt the solid outline of the invitation card in a side pocket and called out gleefully, 'Here it is!'

The man walked back and took the card, scanning it with the precision of a barcode reader. 'I'm afraid you were, uh ... meant to be 'ere at seven thirty ... sir,' he said, bowing slightly in Methuen's direction. 'The last person with this type of card arrived 'alf an hour ago. Would you please follow me?'

Emerging from the passageway into an ornate high-ceilinged room, Methuen stepped back in surprise, as he saw a multi-coloured mass of exuberant young adults packing a wide, elegant staircase that curved upward and out of sight.

'I'm afraid I can't get you through this lot – you'll 'ave to queue 'ere,' the man said, walking away.

At over two metres in height and younger than most there, heads turned as Methuen arrived at the foot of the stairs and dropped his satchel on the floor.

'Hi, how you doin'?' he said to a group of young women in front of him, kitted out in matching scarves and gloves. *All with designer labels*, Methuen thought, chuckling to himself.

A rough-looking gang of young males arrived and began laughing at him as his coat fell open, revealing the sapphire blue jacket and trousers that the school inflicted on its sixth-formers. Ignoring them, he looked up the stairs for the end of the queue but found his view blocked by a man shouldering a large backpack covered with hand-stitched badges.

Modern war medals, I guess ... though rather than Basra or Musa Qala, it's what? He twisted his head and read: Twyford Down, Newbury Bypass, Finsbury Square Camp and then at the bottom: Stop Esso and St Paul Anti-Fascist Action Group.

As he continued to scrutinise the self-conferred decorations, a young woman beside him said, 'Impressive, huh?'

He went to reply but was cut short by the male backpacker, who turned to the woman and began recounting stories from his various 'campaigns'. Methuen listened politely at first but then, noticing that the man had left a space next to the railings, edged himself over and again looked up the staircase. His shoulders dropped in exasperation as he saw the queue had stalled outside a pair of half-open double doors. *This is going nowhere ... what was I thinking about in the church?*

But as he tried to return to the Segmented World, his thoughts drifted again, first to the text message from his brother and then to a more deeply scored memory. *I'm sitting in the front seat of the car, next to my mother, who's driving. My two older brothers are in the back. We're returning from a school open day where I've just given that speech on 'The End of Economic Growth'. I'm excited by all the applause I got, but the mood in the car is quite different.*

'All this studying at your age isn't good for you – you need to get a life!' shouted his elder brother, followed by the other saying mockingly 'I think it's boring ...'

'Boring! Boring!' Methuen found himself voicing the words aloud and glanced around, embarrassed in case those near him on the stairs might have heard his outburst, but it seemed that no one had noticed. The gang behind him were now interacting with the young women, who had started squawking like a flock of para-keets over the attention they were receiving. Leaning back on the stair rail, Methuen returned to the argument in the car, at the point where he had unbuckled his seat belt and was wagging a finger at his brothers in the back.

'I'll tell you what's *boring*: neither of you thinking about the future you're going to inherit,' he said.

'What d'you mean by that?' his older brother replied resentfully.

'Every time you hear a government minister proposing a new policy to win your vote, just ask yourself: where does the funding *actually* come from? I can tell you now, it won't be from *boring old economic growth* in the future. It'll have to be underwritten by you paying more tax for the bigger and bigger interest payments on the national debt.'

'So what?' the younger one barked.

'I'll tell you what. When we eventually reach the limit of borrowing to fund growth, you can forget any new increments in state provision to the NHS, the education system and social care payments. That's why the decline of economic growth is not boring, brother.'

'Sit back and buckle up, Methuen!' his mother screamed at him.

But she didn't tell them to shut up. So unfair, not defending me after I had defended her all those years against my father.

The queue started to shuffle forward and Methuen moved up the stairs, his thoughts elsewhere as he continued to brood over the argument in the car.

That's when I shifted from my family to my work, and to Mr Demming, of course. He'd always been a strange one – the grave runner. I bet our Head never realised quite how much he'd done for dear old Demming's reputation by ticking him off for using the graveyard next to the school as a shortcut. But it's not just his petty rule-breaking that makes him so popular with us. There's also that rumour about him being wanted by Interpol because he won't go on school trips abroad – something to do with him being an arms trader or so they say? What no one questions, though – not even the Head – is his brilliance as a teacher. I never know whether I'm in a maths or philosophy class during his lessons.

'Mathematics is nothing more than a tool, ladies and gentlemen. Don't get too excited about it. The real fun in life is in

recognising the paradoxes and deceits all around you. Learn
to identify them and then, if it's appropriate, use mathematics to help you prove or disprove your conclusions.'

*All that teaching to the unconverted didn't mean much until that
lesson on the intricacies of the exponential function. I can just see
it now, him moving away from a board covered with equations,
and posing a question.*

'The total output from the world's mines has grown expo-
nentially over the past one hundred years. Here's the data.
Plot it and tell me how this has been possible?'

*It didn't take me long to work out that the main reasons were due
to improved exploration techniques and increased recovery. As
a bonus, because he always gets excited when we do something
extra, I applied a similar analysis to several other key commodities and used the extrapolation technique he'd taught us earlier in
the year to define a few likely outcomes. I thought I'd made some
error in my calculations because in every single case, the increased
production plateaued – and over the succeeding decades there
was a steady decline in resources such as crude oil, phosphorous,
tin and lead.*

*About a week later, he asked me to stay behind at the end of
a class. That was the moment that changed my life. I can see him
now, marching over to the blackboard, taking off his gown, and
drawing one graph after another, showing more and more examples of the expected decline in natural resources up to the end
of the century. He then pulled across another board and began
making fresh graphs of things I knew nothing about at the time:
birth and death rates, per capita food production, ditto industrial
output. But it was when he finally turned to face me that he got my
full attention: instead of his usual enthusiastic, bouncy persona, he
looked troubled and uncertain.*

'We live in a finite world, Methuen, which we exploit as
though every part were self-replenishing. I will be spared

the worst excesses of this foolishness but you will not, and nor will your children, nor your children's children.'

That statement alone would have been enough to stimulate my curiosity, but the emotion in his voice and his use of my first name nailed it for me. That was what, early 2009? By the end of 2010, with his help and his urging me with lines such as – If you don't know what connects and controls things, Pryce, then start by correlating until you find the causation – I managed to get hold of what seemed like back then vast amounts of data, along with systems software allowing me to reproduce not just the projections he had hurriedly chalked up on the blackboard, but also a way of revealing just how these might interact over time. Then in early 2011, thanks to his lobbying, I was selected to lead the school at the quarter-finals of the UK interschool debate. The talk was entitled 'The Time of Less', a term with a certain ring to it that came to me as I was preparing the talk. But when I received back my eight-minute script from him without a single red mark on it, I was worried that this was a sign of his total rejection. Instead all he said was, 'Not bad, Pryce. Carry on.'

Methuen looked up and saw that the queue was still barely moving, while behind him the gang of young men had started the predictable chant of 'Why are we waiting?' He rested his arm back on the stair rail and returned to his thoughts.

I'm standing at the debating table, flanked by my team. In front of me sits a jury of three men and three women, all with encouraging smiles. Behind them is the audience, mainly made up of parents and pupils from rival schools – all waiting to grill me once the panel had finished. I'd planned the talk carefully, topping and tailing it with two blunt statements. I also had a surprise up my sleeve, having decided to break the rules and include several graphic images behind the projected words of my speech. I got a real buzz as a gasp ran round the room when the bright red capitals on the first slide came up.

I'M NOT SO WORRIED ABOUT CLIMATE CHANGE ...

NOR EVEN THE DEPLETION OF KEY COMMODITIES
BY THE MID-CENTURY ...

WHAT DOES CONCERN ME IS THE IMPACT OF THESE
ON THE ECONOMIC GROWTH WE REQUIRE TO
FEED THE EXTRA FOUR BILLION

I moved now to the front of the table, again breaking the rules, and clicked the controller to highlight the graph behind the words, showing world debt against economic growth over the past fifty years. It was time to talk.

'Global economic growth today is propped up by unsustainable borrowing that like any addictive substance is becoming less and less effective in producing the required stimulation. Look at the balance sheets of countries around the world. How much will repayment of debt, cost in the future? The same as defence? The same as defence and education? Or even the same as defence *and* education *and* health? And what happens when no one wants to lend? That's surely the point when the Great Defaulting begins.'

I gave them a few seconds to absorb this and then flashed up my second slide, this one in even bigger letters.

ECONOMIC GROWTH IS A LIE
DON'T BE HOODWINKED!

A few people in the audience started to object, so I quickly showed a third slide.

THIS ONE'S FOR THE GROWN-UPS LOOKING FOR
A GET-OUT-OF-JAIL CARD

IT'S TOO LATE FOR TECHNOLOGY TO SCALE UP

THE ONLY FIX IS EACH OF US
CHANGING OUR LIFESTYLE

It was time to put on my serious face and draw my conclusion.

'Civilised human society will degenerate and die unless we do something now. We must act on this reality by finding a more sustainable way to live ... This is the only remedy we have to prevent chaos.'

As I ended the speech I glanced over at the jury. Its members were alert but pensive; one was chewing his nails while two others sat with their chins propped on their hands, staring up at the last slide. Each spoke in turn, praising my 'passion', 'originality' and 'sophistication of the thesis', with absolutely no reference to my having trampled on procedure. The trouble only began when the questions were opened to the floor.

'... dethroning the idea of economic growth is a classic case of scaremongering ...'

'... spreader of a false belief ...'

There was also a barrage of personal stuff at the end, with one comment, parodying the title of the talk, eliciting a loud round of applause.

'Less of your time will save a lot of our time worrying over nonsense like this.'

I was stunned – I had expected criticism from older members of the audience, but this had come from my peers. I stared down at the faces alongside me and knew I'd blown it. On the bus going home, Mr Demming did his best to ease our disappointment at losing the debate and not progressing into the semi-finals.

'In life, ladies and gentlemen, failure often provides greater long-term rewards than the short-term thrill of winning.'

'Good old Mr Demming,' Methuen said aloud, and then looked up and realised he had reached the top of the stairs.

Peering over those in front of him, he stared into a packed room which seemed to be discharging frosty air. In the centre he spotted a seated area, which he assumed was reserved for those like him with an invitation.

'It's like a bloody fridge in there,' he murmured, noting that many who were seated wore blankets draped around their shoulders and appeared to be clutching hot-water bottles while those standing were snorting out dense clouds of condensed air – *like horses waiting to race on a chilly winter's morning*, he thought to himself.

Once inside, he worked his way along the back of the seated area, having spotted a single unoccupied chair with a neatly folded blanket and what he imagined would by now be a tepid-water bottle. As he went to claim his place, a powerful set of lights illuminated the front of the room revealing seven cushioned chairs positioned behind a solid line of glass tables beneath which convector heaters could be heard blasting out, what he presumed would be, warm air. While he mulled over this contrast in comfort, a group of lightly dressed individuals filed out from a side door, led by a spindly youth, his hands hidden within the folds of a shapeless black woollen jumper.

As the new arrivals settled back in their padded seats, the young man, who Methuen decided must be a member of the theatre staff, began to reel off a set of safety instructions with all the verve and joy of a late-night station announcer.

For goodness' sake, you don't kick things off like that! You say, I'm sorry for the lack of heating, blah blah blah ...

But the youth blabbered on, eventually taking a crumpled sheet of paper from his pocket and reading out names, positions and general introductions for those seated behind him.

Methuen felt a fresh upswelling of irritation as the presenter seemed finally to draw breath with a last fawning comment: 'And now will you please welcome your panel for this evening.'

'You're not introducing some bloody gardening programme!' Methuen grumbled, but was then taken aback by the loud applause the announcement received.

More like a sodding football match – unless this invitation is some kind of prank? This thought caused him to look around for a means of escape, but it was too late. The doors had closed and the young man, who had described himself as a 'sort of convenor', now, to Methuen's despair, embarked on yet another dreary monologue. With nowhere to go and the chair too high to climb over, Methuen folded his arms in resignation and turned his attention to the two most senior panellists – a man and a woman – who had taken seats behind the youth.

Their choice or his? he wondered and then looked up in annoyance, as the young man started talking on a new topic – outlining the format of the evening.

Studying the seniors more closely, he observed that the man, who was dressed in tweeds and clearly the older of the two, seemed to be sitting back and deliberately avoiding the gaze of the audience. *He looks like he's dressed for a country house weekend, though the natural greens and browns blend rather well with the colours of the parakeets on the stairs.* He chuckled at this thought and then turned to the woman, who in contrast was wearing a slick, charcoal-grey trouser suit and, unlike the man, leaning forward and actively studying the crowd facing her. *She's definitely older than my mother.*

The colourless compère now ended his round of announcements, passing the microphone on to a female panel member, requesting her to make an opening statement. Methuen listened with interest as she talked about the circular economy: 'slowing down resource depletion', and then the next presenter, promising advances in agricultural productivity: 'feeding the growing population'. Several others spoke on energy-saving actions, ranging from electric cars to new developments in turbine and solar technology: 'replacing the use of damaging fossil fuels'. The tone of each was upbeat, but as they concluded, the mood of all became more sombre, laced with dire predictions should their particular idea not be adopted.

This single-issue outlook is too easy. We can only solve these things holistically, and that means compromise. But despite his reservations, all he heard after each speech was rousing applause from the audience.

The elderly man in the tweeds now took the mic. As he stood up, Methuen noticed an unmistakable drop in the level of background chatter. Eager to understand what commanded such apparent reverence, he sat up and cupped his ear. The man's opening lines though were a disappointment: '... the sheer ineffectiveness of politicians and the political process ... the irresponsibility of the corporate world ...'

The same old rhetoric from the constituency of blame. We're all to blame, mate! We're all accomplices in this unholy mess. I'm getting fed up with this. He looked again towards the door and was just reconsidering his options for escape when he heard the man's voice grow more strained, reminding him of the way Mr Demming had spoken when they first talked about the future.

'The fundamental problem we face is common to us all,' the man said gravely. 'It's our own faulty wiring that leads us under stress to abandon cooperation as the best solution and seek to gratify our immediate needs, making us incapable of acting on anything beyond the *Bloomberg Horizon*. We must force ourselves to acknowledge that the common good does not extend much beyond our own family when times are hard.'

The man then stepped forward, spread his arms wide with his palms to the audience, and in a breezier tone of voice said, 'We *must* rethink these shortcomings, we *must* find a common purpose and we *must* solve these problems by all working together.'

Watching him take his seat to the loudest applause of the evening, Methuen bowed his head in his hands. *Don't give us all that rallying the troops guff! Say more about the real causes you were outlining and what we can do about them.*

But it was too late – the next speaker had taken the mic.

She can't be much older than me?

Any sympathy the speaker might have stirred in Methuen, though, quickly evaporated as her Gatling-gun delivery electrified the room.

'We've started the campaign to destroy the shareholder value of the fossil fuel companies – let's now finish it! The tarring and feathering of their outlets will continue; the names and addresses of all the executives are on our website. Do what you must!'

Hmm, wouldn't have been out of place at a Nuremberg Rally. This thought was then reinforced as a high-spirited group next to him began chanting, 'Do what you must, do what you must ...'

Methuen was stunned at the evident satisfaction in the speaker's voice as she described each act of destruction, as well as the loud support coming from the audience. 'What's the point of all this?' he muttered to himself, loud enough for a well-dressed man seated on his left to turn and stare at him.

Then, without any invitation from the compère, the suited man stood up abruptly and in a patient, controlled voice asked the Gatling-gun girl, 'Your tactics are aimed solely at the IOCs. What about the NOCs?'

Oh, that's interesting – the old guy in the tweeds has come forward to see the audience's reaction.

The young woman, visibly unsettled by the remark, said, 'I'm sorry, I don't know what you're talking about ... What are IOCs and NOCs?'

Methuen heard the man mutter something angrily under his breath, but then respond calmly. 'IOCs are independent oil companies – the sort you want to "tar and feather", while the NOCs are national oil companies, who own eighty per cent of the remaining crude oil reserves. If you fancy going to their country and tarring and feathering their outlets, they'll likely throw you in prison ... and some may even cut off your hands!'

A wave of shock ran around the room at this last remark. Several of the panellists shuffled in their seats, all looking rather grim, while the convenor, after vigorously tapping into his mobile, stared into the lights and asked nervously, 'Err, could you explain what you mean?'

The man replied instantly. 'By destroying the IOCs, not only will you jeopardise the free flow of fossil fuels and potentially destabilise civilised society – which I might add you rely upon to allow your protests – but you will also have closed down the only effective channel you have remaining with which to influence the oil and gas industry in any meaningful way.'

Methuen noticed the old man turn to the convenor and gesture for him to move on to another question. But before anyone could respond, the woman in the trouser suit, sitting next to him – who had introduced herself as a professor of atmospheric engineering and given a vexatious update on climate change – jumped to her feet.

'Fuck the IOCs – cripple them! We have to start somewhere,' she said slowly and emphatically.

Around him, Methuen heard a few cheers of support, although most people, including the other panellists, stayed silent. *It's like Mr Demming waggling his finger at me after I'd been too fierce in that school debate a few years back. What was it he said? Oh yes: 'Goldilocks passion, Pryce – not too much and not too little.'*

But in that instant and before he'd had time to construct a reasoned reply, Methuen found his hand in the air and the convenor inviting him to speak. In the split second before he began to talk, he saw several of the panellists smiling at him.

Are those smiles of welcome, or relief that someone's going to ask something less contentious?

'All I've heard this evening is what each of you *object* to,' he said, speaking in the deeper tone of voice he had developed to defend his mother in family disputes. 'What I'd like to know, speaking from your environmental point of view, is precisely how you propose we move towards the more sustainable, low-carbon society we all favour? It seems to me that any plan requires the involvement of all players, including those whom some here want to destroy. So can you tell me, please: what is *your* plan for the transition?'

Without stopping to confer with the others, the physicist stood up and pointed at him. 'This problem is far more urgent than you realise: we desperately need to stop pumping all this crap into the atmosphere and *now*! We'll start with the easy targets and move forward from there – that is our plan.'

Out of the corner of his eye, Methuen saw the suited man shake his head despairingly, while on his other side, a slim young woman in an elegant black velvet coat turned in his direction and stared at him over a set of pince-nez.

Undeterred by the ferocity of the physicist's reply, Methuen said, 'What you're advocating will make the problem worse, not better. Oil and gas accounts for a huge percentage of the primary energy that the world uses today, and it's going to stay like that for a long time. If you remove its availability too fast, people will burn wood and coal. That will add proportionally more carbon dioxide and other noxious substances to the atmosphere and accelerate the degradation of our environment. Also, I'm no expert, but everything I read tells me that alternatives such as wind turbines and solar panels will never be able to *reliably* provide more than forty per cent of the global energy requirement. If we use the remaining, cheap fossil fuels wisely enough, we might have enough to keep civilised society together while we develop affordable, alternative solutions that *everyone* can benefit from.'

He thought about ending it there but so much was buzzing through his head that he found himself compelled to keep going.

'It'll take time before enough people on this planet have similar access to these alternatives as they do to fossil fuels today. Without a global transition plan, you're condemning billions of people to energy poverty, aren't you?'

Turning away from the physicist, he went to address the Gatling-gun girl, but as their eyes met, he felt an inexplicable pang of remorse as he saw her shrink back into her seat, and a voice in his head said, *Please, please don't ask me.*

He turned away from her and directed his comment to the panel as a whole.

'I'm not sure if it's already too late to stop the worst excesses of climate change and find a more sustainable way to live, but one thing I'm certain of is that it's way too late simply to wave your banners and protest—'

'*Nothing* happens unless we protest!' a harsh voice shouted from across the room. Methuen turned in the direction of the remark but resisted the urge to respond, as further comments were hurled at him. 'Who the hell does he think he is?' and then, triggering widespread laughter, 'Daddy probably works for an oil company ...'

As he reluctantly sat down, he saw the woman to his right, stand up; place her pince-nez in a top pocket and then turn in his direction. Tall and imposing with a bundle of neatly coiffed black hair, she fixed her eyes on him and then, to his astonishment, clapped, slowly, three times before saying loudly, 'Well done – well done!'

Engulfed by a crimson tide of embarrassment, he was about to reply when a distant bell rang, causing the convenor to jump to his feet – with more fervour than he had shown for the past hour or so.

'For anyone with tickets, the evening performance will begin in thirty minutes; for those who aren't so lucky, the bar is—'

Before he could finish, the room erupted with the sound of scuffling feet and screeching chairs as people made a dash for the stairs and the prospect of something warmer and more convivial below.

As the room emptied, the suited man reached over and shook his hand but left without saying a word. Methuen then turned to where the clapping woman had been seated but saw she had moved to the front of the room where she was now remonstrating with the physicist.

Picking up his bag, he joined the queue on the stairs. As before, no one greeted him, although this time he sensed that everyone was aware of his presence. As he stood there, a hatchet-faced young man with a rigorously trimmed moustache turned towards him. 'So what are you then – one of these ecomodernist lackeys?' he asked.

Unsure of what he meant or how he should respond, Methuen shrugged but remained silent.

The man tried again, this time with more hostility in his voice. 'People who sit on fences, laddie, eventually get pushed over.'

I can't let that go. You may be five or ten years older than me, but I've seen you before, whether as my father bullying my mother, or now my older brother trying to keep me in line.

'The problem is greater than a single issue and destroying things really isn't a solution,' Methuen replied sharply.

'It's a fight between the vested interests of capitalism and the rights of the ordinary people,' the man snarled.

'It's not as simple as that,' Methuen said, shaking his head wearily.

'You arrogant bastard! Are you calling us simple?' shouted a heavy-set youth pushing his way through to Methuen.

'Excuse me! Excuse me,' he heard someone call out urgently from behind. Before he could react, he felt a hand grip his elbow and propel him forward. Glancing round, he saw alongside him the clapping woman, who then began to wail like a police siren, steering him towards the stairs.

'Please make way! This is an emergency, emergency, emergency …'

Her piercing voice unzipped the crowd ahead, creating a narrow pathway down which they descended unhindered into the foyer.

'Hah! I enjoyed that ... didn't you?' she said, squealing with laughter, and then pulling out her pince-nez to peer over the heads of the assembled theatregoers.

Methuen laughed shyly as she waved to attract the attention of the commissionaire.

She's only a few inches shorter than me, with straight shoulders and a dark complexion – Arab or Iranian maybe? But definitely in charge.

'We need to talk!' she shouted as the commissionaire moved through the crowd towards them. 'We could head to the bar but risk bumping into those idiots on the stairs. I suggest we go to my car.'

Her car?

Methuen's head started to spin but before he could decide what to do, the woman had grabbed his arm again and dragged him through the crowd – ably assisted by the commissionaire making judicious use of an unfurled umbrella.

Out on the steps of the theatre, the man pulled a whistle from his top pocket and waved at a limousine parked on the other side of the snow-covered street.

Inside the red-painted barn;
Hardin, Montana, NCSA, FSA

09.45 hours, 15 June 2050

'Is that it?' Lianne called out.

'Yep. You want to go straight on to the next one?'

'That was incredible – where were you standing?'

'I put myself by the door – I could see everything from there,' he said, sitting up on his elbows. 'What about you?'

'I went down to the front and watched that ghastly woman being rude to Methuen. He had real balls defending himself like that,' Lianne said, removing her glasses. 'Did you ever view that YouTube clip of the interschool debate – the one that went viral? I was only twelve at the time. I knew about climate change, but he seemed to be saying that the problem was more fundamental than that. Not something that anyone wanted to admit back then – no wonder he was struggling to be heard.'

'But he *was* heard.'

'By the foreign woman you mean?'

'Yeah, and that's what the next scene is about,' Nick said, using the remote to select another file.

'Before you do that, explain to me how it's possible to get so much detail about something that took place nearly forty years ago – you didn't have these new AA Plants then!'

'In Methuen's case, it's not too difficult because of his diaries. Did you know that he's written at least one page of A4 every day since he was eight years old? How many people in history have done that and then kept all the documents? If you add on all the usual stuff, such as this new memory-downloading, you have more than enough material to make a plausible reconstruction.'

'Plausible or true?'

'Hmm, shall we call it a highly verified account?'

'Verified by whom?'

'The main players.'

'That must be enormously time-consuming?'

'Sure. That's why this idea of creating Embodiers – Exemplars with memory – never took off previously. But now we have these AA-Plants that download everything from their user, along with the Storymaker IA—'

'Intelligent assistant,' Lianne confirmed.

'That's right … automating the reconstructions. Actions, places and even thoughts are recorded – all you need to decide as an observer is who you believe. Shall we move on and find out what happened when an attractive older woman invited a schoolboy into her car?'

'Purely intellectual, I'm sure.'

'Umm …'

AA-Com File:
'... a little more towards Heaven ...'

Outside the Trent Theatre, Nottingham, UK
Late evening, 10 February 2012

Virtual Scene snapshot: A sleek black limousine is parked alongside the theatre steps. It is snowing heavily. The commissionaire, holding up an umbrella, is escorting the Clapping Lady to the far rear door of the car, which is being held open by a uniformed driver in a smart cap and long leather boots.

Alone at the top of the steps, Methuen experienced a twinge of anxiety as he recalled childhood warnings about cars and strangers. But his concern quickly faded as the driver, smiling, walked over to him with his hand extended.

'Your bag, sir,' the man said, opening the car door with the other hand.

Slipping inside, Methuen heard a syrupy click as the door closed and he sank down onto a heated leather seat. In the dark interior the air was fresh, save for a faint floral fragrance from the woman silhouetted against the window.

As they pulled away, with the commissionaire bowing repeatedly, the woman switched on a small light and without turning to face him, began to talk.

'This is much better. I'll drop you off at your home – that should give us enough time.'

She then opened a cabinet in the back of the seat facing her, took out a cut-glass tumbler and placed it on a lacquer-topped armrest between them.

'After all that excitement, I think I could do with a little liquid refreshment. How about you?' she said, unscrewing a miniature bottle.

'Err, do you have beer?' Methuen replied a little bashfully, stealing a glance at his host.

The woman paused as if she had not understood him. He was about to change his order to a glass of water when she pressed a small button beside her and repeated the request to the chauffeur. The car slowed, and after a few seconds, a can of lager appeared at the privacy hatch, which was then closed.

Methuen fiddled with the ring pull as the woman asked more eagerly, 'So tell me ... what is *your* transition plan for the future?'

Despite the deference shown to her by the commissionaire, the attentiveness of the chauffeur and the opulence of the car's interior, Methuen found himself surprisingly relaxed in her presence. *She's like Mr Demming – dispensing with the niceties of introductions and going straight to the critical question.*

He ignored the glass the woman had placed on the armrest for him and took a swig from the can. 'Actually, I don't have one,' he said. 'I was simply curious to know whether those who seem hell-bent on disrupting the current system had come up with anything better to replace it.'

He was keen to say more, but out of politeness waited for her response. When none came, he sat up and continued, 'You could say we've been in *transition* ever since the population exploded after the Second World War. Did you know that the seven billionth person was born on the thirty-first of October last year? Seven billion on a planet that some authorities believe can only comfortably sustain less than half of that in the future. There have been endless warnings since then about the problem we're creating, but here we are, twelve years into the new millennium, and we're still running the global economy as if living standards can rise forever.'

He heard what he took as a murmur of agreement and was about to say more when the woman replied in the theatrical voice of an old sage, '"The old ways will not die and the new cannot be born; we are in an interregnum when a great diversity of morbid symptoms will emerge." That's how someone described the world when the last great global event was upon us during the late 1920s,' she added quietly.

Event – what is she talking about? 'Uh, I was referring to something more far-reaching than that,' he replied firmly. 'This transition will change everyone's lives – old and young, rich and poor, wherever they live.' He sat back, the can between his knees. 'I fear it might be too late to do anything about it. That's why I have no transition plan.'

The woman remained silent for a few seconds and then said thoughtfully, 'Ah ... now you see, on that last point, you and I are *not* on the same page.'

Mr Demming again, cutting to the chase: neither questioning nor denying the inevitability of change, but focusing on the important bit – the timing? Invigorated by her response, Methuen said, 'Even if we did have more time, you only need to listen to what the old guy said tonight to realise how tough it'll be to get the majority to alter their way of life.'

'Remind me?' the woman demanded gently.

'Well, before he launched into that ridiculous tribal cheerleading stuff, he said something that struck me as particularly important: that all our problems track back to fundamental failings within ourselves. How did he put it? "... a general inability to act beyond the Bloomberg Horizon". And then there was his statement that "... the common good does not extend much beyond our own family when times are hard". Don't you agree that these inbuilt biases limit what we can do?'

'Some people would take issue with that,' the woman replied equably. 'They would describe examples where humankind has successfully acted as one to solve big problems. Take the banning of CFCs to protect the ozone layer – didn't that show how the world can come together and act for the *common good*?'

Methuen shook his head. 'That's what I call a *moon landing argument*: "If we can land people on the Moon, then we must be able to ..." You know how it goes. Those who reason that way both overestimate the challenge that flying to the Moon actually posed and underestimate the far greater complexity of the problems we face here on Earth. Take the CFC issue. That was actually relatively easy to solve. All it required was for government heads to ban one single chemical and replace it with something inert. I wonder what would have happened if the only answer had been for everyone to forgo the luxury of refrigeration? Landing on the Moon was an incredible feat certainly, but *just about* within our capabilities, whereas switching billions of people from a lifestyle based on growth to one of sustainability is several orders of magnitude more complex – and at present well beyond our collective ability.'

Again he heard what he took to be a murmur of assent and as she remained silent, he continued to talk but now in a lighter, more engaging voice. 'I think of our current predicament as similar to that of the little tin soldier – you know the story? There he is, innocently floating down the gutter in his paper boat, standing steadfast at the helm and gazing straight ahead. Unfortunately, he's not reacting to the pickup in the current that's rushing him along, nor the sewer drain that he's heading for.'

'So that's what The Time of Less will be – a sewer?'

Hearing a key phrase from his own work, Methuen turned to her, only to be caught by her dark eyes staring back at him. Embarrassed by the intimacy of their exchange, he went to look away but then turned back and smiled as he heard her laugh in the same carefree way she had done earlier in the evening.

'Don't look so worried – I watched the YouTube video of your speech! I must say, "The Three Indulgences: Grew too much. Consumed too much. Polluted too much." was a great opening line.'

'That probably means you also read the online comments when it went viral and the handle they gave me ...?' he said uncomfortably, leaving the question hanging in the air, before adding in a ghoulish voice, '"Doomboy"?'

She sipped from the glass and then, widening her eyes at him, said with mischievous giggle, 'And *are* you a Doomboy?'

Methuen smiled back in response to the teasing tone in her query. 'People say I can get a bit heavy when I'm talking about the future as I probably did in the meeting tonight, although on that video, I did try to be more upbeat. Even my family were surprised at how positive I came across. It was only afterwards when everything had quietened down, that I realised it wasn't just me who had prompted the Doomboy label. There's no real generation gap when it comes to judging how people view the future, despite all the supposed differences between the Millennials and earlier generations. We all seem to have a default anxiety setting. The pessimism I was accused of was as much to do with people's own feelings about the future as my own predictions.'

'*Mokita*,' the woman exclaimed.

'Pardon me?' Methuen replied, frowning at her.

'"A truth we all know but agree not to talk about." You need to go to a tribe living on a small island off Papua New Guinea to find a single term that fully describes such a concept.'

'A form of ... culturally sanctioned lying about reality?' he asked, still frowning.

'Not lies, it's more like denial – a sort of unutterable zeitgeist. And it's not confined to any one culture, it's planetwide – the *mokita* of our modern civilisation,' she said, nodding. 'It's a form of protection against the terrifying thought that we're in the process of destroying ourselves. You even find it among folk who worship reason and sing the praises of our enlightened world. Try telling *that* kind of person that the physical conditions on which progress has been built are about to come to an end and just watch how advocates of rational thought very quickly become quite irrational in their own response.'

Taking a sip from the can, Methuen nodded slowly in agreement. 'I only have anecdotal evidence to support that, but I get what you're saying.'

'Does it trouble you that there's so much resistance to taking your ideas seriously?'

He laughed dismissively. 'After all the kerfuffle over the YouTube video, I went to my tutor and said I was giving up the modelling project to concentrate on my A levels.'

'Oh, I didn't know that.'

Why should you? He looked out of the window, puzzled at her remark, and noticed that for some reason they were now on the motorway. *Why are we going the long way round – or are we off to somewhere else?* His anxiety levels shot up again but just as he was about to enquire as to where they were heading, the woman turned to him and asked, 'So what was his reply?'

'He was a bit irritated at first, saying something like, "This work is bigger than you, Pryce." And then he twisted the knife with, "Do whatever you must, but abandoning the most important issue ever facing humankind will make everything else seem pretty trivial by comparison". Here was a teacher telling me that my schoolwork should take second place to my private obsession – well, I couldn't ignore that, could I?' he said with a forced laugh.

'So what did you do?'

'For a time I carried on gathering information on all the main factors controlling economic growth, but then two other things happened in quick succession that changed my whole approach. After attending the interschool debate and viewing the video, my mother introduced me to one of her friends who had just finished a novel set in the near future. This woman went to great lengths to dismiss the timing as "just the backdrop", but nonetheless I started quizzing her on how she had imagined life would be – I think it was in the 2030s. To my surprise, this intelligent and articulate individual became quite agitated and said something I found very revealing: "I was relieved to get away from the future. It made me so depressed. All I wanted was to get back to reality." Like many of the people I interacted with online after the video, she was capable of understanding the implications of declining economic growth but unwilling to incorporate it within her daily sense of reality, let alone take any personal action.'

Methuen glanced at the woman, who was staring back and seemed to be willing him to continue.

'The other thing sounds rather more trivial,' he said. 'It was a comment made by the younger of my two older brothers. During one of his many rants, he came out with, "No one cares when you talk about the effects of all these changes on the planet or humanity." I mumbled that it was everyone's responsibility to make a contribution, but his next remark stuck in my head: "It's way too big and difficult for any single person to grasp – it's something the UN or some other global agency should be dealing with, not ordinary people like us."'

'And what did you say?'

'I didn't bother. I can't reason with him when he's so damn sure of himself, but it did make me realise just how essential it is to get everyone on board with my idea. Governments can deal with straightforward single-point issues, but what we are facing is something so broad and so complex that it can only be solved by *all of us* acting together. I put this to him eventually, and he repeated his argument about the ineffectiveness of the individual. I countered, emphasising the power of the crowd – multiplying the small contribution that each one of us can make by the billions on the planet. But he'd stopped listening – like my mother's friend, he just didn't want any change to his perfect little life.'

'So, what did *you* decide to do?'

'I went back to my tutor and told him I would carry on with the work but needed his help because I wanted to change the way

I was modelling things.' Methuen looked at her, expecting another question but again only saw her silent nod.

'I grew up a bit after failing in that school debate. I realised there was another challenge: I needed to find some way of properly explaining this concept of a non-growth world to grab the attention of people like my brother, my mother's friend and all my contacts online. Wrestling with this thought, I came back to my brother's comment. I accepted that part of the problem lay in the way in which the ideas of economic growth are always referenced to humanity or the planet, after all that's the scale on which the drivers of growth operate. Barring a few tree-hugging romantics though, the thought of the planet or humanity as being under threat simply doesn't stir up enough concern to bring ordinary folk onto the streets, never mind change their lifestyles. I realise that makes me a little odd because I myself have no doubts at all ...' Methuen hesitated as he glanced at her and felt himself blush at the boldness in his voice.

The woman sipped from her glass and then said, 'But you continued.'

He nodded back and, after taking another swig from the can, said, 'The modelling already shows that momentous change is coming – and soon, but most people need more than that. They need the problem brought closer to home – on a scale where they can see directly how it will affect their daily lives. That led me to ask myself: what would be the largest social group that might actually grab people's attention? If not the planet, then maybe the nation-state – good old Blighty and all that. With my tutor's help, I drew up an example of a fifty-year balance sheet for a nation-state, guided by the projected economic trends emerging from my model. I created a few examples and compared them with budgets based on the assumptions of *continuous growth* and *limitless resources* – which most governments around the world assume today for their long-term planning. What I found amazed me: every single economy I analysed in this way failed by the 2040s – with profound social and political knock-on effects. I realised that I'd finally given substance to my phrase "The Time of Less".'

The woman nodded, and then asked a little sceptically, 'Weren't you concerned at the sheer size of the task you were undertaking? Not just refining your model, but building fifty-year balance sheets for *every* nation-state?'

Methuen waved his finger at her and smiled confidently. 'That was of concern to me, naturally, but I had one of my *imaginings* – a sort of vivid awareness that sometimes appears in my head when I'm struggling with a difficult problem. I realised that it wasn't necessary to model every nation-state to get close to the answer.'

'Aha!' the woman responded, but again in a way that perplexed Methuen. It felt as if he was filling in a story, the guts of which she already knew. He glanced at her, but she sat back again, waiting for him to continue.

'I saw the nation-states of the world like the players in a huge game of musical chairs, but at a point in the game when the sound system has broken down and won't restart. Even before the music ended though, many of the nation-states in this imagining had stopped dancing. They had failed to find a chair, enfeebled by things like natural catastrophe, military conflict and curtailment of external aid. All they could do was sit on the sidelines and try to survive. Those countries still dancing had found a way to remain economically viable, at least until the music finally stopped. At that point, to their dismay, they saw that the five chairs remaining were already occupied. Their choice then was either to join the ranks of those already out of the game and accept falling living standards or arrange to sit on the lap of one, possibly two, of those with a chair.'

'I suppose this core of seated players is made up of the US, Europe, India, China … but what is the fifth?' the woman asked curiously.

'The modelling always places Russia in that top group. It's a minnow in economic terms but retains a powerful nuclear capability to protect its great commercial advantage: a significant proportion of the planet's dwindling natural resources.'

'What you're saying is that you will make predictions about the future of the world by modelling the outcomes for just five … I was going to say states … but what you're talking about are *superstates*, aren't you – which over time will bring other countries under their control?'

'Sitting *uncomfortably* on their laps,' Methuen clarified.

'Think your average man or woman will relate any better to these new entities than they already do to the planet or to humanity?'

'Well, it's a start – at least in the case of those living in the superstates.'

'Meaning?'

'Meaning that if I can understand how each superstate is likely to react to a non-growth world, then it should be possible to drill down into their national, regional and even city structures and work out what it'll require in these smaller units for people to live with dignity.'

'That's good,' she said quietly, nodding her head in agreement.

He smiled back. *Just like Mr Demming when I give a full answer to a question in class.*

'And what is the current status of the model?' she asked, in a more detached, business-like voice.

'At present, I'm defining the main drivers that will control events up to the mid-century, but I have also begun populating the database for modelling the fifty-year budgets of the superstates.'

Only the faint sound of the car engine accelerating and decelerating through the evening traffic could be heard as they both fell silent.

She not only follows what I'm saying but at times is ahead of me. Who the hell is she and what does she want? He peered through the snow-flecked window, trying to formulate a question, but it was the woman who spoke first, now in a more reflective voice.

'It's not easy accepting the changes we envisage, Methuen.'

We? he thought, leaning back against the seat.

'Before coming up here to see you,' she said slowly, 'I went for a walk along the South Bank on one of those gorgeous winter after-noons, with a chill in the air and a welcome blast of sunlight. I was among people of all creeds and classes enjoying themselves. I could see cranes rising above half-built, high-rise blocks, all seeming to point confidently skyward, while on the river there were leisure craft and working boats busily going about their business. It was a buzzy exciting place, and I thought to myself, how can this possibly end? How can I imagine, let alone prepare for, an alternative way of living? And that was *me* speaking – someone who could scarcely be more aware of the future. I was still asking myself that question when I walked past Southwark Cathedral. I'm not a believer, but something pulled me inside. As I stood there watching people take the sacrament while others knelt in prayer, I realised that the prob-lem we face in explaining these changes is not just one of raising *awareness* – there are many ways we can do that. It's more to do with the next step, of gaining *acceptance* – in the way those around me had come to unquestionably accept the tenets of their religion. I wandered off, knowing I had no place there, but convinced that in order to gain acceptance for the changes ahead, we needed to find something to capture people's hearts and minds – a compelling explanation of what is to come and a *guide* as to how we may still live a rewarding life in what you call The Time of Less.'

'But it's still a World *with* Less,' Methuen chimed in. 'What do I say to my steadfast tin soldier? "Look! There's a ledge next to the drain where you can survive. Prepare an evacuation plan to jump off and settle there." Do you think that would be enough?'

'Of course not,' the woman fired back, then paused before adding, 'You would also have to paint a graphic image of the chaos that awaits if he *does nothing* – and tries to ride over the drain. Only with those twin visions in his head will he be brave enough to make that *noble leap* that will take him ...' She paused again, and then in a quieter voice said, '... *a little more towards Heaven than Hell.*'

They sat in silence for a few seconds before the woman said more buoyantly, 'You're lucky, Methuen – even at your young age, *you* have made that noble leap. That's why I'm here talking to you this evening. There are lots of people who can model the future, but few who can do it with the passion and persistence that comes with having already internalised the inevitability of the changes ahead.'

Leaning over the armrest, she placed her hand on his. 'People like us have a duty not just to make others aware of what is to come, but to provide them with a path they can follow. Not one sugar-coated with promises of a more prosperous future as many of the political manifestos of the future will do, but one grounded in a reality that will allow us to survive and, in the fullness of time, thrive in the world ahead.'

'And you think we'll have time to do all that?' he said, retracting his hand.

'I think so. This new "G5" you talk of, whether they come together or do their own thing, will not readily promote the process of *acceptance*. They are the masters of the old world and have a personal stake in preserving the status quo—'

'The old ways will not die, and the new cannot be born,' he said, attempting to mimic the sage-like tone she had used.

The woman caught his eye and they both laughed. 'I can see why your tutor likes you,' she said brightly, adding, 'This affluent core will indeed show great resistance over the next few decades, but that gives us time to present our argument and build the case for change, with those who are willing to act.' She nodded again, arching a dark eyebrow. 'I think there's enough time for you to persuade that steadfast tin soldier of yours to make the leap onto the ledge.'

Methuen scratched his head. 'But I see my purpose in life to be the seeker rather than the seller of truth. I'm neither a politician nor even much of a public speaker – all that debating stuff is just a charade. I can't go out and preach all this: my place is to think, not do.'

'No, Methuen Pryce, you are not getting away with that,' the woman said, pulling herself upright and facing him. 'You've already proved your tenacity tonight in front of that confused mob. Besides, I'm not suggesting you become the front man – there are plenty of others who can do that. Your focus must be on developing the new model with the sole intent of convincing people that it's better to accept a "World of Less" with all of its challenges, than the absolute hell that awaits them if they do nothing.'

Methuen was still reflecting on her remarks when the car drew to a halt. He looked out and saw the front gate of his house and the lighted porch at the end of the garden path. The woman instructed the chauffeur to switch off the engine and then, leaning over, kissed him on the cheek and handed him a name card from a small silver case.

'To *know why* is the most important question,' she said softly. 'It determines purpose, explains cause and fosters belief. In the years to come, you will need to remain clear and, like your little tin soldier, steadfast on all of these.'

As the car drove out of sight and cold air started to seep through Methuen's untoggled coat, he remained rooted to the spot, contemplating not just the extraordinary events of the evening, but also the realisation that his ideas had come to the attention of someone as impressive as the Clapping Lady.

As he walked up the path, wiping her lipstick from his cheek, he looked at the card. Under the light of the doorway, he read in bold typescript, CONSILIENCE FOUNDATION, and below that, in small italics, *The Consilience Fund/Chief Strategist*. No address, no name – although in the top right-hand corner he spotted the same NOY insignia he'd seen on the invitation. As he went to stow the card in his top pocket, he noticed on the other side, another line of italic print: *Promoting the global transition to post-growth sustainability*. Taking a deep breath, he turned the key in the front door and entered the house.

'Where've you been? Didn't you get my message?' shouted his older brother, as Methuen flung his satchel down in the hallway. 'We're still responsible for you until you're eighteen, you know!'

From the end of the hall, a woman hobbled towards him, reading glasses dangling from a cord around her neck, her walking stick in one hand and a book tucked under the other arm.

'Evening, Mother,' Methuen said cheerlessly, following her into an adjoining room, where an open fire burned in the grate.

'Methuen, why in heaven's name didn't you reply to your brother's text? We've been so worried about you. You must let us know where you are.'

'Sorry, Mother,' he replied in a monotone as she sat back down placing the book on her lap.

'It was bad enough when your father was alive, never knowing where *he* was,' she said bitterly.

Methuen made no reply and bided his time until she became engrossed in her book. He then crept over to the door, the fire crackling in the background. 'Night then, God bless,' he said in the same dispassionate tone.

Out in the corridor, his elder brother tried to engage him more amicably but Methuen's mind was elsewhere. Without responding, he bounded up the three flights of stairs to his attic bedroom and after locking the door, grabbed the laptop from his desk and jumped on the bed.

Feeling cold, he pulled a blanket around his shoulders before logging on to the website printed on the woman's card. As soon as he pressed the return key, the screen went blank and a table appeared, requesting personal information and a three-letter code. Recalling the NOY insignia, he typed in the letters.

Instantly the router on his desk sprang into action, while the screen on his laptop first dimmed and then went blank, again. After a few minutes with no change, he lifted up his satchel to hunt out the invitation card to see if there might be an alternative code.

Placing the bag on his knees, he saw that the straps were more extended than normal and found that two books had been stuffed inside. One was a primer on Pericles with a bookmark sticking out, on which his name had been scribbled in the same hand that had written the note attached to the invitation card.

He opened the book at the marked page and read aloud a sentence that had been underlined. 'The bravest are surely those with the clearest vision of what is before them … and yet notwithstanding go out to meet it.' *Blimey, is she trying to spook me?*

He turned to the other book and again read the title aloud. '*The Age of Anxiety* by W.H. Auden.'

He glanced back at the screen and to his relief saw a small cursor blinking in the top right-hand corner. Returning to the book, he found the first few pages difficult to follow, but noticed that a whole stanza had been highlighted.

We would rather be ruined than changed
We would rather die in our dread
Than climb the cross of the moment
And let our illusions die.

He was about to reread the poem when the screen lit up and a mechanically filtered voice began to speak.

'Hello, Methuen. Welcome to the Consilience Foundation. Glad you were able to make a connection. I am here to answer your questions. For security reasons, there is a limit of five minutes on this interaction. After that, the link will close and you won't be able to access it again. I need a written record of our dialogue, so please type your questions below.'

Methuen sat up, set the timer on his watch, and taking a writing pad from his satchel scribbled some notes, before typing: What is the Consilience Foundation?

After a pause, the mechanical voice said, 'We are a non-profit, philanthropic organisation that seeks to accelerate the unification of knowledge for the betterment of humanity. We have no political affiliation or aspiration. We see no line separating the arts from sciences or the humanities. Consilience identifies inspiring young people already with the rudiments of meaning in their lives. We then help them to foster their ideas. Our only belief is that reason is the key to human progress.'

The explanation ended and a new box appeared, inviting the next question. In response Methuen typed: Who funds all this? There followed a brief delay before the reply came from the human or machine – he was unsure which.

'An important aspect of the Foundation is anonymity. We do not supply the names or addresses of our representatives. You may create names for them if you wish and I am sure that anyone contacting you from the Foundation will be happy to use them.'

Methuen checked his watch and was surprised to see that half the allotted time had already passed. He was eager to ask questions about the Clapping Lady, but more urgent was his need to find out how he might fit in.

He typed: Why have I been selected?

'You have not been selected, you have only been shortlisted.'

Silence followed, and then like a speaking clock filling in the specific time the voice continued, '... because of your exceptional forecasting skills.'

There was another pause before the voice spoke again. 'If selected, the level at which you are deployed will be decided once you have completed a questionnaire that will appear on the screen after this interaction.'

The response reminded him of the school's Junior Army Cadet Group, which he had considered joining as a last-ditch attempt to win favour with his father.

How will the Consilience Foundation help me? As he typed, he recalled asking a similar question of the recruiting officer at the interview to join the cadets. Unlike the long-winded reply he had received back then, the answer he got now was short and to the point:

'Data, networking facilities, logistics and finance.'

'Data!' he exclaimed and was about to ask for more information when the timer on his watch began a thirty-second countdown. He looked at his notes and saw a word written out in large letters: CONTROL.

What constraints will you place on me?

The reply came back at once: 'There is only one constraint, that humane reasoning guides all your ideas and actions.'

Methuen was about to ask how he would stay connected with Consilience when the screen went blank. Concerned that he might have lost school and project work files, he rebooted the machine, finding, to his relief, his personal data restored. Searching through the system files though, he could find no trace of any link to the Foundation and was about to shut down the laptop, when he saw in the top right-hand corner a small blue file inscribed with the letters NOY. Resisting the impulse to click on the icon, he walked over to his desk, connected an external drive and instructed the machine to make a system save.

Back in bed and with the drive now disconnected, he clicked on the new icon. As before, the screen lit up and then went blank, as once again the lights on the router blinked frenetically, connecting him, he presumed, to the same network that would leave no trace. He was still mulling over the implications of privacy and control when what resembled an examination paper appeared on the screen, along with a set of instructions requiring him to complete the questions in a single session, at some time in the next three days.

Inside the red-painted barn;
Hardin, Montana, NCSA, FSA
10.15 hours, 15 June 2050

'Did you know about any of that?' Lianne asked, as Nick checked the external cameras.

'You mean the Consilience woman?'

'No – about Methuen's home life. Elizabeth's never mentioned it to me.'

'Nor to me,' Nick said absent-mindedly, pointing the remote towards a monitor at the end of the bed.

'I knew his father had died early and that he seems to resent his mother terribly ... What is it?' she asked, seeing him bend forward and stare intently ahead.

'The radiation level's not fallen, even though it stopped raining some time ago; it's over 200 millisieverts inside this barn,' he said, sliding back the bedroom door and swinging his feet into the stairwell.

Lianne followed him up into the driving cabin, where an alarm was now sounding – automatically switching on all the external cameras. On the front camera monitor, beyond the wall of collapsed bales, a shaft of light shone through a gaping hole in the timbered roof, illuminating a mangled heap of metal on the floor of the barn.

Seeing her attention focused on the image, Nick said soberly, 'It's a tractor engine, it must have been hurled through the air during The Incident. I saw it when I positioned the drone inside but didn't want to worry you.'

'Oh Lord – those posters,' she said, holding her hand to her mouth. 'We must be at the centre of one of the explosions.'

Another alarm went off, making them both jump up. Nick steered the camera around the inside of the barn and then laughed aloud as a family of raccoons came into view, walking nimbly in line along a wooden beam above the remains of the tractor engine.

'The radiation doesn't seem to worry them and nor should it worry us that much,' he said, pointing to the counter on the screen. 'We're perfectly safe in here. Fancy something to eat or shall we view another scene?'

'I'll bring something down,' she replied, heading into the kitchen and opening the fridge.

Back in the bedroom, Lianne placed a tray between them. 'I've been in some peculiar situations with you, Grady, but none matches this – sealed off from the outside and immersed in the past. So, what do you have there?' she asked, as he went through a list of titles on the screen.

'It's three years on, and I see that Elizabeth has contributed to this one.'

'Oh good. Do we get to hear it from her perspective?'

'I'd rather stick to Methuen for now if you don't mind?'

'Can't we play both?'

'Sorry, our on-board processing capacity won't allow that. Let's go with Methuen for this one and then maybe Elizabeth next time.'

AA-Com File: The Odd Couple

University Hall, Edinburgh, Scotland, UK
Evening, 18 December 2016

Virtual Scene snapshot: Methuen, dressed in an ill-fitting dinner suit and holding a pint glass in his hand, leans against a doorway opening into a festively decorated stately hall. Approaching him is a man sporting a jester's hat, a garland of plastic flowers and bearing a bottle.

'Hi, Hamish,' Methuen said raising his glass.

'Hey, mate, come and join us,' the man called out, laughing merrily before bursting into a random snatch of song.

Waving away the request, Methuen moved to the wall closest to the main exit. *What am I bloody well doing here?* he thought, as the hall filled with inebriated engineers and medics, obliged by austerity cuts to combine their year-end faculty parties. *I could have gone anywhere, on any science course, with my straight As. Why in God's name did I choose this place?*

> 'Why engineering and why Edinburgh of all places? It's so far away,' his mother asked, holding up his college acceptance letter.

That was a telling moment for both of us: me staring back at her without responding and her realising that the question she had posed also contained the answer. The choice of subject though was more difficult, especially when it brought about a temporary alliance between her and Mr Demming.

> 'I think you should follow your tutor's suggestion of a pure science subject – you would also be continuing in your father's footsteps.'

What, so he would still be exerting influence on me – even from beyond the grave? She never got it, did she? That's why I chose Grandad's profession and adopted his philosophy of 'making something useful was the best way of … being someone useful'. She had no idea, of course, that by then, I was living in another world. Once I'd been accepted as a member of Consilience, CL – why do I still call her the Clapping Lady? – took over from Mr Demming as my main point of reference.

Methuen glanced up as the music increased in volume and seeing people begin to drift onto the dance floor, he moved towards a more dimly lit corner of the room. *Nobody knows how much my life has been guided by Consilience. There was the access CL arranged to the Nottingham University Computer Centre. And when I asked her about my college place, it was she who suggested Edinburgh and systems engineering.*

> 'You need to understand how technical and human-centred systems interact, Methuen. That will be the biggest test of your model.'

Too right, ma'am! Her involvement didn't end there, though. During Freshers' Week, while everyone else was partying and signing up to various clubs, I was told to put on a suit and was then transported to a grand Georgian house in the old part of the city. The wide hallway smelled of polish and was lined with heavy Victorian furniture. There was even an aspidistra on the hall stand – not that I knew what it was called at the time. At the far end, I was shown into a dark wood-panelled room filled with … How did I describe them in my diary? Oh yes, 'wonderfully refreshing, intellectually borderless individuals from all walks of life'. As I entered I saw her, in the centre of the room, CL – slim, tall, dressed in black lace – her arms open in welcome towards me. But that wasn't the biggest surprise of the night; that was provided by the person standing beside her, unrecognisable in a smart jacket and looking more like the spy

*we'd all imagined him to be. I was gobsmacked. My brain went
into overdrive, with as many new questions about Mr Demming
as old ones were answered. Before I had time to speak, there
was a tap on my shoulder from the man who'd collected me
from my digs.*

'You must prepare a talk over the next six weeks, so we can
decide what role you will play in our little group.'

'What will you take as your topic?' another asked.

They asked the easy question first? Methuen thought.

'The world of the mid-century.'

'There you are, what did I tell you? We've found our synthe-
siser,' the Clapping Lady said, laughing loudly.

*Things moved quickly after that. A note came from the head of
engineering, informing me that I'd been allocated a room in the
university's IT centre and given full access to the computer system.
I mentioned this to no one, but somehow the news spread like
wildfire around the campus, triggering a few negative remarks in
the bar at the Students' Union. That didn't matter much – what
worried me more was the loss of my anonymity. I tried to play
down the significance of it all, telling people I was finishing off
some project work, but that fooled no one, and so as time passed
I began to be treated as an oddity and someone people held firm
views on – not least Hamish, my roommate.*

'You're obviously a bright guy, and you're tall and athletic.
I see quite a lot of women staring at you but, man – your
clothes! Change your style, give the check shirt and jeans a
rest. You know what they call you behind your back? "The
Lumberjack". And then there are the hours you keep. It
makes me and everyone else in the house feel guilty. You
leave early and return late – really late. You're never going
to meet anyone if you carry on like that.'

*And then last week in the student bar, there was that woman who
started mocking me for the way my voice gets deeper when I'm*

angry. That kicked off a whole slew of remarks from other people about how I drink cheap ale and support the local football team. 'Yes, and …?' I wanted to say, but as usual, I kept quiet. There have been enjoyable evenings though, particularly in my digs: me propped up on a pillow with a six-pack, listening through the night to everyone's views and giving them my ideas about what's coming in the world ahead.

But it's the invitations to attend soirées at Senate House that have been the biggest factor in separating me from those here tonight. I was uncomfortable about it at first. In the early days, I felt like a running back protected by his team. On entering a reception, I would often be intercepted by newer guests who weren't aware of why I was present. If the questioning became too aggressive, one of the regulars – a professor or senior admin- istrator – would take-them-out: politely shuffling them to one side to inform them of my role as secretary of the Edinburgh branch of the Consilience Foundation. It was quite funny to see how, not wishing to show their ignorance, no one enquired as to the nature of the Foundation. Although even if they had, not even I could have told them much.

Taking a gulp from his glass, he glanced up to see his roommate coming over to him again, his head wobbling slightly.

'Not going yet, are you, Methuen?'

Before he could reply, a tumbleweed of yattering, exotically dressed young women rolled up close to them. The spectacle caused Methuen to search urgently for the cloakroom ticket in the unfamiliar pockets of the hired dinner suit. He was about to make some excuse for leaving when he spotted something not quite right amid the ball of chattering, swirling femininity.

A girl – no, more like a woman.

The revelry seemed to revolve around her, but he noticed she wore none of the taffeta or lace of the others, only a plain dress and what appeared to be flat shoes.

Spotting his interest in the woman, his roommate elbowed him in the ribs. 'Forget her. That's Bouverie-Morgan, the daughter of Simone Bouverie – you know, the fashion designer?'

'*She's* a medic?' Methuen gasped with surprise before, supping deeply from his glass.

'Father was a lecher here – sorry, lecturer here, yonks ago. She's followed the family tradition, I suppose.' Then, seeing Methuen continue to stare in her direction, he added, 'She's a real handful – almost impossible to pin down. Likes clubbing, but also a loner.'

As he was speaking, the woman stopped in her tracks and stared in their direction, causing Methuen to turn away as if he were about to go. Hamish held his shoulder and whispered, 'She's a bit of a cockteaser as well – wants to know all about you, but it's never clear if she's just being plain nosey or wants to go further.'

Before Methuen could come up with a response, the woman left the crowd surrounding her and walked over to them. For all his derogatory comments, Methuen noticed his roommate's hopeful smile as she approached, and then how his shoulders dropped as she brushed past him.

'You're Methuen Pryce, aren't you?' she said, waving her finger at him.

Even in the poor light, Methuen could see that his assessment of her had been correct. She hadn't bothered with make-up and, to him, her hair looked as if it had been styled in the dark.

'Yes,' he replied hesitantly. 'How do you know me?'

'I know everyone,' she said with a teasing smile, folding her arms, 'especially when I've heard interesting things said about them.'

Methuen gave a short grunt and then asked, 'And what do people say about me?'

The woman held her gaze and hunched her shoulders. 'That you're a bit ... crazy.'

Methuen let out a huge belly laugh, something that only a late-night drinking session in the Students' Union would normally induce. His roommate glanced at the woman, who remained unmoved, arms still folded but her shoulders more relaxed.

'They also say you've got a big picture in your head about the future that stops you living in the present.'

Methuen paused, his broad grin turning into a wary grimace. 'You have a problem with that?'

'Half of it I do, but the other half intrigues me,' she said, tilting her head to one side.

He leant towards her slightly but made no comment – sensing she had more to say.

'People tell me you're annoyingly confident about the world ahead. What I want to know is, supposing you're wrong ... will you be able to admit it?'

'If I'm *wrong* about *anything* I will always make changes, but right now everything is pointing in one direction.'

'I could never settle on just one outcome – it's too much of a gamble.'

'Not as much as you may think,' he said. 'Besides, I always run with several outcomes. Everything I do is statistical rather than deductive.' He fixed his eyes on her, keen to see how she would react to the precision of his reply.

The woman raised her pencilled eyebrows and without hesitating asked, 'Is this great idea of yours, Mr Engineer, just full of things you can measure and quantify, or have you also woven in things you don't generally have to consider when building bridges?'

Methuen smiled, fascinated by her boldness, but then noticed how her eyes narrowed, as if his facial response had offended her. 'You can only make useful predictions from things you can measure and extrapolate,' he said a little more gently, straightening his shoulders.

'Bollocks!' she replied, tossing her head back. 'What's *trust*, for example, if not a prediction of reliability? You don't measure trust – you *believe* it'll deliver things.'

Methuen found himself taken aback, not by her colourful language nor even her argument, but her readiness to engage in a debate within the setting of a dance floor.

While he pondered his reply, she asked, 'How do you deal with people's reaction to this future you're predicting? It's not what people know intellectually that gets them to act, it's what they value emotionally that counts. How do you quantify that, in deciding on how this new world of yours will turn out?'

Methuen made no response, prompting his roommate to cut in. 'I think you've instigated one of his pregnant pauses.'

The woman ignored the comment, causing the man to walk off.

Methuen, barely aware of his friend's departure, had found his thoughts back in the Trent Theatre with the old man's fatalistic comments on human nature.

'I have to be sure of the measurable things before I can deal with what can't be measured,' he replied at length, staring at her and waiting for her next verbal blast.

Instead, he saw her look upwards – as if in thought. 'I see that, of course,' she said quietly. 'It just frustrates me that academics often find their reality in things that can be measured, while politicians often find it in what cannot. You don't have that choice, I imagine, when you're trying to predict the future?'

What an interesting thought. Who is this peculiar creature? Cupping his hand to his ear, he said, 'I hear you ...' and then laughing aloud, added, '... or rather, I don't. Shall we get away from this racket? I hate all this noise.'

'The louder it gets, the more alone I feel,' the woman said, and to Methuen's surprise, tucked her arm into his, as they walked off together.

In the now empty dining room, they sat across from one another at a table covered in party junk. Before he could say anything, the woman leant towards him and asked, 'Tell me something ... what is your personal god?'

She has the most beautiful eyes. 'Sorry, I'm not following you ... What's yours?'

She placed her hands on the table and fixed her eyes on him. 'To help those who are suffering to help themselves,' she replied, tapping on the table to emphasise each word. She then stared back at him, waiting for his answer.

Methuen swept a hand through his hair and sat up straight. 'Umm, nothing that grand,' he said, screwing up his face, but then after a pause adding, 'truth is important ... and so too is fairness.'

The woman moved forward about to respond but Methuen raised his hand, and smiling at her said, 'More generally though, I would say to *know why* is the most important thing. To never give up until you've answered that question. No ideology of any colour will feed or clothe people for long, nor does it make them feel secure. Lies never last,' he exclaimed, sitting back and spreading his hands out on the table. 'Only the pursuit of truth through informed, rational thought stands the test of time. It's an inexhaustible resource we're all adequately blessed with.'

'Hmm, not bad,' she said, a faint smile breaking out on her face as she poured herself a glass of water. 'I think I need to find out a bit more about this *new world* you're envisaging Mr Engineer and try to decide whether I need to take it seriously.'

Just then, the doors to the dance hall were thrown open by a group of partygoers. Without saying a word, Methuen and the woman stood up and headed for the exit.

Out in the foyer, Hamish reappeared, and seeing Methuen holding a woman's coat said, 'You're not leaving with *her*? No one's tamed Bouverie-Morgan ever. You know she's crazy, don't you?'

Methuen shrugged. 'Then that makes two of us. We should get on just fine.' He turned to find the woman and saw her talking to a man who seemed to be trying to persuade her to join him back on the dance floor.

Despite dressing down, she does have a ... certain casual elegance about her.

'Sorry about that,' the woman said, taking her coat. 'He's a nice chap but lacks depth. I'm Elizabeth by the way.' Shaking his hand, she looked back in the direction of the dance hall. 'My problem is that I'm too headstrong for most men and too unpredictable for most women.'

'And I'm rather quiet at times and keep myself to myself,' he said with a short laugh, before falling silent as she took his arm once more.

'No problem,' she chirped. 'I'm an expert on such things. You should meet my father.'

Inside the red-painted barn;
Hardin, Montana, NCSA, FSA

11.00 hours, 15 June 2050

'Why have you stopped?' Lianne said, removing her glasses. 'I was just getting into that. Wasn't it lovely to see Elizabeth and Methuen meeting for the first time?' She looked over and saw Nick flicking through the other files.

'They've listed these chronologically as well as alphabetically,' he said. 'Would you believe it, on that same day and at that same hour – Eastern Time at least – there's a scene here with me in New York, entitled "Dinner with Sam Harding"?'

'No,' Lianne said emphatically, 'I want to carry on with Elizabeth and Methuen.'

'Okay, okay,' he said, scrolling back up through the list. 'In that case, we may just as well continue with what they did next.'

Nick projected the Storymaker Dashboard. 'This is mainly Methuen explaining his ideas. I think we should stay in *his* Thought Mode.'

'Sure, but at some stage, I want to be standing in one of these scenes and hearing what Elizabeth is thinking,' Lianne said, lying down and putting her glasses back on.

'That's fine,' Nick grumbled, fiddling with the remote. 'We'll watch this one with Methuen, then I'll get it to go straight into the next scene from Elizabeth's point of view. Happy?'

AA-Com File: Basement Revelations

University Hall, Edinburgh, Scotland, UK
00.30 hours, 19 December 2016

Virtual Scene snapshot: Methuen stands at the top of a long tier of stone steps that widen out onto an empty lamp-lit square. Beside him, Elizabeth is wrapping a black cape around her shoulders.

I like this woman. I should be livelier and more upbeat with her. 'Your Batman outfit?' he asked with a grin.

'Well, excuse me!' she protested extravagantly. 'This is silk velvet, I'll have you know – circa 1920. I stole it from my mother's wardrobe before she upped sticks and left us a few years back.' She stopped and looked at his dinner suit. 'You must be freezing?'

'My coat is over there,' he said, pointing to a building across the square.

'Where's over there?'

'The university computer centre, where I have an office.'

'Okay, let's go,' she said, striding down the steps.

Does she really want to go there – at this time of night?

As he hesitated, Elizabeth turned and called over her shoulder, 'You don't seriously expect me to miss the opportunity of visiting the hideaway of the mysterious Methuen Pryce, do you? Come on.'

On the other side of the square, Elizabeth confidently walked towards the doors of a large glass-fronted building.

'No, it's this way,' Methuen called out, opening a side gate above a narrow set of steps.

In the darkened courtyard below, he took a key from his pocket and unlocked a plain metal door. As he patted the wall for the light switch on the other side, he let the door go, almost crushing her as she scrambled through.

'Oh, I'm sorry. I'm so used to coming here on my own, I was thinking about something else,' he said with a nervous laugh and then strode off down a dimly lit passageway, its walls lined with metal pipes.

'I can barely see where I'm going in this rabbit warren,' she called out from behind him. 'And what's that awful smell?'

'I can't smell a thing in the winter – I seem to have a permanent head cold when I'm in Scotland,' he said, unlocking another door but this time holding it open for her.

Mumbling something about the damp air, Elizabeth then squealed loudly, as her eyes were blasted with light from a bank of monitors mounted high on the wall ahead of her.

'How many of these things do you have?' she asked, still shielding her eyes.

Is she impressed, curious or both? 'Thirteen when I last checked,' he said, quickly counting them again.

Moving over to a battered leather sofa, she removed several empty pizza boxes along with a pile of papers. Pointing up to a screen displaying a continuously scrolling set of numbers, she asked, 'What's happening on that one?'

'Oh, that's just routine night-processing. Some of the programs are so CPU-hungry that they only allow me to do continuous runs during these slack hours.'

He picked up a coat slung over a U-pipe coming up from the floor and set off towards the door.

'And where do you think you're going?' she demanded.

'Err, I thought we were—'

'For a clever man you're quite slow-witted over certain things, aren't you?'

Well, no one's ever said that to me before. But before he could come up with a suitable retort, she began a conversation with herself:

'"Where did you disappear to last night?"

'"Oh, I visited the secret lair of that oddball, Methuen Pryce."

'"And what did you do then?"

'"He gathered up his stuff and I went home early for a cup of cocoa."'

So you're not only smart, you're funny as well.

'Come on! My imagination's in overdrive ...' she exclaimed. 'I'm not leaving until you tell me what's going on here.'

Would that create a confidentiality issue with the contract I signed with Consilience? Oh, bugger it – she's not a spy, just a rather fascinating human being. I'd love to know what she thinks about the model.

He flung his coat down on the sofa and drew out a rickety stool from under the long table that ran below the monitors on the wall. 'Great! What would you like to know?'

'Well, for a start, you can tell me what the labels "NR INf" and "NR INi" mean under those two screens over there,' she said, looking mystified.

She's a bit cheeky but I think she really is interested in what I'm doing. 'I'd have to explain how the model works,' he said tentatively, but then saw her eyes narrow just as they had done in the dance hall.

'I think my midnight brain can just about manage that, Methuen,' she replied with a faint smile, her voice dropping fractionally as she used his name.

She's every bit as intriguing as CL! 'Okay ... Well, the six screens on the left, including the two you pointed out, are concerned with finding what we call the *Irreversible Numbers*.'

Elizabeth drew her long legs up onto the sofa and tucked them beneath her. 'I can see this is going to be a long night. What, pray, are "Irreversible Numbers"?'

'INs – that's how we refer to them – are unstoppable, quantifiable, human-induced, global phenomena that in the near term are going to have a profound impact on all of us.'

'And near term is what?' she asked cautiously.

'Anything up to 2050,' he said. 'There are also medium and long-term INs, but for this particular model, they have minor impact.'

She craned her neck towards him and raised her eyebrows as if to say, elaborate please.

Her shoulders are slender but proud, rising and falling slightly as she talks. 'Medium term is up to 2100, and long term after 2150.'

'Ah, so your near term is my long term,' she reasoned, but then propped her elbow on the arm of the sofa, placed her hand under her chin and stared back at him.

'Yes ... That's why it's so hard for people to take any of this seriously and why, to many folk, I seem disconnected from reality.'

'Well, to avoid me falling into that category, tell me more about these Irreversible Numbers.'

Methuen slid off the stool and moved across to the sofa, sitting on the opposite arm facing her. As she turned towards him, her skirt rode up above her knees but he noticed she made no attempt to cover herself up.

'We're approaching a point in human history where every global action can be measured and monitored—'

'You mean a big-brothered kind of planet?' she shot back.

'Sure, I understand the downside, but used in the right way this new level of connectedness also offers the opportunity to understand changes in the key processes and systems controlling our lives. That's what all this is about,' he said, waving up at the screens.

'But irreversible? It's such a bold statement. How can you say that?'

He sat down and, resting his arm along the back of the sofa, became aware of her staring at him intensely. Distracted, he glanced up at the monitors to regain his composure.

'The specific INs define three great global problems which are also, by definition, irreversible in the near term.'

Methuen pointed up to a screen where he displayed a cartoon of a crowded, heavily developed desert island, in the centre of which stood a single bedraggled palm tree. He smiled at her, but seeing no reaction, continued with his explanation.

'The majority of people are already familiar with these three problems, namely the depletion of natural resources, the pollution of the planet and the growth of the global population. This is the stage we currently find ourselves in—'

'What do you mean by "the stage"? You make it sound as if we're on some sort of journey?' she said with an uncertain laugh.

'Oh sorry, it's the way I see all this sometimes. I imagine a conversation between aliens carrying out a survey of exoplanets in the Milky Way at the start of our twenty-first century:

'"This one they call Earth; it's currently growing, exploiting and polluting itself out of existence," the first one says.

'The second one replies, "The usual problem – lack of a proactive long-term imagination?"

'"Inventive species though," the first one responds.

'"What shall we put down as an action?" the second one asks.

"Make another visit in two hundred Earth years?"

'"Far too late,' the second one replies. "It'll go one way or the other long before then – let's put it on the fly-past schedule for the start of their twenty-second century. If they're still bickering by then, the outcome will be crystal clear."'

Elizabeth stared at him and then her face broke into a smile.

Does she think I'm mad or is she just thinking it through? Push on. 'Our focus is on identifying as many of these globally significant Irreversible Numbers as possible and to demonstrate how they will interact and shape the world of the mid-century.'

'Can you give me an example?' she asked, tucking her hair behind her ears and folding her arms across her chest.

'Okay, let's start with natural resources – this is the one people are least worried about *at present*. The fact that they will eventually run out is of less interest to us than the specific rate of decline for each commodity.' He picked up a remote from the table and returning to the sofa said, 'Here is a list of the natural resources whose decline profiles we have fixed – hence the "f" in the NR INf label for that screen,' Methuen said.

'What do you mean, fixed?'

'Where we have a seventy-five per cent plus certainty on the profile.' With the laser light, he pointed to the next screen, labelled NR INi.

'These are the natural resources we're still working on. We call them "incipient" Irreversible Numbers. As soon as our research allows us to reach the threshold certainty on their decline profile, we'll migrate them over to the NR INf file, where they can then be used in the model.'

'So in a way we're both hunting for something – I'm looking for ways to relieve pain and suffering and you're tracking down these Irreversible Numbers?'

Hunters – never thought of it like that before. 'Well, I suppose I am – along with a lot of statistical supply and demand modelling.'

'Meaning?'

Methuen went over to the table and began to search through a list of files on the NR INf screen.

Without turning around, he pointed up to a line plot that had appeared. 'Look at this. Love it or hate it, this is the substance that has done more than any other to raise living standards across the world. Without it, the benefits of the Age of Enlightenment would not have spread across the planet.' He pointed to a title box on the screen that read: ANNUAL QUANTITY (BILLION BARRELS) OF CRUDE OIL CONSUMED EVERY YEAR SINCE 1980. 'In 1980, consumption was about twenty-eight billion barrels a year. Last year, in 2015, it was thirty billion – give or take a few hundred million—'

'I have no context for understanding those numbers. Is that a lot?' Elizabeth asked, placing her feet on the floor and leaning towards him.

What sort of question is that? He laughed but then his face fell, as he saw another disapproving frown from her. *Have I offended her again?* Running his hands through his hair, he smiled warmly and said, 'Let me put it another way: by the year 2000, the world had consumed about a trillion barrels of oil since the beginning of the Hydrocarbon Age just after the Second World War. We know we have another trillion in the ground and have been producing from that since 2000. We consume about thirty billion barrels a year, so that means the current trillion barrels will have gone by 2030.'

'Gosh! So we'll run out of oil in fifteen years' time?'

'No, no. There's still a lot of producible hydrocarbon in the ground waiting to be discovered or that governments have not yet chosen to exploit. We know it's there from modelling and subsurface imaging – most estimates put it at about another trillion barrels.'

'So that could give us another thirty years. Still doesn't seem like much?'

Ah, now that's an interesting comment. Her imagination extends to the medium term. 'You're right,' Methuen said, getting up and walking over to a cabinet wedged between two lagged pipes. Taking out a small bottle and unscrewing it, he came back and wafted it under her nose, causing her to jolt back.

'Don't worry, it's quite safe. It's Saudi light crude. It's stuff like this that over the past six decades has transported, clothed, furnished, warmed, cooled and even fed us—'

'How do you mean, "fed us"?' Elizabeth said, waving the bottle away.

'Try running a heavy-duty tractor on a battery and see how long it lasts. Without fossil fuel-driven tractors, we would never have been able to feed four billion people, let alone the seven we have today. Nor would we have been able to maintain soil productivity without the use of fertilisers from fossil-gas.'

'So ... what's the problem?'

'The problem is that the final trillion – much of which still has to be developed – is in places that are expensive and highly challenging to reach: deep, hot, technically and politically difficult. It will take longer to exploit and be considerably costlier to recover, both in economic and environmental terms. The era of cheap oil – keep that adjective in your head because it's important in any proper discussion – will be over soon.'

'What's the other line on that plot?' she asked.

'That's a running check on that final trillion. It shows the annual volume of what we've discovered since 2000.'

'But that must be' – Elizabeth skewed her head to read the graph – 'less than half of what we've been producing over that same period. Is that right?'

Ah, well spotted ... 'That's right. For the last two decades, we've been producing from the second trillion about twice as much as we've been able to develop from the third.'

'So we're becoming overdrawn at God's Bank.'

Another neat phrase and there's that wicked smile again. 'Dangerously so for humanity because we're so dependent on this stuff.'

'But people often talk about the "end of oil". Aren't those warnings being heeded?'

Methuen returned to the sofa, taking with him a keyboard from the table. 'The most important consideration here is how governments choose to act. As with economic growth, if they assume oil will always be there in their budgeting, then they are effectively saying it is infinite. Most political theorists have assumed that about natural resources – even Marx,' he added, but saw no reaction from her. 'That's why most of their macroeconomic projections for the future are wrong.'

'So what about this thing called peak oil?'

Does she want an explanation or is she testing me? 'That's when the global depletion of the most likely recoverable oil volumes reaches fifty per cent. But let me tell you, that's not actually the crucial trigger point for any of these natural resources – I wish it were because it would make all this modelling much easier. The critical timing is when the Market becomes aware that there's a supply problem.'

'But how can you predict when the Market will react?' Elizabeth asked sceptically.

'Not easily, although given the tendency of the press for eye-catching headlines, it'll probably occur *before* physical peak production. The more subtle point that the press will probably miss is the one I mentioned earlier: when will *cheap* oil peak? Once that is fully recognised, then crude oil will stop being a freely traded commodity as it is today and become a geopolitical weapon second to none.'

'Hang on, I'm confused,' she said, sitting up. 'Petrol prices are the lowest I can remember for years, and I've been hearing stories about this new oil shale bonanza in the States?'

Methuen was about to respond when she added, 'And the other day there was some oil executive on TV saying that demand rather than supply was keeping him awake at night.'

My oh my, not just slick phrases but also a discerning ear. He leant towards her and began to count out the answers on his fingers.

'The lower price of petrol is simply a reflection of the game between the various producers – some are even more short term in their thinking than their consumers. As for the resurgence of production in the US from shale, that will fizzle out. In ten years' time, the hot spots they're producing from cheaply right now will have been replaced by more expensive stuff from the final trillion. It will become marginal in commercial terms and therefore not attractive enough to draw the necessary investment.'

'And the oil executive?'

Methuen made a dismissive gesture but to make sure this time she didn't misinterpret him, he gave a broad smile before adding calmly, 'I wouldn't be at all surprised if after that press conference, his next business meeting was to discuss the details of some major new oil or gas investment. Between now and its global politicisation, there's still a lot of money to be made from crude oil – and thank God for that, or else that final trillion will never be produced, and the crutch on which our civilisation rests will be pulled away even faster.'

'But what about the pollution caused by all these hydrocarbons?'

'Sure, but we need *time* to develop non-polluting alternatives, globally. Collapse society now by withdrawing fossil fuels and you'll see how things like climate change rank in people's list of priorities.'

'So the cheap stuff on which we're so dependent is running out fast with no viable alternative, and for that reason crude oil qualifies as one of your significant Irreversible Numbers. How many other natural resources have you fixed like this?'

Great question. Methuen brought up a new display on the NR INf screen. 'Every fossil commodity is under review, including non-tradable ones like underground water.' He flicked to another screen showing a global map covered in red dots. This is our "drought city" map in 2000.' As he spoke, the map reddened, while the counter in the top corner showed time advancing. 'Scary, huh ...? By 2050, one hundred and twenty cities and a billion people will be left without a reliable water supply.'

A large spreadsheet now appeared on another screen. 'What you see here is the countdown table for every commodity as it passes peak production. It's not just animal species that are becoming extinct,' he said, shaking his head. 'Besides crude oil, there's a whole range of base metals, rare earth elements and water reservoirs that should be on everyone's endangered list.'

Elizabeth nodded, staring at the multi-lined plot. 'What about the Irreversible Numbers arising from the other driver?'

Methuen hit a few more keys. On a green-framed monitor labelled PL INf, a mind map appeared with the letters CO_2 / CO printed in the central bubble.

'On this screen you can see the latest update for man-made CO_2 / CO atmospheric accumulation – the most damaging PL Irreversible Number. These are levels of carbon dioxide and carbon monoxide levels, just to be clear—'

'I know, I know,' she replied, waving at him to continue.

'We think we have a reasonable understanding of how "CO_2 / CO warming", as we call it, will increase in the near term—'

'What do you mean, you *think*?' she broke in abruptly.

He switched to another channel on the green screen, now displaying columns of continually changing numbers. 'We're always unsure as to how Mother Earth is going to behave – other than our own brains, it's the most complex system we can conceive. That's why we're continually scouring the planet for information to check our predictions and identify any new or neglected phenomena. What's running here,' he said, directing the laser pointer at the monitor, 'are permafrost records that came in last week from eastern Siberia ...'

Elizabeth looked up at Methuen, who was smiling at her. 'That's why I let go of the door when you came in – my mind was on this data download,' he said half-jokingly. Seeing her turn back to the screen, he added, 'Currently we expect permafrost mass melt to be a medium-term contributor to CO_2 / CO warming. As with rises in sea level from melting land ice, it doesn't have much short-term impact, but this data, along with new concerns over the stability of deep-sea hydrates coming out of Japan, could change all that. It could significantly increase the likelihood of a three-degree world by 2050.'

'A three-degree world?' she asked warily.

'One with global temperatures fifty percent higher than what we are aiming for in 2050.'

She held her hands to her head. 'So let me get this right: the Earth has reached a point where we have grown, extracted and polluted too much. This is represented in globally significant measurable phenomena you call Irreversible Numbers that ... make your model predict what the world will be in years to come ... How does it do that?'

Methuen ran the laser light along three screens to his right marked: IC ECON, IC POL, IC SOC. 'The Irreversible Numbers give rise to what we call *Inevitable Consequences* – IC for short. I've already mentioned some of the physical consequences of the INs – such as the accelerating permafrost melt due to CO_2 / CO warming ... I could add another, which is the increased cloudiness and weather volatility that reduce the effectiveness of wind and solar-generated power, especially in the northern hemisphere. The consequences I'm showing you on these screens over here, will have a direct impact on our human economic, social and political systems and processes – the very things that define what life will be like for us in the future.'

'So these are predictions from the model?'

'Yes, but only the really important ones.'

Elizabeth hunched her shoulders and held out her hands. 'What makes them more important?'

Methuen raised his hand. 'I'll come to that in a minute,' he said, leaning forward to highlight a coloured world map on the screen labelled IC POL. 'Of all our predictions, the least contested among those of us involved in all this, comes from the geopolitical module. By 2050, all globally important human actions will be controlled by five superstates – what we call Powerblocks in the model. These are China, Europe, India, Russia and the US. Even today they account for ninety per cent of global wealth, contain fifty per cent of the world's population and more than ninety per cent of all military spending.'

She gazed at him and then slid her finger thoughtfully along her lips.

Why's she doing that? Where was I? Oh yes, the superstates.

He tapped at the keyboard and displayed, on the IC POL screen, a set of tables on which numbers were changing rapidly. 'What you see here is an active updating of a fifty-year budget – this is how we judge what's *important*, by the way. 'This is the ...' – he looked up, checking the details – 'US in 2040. We have two sets of budgets for each Powerblock. One is based on conventional planning assumptions such as continuous economic growth, infinite resources, manageable climate change and so on. The other uses the model outcomes to define these parameters, that includes, among other things, the cost of climate change and more realistic resource pricing.'

Methuen tapped the keyboard again, bringing up a new set of graphs. 'What you see here is the impact of different INs on the superstate budget. Pollution INfs have the biggest effect on China and Russia, while the Resource INfs are more critical for the EuroState and the Indian block—'

'And how do you factor in non-economic things such as loss of biodiversity? That's important too, isn't it?'

'That's what we classify as an animate natural resource ...' *Come on, don't soft-peddle on this. You know what she's getting at – tell it to her as it is.* 'If the Powerblocks don't find a way to manage the economic challenges that IN-driven budgets predict, then there's little hope that they'll give much attention to protecting the natural world around them. Few will care about the impact of burning coal or destroying wildlife habitats if it means they have a way of keeping their citizens warm and fed. With modelling on this scale, you have to remove your cosy metropolitan slippers and walk in the bare feet of the impoverished.'

Elizabeth nodded thoughtfully.

That's good. She's not one of those useless single-issue people.

'What about other Inevitable Consequences?' she asked, leaning forward and pointing to the screens.

'Well, let's take the IC ECON. One of the most significant consequence of the INs on human processes and systems is an economic condition called "secular stagflation". We saw it emerge, briefly after the oil crisis in the seventies and then again in 2011 following the financial crisis, but what I'm referring to here is way off the scale.'

She rested her chin on her hand and stared intently at the screen as a set of new graphs flashed up.

'Secular stagflation starts when global prices consistently rise faster than incomes. In the model, this is driven by among other things increasing prices due to shortage of resources. At the same time, a variety of factors contribute to falling incomes, not just competition from a rising population but also significant state actions, such as the termination of foreign aid, the unavoidable capital cost of weather-damaged infrastructure and increased spending on defence. All these begin to take a larger slice of the Powerblocks' budgets.'

Elizabeth joined him at the edge of the sofa and said uneasily, 'And when will that start?'

'That's the *big* question,' he replied, nodding earnestly. 'Currently we have stagflation going global in the mid-2040s, but it's a complex piece of modelling – that's why we carry a ten-year error bar for it at present.'

'So what does that mean for mere mortals like me?'

Like you. You mean, like all of us. 'If not managed properly, stagflation is the most damaging economic environment imaginable. Savings, annuities, dividends all lose their value; currencies become unstable, pushing down the standard of living.'

'Creating a sort of Blade Runner world, with a wealthy elite and a huge impoverished underclass?'

'No, no, no, none of that movie nonsense, please. I don't go in for all that apocalyptic stuff,' he said firmly. 'The world is a big, big place, populated by a highly adaptive species. It takes a lot of time and persistence for anything to have a truly global impact. Providing the pace of change is not too fast and we are well prepared, there's a good chance we will find ways of living with all of this, even something as insidious as secular stagflation.'

'Well, that's good to hear. I was beginning to doubt whether you were going to say anything remotely optimistic at all this evening.'

Ouch! You're being a Doomboy. Methuen placed the keyboard on the floor and reached over to her. 'I'm sorry, I don't mean to be gloomy, but all this,' he said, waving up at the screens, 'is my daily bread. If it's any comfort, it also scares me at times.'

'I'm not scared,' she shot back. 'I'd rather know the likely outcomes now than be surprised later. What about the third IN – population – you've not mentioned that yet?'

He picked up the keyboard and went over to the table, highlighting a screen to his left, entitled P INf. 'Our model pretty much agrees with that of the current UN prediction that by 2050 the world's population will be approaching ten billion. The problem is that even if we assume the continuous growth model that governments currently use, there is no capacity to feed or shelter the extra forty per cent. That will create momentum for people to move en masse, but on a scale we have never seen before in human history. This is what we call "The Resettling".'

'You mean people from Africa migrating into Europe?'

'Oh no ... more, much more than that. As we approach The Time of Less, everyone on this planet will be asking the same question that the shoeless tribesman asks today: Is there a more secure and rewarding place where I can live?'

'You seem pretty certain that 2050 won't be some kind of Blade Runner dystopia, but with everything you've described, I can't imagine it's going to be a world ruled by democracy-loving governments.'

What did Mr Demming use to say? 'Rhetoric is the enemy of the people. Speak your truth; don't play to the audience.' Methuen again ran his hands through his hair. 'You're right, but it's not as grim as you may fear. Democracy is a remarkable experience. Once a culture has tasted it, or even just observed it on mass media, the enticement of freedom is impossible to eradicate.'

Still looking at the screens, Elizabeth steepled her hands against her chin. 'Going back to your geopolitical module, I still don't see how you can be so sure about how it'll emerge in the 2050s?'

I thought I'd been quite clear. Patience, Pryce – spell it out a little more. Methuen pointed back to the IC POL screen. 'We build scenarios based on how the Powerblocks react and interact in response to their fifty-year budgets. As with any other institution, when a superstate is going bust – as is the current destiny of all of them before 2050 – what can they do? Borrow more money? That won't be an option in the future because there will be no organisation capable or willing to lend on that scale. Lower their living standards? One can hope we would all take that seriously, but it's not easy. It requires the type of self-disciplined society that today only exists in places like Japan – and even there it's dependent on continued economic success, which right now is built on excessive amounts of debt.'

Elizabeth got up from the sofa and stood next to him.

She's quite tall, five nine or even five ten maybe, and I think she's older than me?

'They're much bigger than they are today?' she said, pointing to the map on which the Powerblocks had been shaded in.

Shoulder to shoulder, considering things together – how nice. 'That's because by 2050 most of them have exercised one of the responses to the budget deficit that we generally refer to as "contiguous absorption". The US does it passively by merging with Canada; Russia and China, more aggressively with their neighbours.'

'Sounds painful—'

'In the short term it is, particularly for those living in countries being forcefully absorbed, but once they're part of a Powerblock, there's a good chance of a square meal every day, some level of law and order and an opportunity for many of the kids to go to school—'

'But they're not able to travel? They're prisoners.'

'To varying degrees, yes, but compare that to the lives of those outside the Powerblocks.'

'Resource Conflict Zones, StaticLands and Neutral Areas,' she read from the map key. 'What happens in those?'

'In our most likely scenario, the Powerblocks don't engage with one another militarily up to 2050 – largely because of the nuclear deterrent and MACA.'

'MACA?'

'Mutually Assured Cyber Annihilation.'

'You believe that'll be possible?'

'It's a better deterrent for humankind than neutron bombs, although no less disabling,' he said, playing the laser pointer over the map again. 'The main activity between now and 2050 will be land-grab wars that secure borders, protect trading routes and, of course, gain access to remaining resources.'

Methuen pulled up a separate map labelled RESOURCE CONFLICT ZONES. 'Where the potential reward is large, the Powerblocks will invade. These include places like the Congo and even Antarctica, but the main theatre of conflict is the resource-rich "emerging strip" running north-east from North Africa, up through the Middle East and into the 'Stans.'

'What about the local people in these areas?'

'They will survive if they cooperate, but if they resist, they will either be subjugated or eradicated.'

She shook her head in disgust. 'Genocide?'

'By 2050, international law will have weakened. The Powerblocks will do whatever is necessary to maintain their living standards.'

'What goes on in the StaticLands then?' she said, prompting him to project a new map on the IC POL screen.

'Oh, it's nowhere near as bad as in the Resource Conflict Zones. In the blunt terminology of the model, they're regarded by the Powerblocks as mainly "low-utility" countries. They are often poor in resource and therefore don't warrant the cost of military action. With global agency and foreign aid all but gone by 2050, most are in the process of reverting to their ancestral origins – becoming tribal and preoccupied with protecting their territory.'

'And the "Neutral Areas"?'

'There'll be a few countries that are simply too remote. These will adopt an apolitical position and may have relationships with several Powerblocks. Australia falls into this category up to 2050, although in the medium-term model, invasion and fragmentation is the most likely outcome, because of its prize resources.'

Elizabeth stepped away and then turned back to him, holding out her hands. 'The way you describe it makes it sound as if you regard this' – she stared at the map to read the title – '"Powerblock Stand-Off Scenario" as something stable, even desirable?'

'I assure you there are far worse possible outcomes for 2050: Powerblock conflict, Powerblock collapse, single Powerblock dominance, to name a few. Fortunately, none of these is as sustainable as "stand-off". So long as the channels of communication among the Powerblocks remain open, there is always hope.'

'Hope for what?' she replied scathingly.

'Hope that even with the loss of the integrated world of today, global cooperation particularly in science and technology will survive. We need that above all to find solutions to the three great problems facing humankind today: creating cheap substitutes for declining raw materials, countering the effects of global warming and managing the rising population.'

'The global brain still able to move the global hand,' she said, smiling at him.

I love these straplines she pulls out of the air. 'Yes, that's a great way to describe it – I must write that down.' Methuen reached across the table and handed her a loosely bound wad of paper. 'If you promise not to copy it, you can read this.'

Elizabeth took the document and after turning over several blank sheets, came to a title page with the words Progress Report on Scenario F227M94: The Segmented World. 'This is your preferred world view for 2050, I presume?'

'Yes. We submit updates to the Foundation every month – I serve as a collator, pulling it all together.'

She looked at him suspiciously. 'Who is this "we" you keep referring to?'

I shouldn't have said that. Oh, come on – in for a penny, in for a pound, as Grandad would have said. He fired up the screen furthest to the right and instantly a map of the world appeared with intersecting lines dimming and lighting up.

'This isn't all my own work,' he said, laughing. 'I'm part of a network of forecasters compiling the mid-century model. We're managed and financially supported by the Consilience Founda-tion.' *She's frowning at me again – but with barely any wrinkles on her forehead and I like the way her cheeks round out slightly when she's smiling.*

'Never heard of them. What do they get out of it?'

'It's entirely non-profit,' he heard himself reply guardedly and then, seeing her blank stare, quickly added, 'I don't know a lot about them. They could be run by some Mr Big who wants to control the world.' He laughed again but seeing her face still unchanged, added more seriously, 'They've never asked me to do anything I didn't want to do. They provide me with amazing data, like this permafrost file we've just looked at, and facilities that no one else has – other than a few governments and one or two of the top finance houses.'

'Nobody creates an organisation on this scale without wanting something in return – or am I being too cynical?'

'I think you've answered that question already. Who wants to live in a world where the global hand and the global brain no longer work in unison? That's motive enough for all of us to keep working on this.'

She returned to the sofa, chin in the air and arms folded.

Come on, show her everything – make her part of it. He pointed to the far screen on his left and typed into the keyboard.

A young black male appeared, a pair of glasses perched on his head and wearing a T-shirt bearing the words THE SIXTH POWER-BLOCK. Immediately, the man began speaking.

'Yo, my boy – Pryce! You spyin' on me, bruv?' Spotting Elizabeth, the man's tone changed instantly. 'Oh, who do we have here then? I've not seen you before.'

'This is my friend Elizabeth. I'm showing her around the model.'

The man peered into the camera and grinning broadly, said, 'Careful with him, babe. He's a monster in disguise.'

Elizabeth smiled but said nothing.

'Did you get the Panama Papers' transcript?' Methuen asked.

'Too right I did – the Foundation's on the ball as usual. But what came with it has had me working like a dog for the past week. We now have a professor on board from Moscow State with the lowdown on the two gangs that run Putin.'

Methuen turned and caught Elizabeth's puzzled look. 'Enough, enough, Zak. You joining the global broadcast on the model update tomorrow?'

'Wouldn't miss it for the world – even if your lady friend there were to ask me out,' the man said, pushing his face up against the camera with his tongue hanging out.

That's enough, you horny bastard. 'Bye, Zak, see you tomorrow.'

Methuen looked back at Elizabeth and said a little ruefully, 'He's living on a redundant early warning facility somewhere in the Arctic – no female company for months on end. That's the only way I can explain his behaviour.'

'He's rather handsome … sparkling brown eyes. Why's he on his own out there?'

Handsome? I'd expected you to be disgusted at his behaviour or at the very least taken aback, not admiring!

As he stared at her in surprise, she said, laughing, 'I'm joking. What interests me more is what he's doing with the Panama Papers?'

'He works on one of our Pioneering Projects. You may think from our discussion that we only model bad news into these alternative fifty-year budgets, but we also look at positives, such as Zak's work on bribery and corruption. He's already shown that the Russian Block would be forty-seven per cent more productive if B&C were reduced to the global average.'

'Do you have a pioneering project, Methuen?'

'I do – I look at Attitudinal INs.'

'Let me guess, it's some sort of …' Elizabeth threw back her head and laughed. 'No, I'm not even going to try … You tell me.'

Methuen changed the channel on the screen they'd been viewing and brought up another coloured map, entitled Changing Global Attitudes.

'This is more art than science right now,' he insisted. 'If you go back in history, significant periods of change have always been associated with shifts in the way people think and feel. It's arguable which comes first – the shift in public opinion or the change-making events. I call that response "Attitude", whether it's an outburst of inventiveness and liberation, similar to what we had after the Second World War in Europe and the US, or a retreat into something darker like the Cultural Revolution in China. Given what we are about to experience, I think it's highly likely that some global shift in people's "attitude" will occur over the next thirty years.'

'So what's the status of this "artistic" exercise of yours?' she asked.

'Well, there are several angles I'm pursuing, one being the masculine response to hardship.'

'Because women don't figure in your world?' she chided.

Oh, is that her flaw? Is she one of those overly politically correct types. God, I hope not.

'Actually, it's the response of the masculine quality – in men or in women – that I'm interested in. Loss of power, status or some other challenge to the masculine self has always been the trigger for change.'

'And how do you access such a thing?'

'My focus at present is on the behaviour of one particular group that we define as super-rich – those with a net worth of over one hundred million dollars. Don't get me wrong, I have no objection to the acquisition of wealth that is come by legally and is used fairly, but many in this group don't fall in that category. They built their wealth during the early stages of globalisation when regulation was thin on the ground. A few use their money for philanthropic purposes or to fund research and invention – those individuals give us great hope for the future, but sadly most of the super-rich contribute very little to the betterment of human society. They're apathetic to the fate of others. What fires them up is a constant, childish race to the top. They have no army and often no organisation behind them, but exert a disproportion-ate influence within the various superstate power structures. I've started mapping not just the influence they wield within Power-blocks, but also how their behaviour affects global attitudes. I call them "OST-man" – although women feature in this group too, by the way.'

'OST?'

'One-sided thinking.'

'Meaning?'

'Meaning that the questioning voice in their brain has been disabled or stunted by the obsession of wealth building. If you press them into explaining their philosophy, you find that they don't believe human beings are particularly special – except within the clan to which they belong. They pursue things for their own benefit with little concern over their impact on others. And when things don't work out, they distort the truth, to fit *their* reality. Of course, by de-humanising themselves in this way, they have become wonderfully adaptive to surviving in the amoral ecosystem we call capitalism. Again, please don't misunderstand me: I have no problem with capitalism itself – it's the best damn way we can run human commerce. What I object to is the selfish, unregulated version that OST-man promotes and thrives on.'

'You're talking about the alt-right?'

'Not just them. All these ideological groups – left, right, religious – have one thing in common: they opt for simple solutions that are not even utilitarian in their arithmetic, but narrowly elitist.' Gazing at her, he rubbed a bead of sweat from his brow.

'But isn't that type of selfishness present in all of us, especially when we're cornered?' Elizabeth asked, hands behind head, nodding slightly at the screen. 'It's just the way we're made, isn't it?'

'It is, but with one important difference. Most of us have an internal dial set not on maximum personal gain but somewhere in between self and other – two-sided thinking, if you like. A quiet, rational, compassionate voice still talks to us when we get carried away. The people I'm describing are unable to do that. Even though they are often highly educated and well resourced, not just their ability to think in a rational and objective way has been lost, but also their imaginative faculty has been damaged beyond repair. They cannot visualise alternative outcomes, let alone act on them. Not only their private but also their public actions are determined by a single way of thinking. A concept, like fairness for fairness' sake, for example, is simply not in their mindset.'

'So the OST attitude is one of your irreversible phenomena?'

'No, not yet … but were that form of thinking to become the norm in the middle ranks of society, then an irreversible change would indeed be triggered, leading to a Segmented World far darker and more menacing than one I describe in that draft I've given you.'

'But what you've described is already happening, elsewhere? Vast swathes of the younger generation are signed up to social media and create their own reality by "unfriending" anything they don't like or understand, including history.'

'So you're not a fan of Facebook or Twitter then?'

'Well, I suppose it's better than taking cocaine, but I like to learn from the past, and I prefer to have friends who surprise and challenge me – no matter how eccentric their ideas. Many people hooked on social media are retreating into themselves. They seem to have reached an unconscious conclusion that they're—'

'Doomed?' Methuen chipped in with an ironic laugh.

'More like confused – and considering all that we've been discussing, they have good reason to be. The only things they can be sure of are their own thoughts and feelings, and that's why they "friend" those who think and feel the same way. They'll be easy converts to this OST mentality. Getting them to look outside their world and act more cooperatively, as you want, is going to be a huge challenge.'

'Instead of feeling stranded like sheep in the snow, huddled together on their phones with their backs to the world, unsure of where to go,' Methuen said reflectively and then added, 'In the network, I'm the youngest, and part of what the organisation calls the "Transition Generation", but the more I pursue the Attitudinal INs, the more I realise that everyone is ... confused, as you say – young and old alike.'

'I'm glad you said that. You only need to meet my mother to see how many of the older generation are just as lost as their children.'

'Your mother ...' He stopped as he caught sight of the clock on the wall. 'Crikey, look at the time – it's two-thirty. How are you going to get home?'

AA-Com File: Hunter's Tryst

Princes Street, Edinburgh, Scotland, UK
Early morning, 19 December 2016

Virtual Scene snapshot: Elizabeth and Methuen are walking along a street strung with Christmas lights and crowded with young partygoers.

'I can't see a cab anywhere,' Methuen called out, scanning the traffic on the edge of the pavement.

They're right what they say about him – he is a bit odd and certainly obsessed with this modelling stuff. But when didn't I want odd, and why should I care that he's obsessed? At least it's nothing kinky or sad. My father will like him; my mother will detest him – so that's box number one ticked for you, Mr Pryce. 'Doesn't matter. I can take the number five or the twenty-seven to Hunter's Tryst,' she said, pointing to a bus stop.

'Hunter's Tryst? That's miles away,' he replied, but then seeing a gang of young men waiting for the bus, grabbed her arm and said, 'I'll go with you.'

Oh, I wasn't expecting that … or is he just being gentlemanly? 'It's okay, it's not necessary, Methuen. This is 2016, not 2050.' She laughed.

As they joined the queue, a youth covered in tattoos lurched towards her, a can in his hand. 'You comin' wiv us then, darlin'?'

Touch me, pal, and you'll discover the delights of a Mace facial.

Methuen put his arm around Elizabeth and glared at the man, who wavered and then staggered back to join his fellow drinkers.

'I've always wanted to see Hunter's Tryst,' he said, glancing at those ahead of them.

When the bus arrived they found the lower deck full, so had no choice but to follow the gang at the bus stop upstairs and squeeze together on a small double seat by the luggage rack.

'Safer if we look like a boring couple,' he said, cupping his hand under her elbow.

'One of those may become true,' she snorted, 'but I don't think the other will ever apply.'

Her comment provoked a similar belly laugh from him as she had heard in the dance hall, drawing the attention of the inebriated rabble further down the bus. She nudged him to quell his laughter, and together they bowed their heads, sniggering quietly.

As the bus picked up speed, she drew back her cape and checked her watch. 'Do you realise we were busy talking for over two hours in that bunker of yours and except for when your friend Zak came online, never once did either of us say anything about what's going on right now. Where are the signs of this Segmented World you talk about – or are they not yet obvious?'

Methuen nodded, still gazing down at his lap.

I like that nod. He takes me seriously.

'Prediction,' he said quietly, 'is always rooted in the present. A good forecaster is one who can cut through all the froth and select the critical here-and-now events that will shape global systems and processes in the future.'

'So is this *Segmented World* already upon us?' she asked again.

'Not yet. That only happens when the three big problems reach a certain level such that we start seeing the Inevitable Consequences appear, in the form of global phenomena like secular stagflation, resettling and debt-defaulting.'

'So when will that be?' she persisted.

Methuen squeezed his eyes tight as if he were trying to recall something. 'In that draft I gave you, the most likely declaration date for the Segmented World lies somewhere between 2040 and 2050, although there is a wider range possible up to 2060.'

She laughed mockingly. 'A wider range? I thought you were going to say 2080 or 2100.'

'No, no, I think it may actually be closer to 2040.'

'In which case, there *must* already be signs of the Segmented World all around us.'

He hunched his shoulders. 'Well, of course there are. The pressure on resources and the environment began some time back. Many of the older members of the Foundation point to the 1970s as the starting point – when the US came off the gold standard and removed any control on debt. Only that way could the world, or should I say the US, bump up their living standards. What followed was an orgy of uncontrolled consumption, matched by growing levels of pollution and inequality. It was a heyday for the financial community because as population and living standards rose, the only way to stimulate further growth was through more credit – much of which unfortunately was badly regulated – giving rise eventually to the crisis in 2008—'

'Low-hanging fruit that let your OST-man thrive.' *Hmm, he's beaming at me again – he likes my little summaries and doesn't feel threatened by me speaking out.*

'You could argue that the debt-supported austerity that followed the 2008 crash has been a gentle way of preparing everyone in the West – at least – for the falling living standards that are to come.'

Only you could regard austerity as something beneficial. 'So going back to my original question, what signs of the Segmented World can we see today?'

'Since I joined Consilience in 2012, we've been scrutinising an enormous variety of social and political developments to see what they can tell us about our transition into the Segmented World. One way to understand it is through the attitudinal approach we discussed earlier. When humans are under stress, the masculine response tends to come to the fore, mainly triggered by men losing their jobs and with that their self-worth. A steelworker doesn't want to serve in a fast-food outlet but nor does he want to see his family go hungry. Events have moved on so quickly since the financial collapse that mainstream politics hasn't yet diagnosed the problem, let alone found any solutions.'

'Hence the rise of populism?' Elizabeth chipped in.

Methuen nodded vigorously in agreement. 'In democratic societies, populism is being allowed to work itself through the system in a sort of learning exercise, no matter how much harm it may do to the economic and social well-being of us all. In authoritarian states like Russia and China, the governments squeeze out dissent, which may work for now but in the medium term will damage the creative and inventive output from their populations, as has happened before.'

'So you're not a supporter of this new president in the US then?'

'I don't understand him. Here is someone claiming to be a businessman but who ignores a massive business risk: that of CO_2 / CO warming. When more than ninety-five per cent of scientists say something catastrophic is going to happen, then the sensible businessman reacts according to the threat. This chap simply denies it.'

'So you're not a supporter then?' she asked again.

Methuen bent his head to one side. 'The only good thing about these populist leaders is that they often speak the unspeakable and sometimes try the untried. As they flail around to find issues to increase their popularity, they come across the unwritten book handed on by word of mouth from president to president, prime minister to prime minister: the "Book of Very Difficult Issues". In that tome today lie at least two of the main consequences of the Irreversible Numbers: resettling and the imbalances arising from global free trade.'

'What happens then, to things like immigration and trade imbalances in this Segmented World?' Elizabeth asked.

Methuen shrugged his shoulders. 'Well, they're simply reduced or removed.'

'Meaning I can pencil you in as a closet supporter of the current president?' she whispered.

'No one can disagree with the idea that immigration and trade should have checks and limits – it's a question of how you go about it. Putting our head in the sand and pretending it's not an issue is as irresponsible as the many divisive things these tinpot populist politicians get criticised for.'

'So what does your model predict for the decade ahead?' she asked cagily.

'The debate in the network is not so much about direction but the pace of change. As I said before, geopolitics is the easiest to predict. The new G5 has already started to emerge. More difficult to model is how quickly institutions like the UN will adapt to the reality. The idea of one-country-one-vote is stifling enough in the EU – how much more so in these multinational agencies. All leading councils and committees must be restructured around this G5 I mentioned, or else the great post-war amalgamating force of the United Nations will become irrelevant. China, India and Russia are already embracing a more isolationist stance. As for the US, resettling, the trade deficit and the financial cost of playing good cop are now live issues. After bringing them to public awareness, no politician will ever be able to ignore them—'

'You never step into the same river twice,' she interjected.

Methuen nodded his head and said, 'And nor, I fear, will the US ever again be regarded as the world's representative of freedom and justice. What made America Great is being systematically destroyed by the new leader of the GOP.'

'And Europe?'

'The honeymoon is over. Right now, it's held together by its debt-raising ability to lift the living standards of the poorest members. When that falls away over the next decade, we can only hope and pray that the military threat from Russia is enough to keep the member states united. If not, then fragmentation is the most likely outcome.'

He turned and smiled at her. 'Enjoy these halcyon days, Elizabeth, when resources are still freely traded, the effects of climate change are still manageable, and the main concern we have with regards to the growing population is how we provide enough white goods to the twenty million entering Social Class C every month.'

Is there no hope at all for the future, from his perspective? It's all so depressing. 'So it's all downhill from here …' she said with a sigh, staring pensively out of the window.

'We have to hope that a cohort of intelligent global leaders will eventually emerge in the G5 who will understand the mistakes of the past and recognise the vital importance of international collaboration.'

Seeing the top deck of the bus now empty around them, Elizabeth laughed loudly. 'Is that a prediction or just wishful thinking?'

He rested his arm along the back of the seat. 'It all depends on the next two decades. We're entering an utterly unique period in human history. We either collectively acknowledge The Time of Less and come together to solve the huge problems it poses, or we segment, with each entity doing its own thing. To prevent that will be the G5's greatest challenge.'

* * *

Virtual Scene snapshot: Arm in arm, Elizabeth and Methuen walk down the middle of an empty, moonlit road.

'Why do you live so far out?' Methuen asked, pulling up the collar of his jacket against the cold wind blowing off the Firth.

'I'm not really into being a student,' she replied, chuckling. 'I'm a bit old for that.'

He stepped back as she turned towards the entrance to a stylish, polished brick apartment block.

'This is a bit swanky,' he said as she tapped a code into the keypad next to the entry.

'We're all adults and I'm the youngest here – not a student in sight,' she said as they entered a wide foyer with a polished wood floor. As Methuen set off for the lift, she called him back to a drab utility door, where she had started to punch the keys on another wall panel. 'I don't live up there – like your office, my home is in the basement.'

'I'd have expected you to live up in the penthouse,' he said mockingly as he followed her down a bare stairway.

'Well, I have something better than that – a walled garden,' she said. 'It's a bit shrivelled up right now but wait 'til you see it in the summer.'

Inside the apartment, books and papers lay in well-defined heaps on the floor, each with its own distinct collection of glasses, plates and writing materials.

Elizabeth glanced around the room and began straightening some of the books into more organised piles. As she made her way towards a far side door, she pointed at a low-slung modular sofa in the centre of the room. 'Make yourself at home. I need to get out of these party clothes.'

Closing the door to the bedroom, she stripped naked and walked towards the shower, shaking her head. *God, why is this place always such a mess?*

* * *

Virtual Scene snapshot: Ten minutes later. Elizabeth emerges from the bathroom, pulling on a silk kaftan.

She stared at herself in the wardrobe mirror, pursing her lips and scrunching her damp hair. *You could do with a spot of remodelling yourself. You may say you dislike being a student, but that's exactly what you look like. Come on girl, change. Change!*

She frisked her hair up again and padded through to the sitting room in her bare feet. Dimming the lights, she looked over to where Methuen lay stretched out on the sofa, his shoes lined up neatly on the carpet and his jacket folded beside him.

'Fancy a nightcap?' she asked, switching on music and, without waiting for his reply, poured two drinks. 'This is all I have, I'm afraid,' she said, handing him a cocktail glass.

Taking the drink from her, he pointed to one of the abstract canvases on the wall and then to a large metal sculpture in the corner. 'Quite an eclectic mix,' he said.

Eclectic. Is that his way of saying he doesn't approve?

'You also paint and play,' he added, nodding at an easel next to the window and then at a music stand alongside a small harp.

'It's all a bit of a mess, I'm afraid. I hadn't planned on inviting anyone back,' she said, sipping her drink.

'It's great. It has that free-flowing feel of creativity.'

That's a relief. He's not one of those OCD types who wants everything ordered.

'Cheers,' he said, raising the glass, only to splutter loudly and spray a mouthful of drink over the sofa. 'This is neat gin!' he shrieked.

Elizabeth laughed as he plucked something from his pocket to wipe the damp spots from her cushions.

Oh, look at that, it's an actual white handkerchief! 'It was very noble of you to bring me home, Methuen. Don't go back tonight – you can sleep on this,' she said, tapping the sofa. 'People say it's wonderfully comfortable. I'll make you bacon and eggs in the morning, or whatever you fancy.'

Oh, my handkerchief man looks surprised! She sat up and moved slightly towards him. 'Now, tell me this: imagine I have travelled forward in time and lived in this Segmented World of yours for a couple of months. What do I say to people who ask on my return, "What was the biggest change you noticed?"' *Ah, that confident smile – he's been asked that before.*

'I think the one thing you might say is that it wasn't so different from the world of today. Of course, there'll be lots of new gizmos, AI-driven things in particular – but never forget, the world is a big place, a large and complex system that doesn't flip overnight into a dystopian hellhole or utopian paradise …'

I've heard him say that before. Is this the argument he uses to keep himself sane?

'… inequality will have increased,' Methuen continued. 'Not only the gap between the super-rich and the rest of us but more importantly between those who can be sure of a regular meal and those who cannot …'

His voice tailed off and she was about to ask for more details when, to her surprise, he began to recite verse.

'We would rather be ruined than changed, We would rather die in our dread, Than climb the cross of the moment, And let our illusions die.'

'Uh?'

'Your question reminded me of something a few years back,' he said, scratching his head and then sighing deeply. 'One answer is a more widespread feeling of anxiety—'

'What, even with my gallant protector beside me?' she said, trying to lighten the mood.

He gave a short laugh but then looked back at her with a grave expression. 'Not just personal safety, but across the board – income, food availability, reliability of water supply. Things we take for granted today we will value more in the future.'

'Sounds like the world that our great-grandparents experienced in the last century: rationing, make-do-and-mend and all that.'

'You may be right, although that was a radically different time. People in those days knew their place – there was predictability and cooperation. Our society wasn't the patchwork of competing identity groups that it is today – it was something more coherent, built around a single idea of nationhood that pulled people together. In this so-called advanced world we now live in, we aim to maximise our independence by minimising our dependency. We demand our rights without accepting our responsibility. We've lost the discipline of balance and self-regulation.'

'Oh dear, I've triggered something there, haven't I?' she said, laughing nervously. 'Maybe all this angst we're about to face in the future will bring us all back together?'

'That would be a wonderful outcome.'

But one you don't believe will happen. 'How will all your work help to achieve that?' As she said the words, she noticed his jaw drop along with his shoulders.

'We're not quite there yet ...'

'But once you're ready,' she persisted, 'how will you communicate this idea of a Segmented World?'

'Through the Foundation, I guess.'

What a disappointing response ... and that look from him tells me he knows it. She reached into her bag on the floor and pulled out the draft of his report. Bending towards him to borrow a pen, she saw him glance at her exposed cleavage.

Sitting back, she turned to the front cover of the report and put a line through the title, writing above it, Living in a Segmented World: A Progress Report. 'If you're so sure about your predictions, you need to start thinking about this also.' She held the draft out to him so he could read the title and then said, 'Describe to everyone – not just Establishment figures – what this new world will be like and what we have to do to survive in it, not only individually but also collectively.'

She looked up in surprise, as Methuen gave out a small, controlled laugh. 'I've heard bits of this conversation in the past,' he said.

He opened his mouth to say more, but she cut him off. 'You should also think about realigning that personal god of yours too. Seeking the truth is admirable, but it doesn't have enough focus. How about: Helping people to understand the future. Shouldn't that be the minimal aim of all this modelling?'

She saw him hesitate and realised her comment had triggered another of his pregnant pauses. While waiting for his response, she found a blank page at the front of the draft and printed out the word THOUGHT. Showing it to him, she said, 'It's what my father taught me many years ago: Ensure all your thoughts have depth like the vertical line in the letter T, and breadth like the horizontal arm.'

He smiled, pointing to her drawing. 'I presume I'm the vertical in all this – arguing from the model – and you're the horizontal, deducing deeper meaning from the day-to-day?'

You might well have something there, Mr Pryce. She leant over, planted a kiss on his cheek and stood up. 'Sounds like that not-so-boring couple we discussed on the bus. I'll get you a pillow and some blankets.'

* * *

Virtual Scene snapshot: Elizabeth lies in bed, staring up at the ceiling, her hands cupped under her head.

He's different from my father, more willing to consider every angle. She sat up sharply, as the memory of her mother – suitcase in hand, slamming the door, leaving – came to mind.

'I don't want to be like her. I need to settle down,' she said aloud.

Sipping water to take away the taste of the gin, she tiptoed through into the living room, where she could hear Methuen snoring lightly. Touching his shoulder, she whispered, 'Move up, I need to absorb your thoughts into my body tonight.'

'That'll be nice,' he said, shuffling towards the back of the sofa.

'Night,' she replied, snuggling into him.

'God bless,' he murmured.

Inside the red-painted barn;
Hardin, Montana, NCSA, FSA
13.15 hours, 15 June 2050

'Is it over? I was enjoying that!' Lianne cried out.

Nick laughed cynically. 'There you were, a few hours ago, complaining about privacy rights and now you've become a rampant voyeur?'

Lianne lay still for a moment before taking off her glasses and turning towards him. 'I presume Elizabeth and Methuen would have final editorial rights on what we've just experienced? After all, it is *their* memories.'

'On their perspective for sure, but if there's incontrovertible data that something occurred that one of them didn't want portrayed or didn't recall, then the consensus of those there is followed.'

'And what if there is no consensus? Who is the final arbiter – the Storymaker?'

'No, that's only an editing IA; it has no advanced emotional or ethical programming. For the pre-'49 scenes that we're watching – it's the team that assembled all this. But eventually it will be Katharina.'

'Who's that? Have I met her?'

'You will, but we need to go through a few more scenes first. Shall we have some lunch and then immerse ourselves in another one?'

'I'd rather carry on viewing,' Lianne said.

'Hah! It's really gripped you, hasn't it?' he said, searching through the list on the screen. 'There's quite a short one here – all Elizabeth – so we can run it from her perspective. Starts with her … Wow! Looks like some sleazy pull-in off US-1, post-Covid. Could be interesting.'

AA-Com File: Going Around

US-1, Q-Bar, Philadelphia, USA
Late evening, 10 March 2023

Virtual Scene snapshot: Elizabeth, wearing a tight, low-cut dress, is seated at the wheel of a car in a parking lot next to a bar just off the highway. A police car with lights flashing, is pulled up behind and an officer is looking in through her side window.

'Evening, ma'am. I noticed you hit the kerb twice as you moved off. Are you okay?'

Where's the bloody reverse in this car? 'I'm fine, just a little tired, Officer.'

'Are you visiting the States or do you live here?'

Ah, there's the Park. 'Why do you ask?' she said, smiling at the poker-faced young man.

'Well … from your accent, ma'am. Can I see your documents?'

Fuck, where are they? She reached over and searched the map pocket in the door alongside her. Handing an untidy sheaf of papers through the car window, she heard another voice call out, 'Wait a minute, Chuck, I know this lady.'

An older man appeared and leant in at the window beside his colleague. 'It's Doctor Pryce, isn't it? You run the medical centre down by the river in Richmond? I'm Michael Flanagan – remember me? I brought my brother in last year with a knife wound.'

Flanagan. Yes, I remember lots of blood. I can't get out of the car in this dress. 'How is Declan now?' she asked, pulling a coat around her shoulders.

'Oh, he's good, thanks to your quick work.'

The other officer handed back the papers – now organised into a neat pile. 'Is this a regular stop for you, ma'am?'

'I sometimes pull in here to unwind after work,' she said, shoving the bundle into the glove compartment.

'It's just that we patrol this area regularly and have seen you before, or at least this car. It's not the safest place for relaxation,' the man continued, nodding his head towards the front of the bar, where a group of young bikers looked on.

'And where would you be going now?' Officer Flanagan asked.

'Back home to the campus at Princeton.'

'You think you're safe to drive that distance?' the other chipped in.

'I'm fine. I just had a glass of wine and talked with a few people.'

'Once you're on the public road, you'd be happy to be tested?' he shot back.

'Really, I'm fine.'

'Chuck, leave this one to me,' Flanagan said, waving his younger colleague back to the patrol car.

The other man went off and Flanagan leant back in through the window. 'Now, Doctor Pryce—'

'Elizabeth, please,' she said, smiling a little flirtatiously.

'Well, Elizabeth, it's not for me to say who you drink with or where, but these are unpredictable times, and like my buddy indicated, this is an unpredictable place. In the past three years, there's been a twofold increase in the number of people disappearing without a trace, in this county alone.' He stepped back and took a card from his breast pocket. 'I live up your way. If you need any help, call me anytime. Drive carefully now.'

* * *

Virtual Scene snapshot: Elizabeth stands in the centre of a spacious, well-furnished apartment, her bag on the floor beside her.

Once again, he's not here.

She took a remote from a side table and aimed it at a large screen on the wall, bringing up the image of a book-filled room with

Methuen bent over a desk, working. After staring at the screen for a few seconds, she switched it off and threw the remote onto the sofa.

Bugger it, you stay over there in Study House, and I'll stay here – as usual.

She walked over to the drinks cabinet, poured herself a large glass of wine and flopped down on the sofa.

What in the hell has gone wrong? We seemed as one, when we first met. I introduced him to what he kept referring to as my 'eclectic friends', but he always joined in and never voiced any objection to them. He even allowed me to spruce up his wardrobe – binning that awful lumberjack outfit and buying him some open-necked shirts and a few well-cut suits. I also trimmed his beard, restyled his hair and replaced those hideous black plastic specs with a pair of light metal frames. It made him look so handsome.

She took a sip from the glass and stretched out her legs.

I changed too, though. I stopped all that attention-grabbing stuff of dressing down for parties and dressing up for lectures. I replaced the low-cut tops and the thigh-hugging short skirts with dull but respectable two-piece outfits. I even bought a trouser suit, though I don't think I ever wore it.

She twisted her long black hair around a finger and sipped from the glass.

Gone were the wild parties with all the hangers-on. That was the biggest change for me and I thank him for that, even though it wasn't his suggestion. What got me to change was attending that first Foundation meeting.

'And what do you do?'

No one asked that of Methuen – only me.

'I piss around and only study medicine to please my father' *was what I wanted to say.*

Refilling her glass, she spotted the degree certificates on the wall.

It worked though. I started getting up early and astonished everyone by being at the front of the queue for lectures – for the

*first time in four years. Those were heady days. He and I seemed
to communicate without words, making decisions with barely any
discussion – including jumping out of bed one morning, driving
down the M74 to Gretna Green and getting married. It was a
corny thing to do, but so much fun. And there was that moment
in the chapel with the tourists looking on, when he kissed me and
I saw the tears in his eyes. What did he say? Oh, yes: 'Thank you.
You've answered my greatest need.'*

*I skipped out of that registry office and just stopped myself from
making some wisecrack about which part of his project he might
be referring to? I'm glad I didn't. This was something appearing
in him that I'd not seen before, something I wanted to see more
of … But then came the shock, him announcing that he wasn't
going to do his PhD in the UK but go to Stanford – all proposed
by the mysterious Clapping Lady, I discovered much later. I began
to wonder whether he'd even consulted her about me.*

She looked again at the certificates on the wall.

*I could have fallen apart that year we were separated, but I
didn't, and there's the evidence: a first-class degree and my MBChB
medical qualification. Oh, Dad was so pleased at the graduation
ceremony, and so was Kirsten his new wife. It was great to see
them together – until my mother arrived that is, solo, in a camel-
hair coat and knee-high, white leather boots. She said nothing
during the formalities, but then polished off a whole bottle of wine
and ruined the day for me.*

'Darling, you look so prim and proper – what on earth has
become of your joie de vivre? Has it gone up in smoke, like
that man you married?'

*Bitch. Though there was a grain of truth in what she'd said.
Methuen's absence, and then his delay in calling me because of
some emergency meeting of the Consilience Foundation, did upset
me. After that, I started to take his work obsession more seriously,
although thinking about it now, there were plenty of warning signs*

before. Even in Edinburgh, when we felt like the golden couple, asked along to every party, there was something wrong.

It came to a head at that private viewing at the Scottish National Gallery. I knew progressive art perplexed him, but he'd shown no reluctance to accompany me. The problem started as soon as we arrived, with him staring for twenty minutes at the, admittedly rather obscure, conceptual installation in the entrance hall. People arriving thought he was appreciating the work, but I suspected not, that's why I sidled up and asked for his thoughts – a big mistake.

'Why is this artist so lazy that he can't even bother to give some idea of what this is all about? Not explaining yourself is straightforward intellectual cowardliness. Imagine if I refused a peer review of a paper or a novelist ignored their readers – we would be rejected. But this person gets exhibited even though ninety-nine point nine per cent of people here have no idea what it means and will never bother to find out.'

That was when I tried to take the sting out of his negativity.

'It's something different and challenging – like understanding me.'

He turned straight on the attack.

'Answer the question! We're approaching the greatest crisis humanity has faced, art has to play a role – otherwise it's irrelevant.'

He hadn't been rude to me before and I was upset, but had to hide my feelings because our little exchange had attracted a crowd of onlookers.

'This is art for the selfish needs of the artist, pure and simple ... It does nothing to help the world solve its problems. Why doesn't he or she, or whatever created this, use their talent to inform people more clearly about the changes we are about to experience?'

'That isn't normally the function of art. It usually acts more as a mirror on the here and now – getting people to understand who they are, rather than acting as a window on the future.'

'I don't see why something with such limited utility should receive any government support?'

'To give us progress, we need science; to give us hope, we need art.'

'Even if that were true – which it isn't – how can art like this give the world hope when it's so obscure?'

The crowd grew larger as he demanded that 'Art must play its role, just as science and literature are already doing, to alert the world of what is to come' – or something like that. By then the gallery officials had started to close in, and I had to pull him away. I told myself his outburst was a combination of overwork and too many glasses of wine, but even then, I knew that wasn't the case. His modelling project was not just giving shape to the future, it was also shaping him. That became even clearer when I arrived in the States.

'It's so great to see you! You're looking lovely.'

I was, but then so was he, standing at San Francisco International Airport arrivals with an armful of flowers, dressed in the light blue suit I'd bought him for our wedding.

'I've put all my work on hold,' he said. 'We'll have the honeymoon we never had.'

But waking on that first night, unsure of where I was, I saw his profile against the light coming from his laptop. I felt so detached and alone, which was why I pretended to be asleep when he crept back to bed. Things got worse once I was installed in the small apartment at Stanford. His work routine was even more time-consuming than it had been in Edinburgh. Every weekend, every national holiday and most evenings he slipped away, dressed in his check shirt and denim jeans, to work on his project.

She reached out to top up her glass but instead took a long swig straight from the bottle.

I tried to be the little wife, making friends with the partners of other male students. But the normality of their lives – spouses returning home in the early evenings and taking time off for long weekends – only underscored the peculiarity of our own relationship. I began to view his grand obsession like a third person in our marriage – an unsatisfactory ménage à trois in which only two people are content.

She rested on the kitchen worktop and refilled her glass.

I was sad but also angry. It was the only time I ever thought about packing it all in and going back to the UK. That though was what my mother had done – run away. I was never going to do that and end up shallow and rootless like her. But that wasn't the only reason for not leaving – there was also the thought of Methuen on his own, and that somewhere within him there lay a whole reservoir of love and affection, waiting to be tapped.

Walking back to the sofa, she caught sight of the photo albums on the bookshelf that, since their first meeting six years ago, they had stuffed full of not just pictures but also restaurant bills and invitations – all the memorabilia of their time together. Taking down a thick volume marked 2020, she stared at the front cover and the word 'Crisis' that Methuen had written across it, above two underlined Chinese characters, one labelled 'Danger', and the other 'Opportunity'. She sat down with the album on her lap and laughed.

Only Methuen Pryce could see that fucking virus as an opportunity. Hah! here are some notes he's written as an aide-memoire for one of his numerous ZOOM calls.

It's a dry run of the Segmented World – for a year or two, economic growth will be negligible. Covid-19 provides a brief window into what the Irreversible Numbers will eventually impose permanently on the world. This is a dress rehearsal for The Time of Less. ~~Watch how the short-sighted autocrats of the emerging superstates react.~~ See how inequality increases, global trade contracts and the support for global agency falls away. Later, we'll see a Covid-induced wave of Resettling.

He was ecstatic in the way that only Methuen can be – and that only I can understand. On several occasions I had to tell him to tone down the eagerness in his voice as he explained his ideas, for fear that someone listening might have lost their job, or worse.

~~No matter how elegant my model is, few people take it seriously. People only believe what they themselves have lived through.~~ After Covid, everyone will have experienced isolation and the threat to their living standards – conditions that will become commonplace when The Time of Less arrives. What is happening now is a simulation of the Segmented World, driven not by a breakdown of supply but through a lack of demand.

He believed passionately that the crisis would make people more amenable to his vision. 'When everyone understands why they've suffered, then change will occur' was his stock phrase, although by 'change' he was no longer talking about the factors populating his fifty-year balance sheets – that he had handed on to others to develop by then. Instead, his main focus now was on his Attitudinal Study, and in particular, what he called the 'Ascent of OST-man'. For a time, there was an uptick of interest in his ideas – he even got invited onto an online PBS panel discussion about the post-Covid world. What brought him back down to earth was when the rules on self-isolation meant the award ceremony for his PhD was cancelled. Not that self-isolation by itself was a problem for him or even for us as a couple – it had become the norm, long before Covid.

Turning the pages in the album, Elizabeth now came to a photo of a small creek and a grassy knoll, with the Stanford buildings off in the far background. On the next page, she stared at a photo of the same location – now almost unrecognisable.

My favourite spot, devastated. Where I used to sit on the grassy knoll, there was now a wide fast-flowing channel and – the reason for that change – a colossal boulder lying in the centre of the creek, washed down by a storm.

She found another picture, this one looking downstream towards the boulder.

Ah, the view from that overhanging tree … Oh, and here's one showing the sticks I used to drop into the water to see how they would flow around the boulder. Most took the wide channel that had consumed my grassy knoll.

She looked carefully at the next photo.

This was taken a few weeks later, after a small beach had formed on the edge of the wide channel, against the boulder. 'Something constructive is going on,' I remember thinking. I must have thrown dozens of twigs into the water before one of them was pulled into the shaded channel to the right and disappeared – dragged down by currents and eddies undercutting the boulder on that side. Thinking about the two channels that night, it suddenly came to me: Methuen's obsession was like the boulder, distorting the flow of my life.

She sat back with her feet on the sofa and the album propped against her knees. *I went back to that place nearly every day for two weeks: perched on the tree trunk, tying little ribbons around the sticks and throwing them into the water, pretending they were me, and observing their fate. I began to play with the idea as a way of resolving what to do about my relationship with Methuen. I had the option of ignoring it all, equivalent to sitting on top of the boulder and just giving in – as those dutiful wives did on campus. But I had already rejected that – a decision made easier by the peculiar enjoyment Methuen seemed to derive from doing housework. At dinner parties, he would sound off about the restorative powers of routine tasks. It was the image of him happily vacuuming the sitting room one day that convinced me to follow the strategy of the river and flow around his obsession.*

'Going around,' she said aloud. That was the start of my life, for sure. *'Be the wide supportive channel, build a firm base on which the boulder can rest, but let yourself grow also.' That's what I told myself and that was the reason I applied for the fast-track MD degree at the medical school.*

'That's a brilliant idea!' were his exact words when I told him, and that night he didn't disappear into his den to work – an unexpected bonus. He genuinely was delighted that I was striking out, finding something to do.

'This new low-cost computerised health screening that the Consilience Foundation is developing at the School will transform medical care in the Third World. Why not get involved in that?'

His reaction was so over the top that I began to wonder whether it might be more to do with his sense of relief that I was no longer going to be a burden to him. That wasn't fair though and I knew it. I could see he took great personal pleasure in my success, just as the boulder might have been benignly disposed towards the wide channel for depositing supportive sands against it. Whatever the case, two years down the line, I delivered the goods and this time he attended the graduation.

Elizabeth returned the album to the bookshelf and pulled out another, dated 2021. Settling back on the sofa, she turned the pages until she came to a large group photo, with everyone wearing surgical masks and her in the centre, dressed in a college gown and proudly brandishing a scroll of paper. She pulled the album closer. *There's Methuen – with that inane smile he puts on for photos – my father and stepmother, and my mother clinging on to her new conquest – the senior Democrat politician, Oswald Battersby III. With widespread financial insecurity caused by the virus all I heard from Oswald III was his gleeful talk of the Republican vote being split by Sam Hard-ing's idea of a new party. Nothing about principles – just power. 'You're welcome to one another,' I wanted to say to them but this photo records my growing diplomatic skills – smiling, while I grip Methuen's arm.*

She got up and went over to the fridge to pour herself a glass of water.

You've stopped this recollection because you want to forget the great faux pas that occurred next when you heard your mother's new beau talking to Methuen.

'Congratulations on your appointment at Princeton. You know, I'm well in with the board there. Now we're going to be family, we must get together soon.'

I didn't let rip until we'd said farewell to Dad and Kirsten at the departure gate.

'Bloody hell, Methuen! First, I find out I've got a new step-father, and then I learn we're moving to the other side of the country – where do I start?'

He, of course, remained calm and reasonable as ever. This time though, my anger continued to burn – and he could see it, which was why, on the way home – down the I-280 – he suddenly shot off to the right and headed for the hills to a spot we both loved, with the bay on one side and the Pacific on the other. This time, though, he didn't crack his usual joke about 'being on the right side of the San Andreas'. We sat down on our favourite bench and he told me, quietly, about the assistant professorship in alternative energy engineering he'd been offered at Princeton, the hike in salary and the use of what he called the study house. 'I can finalise the book there – and in the same road where Einstein once lived,' he said proudly. I was still furious, demanding to know why he hadn't discussed it with me. His reply was classic, disarmingly honest, Methuen Pryce: 'You were busy with your exams and I didn't want to trouble you.'

That night, though, the thought returned to me that maybe his response to my success was, at least in part, triggered by a sense of relief. That I was a boulder in his river – an obstruction he also had to 'go around' to avoid delays in his work.

Elizabeth returned to the sofa and rested her head back.

Leaving him and going elsewhere was not the strategy of the river, nor would it be mine. That was when the idea of the charity clinic came to me. Plenty of classmates from Stanford days were ashamed of the ballooning number of people with inadequate healthcare cover after Covid. A few friends recommended the leafy districts around Chestnut Hill or Pennypack Park, Philadelphia, as the first location, not so far from Princeton, but what was the point of that? Safe for me, but not where the greatest suffering was to be found. Instead, I chose Richmond – 'Down by the river, full of water, immigrants and the disaffected,' as I quoted to him when describing my plan. He was thrilled with my decision, albeit a little gloomy as well.

'You'll be right near the edge of a Powerblock. When that's starting to fray, The Time of Less will not be far away.'

That was the way he was beginning to articulate everything – as if this Segmented World was now coming at him even faster than he had expected. I must say though, it was gratifying at dinner parties and other gatherings to hear him commend me for my achievements, as if I were now a revered colleague at a similar level to himself. This grew almost into adulation when I announced my plan to expand the charity clinic concept into a nationwide network of voluntary medical centres.

Elizabeth returned the album to the bookshelf and took down a small statue of two outstretched hands, with a citation reading: THE GOOD SAMARITAN 2022. AWARDED TO DR ELIZABETH PRYCE FOR THE CREATION OF THE NATIONAL COMMUNITY CLINIC. She placed it back on the shelf and went over to the kitchen to refill her glass with water.

For me, the only good thing to come out of the pandemic was the groundswell of support for the NCC idea. Seeing all those people being buried in pits woke America up to the truly pitiful state of the Union. Never have the divisions in this society been so cruelly put on display. It was time for action not words.

She took another sip of water. *It was tough though. The clinic may largely have been online during Covid, but after that, when we had to start opening actual centres, I started travelling – lots of travelling. A different hotel every night, always alone, tucked up with a cup of hot chocolate and CNN – that's what setting up the NCC meant. But, of course, that couldn't last. As soon as all the restrictions were lifted and I started hosting receptions and making speeches, the adrenaline began pumping back through my body. Sometimes I simply needed to let the bubbly, rebellious side of myself off the leash a little, although with my new public profile, I knew I had to be careful. There was that meeting in Chicago last Christmas when I bumped into one of Methuen's colleagues. How did I explain away that guy I was with? Oh yes, 'my co-director'. I was frightened by that chance meeting, realising that I didn't want to split up with Methuen, just have some occasional fun. I lay in bed that night, conjuring up the image of the river, but this time focusing on the dark, fast-flowing channel.*

'Some water must go that way for the flow to be balanced,' I wrote in my journal. I knew I had to do this, but with care not to create the eddies and currents that had dragged the sticks down and undercut the boulder. I decided to plan my playful times with the same attention to detail as I had applied to developing the NCC.

Friday nights are best. Changing out of my business suit some-where along Highway One and pulling on a figure-hugging dress, I transform into Simone – to spite my mother. I claim to be a professional dancer, drink neat spirits and beat most men at the pool table. Sometimes the flirting gets a little out of hand as it did tonight with those bikers, but that's a necessary risk for 'going around' on the shady side. I get the thrill I need, which makes living with Methuen and his mistress that little bit more bearable.

Elizabeth switched on the TV news but found only wall-to-wall coverage of Sam Harding's shock decision to form the new Unity Party, with Oswald Battersby III, doggedly rejecting the interviewer's suggestion that a new centre-right party would threaten the ability not just for the Republicans but also the Democrats, to form a majority in either House.

As she hit the off button on the remote, she noticed in her bag Officer Flanagan's personal card. Taking out her cell phone, she dialled his number.

Inside the red-painted barn;
Hardin, Montana, NCSA, FSA
14.00 hours, 15 June 2050

'What webs we weave when we try to accommodate one another,' Lianne said, folding the VR glasses in her hand. 'Did *you* know about all that?'

Nick lay still for a few seconds and then asked, 'Do you think about me in that way?'

'What – that I have to "go around" you?'

'Yes ... Isn't your daily writing routine your version of "going around" – locking the door to your study at eight-thirty and only emerging in the evening at seven?'

'I suppose so ... but there's nothing wrong with "going around" – it's how you go about it that's important. Every couple has their own fix. It works for most people, providing they find a way to excite or delight one another at some point during the day. It's just that that's been a little lacking in our story over the past few years.'

Nick adjusted his pillow and sat up. 'I think *our story* has been even more remarkable than that of Methuen and Elizabeth: a writer and a global executive, living together but often in completely different worlds.'

'Except that I've not actually written anything for a year now,' Lianne replied instantly.

'I know.'

She whirled around to face him. 'How do you "know"? I've never mentioned it to you.'

'Because you quit testing your plotlines and characters out on me ...'

She stared at him, unable to say a word.

Slipping down in the bed and gazing up at the ceiling, Nick added, 'And then you started drinking.'

Lianne fell back on her pillow, hands over her face, rubbing her eyes. 'It was all too much. Just as I was settling down in the UK, you announced the plan to travel to Phillips with the Pryces. I wouldn't have minded if we'd stayed there – but that wasn't part of the plan—'

'We had to get back home—'

'Home, Nick! You call this home?' she said, pointing to a barren landscape displayed on one of the monitors in front of them.

'Come on, that's not fair,' he moaned. 'How was I to know what was going to happen?'

'It's not just The Incident that's changed things. You knew the threat that McFall posed to this country – better than anyone,' she fired back.

'But in early '48 – back when I started planning the trip to Phillips – McFall was under the cosh. The coalition govern-ment had approved the new constitution and the country was moving, not just physically but politically, to the centre. It was time to return.'

'But McFall still scared me. I heard all his propaganda on the news channels. That told me we should stay put in London, or even wait a while in Phillips Cay.'

'It would all have been sorted out, had it not been for what happened,' he said, looking up at the screen on the ceiling and highlighting a new file. 'Come on, let's forget all that and immerse again – this is Methuen and me meeting before the Grand Tour. I've not opened this one before. Oh, wait a minute, there's something before that. It's a raw narration by Methuen, probably for a scene that's not been made yet. Want to listen to that first?'

'Why not?' Lianne said airily as she refitted her VR glasses.

'You don't need those,' he said, tapping her frames. 'There's no immersion with this one, just Methuen's words. I'll play them through the monitor's sound system.'

AA-Com File: Preparing to Present

Professor Methuen Pryce, submission to Allied Answers Corporation, AI Department.

Recorded in the Soft Rush Estate, Sandy Hollow, Southern Governorate, UK

3 March 2049

Before the start of my third year at Princeton, I was instructed to attend a meeting of the board of trustees with my faculty director. There, we were told that government funding for alternative energy research was being reorganised under the New Green Deal. I sat nodding amicably, expecting to hear positive news. Instead the elderly chairman said to me, quite matter-of-fact, that support for my work would be phased out and transferred to another university. I was flabbergasted, even more so when he added coldly that the study house on Mercer Road, where I was completing the first version of the Segmented World book, would also be withdrawn. I knew people were fearful of the Segmented World idea after Covid, but the decarbonisation, non-growth movement – which my work supported – was becoming a powerful political force.

That was why, when the director got up to leave, I remained seated, glaring at the old man and said something like, 'This makes no sense. The conflict in the Middle East is spreading and the post-peak period for cheap oil has passed – now is not the time to disrupt the research into alternative fuel technologies with all this bureaucratic nonsense.' You can access the precise comments from the Princeton board minutes for the first of June 2023. I also have relevant written records of this event and the circumstances surrounding it, in my diaries for '22 and '23, which I have in front of me as I make this submission.

So, here was a Brit, telling one of the most prestigious academic administrators in the US that he was wrong. I remember the old man's face turning red with anger at my presumption, but the certainty in his reply was unnerving. 'This country can ride that storm for many years to come, Professor Pryce. If you object to our decision, then follow the formal procedures and register your complaint.'

I wanted to correct his assertion that the US would not be affected by a curtailment of oil supplies from the Middle East. Like many of his fellow countrymen, he too assumed that tight rock energy was inexhaustible. If he had only bothered to study the reports from his own Department of Earth Sciences, he would have learnt that not only were most of the shale businesses irreparably bust, but the efficient machine called US business had all but depleted the main shale hotspots. Instead, I made the mistake of appealing to his wider sense of responsibility.

I've written down here what I said. 'Our research is not just for the US, but for the world as a whole.' At this point the faculty director tugged me sharply by the arm, forcing me to leave the room.

When I got back, Elizabeth was almost as disappointed as I was with the news. She knew, as I did, that the decision meant we would have to move again, for the third time in five years.

A miserable week followed, but something unexpected happened towards the end of it. She had arrived back early from a conference and taken a call on the home phone from someone identifying himself as the executive assistant to a corporate CEO, whose name was vaguely familiar to her.

'Sorry to disturb you, Doctor Pryce, when you must be so busy packing. Could I speak to your husband?' the man had said.

Elizabeth told me she wanted to ask him, 'Our contact details aren't widely shared, so how do you have our private number?' and 'How on earth do you know that we're thinking of leaving?' But 'something stopped me questioning him' she said, and so it was arranged for him to call back in the evening when I would be home.

The next day when I mentioned to the faculty director that someone called Nick O'Grady from Allied Answers Corporation had requested a meeting, I was stunned by his reaction. In front of my colleagues he insisted – to the point of ordering – that I attend the meeting and report back to him. When I asked for more details about the named individual, I received only the briefest of descriptions – little more than the short biography Elizabeth had already found on the Allied Answers website. Everyone knew Nick O'Grady, but few knew much about him.

Inside the red-painted barn;
Hardin, Montana, NCSA, FSA

'What?' Nick shouted out as Lianne pulled at his shoulder.

'This is all about your first meeting with Methuen, is there no scene dedicated to that?'

'I've not yet made my submission,' he said. '2048 – when we started gathering information for these reconstructions – was a horribly busy year for me, not just with the preparations for Phillips Cay, but also quietly moving much of our Lincoln–based business to Pico.'

'But this was one of the seminal moments in your life!' Lianne proclaimed. 'Couldn't you have downloaded something from the Memory Monitor and given it to this Storymaker?'

'For an event from twenty-five years ago, I would have had to have done a lot of memory-stimulation work. Methuen had his diaries. I didn't even have an Allied record note of the meeting – since it had originally been planned as just a chat to appease the Consilience people.'

'I didn't know that – I thought it was your idea to contact Methuen?'

Nick looked up and scanned the files on the screen. 'No, it was a meeting with a Consilience executive about the impact of Covid on Allied strategy ... Ah, here it is,' he said opening the file. 'It's dated November 2022 ... We'd just released AA-Com I with financial support from Consilience and we had AA-Com II in the pipeline. I couldn't have managed without their funding at that time.'

Scrolling through the scene, he said, 'A lot of this is detailed stuff about our post-Covid contingency plan. What I'm looking for – yes, this is it ... We had moved from the boardroom to my office and started shooting the breeze about the future when, out of the blue, the Consilience guy asked if I knew who Methuen Pryce was. I'll play that quickly before we go back to Methuen's narration.'

AA-Com File: Covid Consequences

Allied Answers, Global HQ, New York, USA
11 November 2022

Virtual Scene snapshot: In an all-glass corner office with views across Manhattan, Nick sits on a swivel chair, hands in his lap, staring at a straight-shouldered man in a well-cut black suit.

'So, he's called Methuen – what kind of name is that?' Nick said with a frown.

'He's English but has just got tenure at Princeton. He's a quiet guy with a big mop of hair and a beard, but when he talks, people listen.'

'So if he's at Princeton, what has he got to do with Consilience?'

'We've built a team around him over the past ten years—'

Nick sat forward and looked intently at his guest. 'For what end?' he asked, sceptically.

'To develop his global model for the mid-century: what he calls the Segmented World.'

Nick folded one arm across his chest and with his free hand began to twiddle his ear. 'Did this model predict the pandemic?' he said with a sneer.

'No, and nor does it predict whether the Giants will win on Saturday,' the executive replied sharply, his amiable smile fading as he stared back. 'Segmentation is the opposite of globalisation. It's what happens when demand from a growing population exceeds the supply of vital resources.'

'Oh, so it's the impact of negative supply rather than from negative demand like Covid?'

'Forget Covid, Nick,' the executive said impatiently. 'I'm talking about something far more profound. This model has real utility for Allied and, from Consilience's point of view, greater credibility than the Expanded Globalisation model you're currently using for your businesses worldwide.'

Nick O'Grady swung his chair a quarter-circle away from the executive and squeezed his chin. 'So you're saying this is a better model for planning the post-Covid future than what we already have in Allied?'

'What I'm saying is that you need to check it out – we can't continue to invest when our ten-year views are so different.'

Nick swung back round, stood up, and held his hand out to his guest, who scrambled to his feet. 'Send it to me and I'll get my people to look at it?'

'Sure, but we also want you to meet Methuen,' the executive replied, gathering up his papers. 'There's more in his head than there is in the model.'

'Once we've taken it apart, I'll do that.'

Inside the red-painted barn;
Hardin, Montana, NCSA, FSA

14.30 hours; 15 June 2050

'That's all I'm getting?' Lianne said, removing her glasses.

'Yup, that's it. I got the model the next day, and within a week my VP for Global Planning appeared in my office and, out of character for him, was full of praise for what someone else had done. Then about a month later, he started a round of internal presentations on what he called the Adjusted World model—'

'He'd plagiarised it?'

'To endorse it, he had to make it his own, but I could see he'd become a convert and that made *me* want to meet Methuen. Before I did that, I took myself off on a mini-sabbatical to the beach house in Nantucket. You remember that, I'm sure,' he said with a loud laugh.

'Oh ... yes. I was a bit suspicious—'

'You seemed surprised when you arrived unannounced to find the sunroom covered in papers without a single busty blonde in sight?'

'Yes ... and little did I know it at the time, that that was the start of it all ...'

'Let's go back to Methuen's narration and see how he remembers it?'

AA-Com File: Preparing to Present *(contd)*

Professor Methuen Pryce, submission to Allied Answers Corporation, AI Department.

Recorded at the Soft Rush Estate, Sandy Hollow, Southern Governorate, UK

3 March 2049

My sense of intrigue deepened further when a few days later, I was taken in an Allied helicopter and flown to the top of a multistorey glass tower in the business district of Manhattan. From there, a tight-lipped company official led me down to a sprawling, sparsely furnished office and sat me at a glass table in front of a stack of glossy annual reports. With my minder clearly not trained in small talk, I started to investigate the brochures in front of me, and spotted on the spine of one, a tiny inscription: NOY. Pulling it out, I saw emblazoned across the front page: '2022 Summary of The Consilience Fund Investment Portfolio'.

With the attendant still making no effort to engage in conversation, I started scanning the pages of the brochure, discovering that the Fund held a significant share in several Allied companies. I was about to scrutinise the financial summary in the appendix when the zombie-like character opposite got up and disappeared, just as a short young man in a neat suit and an incongruous crew cut came through a side door. He raised a hand in greeting, and with a relaxed smile said, in a clear mid-Atlantic accent, 'Sorry to keep you waiting. I'm Nick O'Grady.'

Seeing the brochure open in front of me, he asked enthusiastically, 'Do you have investments in Consilience?'

I laughed in response to the question, but seeing his look of surprise, said self-mockingly, 'On the salary of a tenured university lecturer, I doubt I have the money to buy a single share.'

He seemed not to understand and stared back as if to say: why would you not have money to invest?

It made me feel rather inadequate, which may be why, when he asked me to explain the project, I nervously blurted out a full account of my long association with Consilience. I then picked up the brochure and asked whether he knew the significance of the NOY insignia. This brought about a strange reaction. He shook his head and seemed uncomfortable at not being able to answer my question. Only after I took a pen and inserted a comma after the letter O and said 'know-why', did he get it. For a fraction of a second, neither of us spoke, until he stood up abruptly and pointed across to two lounge chairs facing out onto the cityscape and the bay beyond.

Shortly after we had sat down, refreshments arrived on a silver tray brought in by another deferential attendant, who poured each of us a perfect cup of Ceylon tea. The flavour was as superb as it was unexpected since I was sure this beverage was not widely consumed by those occupying the building, and certainly not from the exquisite porcelain into which it was poured. It was a small but memorable moment in what turned out to be a most eventful day.

There then followed what sounded to me like a well-rehearsed monologue from Nick O'Grady – punctuated by him taking delicate sips from his cup. He described a modelling project that '… has been in existence for the last three years to guide my ongoing business concerns.' He then turned to me and said plainly and without any hint of jealousy, '… but I've been told I should adopt your approach, because it's better.'

I didn't respond because I didn't know what he meant by 'better'. Instead, I kept silent and listened as he resumed his monologue.

'Allied currently operates across the globe guided by an overarching strategy called Expanded Globalisation. But Covid has been a wake-up call. The idea of a world without borders across which people and goods can move freely has started to look wrong.

Then someone told me that this Segmented World of yours was a better way of thinking about the future.'

As he spoke the words, he gave me a sharp questioning look, as if expecting me to react. Overwhelmed by what was happening, I said nothing, so he continued – breaking into an edgier style of speech, filled with phrases that weeks later still rang in my head.

'If we accept your interpretation, all the big numbers for the mid-century are troubling ... Supply breaks will kill us fast ... Civilised austerity will be forever – if we're lucky ... The Market is inadequate to deal with what is to come.' And so he continued, rationally summarising the effects of segmentation from his business perspective.

Once he had finished, he fixed his eyes on me and said, 'That's why some of us would like to see work like yours continue.' The statement excited me. I responded with similarly clipped phrases, expressing my opinion on what he had referred to as the 'troubling numbers'. I went through a simplified version of the Segmented World – not dissimilar to what I had outlined to Elizabeth six years earlier in my office in Edinburgh. I had arrived in this impressive location uncertain of what to say, but now found myself elated and eager to talk – a feeling reinforced by my host's respectful body language, lowering his head and nodding with approval as I spoke, interrupting only where clarification was needed.

Once I had finished, something else took over – a dialogue, fast and furious, laden with acronyms and shortcuts, like two mathematicians at a blackboard skipping lines of equations that each knew the other understood. An hour or so in, I was sipping the last of my now cold tea, when he said, 'So at this stage, you place high probabilities on all your critical numbers thirty years out?'

It was a measure of how far we had bonded intellectually that I had the confidence to wag my finger at him. I don't need to refer to the diary to know what I said in reply. 'Never have the main planks leading to the future been nailed down so firmly as they are now.' I remember saying it quite forcefully, in a way that could have been construed as dogmatic, even condescending, but he remained unmoved. With a thumb on his lips, he slowly nodded in agreement.

That encouraged me even more, so I continued. 'We lack the conceptual framework and even the right words to describe a world with a full-up sign attached to it – evolution didn't design us for that.' And here's another quote in my diary: 'We are quite unprepared for what is about to happen. Most of us choose to ignore it ... or seek comfort in the misleading idea that somehow technology will bail us out in time.'

At that point, he sat forward and took up the conversation, not about the modelling project or even my research, but with questions regarding the structure and management of the engineering faculty at Princeton, along with its funding.

Around seven, when the sun had sunk behind a large tower block, plunging the room into semi-darkness, another black-suited attendant appeared and, without more being said, Nick O'Grady was gone.

On the way back, I had mixed feelings about the meeting. I was pleased that he shared my concerns over the future and that I seemed to have developed a rapport with someone whose background and style could not have been more different from mine. On the other hand, I was disappointed at being unable to report to Elizabeth or the faculty director any new funding arrangements. Even more worrying was Allied's association with Consilience. I began to fear that the meeting may have been a way of Consilience saying through Allied, 'Thanks for all your efforts. We'll handle this from now on.'

Elizabeth had cancelled her NCC meeting for that evening so she could collect me from the Princeton helipad. In the car, I was generous in my praise of Nick O'Grady: 'a true meeting of minds ... non-judgemental – each of us able to express our natural selves ...

rational and objective – someone who seemed to like difficult tasks and wouldn't give in until he found the best solution'.

She listened in silence for a time before releasing her foot from the accelerator and asking, 'But what's he like? Tell me something more than just about his intellectual qualities.'

'What do you want me to say?' I replied. 'A little shorter than you but according to the company brochure, he's the same age.'

'And his appearance?'

'Keeps himself fit; he's muscular, tanned, wears casual-serious clothing, and keeps his hair short because I think it's already receding.'

'And he's married?'

'He didn't say much about that, though he did refer to someone studying at Columbia – Lianne, I think her name was. He knew about you though, through media reports of the NCC project, and seemed extremely impressed.'

'I can't wait to meet him and … what's-her-name,' I remember Elizabeth adding, a little dismissively.

My concern, that the meeting with Nick O'Grady had been about closing doors, though, was soon put to rest. On arriving at my office the next day, I found the faculty director waiting outside. Much to my embarrassment, he embraced me in front of everyone and said in great gasps, 'Late last night I received notification of a highly significant grant that will fund your research programme here, for at least another ten years.' He then added smugly, 'It will place the faculty at the forefront of global alternative energy research – and entirely independent of government funding.'

Getting back to the apartment, I knew I had two important things to settle before going to bed. The first gave me an enormous buzz.

I called Elizabeth, who had gone to a conference in Chicago. I could tell from all the noise in the background that she was with a lot of people and a bit woozy. To get her attention, I shouted down the phone, 'You want the good news or the bad news?'

'Bad!' she shouted back.

'I'm going to need a business suit.'

'And the good news?' she said, suddenly sounding more sober.

'You can carry on with taking the charity clinic nationwide. I have a sponsor for the next ten years.' I heard hoots of laughter as she relayed the message to those she was with, and then I put down the phone, keen to complete the second, more difficult, task.

I logged into my Consilience account and requested a meeting. I'd been worried that I might have spoken too openly to Nick O'Grady about the project and Consilience. This concern increased when rather than one of the regular staffers appearing, the Clapping Lady herself came online, her hair tucked behind her ears, staring into the camera, one hand on her chin.

'Methuen, it's been too long,' she said, with the same warm assertiveness I remembered from our very first encounter. 'You marked it as urgent?'

With frequent references to my diary, I gave her a blow-by-blow account of the meeting with Nick O'Grady.

Just as she had done in our discussion in the car, she remained silent until I had finished and then, adjusting her seat and leaning forward, said with determination, 'It's time, Methuen. Minds are open. Business as usual is no longer in favour. The campaign we discussed to build awareness and secure acceptance from the public must begin here.'

I was about to answer when, uncharacteristically for her, she held up a hand to stop me and said firmly, 'However, as you pointed out all those years ago, being the frontman for explaining the Segmented World may not be your forte. That is our hope for what Nick O'Grady may yet become.'

I was relieved that she already knew about the meeting, but before I could respond, she said, 'For your information, Nick

O'Grady is not a member of the Foundation, but we did send one of our senior fund executives to whisper positive messages about you in his ear. It's up to him now to make the next move. If he decides to work with you, we have indicated we would be willing to financially underwrite the cost of a tour for you both to present the model worldwide.'

I pondered the idea with some trepidation, as she continued, 'Independently of all that, we would also like you to finalise the book you've been writing on the Segmented World. It will reinforce the message once the tour is over.'

'I want to do all that but it's the time I would need,' I mumbled.

She waved away my concern with a comforting smile. 'That's all taken care of – Princeton will give you a two-year sabbatical to participate in the tour and after that to complete the book.'

'That's great, but how did you get them to agree?'

'There was a little resistance from those who want to preserve the place in aspic, but these days money speaks louder than ever before – and besides, you have the respect and support of the academic members on the board,' she said.

I stared back at her, wracking my brains to find any flaw in the plan. 'Why would the CEO of one of the fastest expanding tech organisations want to go on a lecture tour with me?'

'That's a good question, and one I can only answer by telling you a little story about him.'

I saw her sit back and knew it was time for me to shut up and listen.

'His parents are from an old family in Vermont,' she said. 'Nick is the only child – they had him late. His mother, who is still a rising star in the US judiciary, was thirty-eight when he was born; his father, from a very wealthy family and a senior official in the Defense Department, was forty-four. They invited me over to a party once. Nick was there, dressed in a tuxedo, even though he was a young teenager at the time. After dessert, the subject of earliest memories came up and someone asked him for his. The story he told tells you everything you need to know about Nick O'Grady. He was five years old – "dressed in a white tunic with a blue-and-white-striped tie", his mother proudly interjected across the dinner table. He described the experience of walking into a reception room filled with a lot of "well-groomed adults". As he entered, his father called out, "Please welcome the future President of the United States!" People applauded, women curtsied, men bowed, and as each of them approached him they said, with great sincerity, "Good evening, Mr President." The whole charade was in fact staged by his parents not for their entertainment or that of their guests, but as a powerful means to inculcate in their son's mind his destiny: not to succeed nationally – after all, they were already doing that – but to win recognition on the *global* stage. What they implanted in his young mind that day is the target he will try to achieve over the course of his life.'

'How ghastly,' I remember saying.

'Ah, Lesson Number One with regards to Nick O'Grady,' CL replied firmly, 'before you feel sorry for him, make sure you know the full picture.'

'But how can he be himself if he's always guided by his parents' wishes?'

'By fulfilling them in his own way. A good example is his education. They insisted he went to Harvard, which he did, but rather than reading politics or law as they had, he chose digital technology. Then, after he'd graduated with Honours, his father made a speech praising his son's independence and in front of the media handed him a cheque for $100 million. Nick received it graciously, but then to his parents' dismay announced his intention to create a high-tech company. They had little choice but to accept his decision, and within weeks his father had taken him to a Pentagon-sponsored research centre in Virginia, where he presented Nick with a number of technology projects that required private funding. It's an apocryphal story among those close to him that he selected the project at the bottom of the list: to create a rival to the Internet. When his father openly challenged his choice, Nick is reputed to have calmly replied, "He who communicates best, wins." That, as you know, became the motto for AA-Com – the fastest growing communication network of the Third Decade – with a protocol that prioritises security over communication. Within five years, Allied Answers had been listed and he had become financially independent – buying out the government share and purportedly paying back his father's investment with interest.

'He showed a similar single-mindedness when it came to his personal life, despite his mother's best efforts to be in control. He had already politely rejected her offer to handle Allied's legal work, but when it came to the question of who her future daughter-in-law would be, she was less easily put off. At a reception organised for him to meet the eldest daughter of another well-established Vermont family, he encountered Lianne – her youngest sister, and the wildest there. After years of being one of the most sought-after bachelors in the States, he now seems to have found a match. Once again, it was his choice, not that of his parents.'

'So let me get this straight,' I said, 'you're telling me that he and I, together, will promote the idea of the Segmented World?'

'It's an option we think worth considering. Does that worry you?'

'Not me, but from what you've said, Nick O'Grady is someone who will want to do everything his own way?'

'Sure, but go back to his underlying motivation. What he's being offered is the opportunity to travel to all the main capitals of the world and talk, not to the usual techie geeks about communication networks and devices, but to leading Establishment figures about a vision of the future that involves everyone, everywhere. I don't think he's going to refuse. The main uncertainty, as you have noted, will be how he wants to approach it, and that's something you're going to have to deal with.'

A month after the meeting in New York, Elizabeth and I received a couriered handwritten invitation to dinner, personally signed by Nick and Lianne. A company car arrived to take us to Nick's penthouse apartment overlooking Central Park. They met us in the entrance hall – him dressed in a dinner suit, her in a brightly coloured smock – looking more like the student she actually was. He at once zoned in on Elizabeth, walking ahead with her into his cavernous apartment – immediately tucking his arm into hers, I remember. Lianne was chatty but not flirtatious. Even though our backgrounds were very different, I quickly discovered we shared an interest in sailing and gardening, and as the evening moved on, I began to warm to her. Strangely, she reminded me of my grandfather – someone who didn't just want to know stuff but also to do something with it. I began to wonder whether she was some sort of engineer herself but then, with Nick and Elizabeth still out in the garden, she bowled me over, describing herself as a 'writer in the making'. Her certainty impressed me, although I couldn't see at that time how she and Nick could possibly remain together.

Later in the car on the way back, Elizabeth expressed a similar view, although most of her comments focused on her encounter with Nick. In particular, how he had expressed a fascination over her public profile and late in the evening had declared, 'a weakness for gently spoken English women' – traits that he told her she possessed in abundance.

'I was gracious and accepted the compliments without mentioning my mother's French and father's Welsh origins,' Elizabeth told me, but I could see she was enlivened by the whole experience, talking about 'the lifestyle makeover you are about to be given', as Nick had described it to her.

That night we laughed at the idea, but within weeks our social life had stepped up several gears as a steady flow of invitations came through from the Allied executive office. I also began to receive unsolicited calls from Nick, many outside working hours. Initially, the questions focused on topics relating to the only work requirement of the new grant: to provide a quality control check every quarter on all commodity reserve data input to Allied's new Adjusted World model. I had readily accepted the provision since it required me to do work I was already undertaking as the lead forecaster for the Segmented World's Natural Resource INs. After a time though, our conversations expanded to include issues that bore no relation to the work requirement, leading me to conclude that the checking stipulation in the contract had just been a pretext for using me as a sounding board and even, at times, a strategic adviser. Later I came across another uncontracted contribution. A year into the Allied grant, I found extracts from a paper I'd written entitled 'Twilight Of The US Tight Rock Revolution: Impact And Consequences On Future Global Supply', in an academic presentation by a senior US energy official. Had Allied passed this on without my permission, I wondered? And then a draft of a paper I had emailed to Nick on the geopolitics of aluminium that had ended up cannibalised in an Allied internal release on resource pinch points. The plagiarism flattered rather than angered me, but added to a fear that Elizabeth had begun to express about the growing influence of the Allied organisation on our lives. That perfectly planned cup of tea at the first meeting was never far from my memory.

Inside the red-painted barn;
Hardin, Montana, NCSA, FSA
15.00 hours, 15 June 2050

The audio cut off sharply, causing Lianne to sit up abruptly, resting back on her elbows.

'The Consilience woman describes our relationship as an act of defiance against your parents. Is that how you see it?' she asked bluntly.

'That's the trouble with all these reconstructions. It can stir up too much—'

Lianne collapsed back on the bed and said nonchalantly, 'I only ask because it's what I've always assumed.'

'It's a whole lot more complex than that – as you know. For sure, I wanted to escape the pull of my parents, and maybe that influenced me in lots of things, but after my father died in '36, I had a huge sense of release from no longer being under his thumb. Within three years, I had called a meeting of the Allied board and persuaded them to convert Phillips into a self-sufficient community. That wasn't driven by my parents and nor do they play any role in our relationship today.'

'So what does hold us together?'

'The same things that attracted us to one another when we first met.'

'Hah! You mean the famous dinner party organised by my mother to bring you and my elder sister together?'

'That was the start,' he said, and then turning to her asked, 'While we're revisiting the past, tell me something I've always wanted to know: was it you who set off those five fire alarms during that dinner?'

Lianne laughed. 'No, I wish it was. It was lucky for me though—'

'For us, you mean,' Nick interjected.

'But not poor Eloise. She was so excited, being seated across from you at the table, with our parents either side, keen for the match to go ahead—'

'While you spent the first part of the dinner studying your cell phone without looking up! Your other sister was there also, wasn't she?'

'Yes, Victoria – she was the one who led the panic rush as the alarms sounded. Even you got up to leave—'

'Until I saw you, sitting there, daring me with your eyes to sit back down—'

'And you did. That's when you started to interest me, though I was determined not to show it – even when you followed me into the house towards the supposed inferno.'

'"One alarm would be a worry, maybe two, but five are more likely to be a fault than a fire." That's what you said as we stood on the balcony of your bedroom, watching the emergency services coming up the hill. Do you remember Eloise on the lawn, looking up at us?'

'Sure do. You realise she never spoke to me again? And nor did my parents for several years, after I accepted the invitation to your post-Covid party at the infamous Nick O'Grady beach house in Nantucket!'

Nick laughed. 'The look on your face when you arrived and realised it was a party for two …'

'My first experience of need-to-know.'

'And my first experience of skinny-dipping!' He laughed out loud.

'I couldn't believe it – a private beach and you'd never stripped off and felt the exhilaration of cold seawater before?'

'It was November!' he protested and then, laughing loudly, said, 'We were exhilarated that night all right—'

'I don't think we got out of bed for two days, did we?'

'And remember what we did?'

'Lots of exhilaration as I seem to recall,' Lianne chuckled.

'But in between, don't you recall the conversation?' he asked, turning to her with a deep frown.

'I remember I helped you unravel some problem.'

'Not just *some* problem. I had the draft of the Allied IPO document with me, launching the company on the Market. To my amazement, you grasped all the issues at once.'

'Oh yes, I'd forgotten about that.'

'I went back to New York, threw the redraft at the lawyers and within two months we launched the offering.'

'So?'

'So it's what I told you before – right from the start, you were more than just an act of defiance. Not only did you help me get the wording right, I felt so buoyed up after meeting you – people even commented on how relaxed I looked.'

'Huh, so I helped you solve a problem – and that's it?' Lianne said drily.

'No trivial issue, I can assure you,' Nick said, firmly. 'To have someone I can talk with, who listens generously and is trustworthy – that's meant so much to me.'

'Good God, Grady, are you cracking up or are the Russians right about there being a life-enhancing level of radiation?' She kissed his brow and then lay back. 'So, what's next on the list?'

'We could view the short scene I mentioned before, with Methuen and me talking about the Grand Tour?'

'Ah, your first appearance?'

'Yes, but I don't remember contributing to it. There's probably a request stored on my AVIII. I'll run it in General View.'

AA-Com File: A Meeting at Study House

Mercer Street, Princeton, New Jersey, USA
Early evening, 23 October 2024

Virtual Scene snapshot: A large executive van with darkened windows is parked outside a snow-covered clapboard house, where Methuen, his arms folded across his chest, stands on a colonnaded porch dressed only in jeans, a T-shirt and sandals.

Methuen snorted in derision as the van door opened and Nick O'Grady, seated at a desk and dressed in a shiny dark blue suit with a crisp white shirt and a pair of gleaming black shoes, looked up in surprise. Rubbing his hands against the cold, Methuen watched as the chauffeur carefully wrapped a heavy coat around his master's shoulders and then hand him a small attaché case.

Ignoring the slippery conditions underfoot, Nick bounded up the steps, and patted Methuen on the shoulder, saying nothing as he disappeared inside.

In a small front room, with papers strewn across the floor, Nick walked over to a mirror, running his hands through hair still resembling that of a young Marine: close cut on top and sheared to near-baldness on the sides.

'I gather congratulations are in order?' Methuen said, entering the room.

Nick looked up at him with a questioning stare as he shook out the crease in his trousers.

'Elizabeth heard it from Lianne – your engagement?'

'Oh that, yes. We didn't make too big a deal of it. How is Lizzie? It must be getting close to her time?'

Methuen parked his backside against the window on which snow had started to gather in small strips along the outside sills.

'Still a few weeks to go,' he said, as Nick took out a glossy booklet from the attaché case with the words THE ADJUSTED WORLD artistically scribbled across the front.

Methuen took the document and flicked through it before placing it on the table beside him. 'Looks like we're staging some global rock concert rather than a serious exposition about the future,' he said, clamping his arms around his chest.

'People like all this razzmatazz – it's the way to lure them in. You provide the substance and I'll provide the style,' Nick said, laughing as he held out another booklet. 'These are the presentation summaries; we need to go snap on them tonight so my office can make the flyers.'

'You know my view on this – the picture we're creating is too optimistic,' Methuen replied grumpily.

Nick shook his head in disagreement but before he could comment, Methuen, studying the document, said, 'The first part is fine – it gets the message over that we're in transition, but the action plan that follows is based on the mistaken idea that all we need do is make a few minor tweaks to our current way of life. You know very well, Nick, that this does not reflect what the modelling tells us. No wonder Consilience pulled the plug on their funding.'

'They didn't pull the plug,' Nick objected. 'Allied decided it was such an important event that the Corporation should bear the main cost. Look at the front of the booklet – the Consilience Foundation and Fund are listed at the top of the sponsor list. As for the "mistaken idea",' he said, gritting his teeth slightly, 'it's all part of a process of lowering people into this new reality.'

Seeing Methuen still unmoved, he added, 'You don't reshape something by hitting it hard – that's likely to break it. Slow gentle taps in the right direction will get us there. Remember your Brexit process: you didn't get all you wanted at the start, but slowly, slowly, you remoulded your relationship, so that today you've got the level of independence you were seeking and your ties with the EU are as strong as ever – some would say even stronger.'

'But what we're predicting is not what most people on the planet will experience in the future,' Methuen replied stiffly, flicking through the presentation summaries. 'It lacks balance. Here, for example, you're talking about "safety" in gated communities, "credit trading" to replace unreliable cash and a "bot-dominated" world doing everything from cooking to accounting. You know as well as I do that what you're describing is the world of the affluent – not even for those in the Powerblocks – just the privileged minority who for a time will be able to use their wealth to buffer them from what lies ahead. And by the way,' he added, closing the booklet and waving it at Nick, 'even that description is wrong. There'll be restrictions on movement for the whole of society, and the idea that the current credit-trading schemes will give anyone immunity to secular stagflation simply doesn't stand up to analysis.'

Still smiling amiably, Nick raised a finger at Methuen. 'Look, the whole purpose of these presentations is to shake the movers whether they're living in the Powerblocks, Resource Conflict Zones or wherever the hell they are. We need them to buy into this post-growth scenario and then go out and convert their constituencies. We can't do everything ourselves,' he insisted, and then, with a grin breaking out on his face, said, 'Even Jesus needed disciples.'

'Well, this may work for the executives and government officials you'll be talking to, but my audience is mainly academic. They'll demand answers on exactly how this plan works – for the many, not just the few, to quote a phrase.' Methuen then took a seat opposite Nick and tossed the document back on the table.

Shaking his ahead in disagreement again, Nick said, 'The louder they shout for their new socialist revolution, the keener the Establishment will be to adopt our less disruptive ideas.'

Methuen raised an eyebrow. 'We do run the risk that what we're doing is providing the wealthy and powerful with a blueprint for their own survival, laying the groundwork for a global society of fiefdoms and vassal states.'

Nick frowned and holding his hands up said firmly, 'You know that's not true. The whole reason we're doing this is to show any selfish bastard who thinks of heading down *that* path that it's not sustainable. What do you call them in the book?'

'OST-man.'

'Well, your OST-man will continue to dominate unless we find persuasive ways to show him that greater cooperation offers the bigger payout. That's all I'm trying to do over the next nine months or however long it takes.'

Methuen made no response. He had heard the argument before and knew the determination of its advocate.

Nick picked up the booklet. 'It's too late to change the content now – we need to get on with this.'

'I'm also not sure about this plan to begin the tour in the East and then head West. The US won't exactly welcome the idea of coming last on the list?'

'Well, to anyone who makes that claim, I'm spinning it the opposite way,' Nick replied sharply. 'I'm saying privately to the US and Euro people, "By doing it like this, we're giving you the advantage of knowing how the others responded." The bigger concern for me is being able to stick to the timetable.'

Methuen went over to a radiator. 'Heating's off again. Let's move to the other room.'

* * *

Virtual Scene snapshot: Methuen and Nick sit in front of a roaring fire; a whisky bottle and glasses lie on a small table between them.

'Is that real?' Nick asked, pointing to the fireplace. 'We have a complete ban on any fire with a flame these days in New York – even from gas.'

'No, it's all electronically simulated. We've also gone green bigtime over here in Mercer County – even though over fifty per cent of the electricity still comes from fossil fuels,' Methuen said, refilling their glasses. 'So, how's Allied coping with the after-effects of Covid?'

'After a little lift in '22, it has become quite punishing. Many of our traditional supply lines faltered and demand on all our products is down by forty per cent. The only good news is that the order book for version II of AA-Com is full.'

'I still don't understand AA-Com,' Methuen said. 'It started as this new protocol for electronic communication, but now seems to be so much more?'

'Sure. The aim was always to make it a totally independent system. I had the late starter's advantage,' Nick said, with a broad smile. 'Everyone knew the security protocols on the internet had to be improved but what we're moving onto now is something even more radical. Increasing miniaturisation may have brought about the creation of the smartphone but moving even faster were the number of things we wanted to include on it. That was when we had our brainwave to split the smartphone, placing the communication in our head and the computing in this device, which we can carry around in our pockets—'

From his bag he pulled out a hand-sized black cube. 'This is my new baby,' Nick said excitedly, handing it to Methuen.

'But who wants more things to carry around with them?' Methuen said, twisting the object around and then judging its weight in his hand.

Nick smiled smugly. 'Everyone, when they realise they don't need cell masts any more. These can communicate locally over fifty miles and connect directly with a huge constellation of satellites we've signed contracts with.'

'What's this cell phone in the head then?'

'The teleplant. All the big techcoms are working on similar devices. We already have a functional device that fits within the ear, but we're also working on something that will eventually be inserted just beneath the skull on your forehead.'

'God, who'd want do that?' Methuen exclaimed.

'Same answer. Everyone, once we've cracked the thought control issue. We already have test models sending information from, and to, the network via this AA-Com cube, all controlled by thought alone,' Nick said, with a sudden burst of childlike enthusiasm.

'But a network of satellite communicators – that's going to be slow and expensive, surely?'

'Ah, we're working on that as well, something that'll replace satellites.'

Methuen took a sip from his glass as Nick continued with increasing excitement in his voice. 'Then there's the crowd of people I have working in my Health Department. I went to a meeting a few days ago where we decided to go ahead with testing brain plants to recover lost memory – something I could already do with!' he added, laughing. 'The only thing that's taking time to bed down is the strategy for the Longevity Division – quite a lot of discussion on which path to follow – transplant versus enhancement. Oh yes,' he said, his face lighting up once more, 'and last week I launched the *Allied Clipper* – would you believe it, we're building ships again, albeit multifuel, superfast ones. High-tech solutions for old ideas: I see it all the time these days.'

'Oh, to be part of the affluent few,' Methuen said aloud, but seeing a tired frown on his colleague's face, added quickly, 'So what about politics? There are all sorts of rumours about you and this Unity Party.'

Nick took a short sip from his glass and then looked squarely at Methuen. 'Well, just between you and me, I've joined up with Sam Harding and become the main sponsor for his new Republican Party – though I'm not releasing that information yet.

'Why not?'

'My priority is to get the key people signed up to this post-growth idea, and for that I need to be regarded as apolitical.'

'"Fairness at Home, Fairness Abroad",' Methuen said, echoing the widely promoted slogan of the new party. 'It's a good soundbite, but breaking the mould of two-party politics in the US is a bit unlikely, isn't it?'

'You can't break something that's already broken. The Unity Party describes itself well: a party to bring the nation back together, but through honestly costed policies. Trump did more than just crater the GOP; he also single-handedly destroyed people's trust in the very things that make this country great – our institutions and the democratic process. What this country needs to get it back on its feet is a dose of objective leadership and sound economic management, rather than all this right-wing nationalism and token socialist and multiculturalist gestures we're getting from the Democrats. There shouldn't be any fucking "ists" at a time like this. We don't have the choices we had before: debt repayments are killing everyone, even the US. We're spending more on interest than we do on education and social services combined. And if the dollar loses its reserve currency status—'

'I agree it's madness,' Methuen cut in. 'I just can't understand how all those clever economists who advise the Democrats square the idea of promoting more borrowing while talking about sustainability? The two ideas are in conflict, surely.'

Nick shook his head. 'I told everyone in Allied we had to lower our debt to equity by being more effective in everything we do. But the most important thing we had to do was to add more value per capita.'

Methuen hunched his shoulders and frowned.

'Hire good quality people who are broad thinking, work hard and want to learn. I don't care what colour, creed or other persuasion an individual is – I just want rounded, talented people in this organisation. We should apply that nationally, making sure we properly educate those who want it, while for those who won't engage, either conscript them or let them slip away.'

'So that's "Fairness at Home", is it?' Methuen said with a sarcastic laugh.

'There's a need for plain-speaking, Methuen. As you know very well, the sums just aren't adding up any longer. Someone will have to explain eventually that there are no simple fixes. Living standards must fall. All we're doing in the Unity Party is trying to avoid there being a free fall – into chaos.'

'You think Sam Harding will retain his seat in the Senate, even though he left the Trumplican fold?'

Nick placed his glass back on the table and stood up. 'I'm pretty certain. He's a good man – articulate and thoughtful – although in this polarised society he has one big disadvantage: he's white and wealthy. The only way he can win over those who are not white and not wealthy is by being honest and fair – that's more than a slogan, I can assure you.'

'That'll be interesting to watch. And what does Harding think about the Segmented World scenario?'

'He's interested. In fact, he asked whether he could read something about it – which reminds me, how's the book going?'

'I have the latest draft for you here,' Methuen said, handing Nick a memory stick. 'Like you though, I'm going to hold back on publication. I don't want the presentations to be interpreted as a book promotion tour.'

'Yeah, that's good. It'll also give you the chance to incorporate any useful feedback we get from this jamboree we're about to embark on.'

* * *

Virtual Scene snapshot: Large flakes of snow are falling as the two men stand side by side on the porch.

Nick turned to Methuen, shook his hand and patting him on the shoulder said, 'All shall be well, all shall be well. Let's get our leaders on board first.'

'What if it fails? What's our Plan B?' Methuen called out as Nick walked down the steps under an umbrella held by his chauffeur.

Without turning around, Nick put his hand up in the air and shouted defiantly, 'It mustn't and it won't.'

Inside the red-painted barn;
Hardin, Montana, NCSA, FSA
15.30 hours, 15 June 2050

'"It mustn't and it won't"? Were you that certain that your grand tour would trigger something significant?' Lianne asked, turning towards him.

Nick removed his glasses and gazed up at the white padded ceiling. 'Of course not,' he replied calmly. 'Even before Consilience placed Methuen in front of me, Allied had done enough modelling to identify many of the phenomena he called Irreversible Numbers – it's just that he was so incredibly insightful and also thorough in how he quantified everything.'

'So you understood there was a problem ... And that's why you hedged your bets, alongside setting off on the tour?'

'What are you trying to say?'

'You kept the political solution alive.'

'Lucky I did, considering the fiasco the tour turned out to be.'

'And whose fault was that?'

'Everyone's – including mine,' Nick said quietly.

Lianne slumped back on the bed. 'You tried hard though ... particularly in China.'

'Yeah ... They didn't show it, but they were pleased we'd decided to start with them – even more so when we took a few extra days to examine their own post-growth model, which had a scenario resembling the Segmented World.'

'And then after that much publicised overstay, everyone wanted to see you?'

'Umm ... but we had to stick to the plan of focusing on the superstates. India was polite but embroiled in creating its new identity so we didn't get much back from them. Russia, of course, tried to get political mileage out of our visit—'

'Being seen with the President of the Federation raised the hackles of those in Brussels and Washington. Why did you allow that to happen?'

'We had no choice. The message we were delivering required all the superstates to act as one. We had to engage with all of them, irrespective of their values or behaviour.'

'I was at my first book launch in Los Angeles when I saw you being grilled on TV by a Senator from the House Committee on Foreign Affairs. He was waving his finger at you—'

Nick held up a hand and muttered something into his teleplant. 'I have a transcript of that,' he said. Within seconds, a text appeared on the screen.

The goal of US foreign policy, sir, is to build and sustain a more democratic, secure and prosperous world for the benefit of the American people.

Then a second appeared.

The world you are advocating will not be democratic, secure or prosperous. Others can choose to live with lower standards for a greater good, but that has never been, and never will be, the American Way.

'He might just as well have said, "We can do this alone – we don't need others",' Nick reflected.

Lianne laughed cynically. 'And that coming from a representative of the Democrats – their anger made them look weak. No wonder the Unity Party stole votes from them in later elections.'

'The most positive thing to come out of it all was that during the long process of selling the idea, I myself became a true convert,' Nick said, staring up at the ceiling. 'I finished the tour with no doubt in my mind that the Segmented World was already taking shape and that the future of Allied was significantly under threat.'

'The future of Allied,' Lianne said derisively. 'What about humankind?'

'The two are intertwined – little point in having products without customers,' he said, laughing uneasily. 'My idea in those days was that the solution should be top-down, requiring governments, institutions and entities like Allied to act, together, on a global scale. When you talk about fault, mine was to think that a lecture tour would be enough to fast-track global acceptance. How naive was that?'

'But at least the failure didn't deter either you or Methuen from continuing to seek solutions – even though you went your different ways.'

'He never believed in top-down; he always maintained that the change required was one of attitude and that that could only be achieved by getting "each and every individual to act", as he used to say. He wrote that booklet – remember? – *How to Live Responsibly*, giving each individual a personal checklist for sustainable living—'

'I had a copy myself,' Lianne chipped in. 'I was amazed at how much I could reduce my energy consumption through simple things like not overfilling a kettle and switching off the dishwasher.'

'It didn't work though – and I don't mean only for those who objected to it, like the manufacturers of white goods and those in the package holiday industry. It just never took off. There was too much, short-sighted, political and Union objection. Greed, jealousy and all sorts of other bad behaviours – are what drive economic growth. People being frugal and sensible was bad news for the power brokers of the old model. But the failure of his little booklet also had to do with funding. Even though Methuen kept costs down, it had to be distributed to over fifty million, just to reach the UK adult population. And there was a bigger problem: the printed word – even with the cartoon images he used to illustrate it – was the wrong medium for a population obsessed by online social media. That's why he turned to VR and the development of the SWVRP – which finally worked.'

'Yes, but only for a short time, otherwise why would you have embarked on the Phillips Project?'

'Let's move forward,' he said, pointing the remote up at the ceiling. 'This is the first scene based on direct data from my AA-Plant – you'll recognise the location. It's also time to introduce you to Katharina—'

'My new rival?'

AA-Com File: A Day at the Office

St John's Gardens Apartments, Inner Westminster
Engatement, London Governorate, UK
07.30 hours, 6 December 2049

Virtual Scene snapshot: In the centre of a bedroom, Nick stands naked in front of a mirror, frozen in the Tadasana pose.

There's something incredibly peaceful about standing straight as a brush, he thought, and then said aloud to his mirror image, 'You look all right, O'Grady – still a firm stomach at fifty-seven.'

As he continued the exercise, the sun peeped out from behind a tower block in the City, lighting up the room, while through the open balcony doors, the rising sound of river traffic could be heard wending its way under Lambeth Bridge.

Readjusting his feet, he settled back into the position. *Phillips Cay, two months from now, crossing the Atlantic with Elizabeth and Methuen – the start of Project 2150. Come on, O'Grady, clear your head. Why is this wretched journey bugging you so.*

Because everything you've done since the board sanctioned P2150 relies on this first step being successful, he heard himself reply.

After a few more poses, and with a procession of worries still marching through his head, he stepped off the mat and collapsed into an armchair. Looking up, he saw a green light flashing on the wall, showing that the new model of the Allied Memory Monitor was ready to use. He focused on the screen, waiting for the image to emerge.

Now remember what the instructor said: Don't think, just relax. Lie perfectly still … Wait for your AA-Plant to create a link between your brain, the AVIII and the monitor.

Ah, it's working. Who's that? Oh dear ... it's my mother ... Why's she waving that newspaper in the air?

> 'Telling the Establishment which way is up through this global jamboree will win you no friends, Nicholas.'

Oh, now it's my father, also looking upset ... pointing at some picture in a magazine. Oh yes, it's the one of me and Methuen taken on the Great Wall in '25.

> 'O'Gradys don't fail – and don't associate with failures.'

Well, you were wrong about that, fella.

The screened blanked and then another image of Nick's father appeared shaking his fist.

What year is this? There it is, March '26. What's he getting so worked up about again? Oh yes, I remember – his discovery that I was funding Sam Harding's new Party. He turned his head to read the headline that his father was pointing to on the TV:

BUSINESS PARTY POINTS THE WAY

'Business Party! The country was paralysed – the Democrats had scraped in but lacked direction ... We were just trying to propose ways for economic activity to get going again after the Covid disaster!' he shouted at the monitor, just as a commentor started up.

> 'An ideological war is raging in our country today between right and left: Trumplicans versus Sharia Socialists – as some have described the more extreme political representatives in the House. The only winner seems to be the new Unity Party led by the popular senator from Colorado, Sam Harding, that gained a significant number of seats in the Senate in the last election, mainly along the eastern seaboard, including the south-east state of Georgia, represented by the breakaway Republican, Ron McFall.'

A new image, of a funeral cortege, caused Nick to look down in his lap.

Sam's death – no I don't want to see that.

He shook his head, causing the screen to blank and then bring up the image of a large jovial man standing on the balcony of the White House.

Gonzalez, the first Hispanic president and there's Sam Harding's son alongside him, a year after the '36 election, announcing the formation of the new Coalition Party. Oh, and here's the famous map scene. There he goes, pointing at a huge projection of the US, like a schoolteacher in front of his class.

> 'We have East, we have West, but we also have a centre – and that's where a government that represents the people must be based.'

Look at the press, they're totally baffled – even more so as Gonzalez puts down the pointer and embraces Tom Harding. Why weren't you there alongside your mentor's son? Pride, Nick O'Grady. Just because he didn't involve you in the kick-off discussions about constitutional reform, you sided with McFall and allowed him to take charge. What would Sam have said about that?

Short clips of Ron McFall, dated '37, appeared in quick succession and a newscaster began speaking enthusiastically.

> 'Today, at the sprightly age of fifty-seven, Ron McFall assumed the leadership of the Unity Party after an earlier vitriolic internal fight with the founder's son, Tom Harding – the, now, newly appointed Vice President of the Coalition Party.'

An image of Lianne shaking her head.

> 'If you don't own McFall, he'll own you, Grady.'

An aerial shot of the warehousing at the Allied Answers yard in Portland, Maine, now flashed up. *What was it that McFall's manager said in '43? 'We need a place to store election equipment', wasn't it? Why did you believe him? Hell, you were under McFall's spell by then.*

Newspaper headline: UP loses half their seats on the Senate to the enthusiastic Coalition party, as Gonzalez names Tom Harding as his candidate for President in the '44 election.

Another video clip. *Ugh! It's McFall embracing me.*

'Today I'm announcing my decision to appoint Nick
O'Grady as the Unity Party's new chief spokesman – and
my future running mate for the presidential election in '44.'

*What's this? It's the Unity Party Spring Conference in '43 ... and there
I am, sitting next to McFall. Hah! Just look at his nameplate – it
tells you everything:* PARTY LEADER AND CHAIRMAN. *And look at him,
pretending to consult me in front of everyone – whereas the only ones
he took any actual notice of were those gibbering young apparatchiks
on either side of us, with their business-school smiles and synchronised
nods of support for every word he utters. And who is this now ...?
Oh, it's Lianne in the penthouse, hands on hips, looking angry.*

'You're too popular with the grassroots, Nick. McFall
won't tolerate it.'

*What am I seeing now? Phillips Cay. It's the Opening – early summer
'44 – and there's Methuen and Elizabeth. Oh! and there's the McFall
entourage, bossing everyone around. Little did any of us expect that
McFall would not even make the run-offs and that Harding would
become the last President of the United States of America.*

The Memory Monitor began to play another newscast, showing dignitaries in a large marquee in the grounds of the White
House, with the date stamp December 2045.

*Oh, I can never forget this: US politics was about to change
forever. There's Harding, the new president – he'd just announced his
plan to form an all-party working group to consider a new constitution. And where's McFall? Ah, there he is ... right at the back with
his new, Trumplican allies ... and here he goes, pushing his way to the
front ... grabbing the microphone from Harding's press secretary –
who looks dumbfounded ... Oh, I've not seen that before – a troop
of McFauns, forming a barrier between their Il Duce and the rest.*

'Western civilisation went into decline when the dulling
effects of overindulgent liberal democracy replaced the
heroic aspirations of our past. We are now in a time of

unavoidable sustained austerity ... For America to survive, we must reinvent the pioneering spirit that projected us forward before ... We must return to the values and ways of those who created this great country. Today I am announcing the birth of the Restoration Party – a voice for all those who wish to see our country regain its status as the greatest nation on earth ...'

Here goes Harding trying to take the microphone, only to be shoved by two hefty McFauns. That's when it got nasty. Ouch! There are the secret service guys smashing the McFauns to the ground with their rifle butts – in front of the world's press. What a disgrace. I still feel ashamed, watching it – even after all these years.

A headline from *The New York Times* appeared: AMERICA UNDER THREAT – but from what and from whom?

Another conference! Oh yes, the Restoration Party 2046 Spring Conference. It was scary being there, but I had to show my face, we were still making the arrangements to escape and expose McFall. There I am ... still at the top table but relegated to one end now. The apparatchiks had taken charge, sitting either side of the leader – 'The Twenty', as the press called them, or as I began to privately refer to them, 'First of the Übermensch'. They had started forming a shield around him – all those meetings in private – and then, the ultimate insult, passing on press briefings for me to deliver without my input.

More headlines: WHITE UP OR YOU'RE OUT. MCFAUNS STEER A NEW DIRECTION FOR THE NEWLY NAMED RESTORATION PARTY.

An image of McFall: thumbs up, amicably dismissing in his strong southern drawl any accusation of white supremacy.

The screen's gone blank – what's happened? Wait a minute, that's the voice of Tom Harding, calling me on my teleplant.

'It's going to get tough, Nick. Either you're with us or against us. All Parties have agreed to convene a meeting of the Constitutional Council. All that prevents that happening is McFall – you've got to help us.'

I know what this is, it's that meeting Lianne organised ... and there's my favourite diner on 42nd Street and Harvey Seingold smoking one of his huge cigars – that should have killed him years ago. He's from my parents' generation: built General Abrasives from nothing to be the biggest and best – just as I'm trying to do with Allied. Oh, why has the image gone?

'Please relax. Forcing the imagery scrambles the brain signal,' came a voice from the monitor.

'Okay, okay.' *Ah, there's Harvey. Ha, I'm smoking one of his Cubans while we stand together in the snow. It's January '46, I'd just found out what McFall was actually storing in that warehouse in Portland ...*

'I'm not a political animal, Mr O'Grady ... but the line between good and bad has been drawn ... We need to stop him ... I'll make the first move since it's my son who's sanctioned the funding for McFall ... I promise the remittances from GA will terminate this week.'

Nick turned his head away as a video clip flashed up, showing dead American soldiers in the desert, some eviscerated. *'Oh God, that's disgusting. Where's that memo from the Ethical Team? Ah, here it is.'*

During test sessions, the new Memory Monitor created some exceptionally graphic images that invoked strong emotional reactions in a number of participants. Before releasing this version, we must develop a clear set of guidelines, particularly for younger users where there could be exposure to significant legal challenge.

Nick looked back at the screen, where the images of the battlefield had been replaced by a map showing the position of the

Russian-backed Iran–Iraq militia from Musandam down to Ras Al Khaimah: '… blocking the export for more than eighty per cent of all liquid hydrocarbons', a reporter was heard to say.

The sound of a running machine and the voice of a robo-trainer coming through the passageway into the other apartment, caused Nick to glance up.

Lianne – she must be awake, going through the motions of her schedule but not writing. She's upset about leaving but what can I do? I must be in the States for the Harding inauguration. They'll sort out McFall and then we can return to New York – she'll like that – it's her real home.

* * *

Virtual Scene snapshot: Nick lies face down on a therapy table in the adjoining apartment – a man is massaging his skull.

'Watch it! That's where my new AA-Plant has been inserted,' he said to the attendant, who muttered an apology. As he tried to relax again, the sound of handbells filled his head, announcing the hour. Closing his eyes, he called up the only newsreel he could trust.

'This is the BBC World Service.
The News at 08.00 hours GMT on 6 December 2049.

Increased tensions between US and Russian Federation-backed forces along the eastern half of the Arabian Penin-sula continue to cause widespread concern. The Chinese self-named Peacekeeper Force has consolidated its position around Ras Al Hadd in north-east Oman and offered to act as a mediator to resolve the most recent flare-up, triggered by the massacre of US soldiers in the Empty Quarter.

In the United States, the twentieth of January 2050 has been announced as the date for the implementation of the new constitution, and instalment of the government – the newly named CENHQ – in Minneapolis. On the fourth of March 2050, the Inauguration will take place of the first President of the Federated States of America, Thomas Jefferson Harding. President Harding was elected through an open vote of the Senate and House of Representatives. He has vowed to bring unity to the country and an end to the conflict in the Middle East. The only discordant voice has been that of Senator Ron McFall, leader of the Restoration Party, which controls a large swathe of seats along the eastern seaboard of the United States. The Party remains implacably opposed to the new constitution. At a New Year rally of more than a million people in Atlanta, Senator McFall stated that he would not permit the creation of the seven new state bodies – the State Associations – 'in any areas where the Restoration Party received the majority of the popular vote'.

Turning to global matters, the "State of the Planet" forecast for 2050 has been issued this morning. The report confirms that three well-publicised milestones will be passed in the coming year. The world's population will reach ten billion – although the report notes a continuing sharp decline in most developed countries. Global temperatures show no sign of decrease, with official confirmation that the Three-Degree World (referring to the rise of average global temperatures above pre-industrial levels) will be reached by 2070. Finally, 2050 will mark the tenth year of successive negative global economic growth, raising renewed concerns for people's living standards across the world.

Other noticeable predictions from the report include the continued change in the ethnicity of major population centres – most notably in the US, where people of Hispanic origin will by 2060 exceed thirty-five per cent. In the

European Confederation, peoples of African and Middle Eastern descent are predicted to form close to a quarter of the population, while in the Russian Federation, migrants from the FSU – the former satellite states of the old Soviet Union – are now estimated to exceed forty per cent.

In the environmental section of the report, there is a startling prediction that by the end of the next decade, more than sixty per cent of the Amazon Basin will be deforested, while in the North Atlantic traditional fish stocks will have declined by fifty-five per cent, due in large part to the decrease in strength of the North Atlantic Conveyor Belt, also known as the Gulf Stream. Perhaps the most marked change, however, comes in the significant increase in the number of commodities at risk, due to a combination of natural depletion, geopolitical disruption and lack of investment. Oil remains the most significant concern, although the report also highlights surprising shortages in materials that have hitherto been regarded as readily available, such as aluminium and iron.

In other news, officials from the US–EUCON Commodity Credit System have announced satisfactory progress in discussions with the Chinese financial blockchain operator Red Star – which currently accounts for more than seventy per cent of all financial transactions within the PRC. Welcoming this progress, President-elect Harding stated, "This agreement demonstrates the ability of G5 members to act together in the interests of global stability."

And now for a summary of UK news.

Following the UK's decision to fully integrate its foreign and defence policy with the EMA – the European Military Alliance – the British Government will issue a White Paper promoting a national debate on the extent and timing of future relationships with the European Confederation. A government official strenuously denied media reports that discussions over the full social, economic and political integration of the UK with the military-led EUCON State were already at an advanced stage, with full incorporation possible as early as next year.

Many people are expected to gather in London today to protest over what they see as the divisive impact of the new Governorate structure introduced throughout the United Kingdom in 2046. Under the banner "Give us back our Nation State", protesters are expected to be joined by many MPs calling for a return to national control of education, health and social service budgets. A counterdemonstration in support of the regional devolution to the Governorates is also planned.

Weather: The intense cold that has held parts of the UK in its grip for the past four weeks is set to continue well beyond Christmas, according to the Meteorological Agency. Parts of Central England and the South East have reported their lowest winter temperatures for almost ninety years. By contrast, the Agency said, "In the far south-west of the UK, where the influence of the Gulf Stream remains strong, average temperatures last month were a balmy 10 degrees centigrade."

Restrictions on travel remain in place in some parts of the South West, North East and Central North Governorates of the UK, because of civil disturbance. The Government has this morning issued a warning that anyone seeking to travel through these areas must obtain the relevant permits well in advance to avoid being refused entry.

In sport, England have taken control of the first Test match against Australia in Brisbane. To win the match, Australia will need to make two hundred and fifty runs on the final day with only four wickets left standing.'

Nick felt a tap on the top of his shoulder, a signal from the attendant that he should move to the sun cabin, next to the window.

Lying face down on the treatment bed he put on a set of transmission glasses linked to his AA-Plant. Several messages flashed up in the left lens from his Head of AI, one, a reminder that, today was the day when he was due to start testing the new AGI module. In the other lens, a line of text appeared.

Role of the new AGIM (Artificial General Intelligence Module):
(1) Help the user to listen more carefully to their internal voices before acting;
(2) Think through the consequences of any conclusions;
(3) Assist the user in deciding on the optimal action.

'Please activate,' Nick said aloud, but the only response came from the attendant, who had slipped in quietly and had begun kneading his shoulders. As the man pulled back, Nick beckoned him to continue, while he opened up another message from his Head of AI. At the end of the document he found an errata statement, explaining that temporarily the AGIM could only be activated or shut down using specific physical actions. Following the activation instruction, he raised his head off the massage couch and looped it clockwise three times – again causing the personal attendant to draw back.

'Good morning, sir,' Nick heard. 'I see you have read the introductory note. Is this just a familiarisation start-up call or is there something specific I can do?'

Sounds like Elizabeth Pryce. Has someone done that to encourage me to use this thing?

'What do they call you …? And if you say Elizabeth, I will change it at once,' he said aloud, attracting a bewildered look from the attendant.

'We were permitted to select our names, so I chose Katharina because it was one I did not find in the list of Allied Associates or their family members.'

'Well, I hope you realise the critical role you and your electronic buddies are expected to play in order to make Phillips Cay a success?'

'It's comforting to know you have so much confidence in us, sir.'

'Look! If you're going to be in my head for the next three days, call me Nick.'

'Thank you, Nick. That makes me more relaxed. You may call me Katharina if you wish.'

'Oh, thank you very much,' he replied sardonically. 'But wait a minute, you don't feel anything – you're just a piece of software?'

Before the AGI module had time to reply, the attendant, clearly put out by the continued one-sided interaction of his client, announced that the massage was complete and Nick could now put his clothes back on.

* * *

Virtual Scene snapshot: Nick steps out of a lift into a minimally furnished foyer with a shining marble floor. A concierge is approaching from the far end, accompanied by a small servantbot dressed as a bellboy.

Taking his bag, the bot raced ahead while the two men strolled towards the exit.

'Now you be careful how you go this morning, Mr O'Grady,' the man said, in what Nick had been told was a strong south-west accent. 'Everything froze again last night. You can't rely on those streetbots to make it safe underfoot.'

At the exit, the man stepped back from the double doors. 'Are you tucked up enough, sir?' he asked, pointing to Nick's coat.

'It's nano-cloth. It adjusts according to the ambient temperature and humidity,' Nick said.

'Is that so?' the man replied vaguely as the doors swung open.

There's no point in saying any more. He's likeable enough but he's from a section of society that will never be able to enjoy products created by companies like Allied. I hope he takes the new government pills, Nick thought as he walked out into Dean Ryle Street.

'If I could stop you for a moment, Mr O'Grady,' the man called out, 'I need to inform security that you're leaving.'

Nick made no reply but stood waiting on the pavement, his mind drifting back to the dinner party of the previous evening, when several of his guests had predicted an imminent nuclear exchange between EUCON or the US with the Russian Federation. There was bitter laughter around the table at the mention of the Hundred Years Since Nagasaki anniversary celebration, back in '45. No one was in any doubt that small-scale nuclear devices had already been deployed in several conflicts, most notably to destroy, years ago, the uranium conversion facility at Isfahan. For many, that had been the critical event triggering the regional security pact between the Federation and Shia forces along the northern side of the Gulf.

Growing impatient with the delay from the concierge, Nick set off cautiously along the pavement, still ruminating on the origins of the prolonged war in the Middle East. A few steps along, he stopped and called up the AGIM.

'Keep me up to date with the latest Test match score, and before I go into Thames House, give me an assessment of the likely outcome,' he said, adding, 'Knowledge or even better an opinion on the state of play is a sure-fire way to start the day on the right foot with my senior British colleagues.'

'Thank you,' said Katharina. 'That is a remarkably interesting cultural observation that I will need to study further.'

Why did I explain all that to this silicon citizen? Nick turned around and saw his regular minders following him. *Ah, there's the orange MOD car and ... there's my Allied securobot.*

'Excuse me, Nick, you are walking towards Horseferry Road. Your usual route is to the right, down Page Street.'

'I know, I know. I just wanted a change.'

'I understand your need to break routine, but since those media reports linking you to the leaks regarding illegal funding of the Restoration Party, you've received several death threats and there has been a steady flow of attacks on Allied Answers buildings—'

'Is this how you normally operate – ordering people around?' he asked.

'I'm sorry, that is how I am programmed. Whenever your anxiety indicators go above a certain threshold, I have to alert you.'

'My anxiety levels?' Nick shouted.

'If you like, I can adjust the settings?'

'No, leave it as it is. I need to stick with your current set-up even when you annoy me.'

'In that case, could I ask what your intention is?' Katharina enquired coolly as Nick turned into Horseferry Road, followed by his security entourage.

'My intention, madam, is to have some time to myself in this public garden,' he said, opening the gate to the small park behind the apartment block. 'Away from the prying attention of my overseers, and that includes you!'

'You are aware, of course, that all your AA-Plant conversations are recorded wherever you are?'

'Is your attitude module properly adjusted?' he asked gruffly. 'You seem far too assertive for my liking.' He noticed a slight delay in the device's response as he sat down on one of the wooden benches surrounding a fountain in the centre of the park, its basin thick with ice.

'I am who I am,' Katharina responded.

'What you are is my servant. Let's both be clear on that,' he said, looping his head anticlockwise three times to shut down the AGIM.

Gazing up at the bare branches, each outlined with snow, Nick recalled the cool shady green dome of the previous summer, which had screened out the apartment block and given him a sense of being back in the hills of Vermont. Looking around, he saw icicles dripping from the dolphin statuettes in the fountain, while in the flower borders, a few limp hellebores gave a welcome dash of colour between the patches of snow. Pulling his coat around his knees and adjusting his gloves to leave no skin exposed, his thoughts turned to the interaction with the AGIM.

Here I am, losing my temper with a piece of software called Katharina. She's right, of course – I'm all wound up ... I wonder if she knows why?

He looped his head to bring Katharina back online.

'I'm worried about the AVIII problem – any ideas?'

'I am happy to help you—'

'It's our star product,' he said, looking up at the glass wall of Millbank Mirror – the two-hundred-storey tower block next to Thames House, where the HQ of Allied NW Europe was housed on the upper floors. 'Over the past decades, income from AA-Com has allowed me to build up the other businesses: Health, Livings, and most recently your birthplace, AI. All that is now threatened because this new AVIII interferes with all previous AA-Com versions.'

'Can you explain a little more about the ... AVIII?'

'We're developing two versions. One is commercial, with a whole lot of new capabilities: holographic projection, mind-map reading, new data projection and loads more. To get the best out of it, you also need to have installed the new AA exo-cortex teleplant, which allows the thought functions to operate most effectively. It communicates using the Allied network of dirigibles, along with some of the leading satellite-based organisations. It's way ahead of anything on the market at present. The second is a private version with all these features, but with the added capability of interacting with the Hub Tool Boxes – your residence – allowing you and me to communicate right now. The problem is that both versions cause interference with all pre-AVIII AA-Com models. It's most severe when an AVIII and a pre-AVIII are communicating through the same dirigible.'

'Does this problem also appear when the different versions are using the same satellite?'

'I'm afraid so. It's a nightmare. We've already distributed forty beta AVIIIs to Allied Associates and have had to send out an instruction for them to revert to their old AVII's until we find a solution.'

'Are we causing interference at present?'

'Not in this location because we have a special dirigible above Millbank Mirror that only AVIII users can access. But if I use the Central London Dirigible, for example, all pre-AVIII devices using it at the same time will be severely affected.'

'I understand.'

'And to make it worse, the PRC has a rival product coming to market with its own Blimp network. I know it won't affect our contracts with the US or EUCON governments, but it could knock out a lot of our private customers.'

'I will create a project to study this business risk and make sure you are immediately informed of any developments.'

Somewhere in the distance, Nick heard a church bell ring, while closer to him the whirring sound of a parkbot started up, clearing snow. He sat back and for several minutes practised the meditation routine his yoga instructor had recently taught him.

'You seem more relaxed now.'

He sat up, surprised by the AGIM's comment. 'So let's get this straight – you're evaluating my thoughts and feelings as well as my words – even when I'm resting?'

'That is the default position when I am online. You can adjust it so that I respond only to spoken words, for example.'

'But you're still reading my thoughts even then?' he said.

There was a small but noticeable pause before Katharina responded. 'Yes, unless you switch me or your AA-Plant off.'

'I'm also not comfortable with you reading my feelings. How are you able to do that?'

'I'm fitted with standard emotional algorithms linked to your blood chemistry, minute quantities of which are accessed by your new exo–Plant. From several research papers I have read, I am aware that Allied AI are developing a more advanced version of the AA-Com VIII to detect an even broader range of senses. That will greatly enhance my understanding of your behaviour.'

Nick nodded, aware of the 'Wet Pyramid Project' – as it was called in Allied – as well as the debate it had prompted over the implications of further increasing the power of the new AGIM.

The sound of traffic on Page Street caused his thoughts to turn to the BBC broadcast and the news of restrictions in the South West Governorate.

'What's the status of the travel arrangements down to Falmouth?'

'The final paperwork for you, Mrs O'Grady, Elizabeth and Methuen Pryce to travel in early February to Falmouth, was submitted last week. I have electronic confirmation that it has been approved, but the Home Office insists that you appear in person to receive hard copies. Without these, you may have problems in areas of restricted movement.'

'The bureaucracy in this country is getting ridiculous. What about the vehicles for the journey?'

'As you instructed, two Retro-Level-1 vehicles—'

'But in reality, Level 5 – fully driverless – right? I doubt whether Methuen or Elizabeth have manually driven anything for years.'

'That is correct. Anyone looking at the vehicles from the outside will probably assume they're run on regular gasoline, so they shouldn't attract too much attention.'

'And what about protection against someone using one of those laser guns to run SDVs off the road?'

'All taken care of: both vehicles have the latest external beam protection that will ... Wait a minute, you have a call coming in.'

'Mr Nick, this is Marco, from the *Clipper*,' Nick heard in his head.

'Have you sorted out the problem of the departure visa with the port authority yet?' Nick asked hastily.

'That's what I'm calling you about. You need to push from your end. I'm, umm ... getting nowhere with them – they just don't want to talk to me. They treat me like I'm no one,' Marco said indignantly in a thick Portuguese accent.

'All right, all right, leave it to me. You focus on getting everything on board and tied down.'

'I'll find out who you need to speak to,' Katharina said, after Marco had rung off.

'Thank you,' Nick replied, more pleased at that moment with Katharina's response than with that of his senior engineer. He sat back, recalling the board discussion after he had introduced the AGIM concept. 'Will it not eventually relegate the majority of our staff to the role of performing manual tasks that the AGIM requires to be done?' he remembered someone asking.

A beam of sunlight burst through a gap between apartment blocks, and as he glanced up, he saw Lianne on the veranda of the penthouse.

'You're worried about Lianne. Do you wish to talk about it?'

'What?' he called out. 'I forgot you were online again. Don't you have some discretion setting to tell you when to shut up – or even better, turn yourself off?'

'I am not set-up that way. As you said, I am a servant. I go when you tell me to go.'

'Well, that's another programming modification we need,' he retorted sharply. 'What do you know about Phillips Cay and Project 2150?'

'If you're referring to the Phillips Cay Project, then I am expecting to get my full briefing later this week. As for Project 2150, I lack any data.'

'Good. There's nothing you should know about *that* at present.' Then, in a more friendly voice, he asked, 'Have Bradley and the others arrived on Phillips yet?'

'I sometimes have link problems with the AA-Com VII set on Phillips Cay, but a conversation between the Phillips General Manager Wallace Adams and Allied Livings two nights ago produced a list of new arrivals that included one Bradley Raymonds, his wife Belinda and several other members of the team who I understand will be working with Professor Pryce.'

Belinda – his wife? Surely not that Belinda. How did that happen?

'Sorry, I don't understand the background to that concern,' Katharina said.

'Never mind … Any other news?'

'The report did include a reference to the arrival of four unregistered vessels in Reception Bay. Like the others moored there, they are seeking approval to enter the marina.'

'Well, they're bloody well not going to get it. Send a message to Allied Livings, reminding them, "No more boat people".'

He waited for the usual acknowledgement of his request but heard none. *Did the use of a British expletive slow her response or is she practising some form of anger management on me?* Still hearing no reply, he asked more calmly, 'What about the Pryces? Are you aware of any issues they have regarding the journey?'

'I noticed that neither Methuen nor Elizabeth have signed their employment contracts yet.'

'He will, and Lizzie's gagging to get her hands on the health-care clinic we've sent out to Phillips for her.'

Again no response – why's that? I wasn't angry this time. In fact, the thought of seeing Elizabeth again makes me feel quite chipper. 'Oh, that's another thing I have to deal with today. Lianne asked me last night about the status of Bliss's Intervention Treatment. Got any information on that?'

'I have limited data. There is a conversation involving Bliss, Lianne and Elizabeth in May 2047, just before Bliss went to Lady Caroline's School. In it, agreement was reached that she would apply for the Treatment. Then at the start of the 2048/9 academic year, there is another communication informing her that she had been selected and given a slot in the January 2050 programme at the school's biomedical centre.'

'I know all that. How could I forget? Have you seen the commodity credits required to fund it?'

'Sorry, is that a rhetorical question? I am, of course, well informed about anything that passes through your account. I agree it's a substantial amount of money when compared with the average household—'

'And may change our delightful little girl forever. Like her father, I'm now sceptical about all this Treatment stuff.'

'It may be too late to change it now and besides, I understand that Bliss herself is eager to proceed.'

Nick rotated his head to turn off the AGIM. *There's only so much I can take from this thing. I need to return to the world where I only have to answer to one voice in my head.*

He walked out of the park and towards Thames House, looking up at Millbank Mirror soaring impressively skyward to his right. Noting the line of staff queueing at the drab rear entrance of the older building, he recalled standing there in the rain on his first day with a stiff-shouldered official, inspecting his security badge and politely instructing him to use the main door. *Why couldn't he just let me go in through that entrance?* he thought. *This place always makes me feel as if I'm back at school.*

Walking along the passageway between the two buildings, Lianne came into his mind and his comment after his first day at Thames House: *'like being in a well-appointed prison in a quirky little country.'* And then her unusually acerbic response: *'I'm going along with all this, Grady, not just to protect you but also myself. We should be grateful to have somewhere safe to go.'*

Crossing the main road, he sat down on a low stone wall, breathing in the smells of the river.

That was a decisive moment for us. Until then, she had focused on her work and been pretty successful in building up her readership – she quickly didn't need my support or social connections. But staying with McFall when he took charge of the Unity Party in '37, stirred her into action. The arguments between us increased and she refused to attend any political events involving 'that bullying misogynist', as she called him. But she didn't know the half of it and I chose to ignore what I knew. That was until the Party failed to make the run-off in '44 and then that shocking bust-up McFall had with Harding in the White House garden a year later. That was when I knew I had to take action. The question was how to do it and that's when Lianne played a blinder. How long was she planning it before I met Harvey? I was rather disparaging at first over her claims of corruption in the Party, saying that supporters who favoured racist policies would scarcely worry about a little bit of financial mismanagement. But then intriguingly she suggested a trip to the beach house. We didn't skinny-dip, but we did spend a lot of time in the same bed we had occupied all those years earlier, this time going through the Restoration Party accounts. She'd done her homework; the scale of the illegal funding was staggering, with General Abrasives as the main funder. Cutting that cashflow would cripple McFall. After that, I simply fell in line with her plan, which she had meticulously constructed like the plotline of one of her novels – beginning with my private trip to London to arrange our new life over here, and then helping Harvey to orchestrate the publicity blitz. No wonder the McFall supporters hate me so much back home.

Turning around, he noticed that the MOD security vehicle had blocked the cycle path ahead to monitor his movements. He looked across the road, contrasting the pre-war stone fortress of Thames House with the all-glass exterior of the adjacent tower block.

Typical Brits – all smoke and mirrors. I entered that antiquated monstrosity on the first day, expecting something fusty and dull, and what did I find? The old interior gutted and replaced by an airy atrium, full of bustling bright young things, the smartest of whom had undergone the type of Treatment Bliss will soon experience.

Walking towards the main entrance, he brought Katharina back online, requesting her to supply personal data on anyone approaching him in the building. As he went through the usual security checks, Katharina fed a selection of his favourite tunes into his AA-Plant, and then just before reaching his office, her update on the cricket: 'It's taking spin; it doesn't look good for the Aussies.'

On the top floor, the fast-moving, energetic mood below gave way to a slower pace and more traditional décor, with paintings on the wall and a select scattering of decorative, albeit redundant French furniture. Entering his own office, however, his attention was drawn not to the view across the river or the choice of artwork on the walls, but the two objects on the table in front of him: a blue-lit cube and a small black pyramid – the iconic forms of the old and new AA-Com devices.

Nick drummed his fingers on the table as an Allied Comms test report on the interference problem appeared on the screen behind the pre-AVIII device. Leaning over, he activated the AVIII pyramid, immediately causing a dense web of lines to spread across the AVII-connected screen. Switching off the AVII, he turned to the AVIII, bringing up a file – marked with a large red cross.

Project 2150

Progress Report

(6 December 2049)

<u>Not for distribution without the signed approval of the CEO</u>

<u>of Allied Answers</u>

Flicking to a section entitled 'Phillips Cay Project Update', he began to read.

Inside the red-painted barn;
Hardin, Montana, NCSA, FSA
17.00 hours, 15 June 2050

'So just as I'm conjuring an image of Katharina as some beautiful blonde android, you introduce me to something in your head that sounds like Elizabeth and irritates you,' Lianne said, tapping a panel on the wall and taking out a glass of water from a small recess.

'It was the AA-Com problem that made me grumpy,' Nick said, removing his VR specs. 'As for Katharina, after a few days I was hooked. I didn't switch her off again until we left for the Pryces' in January.'

'Where did she come from?'

'Long story. The Exemplar is what started it. After Methuen handed over the SWVRP to us in '33, we decided to refocus Allied AI activities from developing androids to concentrating on various types of IA. At the time, if you remember, there was a lot of pushback on the surgical and chemical approaches being developed for cognitive enhancement. The IA software in the Exemplar offered a non-invasive option. That's how we developed the market slogan for the new devices: "Add, don't Alter! It Makes More Sense".'

'You call it adding, but from what I've just heard, it's more like controlling – she seemed to have no hesitation in intervening in your life.'

'Yeah, but all that bossiness calmed down as soon as she adjusted to my style – and I began to realise how useful she could be to me.'

'Putting aside the not insignificant question of how she manages to understand you and formulate such sensible replies, where does she get all her information?'

'Five years of an AI team downloading every conceivable piece of data we could find and storing it on the original HTB in Lincoln – you know, the Hub Tool Box I mentioned before. Two years ago, we also started rerouting all Allied Answers communications through the small network of HTBs we'd created by then.'

'Why did you do that?'

'The HTBs aren't just storage units; they also contain an array of specialist IA modules that search for data relevant to their function.'

'And that includes Katharina?'

'Yeah, although she's something special—'

'Is Katharina monitoring us now?'

'Of course not. We're in communications shutdown – our tele-plants are only working locally.'

'Think she's missing you?' Lianne teased.

'Do I detect a hint of jealousy?' he protested, smirking.

'You have to wonder though, Nick. She sounds less like a computer program and more like some woman pretending to be angry to hide her real feelings.'

'I only have eyes for you, my dearest.'

'Hah!' she said tossing her head back and then lying down.

As they fell silent, the faint sound of birdsong started up in the room.

'This avian muzak is driving me mad – can't you turn it off?'

'It's there for a purpose. If I close the two hatch doors in the stairwell and switch off the monitors and AC, the only sound you will hear is yourself. I can assure you that after a short time, it would drive you insane, hearing only your heart thumping and stomach gurgling. I can put on a playlist if you'd rather—'

'What is this Project 2150 that keeps being mentioned?' Lianne blurted out.

'Err, just something in the making – I need to get that erased from the—' Nick sat bolt upright, hitting his head on the ceiling as he pointed to the image of a large pickup tearing down the track.

Lianne gripped his arm as the vehicle reached the forecourt and five men got out – all wearing protective masks and carrying weapons.

'These guys are sure not CENCOM officials,' she said, as one of them, rifle held high, began to walk towards the barn.

Nick rolled off the bed and scampered up the stairs with Lianne right behind him. In the driving cabin he switched on all the exterior cameras just as the pickup started to follow the man down the track.

'They're just a bunch of hicks chancing their luck,' Nick muttered, busily adjusting the displays. 'I hope for their sakes they're wearing more protection under those work clothes.'

'It's not *their* long-term health prospects that concern me right now,' Lianne barked back, staring anxiously at the monitor.

Leaning over the desk, Nick switched to the drone camera on the roof of the stables, focusing on the man with the gun, who was now attempting to force open the barn door.

'Don't worry, they won't be able to get past those two inner locking bars,' he said confidently.

The men in the pickup arrived and one of them could be seen gesticulating upwards.

'Oh ... shit!' yelped Nick.

'What is it?' Lianne said, clinging to the back of his seat.

'The hayloft door – I forgot all about it. They can get in that way.'

'Nick, I'm really scared now.'

'Don't worry, don't worry – there are heaps of things I can do if they get too nosey.'

They watched transfixed as one of the men ran back down the track, returning with a ladder, which he then placed beneath the upper door.

Nick pressed a button on the panel in front of him, bringing the voice of the man into the cabin. Zooming in on him, he shook his head in disbelief. 'The idiot's not wearing a dosimeter.'

Pulling down his mask for a moment, the man at the top of the ladder was heard to say, 'Gimme that rope ... I'll sling it over the bale hoist and pull myself in.'

Those on the ground watched as he hauled himself athletically up the rope, before heaving his body in through the upper door.

'See anything, Gary?' one of the men called from below.

'You won't believe it,' the man said poking his head out through the loft door, 'There's one of those big RVs in here, surrounded by hay bales. Strange thing is ... the barn doors are locked from the inside.'

The man disappeared again, only to pop back out almost immediately. Tugging his mask aside again, he said, 'There's something not right here. On the roof of this thing is some sort of compartment with one of those mini-drones inside. I'm going down to take a closer look.'

Nick switched to the image from the drone on the cross-beam inside the barn. He and Lianne then watched intently as the man scrambled down over the hay bales and lifted the bars from the doors, allowing his companions to enter.

'No door, no windows,' one commented as they hammered at the metal surface. 'What about underneath?' another said, crouching down.

Nick leapt from his seat. 'Stay here,' he insisted, sliding down the stairs.

As the hatch door opened and closed, Lianne turned up the volume on the speaker and studied the group of men.

'Did you hear something?' one of them asked.

'Think there's someone in there?' added the man kneeling on the floor.

'Well, if there is, they must have something worth protecting to go to all that trouble,' the other said eagerly, eliciting grunts of agreement from the rest of the group.

'Oh God ... Nick, Nick, they're onto us,' Lianne shouted, and then turned sharply towards the stairs from where a muffled clanging sound could be heard. Glancing at the screen, she saw the group of men also react.

'You're right – there is someone in there!' one of them hollered.

'I'm gonna have a look,' the one kneeling said, flipping onto his back and working his way under the vehicle.

Lianne, hand on head, moved towards the stairwell but then stopped, as an intense piercing screech came over the speaker.

'Joe, you okay?' she heard one of the men shout.

Returning to her seat, she saw the man emerging from under the vehicle, holding his face and spluttering.

Another held up his dosimeter and screamed out: 'Fuck, what's caused that?'

She watched as he then ran back to the pickup and returned with a large black box.

'Fuck it, we need to get out of here!' he shrieked. 'It's reading more than a sievert.'

Lianne punched her fist in the air, as the men rushed from the barn towards the pickup. But as the vehicle started up, she saw the man who had been under the RV stumble forward and then fall to the ground, vomiting violently. Groaning, he was then dragged into the back of the vehicle that sped off towards the highway.

Lianne walked over to Nick's seat, head down. *What if he doesn't come back or is hurt – how do I get this thing to move? How do I get the communications to work? Come on, lady, you can sort this out—*

Looking up, she saw a light appear on the panel in front of her, indicating the decontamination unit had been switched on. Waiting patiently, she panned around the lower deck but then heard the sound of the hatch door clicking in the stairwell, followed by Nick looking ruffled but calm. She ran over and hugged him.

He laughed with surprise and gave her a brief kiss on the head before catching sight of himself in a mirror on the kitchen wall.

'Man, look how scruffy I am!'

'Are you OK? That's all I want to know,' she said.

Smoothing his hair with his fingers, he went over to his seat and pointed to an image of the pickup disappearing down the road towards Bismarck. 'They won't be back in a hurry,' he said, taking a drink handed to him by Lianne. 'We definitely need to leave tonight though.'

'How did you get rid of them?' she asked from the kitchen.

'The reactor creates a minute amount of radioactive gas that we normally evacuate into a sealed unit. I just released it onto that goon who was ferreting under the vehicle. The undercarriage is our weak point. I can lower the vehicle entirely onto the ground but didn't bother because I thought we were safe with the doors secured.'

Quivering, Lianne asked, 'But are *you* okay?'

'I scanned myself in the decontamination unit – I'm fine.'

'What about the guy under the vehicle – was it a fatal dose?'

'Not immediately,' Nick replied coldly.

'Shouldn't we leave right now? The barn doors are unlocked. If anyone else comes down the drive, they'll spot us.'

'Only if they're not monitoring radiation levels, which most people are – even those rednecks. This place will be humming for days. We just need to stick to the plan and travel at night,' he said adamantly. 'First, I need a shower, then let's go downstairs and do another immersion to take our minds off all the excitement, huh?'

Back in the bedroom, stripped down to his underpants, Nick took the remote and pointed it at the screen. 'It's almost six o'clock now; it'll be dark at nine – we'll leave just after that.'

'What do you have next?' Lianne asked, lying back on the bed adjusting her AA-Com ear plug.

'Any number of post-'48 scenes – all recorded when our

AA-Plants were active on the *Clipper*. They'll mainly show things that you, me, Methuen and Elizabeth got up to.'

'And Bliss?'

'Yep, she's on the next scene, which is set in the Pryces' home, just before they left. Shall we go with that?'

'Anything – I just want to escape.'

'General View is best with these scenes.'

'Just roll it.'

AA-Com File:
'Something still nagging away ...'

Soft Rush Estate, Sandy Hollow,
Southern Governorate, UK
Late morning, 1 January 2050

Virtual Scene snapshot: In a low-beamed cottage living room, Elizabeth is warming her back against a roaring fire in a large open grate. To either side of her are placed two cushioned armchairs, while across the room, Bliss sits on the edge of a polished dining table, studying her appearance in a mirror on the wall.

'Join you on what?' Bliss said, twirling around. 'I love this quilted jacket Auntie Lianne sent me for Christmas.'

Elizabeth, dressed as usual as if she were off out somewhere, pointed to a chair and said, 'Stop fiddling with that coat for a minute and sit down. I have something important to discuss with you.'

'Can't it wait? I'm about to go to the pub with Jack and Martin ... and look ...' Bliss held out a small book and waved it at her mother. 'I'm going to use the electronic diary Dad gave me at Christmas to record my New Year's resolutions with the boys. Isn't it cool?'

'Sit down,' Elizabeth insisted, 'and listen to me before your father arrives.'

'All right, all right, keep your hair on!' Bliss said, slumping down onto a dining chair, hands in pockets.

'You remember the O'Gradys inviting us to the opening of the Allied resort on Phillips Cay five years ago ...' Elizabeth said, pointing at her daughter but then falling silent as a low humming sound announced the arrival of the housebot, followed by Methuen, his sleeves rolled up and face lightly perspiring.

Smiling amiably at his wife and daughter, he deposited himself into one of the armchairs.

Without acknowledging his arrival, Elizabeth shouted instructions to the bot, requesting it to monitor the New Year's lunch.

Bliss stared briefly at her father but then turned back to her mother. 'How could I forget the O'Gradys? They may not have visited us here in Soft Rush, but they've always been in our lives.'

Unrolling his sleeves and buttoning them at the cuffs, Methuen interjected wryly, 'Present without presence – an all too common occurrence these days, I'm afraid.'

Bliss chuckled. 'More like presents without presence – they never forget Christmas. Look at this nano-jacket, Dad. Each quilted area has its own sensor; it's lusciously comfortable, but the cost ...' she said, shaking her head.

'And not just at Christmas,' Methuen added. 'They funded Martin's SWVRP country-mapping in Southern England last year; the deposit on a house for Jack the year before last – and don't forget Lady Caroline's.'

'What were you going to say, Mum?' Bliss said, suddenly aware of her mother staring at her.

'The year before last, Nick approached your father to help him establish a fully functioning self-sufficient community on Phillips—'

Bliss turned abruptly to her father and said, 'Dad! Wha— what's this all about?'

Methuen went to reply, but Elizabeth held up her hand, requesting his silence. 'Your father will have overall responsibility for setting up the community, while I've been asked to run one of the new computerised medical centres – I'm sure you've heard about those on the news.'

'But ... what about your practice in Bentham and all the work you've done to set up the NCC in the UK? Are you going to just walk away from all that?'

'The practice can function perfectly well without me. As for the network of clinics, the organisation is already in place and in any case, they have the US model to guide them if necessary. I've been needing a new challenge for some time …' Elizabeth said emphatically. 'This one looks as good as any.'

'So … how long are you going on this … jaunt for?' Bliss asked, turning to her father.

'Five years,' he replied plainly, fixing his eyes on his daughter.

'And we leave at the end of the month,' her mother chipped in.

Bliss curled up tight in the chair, her mouth open. 'Five years … and leaving at the end of the month! Why are you telling me this now, Dad?'

'I realise it's a bit of a surprise,' he said, holding up his hands defensively. 'We didn't want to bounce it on you while you were at school and meant to raise it the day you came home—'

'Except that that was the day your father got caught up in the bomb explosion in London,' Elizabeth cut in. 'You didn't see him when he came back – he was in a terrible state. And then, once he'd started to recover, it was close to Christmas, and that was another thing we didn't want to disrupt—'

'I bet you told the boys though,' Bliss shot back angrily.

Elizabeth and Methuen looked at one another, as if unsure as to who should answer. 'They got to know about it because they asked,' Elizabeth replied eventually. 'We gave out plenty of signals that we were thinking of going abroad.'

Bliss shook her head and, close to sobbing, said, 'I'm sorry, but it's ridiculous to bounce this on me now, just before I start this … Treatment.' Then recovering some of her composure, she added, 'I don't see how you can leave within a month. Surely there's too much to do?'

'We've only just signed the contracts,' Methuen responded, 'but while Mum and I were chewing it over, we made all the necessary preparations, so we could meet Allied's deadlines if we decided to go.'

Bliss folded her arms and shook her head again. 'You're just digging yourself in deeper, Dad. If you went to all that trouble, it meant you've been seriously considering it for some time, in which case my question still stands: Why are you telling me this now? Why didn't you let me know during the year?'

'Dad had decided to make the move, but I hadn't,' Elizabeth interjected, pointing at her chest.

'But you've taken a huge decision without even consulting me!' Bliss yelled back at her.

'I understand this comes as a bit of a shock,' Elizabeth said, holding up her hands and speaking more slowly. 'What I suggest is that you talk it over with Jack and Martin in the pub and then we can all discuss it over lunch.'

'Sounds like there's nothing to discuss,' Bliss said, standing up and ramming the chair under the table just as the housebot reappeared.

'Ex-cuse me. There is a smell com-ing from the ov-en that I do not re-cog-nise. What should I do?'

'What? Why did you ever think of supplementing Mrs Rawlins with this circuit board on wheels?' Elizabeth shouted, and turning to the bot said, 'Just switch the bloody thing off!'

'Elizabeth, patience, please, it just needs training. If you get angry, it'll revert to its low-risk performance algorithm, and then it'll be no use to anyone.' Methuen pulled himself up from his chair, rolled up his sleeves again and followed the bot out of the room.

Bliss leant on the back of the chair and said, 'You sure about this, Mum? Cooped up on an island with Dad and a crowd of strangers. No conferences or clinic openings to get away to. I've seen you at work – you're a different person there …' She paused as she saw her mother stare back attentively. 'You need your anonymity.'

'I don't know what you mean.'

'Yes, you do!' Bliss replied sharply, inducing another silence, before she asked, more calmly, 'and what'll happen to Soft Rush?'

Elizabeth walked over to the table, pulled out a chair and invited Bliss to take a seat. 'We've already made arrangements to close the Visitor Centre – we definitely told you that. As for the estate, Grandma and Grandpa will take care of things until we return – they can't go back to Marseilles with the situation as it is over there.'

Pulling out a dining room chair and sitting back down across from her mother, Bliss said, 'And what do I do? I have to be at Lady Caroline's for the next two terms, initially for the Treatment and then to do this as school president thing.'

Elizabeth smiled and reached across the table and took her daughter's hand. 'We're so proud of what you've achieved. You must see it through. At half-term and during the Easter break you can be here with Grandma and Grandpa. After that something is being arranged this summer so you can join us. You can then decide whether to stay with us on Phillips or come back here to live.'

Methuen appeared at the door, patting Bliss lightly on the shoulder as he returned to his armchair.

Bliss looked at him, shaking her head. 'I still don't get it, Dad. Why d'you need to go halfway around the world to build a self-sufficient community? You've got it, right here.'

Methuen waved an arm towards the window. 'We put all this together for the TV series in the late 2020s and then the roll-out of the SWVRP in the mid-thirties. It's just a collection of survival technologies laid out across the estate for demonstration purposes. On Phillips it'll be for real. We'll be starting from scratch, building a new sustainable community in an isolated location. It's a unique opportunity.'

'But at a time like this to do something so risky, and in the Caribbean of all places. Why not choose a nice safe Scottish island or even the Isle of Wight?'

Not reacting to the angry, sarcastic tone in her voice, Methuen replied earnestly, 'Because it's something we *need* to do at a time like this. The world is not standing still. Segmented Lite, despite all the high hopes we had of it persisting, is now struggling. We have to examine other solutions.'

'It still sounds wacky. What if you run short of food or water, or there's a power failure?'

'Allied has made a big investment in the infrastructure. It's no longer the glorified holiday retreat we showed you pictures of after our return from the Opening in '44.'

'And speaking for myself, Bliss,' Elizabeth interposed, 'all my life I've had to run practices on shoestring budgets. Now I have the chance to try my hand at this new concept – everything provided by Allied ... with the whole community wired up and continuously monitored, whether they're ill or not. It's an exciting challenge, moving from being reactive to proactive in people's healthcare.'

'I think you should be more worried about the other challenge, the one you and Dad are going to face,' Bliss said bluntly. 'Isolated and living together without *your* writing cabin and *your* conferences?' she said, addressing each of them in turn.

Elizabeth and Methuen glanced briefly at one another but before they could answer, a clattering sound could be heard from the kitchen.

'That bloody machine again!' Elizabeth said, charging out of the room.

Bliss came over and sat on the rug next to her father. 'Sorry, Pappa, I shouldn't have said all that, but it seems to me like you're both taking a huge risk and I don't mean the usual survival stuff – if anyone can deal with that, you can. It's just that you and Mum have never lived that closely together before.'

Methuen took his daughter's hand and squeezed it softly. 'Don't worry about us. You're right when you say we do have some things to sort out, but maybe this is the opportunity to do just that.'

Bliss shifted across the floor and leant against the leg of the empty armchair. 'The other thing that worries me is that while I know you won't do anything silly, I'm not so sure about Uncle Nick. His … trickiness is one of the few things Mum and I agree on. Look how he got involved with that lunatic McFall and had to come to the UK to get away from him. You sure this isn't just some kooky experimental thing he's thought up for his own amusement?'

'There's nothing kooky about it, Bliss,' Methuen said firmly, his face straightening. 'I've been working with the Allied team on the Project for the best part of four years now. We'll build slowly towards self-sufficiency with Livings …'

Seeing her frown, he added hurriedly, 'It's the Allied department that will manage all this. They'll always be at the end of a line, backing us up, twenty-four seven.'

'But why are they doing it? That's another thing I don't get. No one could describe Uncle Nick as philanthropic exactly, let alone Allied Answers. You know my views on people like him. He may have been generous towards us, but for me he still qualifies as one of your typical OST-men.'

Methuen waved his finger at his daughter. 'You have to take each person on their own merits. In Nick's case, I recognise the convergence of his interests and mine—'

'What, between an altruistic professor and a global businessman? How does that work?'

'There's actually more that joins us than separates us. Our focus is different, but the subject and scope are similar. We believe that progress can only be possible if we create a world where human spirit and ingenuity are liberated. I pursue it for its own sake – Nick through his need to ensure the survival of his business. Think of it like this: Allied Answers survives on ideas; that requires a world in which its employees must have the freedom to think and act independently and one where Allied can tap into global talent unencumbered. Doesn't that sound like a world you and I also want? Like all big businesses, Allied know that the Fully Segmented World – which I'm sure you've experienced in the SWVRP – is like a lobotomised brain: it functions just about, but is feeble in comparison to the whole thing working together.'

'Sorry, Dad, you've lost me. How can you possibly stop a world becoming fully segmented by building a community on a remote Caribbean island?'

'We've tried everything else. We made presentations to the Establishment during the 2020s and when that failed, Nick tried the political path, while I built the VR model to inform ordinary folk of the world to come. But the reality is, none of that has significantly changed the way in which people think or live. We did a good job of raising awareness but a lousy one of gaining acceptance. It's time to try something new, and this is it: a living example of how a sustainable community can not only survive but eventually thrive—'

'Sounds like some eighteenth-century Swiss Family Robinson fantasy to me,' Bliss said.

'Far from it. We've carried out a VR simulation which has helped provide a detailed implementation plan. Once we get the community up and running, it can act as a blueprint for others. What else can we do? Rely on this new G5 World Council to find a solution?'

Bliss smiled affectionately at him. 'Always a new idea, never dwelling on past glories – that's what I love about you, Pappa.' She returned to the dining room chair and placed her hands on her knees. 'Come on then, tell me more about it.'

Methuen sat forward, energised by her change in mood. 'The Project requires three things. The first, Allied Livings can already do – that's the construction of a living facility to accommodate the new community on Phillips—'

'Sounds rather grand – why d'you need a new living facility?'

'This is not a short-term project, Bliss. Like many low-lying islands around the world, Phillips will be largely flooded and uninhabitable within fifty years.' Raising his finger he said, 'The second challenge is funding. Allied has managed to secure that, but the consortium involved is unwilling to invest before we achieve the third thing: showing that we can create a harmonious community.'

'And that's what you're being recruited to do?'

'Not just me; there's a team of professionals converging on Phillips right now who will help.'

'This is bizarre. A group of people who I bet are mainly techies like you, all strangers to one another, dropped off on a remote tropical island, living in an environment that probably none of you have experienced before and given five years to build a community. You're a civil, not human engineer, Dad.'

'My career may have started like that, but everything I've done in the past few years has been about helping communities achieve self-sufficiency. Now I have the chance to put it into practice on a large scale. Can you see how exciting that is for me?'

'But it's a huge step to go from advising to doing, and besides, what does a high-tech organisation like Allied know about building a community?'

'That started many years ago when Livings were fabricating private retreats for the wealthy. They found their clients were asking as much about "how they could live together" as "what they were going to live in". So when the Allied main board sanctioned a change in the Livings role, allowing the Phillips Project to go ahead, they also changed the organisation. One day there were floors of engineers and technocrats designing physical things, and the next, there were psychologists, neuroscientists and people from our AI department sitting alongside them, all tasked to create what we call the Phillips Community Plan.'

'I hope those AI experts create something more like Mildred in the SWVRP than that useless housebot we have here,' Elizabeth grumbled as she returned to her seat by the fire.

'You've not yet seen any of the new AI products,' Methuen replied undeterred. 'They're our secret weapon, something the Swiss Family Robinson never had. Intelligent aids will be helping with every part of the Plan, including all the laborious stuff, like reporting back to investors.'

'What happens once you've finished your calibration and the Community Plan has been implemented?' Bliss asked.

'Once we've demonstrated to the investors that we have a sustainable and happy community—'

'Woah! Wait a minute,' Bliss said, holding up her hand, 'sustainable I can understand, but happy? How will you measure that?'

'No community is sustainable unless people want to stay there. For that to happen, they must address the question that many of us have been asking ourselves over the past few decades: "Am I better off here than elsewhere?" For better off, read relatively happy.'

'Hmm. That sets the bar rather low, doesn't it?'

'It will change as we implement the Plan—'

'And that'll take more than a few months,' Elizabeth chipped in.

'So for five years you're going to be like animals in a zoo, visited and probed by people trying to decide whether you're a viable investment or not?'

Elizabeth tut-tutted loudly. 'You know us better than that, Bliss. If increasing the profits of Allied was the main purpose of all this, neither of us would be going.'

Methuen rubbed his face and ran his hands through his hair. 'I've done everything I can to try and show people how living more cooperatively benefits them, but nothing has worked. This is my last attempt.'

Bliss looked kindly towards her father, whose face had reddened again. 'Something still nagging away, huh …?'

Both Elizabeth and Methuen stared back in silence, leading Bliss to add, 'It's a sort of guilt you carry, Dad – a deep feeling that you should have done more about the Irreversible Numbers and

Inevitable Consequences. I say, just let go of it. You did your best to alert the world of what was to come—'

The sound of the front door opening caused everyone to look up as a voice called out, 'Issy, Issy, it's now or never if you're going to the pub with Jack and me.'

Buttoning her coat, Bliss turned to her parents. 'Why don't you come with us and talk about it?'

'I agree with your mother – it's best you speak with your brothers first,' Methuen said, as cold air from the open door surged into the room.

'Besides, I would rather cosy up in the warmth than brave the elements right now,' Elizabeth added, warming her hands at the fire.

'There you are,' Bliss snapped back, picking up a pair of gloves. 'That's what you should *really* be doing – staying at home rather than venturing outside.'

* * *

Virtual Scene snapshot: Elizabeth is untying the strings of her apron as she returns from the kitchen, while Methuen pokes at the sim-coals in the fireplace.

'It still gets to you, doesn't it?' she said, lifting her head towards him.

'What?'

'Anyone who triggers the fear that you should have done more.'

Methuen poked the fire again. 'Remember how we once talked about our personal gods?'

'Sure – when we first met.'

'Yours was something like "to help those suffering to help themselves". And that's precisely what you've done. I've always admired you for that. But my big life purpose changed. Do you remember what I originally told you mine was?'

'*Knowing Why* – aimed at completing your model, I seem to recall.'

'But over the years it came closer to yours – more like *Knowing How*. It was the impact of the Full Segmentation scenario in the VR reconstructions that did it. I began to get these apocalyptic pictures in my head and even sometimes in my dreams, of a vast chorus of wailing voices calling out for help as they slipped into a hellish abyss.'

'It gave you nightmares?' Elizabeth said, sounding concerned.

'It did at first. I used to wake up with a sense that everything I took for granted, everything that defined who I was, was under threat.'

'Oh, how horrid. You've never told me that before. Have you discussed it with anyone?'

'No one – other than Nick, who told me he had a similar response to the Fully Segmented scenario, although for him, it usually focused on something going catastrophically wrong for Allied.'

'Typical,' Elizabeth said with a dismissive laugh.

'Umm ... but without Nick experiencing the Fully Segmented World, this new idea of creating a template for sustainable living would never have come to life. It's the boldest thing he's ever done, with none of the strategic hedging of the 2020s. This time it's all or nothing for him.'

'But with business coming before any concern for people, just as Bliss said.'

'No, it's more subtle than that. He's developed an empathy for the future, as have I, including the fate of those around us.' He poked at the fire and then, looking up, asked, 'Do you think Bliss has bought into what we're about to do?'

'Us leaving? Yes. But as for her joining us?' Elizabeth shrugged. 'Who knows what she'll choose to do after the Treatment. That reminds me, did you see the response from the LCS medical director to our questions?'

'I'm sorry, I've not read anything since the explosions. Why didn't he send it through the Internet to my AA-Plant address?'

'Methuen, no professional body uses the public Internet these days, and we don't advertise the fact that we're on the AA-Com network. Let me get it,' she said, walking over to a small bureau.

Returning to her seat, she opened a file and handed him the letter.

The Medical Director
The Lady Caroline Biomedical Centre, Herefordshire
Central West Governorate, UK

Dr Elizabeth Pryce and Professor Methuen Pryce
Soft Rush, Sandy Hollow
Southern Governorate, UK

SUBJECT: Intervention Treatment for Bliss Pryce
Date: 18 December 2049

Dear Dr and Professor Pryce,
Thank you for your questions regarding the forthcoming Intervention Treatment that your daughter will undergo in the New Year.

As you know, I am bound by confidentiality with regards to all my patients, but in your case, I have a waiver form signed by Bliss that allows me to respond to your queries in a little more detail than usually would be the case.

Is the Treatment safe?
About 50 per cent of all applicants for IT are rejected. This is mainly due to age (not applicable at LCS, of course) or physical abnormalities, such as incipient tumours and/or 'below-threshold' neural pathways. Psychological disturbances may also influence the decision. I'm pleased to say that in Bliss's case, we found no physical or mental reasons for not offering her the Treatment.

<u>Is the outcome of the Treatment predictable?</u>

Worldwide, almost one million Standard Interventions have been completed. The outcome from these is shared anonymously by all the private companies involved. For each personality type, there is what we call a 'high-probability development path'. (Please note that all my comments refer to the Standard Treatment. More advanced treatments are now being offered on the Market, but we do not currently undertake these at LCS.)

<u>If so, what is the predicted outcome and timing for Bliss?</u>

Bliss is twenty years old. We would have expected her to reach mental maturity by her thirtieth year. We now expect that to be achieved by the time she is twenty-five, or a few years earlier even. As a minimum, the Standard Treatment will do no more than accelerate the communication between the various sectors of the brain responsible for her main personal functions. She has a well-developed dominant Introverted Feeling function, balanced by auxiliary Extrovert Sensing. For her age, she has above-average development of her third function – Introverted Intuitive – and despite it being her weakest, there are signs of her Inferior Extroverted Thinking mode beginning to develop positively. From the detailed PPIS (Personal Pre-Intervention Survey), the development of these later functions (which are still at an early stage) appears to have been induced by experiences within her family and educational environment. This provides an excellent platform for the rapid, post-Treatment development of these two less well-developed qualities.

<u>How will the Treatment change her behaviour?</u>

The Treatment is not about changing behaviour. It is a physical process that accelerates the natural growth of her brain. How the individual chooses to use this accelerated ability (in particular, with reference to how they behave) will be determined, in our

experience, largely by environmental factors. The Social Adjustment Programme, which Bliss will undertake for three months
after the Treatment, will be tailored to her specific requirements.
In Bliss's case, helping her with her two less-developed qualities:
her intuition and rational thinking.

Are there any side effects or unexplained outcomes arising from the Treatment?

Customer satisfaction surveys, which are independently
conducted throughout the life of the participants (and securely
stored on our central computer), show a high degree of satisfaction since we began the Treatment five years ago. The only
side effect, if you may call it that, is occasionally unexpected
enhanced abilities. We are currently conducting an extensive
research programme to improve our understanding of this.
We have recorded no significant negative physical symptoms.
Indeed, there are many examples of customers expressing their
delight in finding new skills, both mental and physical: greater
sociability, intellectual acumen and artistic endeavour, to name
but a few. These seem to relate to previously suppressed
(unconscious) personal functions that have found positive
conscious expression in the lives of the individuals involved.

I hope these answers have reassured you regarding the
significant investment you have made in providing Bliss with
this Treatment.

The Treatment forms part of a more comprehensive
programme at LCS which aims to create the next generation of
women who will play their role in shaping the world ahead.

'Oh, he's added a note about after-effects at the bottom of the
page,' Elizabeth said, as she took the letter from Methuen. '"We
have found that for clients with a strong intuitive score (i.e. as their
first or second functions), the Treatment can on rare occasions have

more unpredictable effects",' she read. '"This is highly unlikely to affect Bliss since, as I have already mentioned, her intuition is located in the third function."'

'Well, you understand all that better than I do,' Methuen said, staring into the fire. 'Whether it accelerates or enhances her abilities, is it worth the risk of losing the sensitive and artistic soul we have nurtured all these years?'

'Why is it that it's the men in my life who object to this Treatment for Bliss?'

'That's not true. Martin has put his name down for the new beta trial, and if you're referring to Jack, you can hardly expect our conservative elder son to agree to anything of this nature.'

'I wasn't thinking of the children; I was referring to Nick. Lianne tells me he's now having second thoughts, not over the cost or the Treatment per se, but how it may change Bliss. She may mistrust him, but she's managed to work her way into his sympathies over the years – as she has yours.'

'Nick has seen what I've seen, and perhaps also what the school has spotted—'

'Which is?'

'One minute, she's spontaneous and responding to everything around her; the next, she's rigorously defending some principle or moral position. That's something that's enthused him as much as it's amused Lianne. I don't want to lose that and neither should you.'

'She's already changing,' Elizabeth said. 'What you're describing is the Bliss of several years back. Didn't you notice how she's not met up with her old art school crowd this holiday as she's done every year since starting there? Lady Caroline's has had a big effect on her. I even popped into her room a few days ago and found it tidy! I didn't do it and nor did Mrs Rawlins. Our beloved daughter seems to have already become more self-contained and, dare I say, more logical.'

'Isn't that just the way she behaves when she's stressed?'

'No! It's what being at Lady Caroline's has brought out in her. She's gone from wacky art student to school president of that privileged set in a mere two years – it's quite remarkable.'

'I'm not going to celebrate any transformation that replaces spontaneity with tidiness,' Methuen huffed.

'You forget how out of place she was when she first went to LCS. The principal questioned whether she should even return for a second term, let alone be accepted onto the Treatment course. Whatever that medical director said, if the principal doesn't think a student is socially suitable – whatever that means – then she wouldn't be offered the Treatment.'

'Hmm! If I celebrate anything, it's this insidious place accepting someone who may ultimately challenge the morality of selling cognitive advantage like a commodity.' Scanning the letter, he asked, 'Why does this state-of-the-art medical centre still use old personality terminology? What about this new neuro-genetic approach?'

'The two systems actually have quite a lot of compatibility, just that at present, the old method is what most professionals are still most familiar with.'

Waving the letter at her, Methuen said, 'So what's your professional conclusion, Doctor Pryce?'

'It's not my field, but from what the director said, her intuitive self is still in its infancy, so the best that can happen, I suppose, immediately post-Treatment will be an acceleration of her normal development without any of this enhancement that his note referred to. But having said that, if the director's predictions are correct, we may gradually see some evidence of the rational and intuitive side begin to emerge.'

'Still sounds as if we're going to lose our buoyant flute-playing little girl.'

'That's another thing to let go of Methuen – she is no longer your "little girl".'

Ignoring the note of irritation in her reply, Methuen asked, 'What about the boys? Think they'd consider coming with us?'

'Martin and Beth have their careers and the kids' education to consider. They want to get out of London, but moving abroad now ... I doubt it.'

'And Jack?'

'You know the answer to that – he'd view leaving the UK as an act of betrayal to that commune or whatever it is he's helped to set up in Kirkwood.'

'It's not a commune; it's a formal council set in a garrison town – the walls of the place ooze independence and self-sufficiency. He must carry on with that. I'm so proud of what he's trying to do there.'

Both stared briefly into the fire until Elizabeth got up and set off towards the kitchen. 'So that's it then,' she said, turning back to him. 'We're on our own.'

'Together,' Methuen called out cheerily, but as she left the room, he heard her say, as if to herself, 'I hope so.'

Inside the red-painted barn;
Hardin, Montana, NCSA, FSA

18.45 hours, 15 June 2050

'Is that it? I thought you said there was continuous recording for all the post-'48 material?'

'There are hundreds of records from Methuen's AVIII in Soft Rush, but not that many that the Storymaker has turned into scenes as yet. The ones I've viewed are mainly Methuen and Elizabeth reminiscing in front of the fire.'

'About what?'

'Things that happened to them after they returned to the UK in '26 – stuff that's only interesting if you were part of it.'

'Such as?'

'Oh, the story of how they found a rundown property in Southern England and converted it into what became the famous self-sufficient estate of Soft Rush. Then there's a whole load of stuff on Methuen's short-lived media career – you must remember that public bust-up he had. It was another YouTube moment for him, though one, I guess, he prefers to forget.'

'Can you find that?'

Nick ran through the current scene and then stopped at the opening frames of a new section. 'I've been through this before. It starts with Methuen and Elizabeth reminiscing – with a pile of his diaries on a table between them—'

'Didn't he have one of those Memory Monitors?'

Nick laughed as he displayed a snapshot of a scene and turned to Lianne. '"Lazy man's diary", is what he calls that device. Here they are talking about entries from his 2029 tome – you can see it bulging at the seams. They've been renovating Soft Rush for three years, Methuen's started teaching at the university, and Elizabeth is setting up the NCC equivalent in the UK. Shall we immerse?' he asked, but as he turned around, he saw her with glasses on, waving her hand, impatient for him to start.

AA-Com File:
'Something still nagging away ...' *(contd)*

Soft Rush Estate, Sandy Hollow,
Southern Governorate, UK
Early afternoon, 1 January 2050

Virtual Scene snapshot: Methuen and Elizabeth are seated around the open fire. A pile of diaries lies on a side table, several with the spines torn or missing.

'There was so much going on ...' Elizabeth said, taking a lime-coloured volume and flicking through the pages. 'That was the year your fledgling media career in the UK came crashing down. I was upset about that. You'd started to attract a huge audience – particularly among the young.'

'Hmm. They were drawn as much by my American twang and that new wardrobe of clothes you bought me,' Methuen smirked.

'Oh, stop being so boringly modest. You were someone people trusted, while your book provided them with a comprehensive guide for living sustainably.'

'But the more the public warmed to me, the more that mainstream politicians regarded me as a threat – and treated me accordingly.'

'Because none of them could pin you down – you were pro-Market but supported limits on wealth accumulation; you believed in the importance of individuals but argued strongly for community participation. Then there was the fracas with the retail finance people, when you told that university audience to ... What was it?'

'Invest in land rather than waste their money on pension products that will never pay out,' he mused. 'But it all ended as quickly as it had begun – because of that cock-up with the microphone,' Methuen retorted with a light sneer.

'It was a pity because that day you were winning the argument, especially when that old fart of an ex-Chancellor began accusing you of fear-mongering.'

'It wasn't him that stirred me up,' Methuen replied sharply, 'it was that interviewer, cutting me dead and letting the politician ramble on, talking about "bright uplands that lie ahead ..." and other such sanctimonious claptrap.'

'Now where's that entry, I wonder?' she asked, thumbing through the tattered volume. 'Here it is!' she exclaimed with a smile, balancing the diary on her lap and sitting upright. '"I know you modern types see people like me as Luddites,"' she read out in a pompous voice, '"but I'm proud of that name if it means that I'm upholding our noble traditions and well-earned way of life." Remember what you said in reply?'

Grinning at her impersonation, Methuen nodded for her to continue.

'"There is no worthy comparison between the Luddites and individuals such as yourself. They were honourable people fighting for their survival, compared with your squalid efforts at self-promotion,"' she read, now mimicking Methuen's deeper voice. 'I remember the audience rising to applaud you as the credits rolled, and then falling silent as they heard you tear into the interviewer, accusing the network of bias and colluding with ... What was it you called that guy?'

She looked down the page to find the quote, but Methuen chipped in. 'Publicity Pervert. The idiot was still denying the reality of human-induced climate change, even in '29 – simply to draw attention to himself. It was only the reaction of the audience that alerted me to the fact that a microphone remained switched on and my comments had been transmitted far and wide.'

'We all cheered your outburst, and most people I spoke to at the clinic the next day congratulated me on your boldness. Except that the network took a different view, of course ...'

'It was of no consequence – it was high time to change.'

'You were upset though. It was the first and last time I have ever known you to call in sick. You were away from work for more than a week, spending the whole of that time in your writing cabin.'

'When you describe it like that, it sounds as if I was running away – but I wasn't.'

Elizabeth raised a quizzical eyebrow. 'Umm, there was an element of that, Methuen Pryce – your daughter has a similar tendency to prefer solitude when things aren't right for her.'

'For a day maybe, but for the rest of the time, there was only one thought in my mind: what can I do to prepare ordinary people for the Segmented World? I don't recall if I mentioned it to you, but around that time, I had several lengthy discussions with the woman from the Foundation—'

'Ah, the enigmatic Clapping Lady,' Elizabeth said a little testily.

'She was the first person I talked to about the idea of representing the Segmented World in virtual terms.'

'Hah! I always thought that was me. I suppose she was gushingly supportive as usual?'

'She was curious,' Methuen said thoughtfully, 'and interested enough to finance the construction of the VR shed as well as all the new optic cabling.'

'How little I knew of what you were up to – I thought Nick had funded that. At the time, it seemed like a barmy idea, taking something from the entertainment sector and using it to inform people about the future.'

Methuen took back the diary and began searching through it. '2029 was as much your year as it was mine. Bliss was born in the July and by November, you were already launching your first community clinic in the UK – I have it right here.'

Elizabeth sat back in the chair, warming her feet on the fire. 'It was no big deal. I'd done it before – travelling up and down the country, opening clinics. It's just that in the UK I had the added joy of the Unions protesting outside, saying it would undermine the NHS, when what they actually meant was that it would undermine their power base. How dare they, I thought – but it was an important detail that I mismanaged, allowing them to cause a lot of damage.' She looked over at him and laughed. 'That was when you picked up the apron again.'

Methuen hunched his shoulders. 'It suited me. After Covid, most of my university classes were online, and with the new comms installed, I was able to start developing the SWVRP.'

Inside the red-painted barn;
Hardin, Montana, NCSA, FSA
19.10 hours, 15 June 2050

Lianne sat up. 'Why did you stop?'

'Oh, the rest is a bit tedious: Allied taking over the SWVRP in '33, and Methuen signing a consultancy agreement to help develop it with my AI people,' Nick said offhandedly.

'Is there a scene dealing with the Phillips Cay Opening in '44? Methuen and Elizabeth weren't happy with you after that, were they?'

'There's nothing, I'm afraid. We had a media ban in operation because of McFall being present.'

'Maybe you should reconstruct it in the future with input from Methuen and Elizabeth – you came pretty close to losing them back then, insisting that they mix with all those hideous McFauns.'

'It was a tricky situation. But using it as a hospitality centre for someone high profile like McFall allowed me to draw attention away from what I was really up to on Phillips.'

'But you got Methuen back on board after explaining about the new project and putting him at the centre of creating the Phillips Community Plan in '48.'

'Did you know that he quit his university job before telling Elizabeth?' Nick said, sounding impressed.

'No wonder she resisted your next big proposal, at the end of that year, for them to travel to Phillips and for him to lead the project in 2050.'

'Yeah ... That delay created a lot of problems for me. I even started to recruit a new team just in case he didn't accept the job.'

'But it all came good at the meeting you had with him in that restaurant near the Liverpool Street-Moorgate exchange in December?'

'The meeting when the bomb went off,' Nick replied grimly.

Lianne turned her head towards him. 'As you would both have been wearing the new AA-Plants by then, the whole event should be recorded and may have been made into a new scene or section on that file?'

Nick slid to the end of the bed and typed a command into the keyboard. 'That's in a different scene – I need to flick through this until I see ... yes, here it is. Yeats.'

'What?'

'Don't you remember that compilation of Yeats's poetry Methuen gave me?'

'Oh yes. I thought for a moment it might soften you up a bit, but then you picked out all the gloomy passages.'

'Here it is,' he said, pulling down his glasses.

AA-Com File:
'The centre cannot hold ...'

Restaurant, Liverpool Street-Moorgate Exchange, City Engatement, London Governorate, UK
Lunchtime, 18 December 2049

Virtual Scene snapshot: In a restaurant full of diners, Nick, dressed in a dark suit and carrying a small briefcase, is making his way around the tables to Methuen who is seated in the far corner, also wearing a suit.

As Nick sat down, he pulled out two documents from his bag and placed them on the table.

'Here are the contracts,' he said good-humouredly, holding out a pen. 'Let's get this over with quickly so we have plenty of time to sample the excellent house white they serve here.'

Methuen lifted a hand up towards Nick and with the other, reached into his jacket pocket, pulling out a sheet of paper with handwriting on one side.

Nick looked at him in surprise before bursting into laughter. 'Oh, I know what this is – Lizzie's questions that you mentioned a few weeks ago.' Then, like a schoolchild waiting to be interviewed, he placed his hands on his lap and looked up, his eyebrows slightly raised.

Methuen took the pen from the table and read slowly as he deciphered his wife's scrawl.

'Will the journey to Phillips Cay be direct?'

'Yes, it'll take about two weeks,' Nick replied plainly.

'Will the crossing be safe?'

Nick frowned. 'How do I answer a question like that? I can't give any cast-iron guarantees these days.'

Methuen offered no help and remained silent, waiting to record the answer.

'Okay, you can write down: "I've taken all possible measures to ensure we can deal with any threats we encounter on the high seas." How's that?'

'Will there be a proper handover?'

'Yes,' Nick said, his voice wilting slightly. 'We will help you settle in.'

'Please confirm that Methuen will lead the new community and I will be given full authority to run all medical services on Phillips.'

Nick pointed to the documents on the table and, looking over Methuen's shoulder, said, 'It's all covered in these things called contracts, Elizabeth.'

'Can you confirm the verbal offer you made me to provide return passage to and from Phillips Cay for the children and other close relatives of the community this summer?'

'I'll do my best – no, scratch that. Yes, I will make the *Clipper* available, Elizabeth,' he said, just as the waiter came over to pour the wine.

Methuen placed the piece of paper back in his pocket, picked up the two contracts and signed them. Raising the glass in front of him, he said, 'This may be the most crack-brained idea you've ever had, but it might just also be your best.'

'I can assure you that it is,' Nick replied as the two glasses clinked.

* * *

Virtual Scene snapshot: An hour on. Methuen and Nick sit in deep conversation – two empty bottles turned over in the wine bucket beside them.

As they talked, a dull thud shook the restaurant, shocking years of dust into linear clouds along the ceiling mouldings and causing a decorative plate in a small alcove to smash to the floor. The diners leapt to their feet en masse, as if they too had been sprung into the air.

'Please don't panic. You're safe here. No need to hurry,' the maître d' called out.

Like the other guests, though, Methuen and Nick took no notice and joined the queue at the cloakroom counter. As they grabbed their coats, another explosion sounded somewhere over-head, rattling through the restaurant even more violently, knock-ing glasses off the tables.

'As if I needed any more reason to leave this country,' Nick said, jostling his way up the stairs to the exit. 'I just hope we can get home in one piece.'

On the narrow side streets above, people were fleeing from the station as the police started to cordon off the area. Separated from his usual collection of securobots and his AA-Plant buzzing with interference, Nick, unfamiliar with the geography of the City, followed Methuen as he headed south.

* * *

Virtual Scene snapshot: At the end of Lancaster Place, Methuen and Nick – both slightly out of breath – are sitting on a bench overlooking the river as people rush past.

With the sound of sirens filling the air, Methuen said, 'You need to walk along the Embankment to the Westminster Engatement. I'm going to cross the bridge to Waterloo.' He rose to leave, but then realised Nick had remained seated.

'Do you recall the first time we met in that same restaurant?' Nick asked thoughtfully. 'We talked about McFall and what it meant for the future of the US.'

Methuen sat back down. 'Sure, I remember you saying you thought he was a good guy at first but then realised he was just

… what was it, "another neatly suited psychopath trying to seize power to satisfy his own inadequacies".'

'While you quoted a passage from Yeats: "The best lack all conviction, while the worst are full of passionate intensity." I went back and read that poem again – the first stanza seems so relevant now.'

Waving his finger in time with each word, Nick slowly recited the lines. '"Turning and turning in the widening gyre. The falcon cannot hear the falconer; Things fall apart; the centre cannot hold; Mere anarchy is loosened upon the world."'

'It's not that bad,' Methuen said, tapping him on the shoulder and standing up. 'Let's get Phillips Cay working so we can show others how a self-supporting community can hold things together … and sustain order over chaos.'

Inside the red-painted barn;
Hardin, Montana, NCSA, FSA

19.55 hours, 15 June 2050

'He's an interesting man, Methuen,' Lianne said, lying with her VR frames balanced on her chest. 'You might have expected someone with such a stark vision of the future to be full of cynicism and negativity, but as I stood there in the restaurant I found myself cheered by his enthusiasm – even when the bomb went off. He gave me a sense of hope, though I'm none too sure why.'

Nick made no reply, allowing the birdsong to swell around them. Eventually he said, 'He thinks long and gets you into the same frame of mind. He doesn't expect quick fixes and sees both success and failure as learning exercises. Look how he bounced back after the tour, creating the SWVRP.'

'But none of it, including everything you tried, has been able to stop the Segmented World from establishing itself.'

'Neither of us set that as a goal. Even in the late '10s, it was clear to a growing number of people that an ever more connected world was creating as many new problems as it was solving old ones. But until Methuen came up with this model, we didn't have a framework for thinking about any alternative. Once we had that, our next goal was to inform people of what was to come, in the hope that this would stop the worse scenario – Full Segmentation – from forming.'

'But that's hardly the current plan, is it, Nick? I know you talk about Phillips as a template for sustainable living that others can follow, but many people will see the project as an example of privileged people running away. Wasn't that what the broadcaster implied, in that global interview Methuen gave before Christmas? Do you have a VR record of that?'

'Actually, it was the morning of the day of the explosion – that's why we were both in suits at the restaurant. It's on a different file. Let me see if I can find it.' Nick looked up and highlighted a title on the ceiling screen.

In Discussion
The Segmented World Revisited
An Interview with Professor Methuen Pryce

'There's a legal note attached to it. "This is a syndicated production by the EUCON Broadcasting Corporation. Copyright protected. Not for unlicensed transmission,"' he read. 'That's why this scene is separate, but we can ignore all that. I watched the podcast and it regurgitates a lot of things we've already viewed. The "running away" comment you referred to came towards the end, when that snooty interviewer – the one who always winds me up – tried to trap Methuen … Ah, here it is.'

AA-Com File: The Interview

**Conway Hall, Holborn Engatement,
London Governorate, UK**

09.30 hours, 18 December 2049

Virtual Scene snapshot: Methuen is seated on a wooden stage opposite a tall slender man, who is wearing a grey suit, beneath which can be seen a brightly coloured waistcoat. Sitting under the stage lights and surrounded by cameras, the two men look out onto a packed auditorium, with many standing at the back and some spreading down along the aisles.

'What then of the future, Professor Pryce?' the interviewer asked. 'Where is this Segmenting World taking us? Are we slipping into a new Dark Age or do you have hope for a more positive direction – a new Enlightenment perhaps?'

Methuen stared upwards, beyond the penetrating stare of his inquisitor. 'The political process of segmentation into Power-blocks, StaticLands and Resource Conflict Zones was always unstoppable. The only question was how far it would go? Our current modelling shows a number of likely outcomes, familiar to all those who subscribe to the SWVRP.' He paused and looked to the front row, where, flanked by two minders, Nick sat expressionless and avoiding eye contact.

'In the Segmented Lite outcome,' Methuen continued, 'the Powerblocks continue trading with one another, albeit selectively; and there remains a semblance of the old world, acting globally. But let's be clear, to a large extent this is happening because the new G5 have recognised that cooperation is the only way to deal with issues that have no borders, such as climate change and some of the nastier pandemics we've experienced over the past few decades. These provide the main incentive for current leaders of the superstates to keep on meeting.'

Expecting a question, Methuen glanced over at the interviewer, but instead saw him listening intently. Sitting back, he continued, 'Equally, there are many forces driving each superstate towards greater isolation. The PRC have adopted their New Path philosophy to achieve national sustainability, which has been commendable in its aim but exceedingly harsh in its execution. India is now in a state of internal disarray caused by religious factionalism and military conflict with its neighbours. Then there is Russia, no longer able to control its vast border with China and with its main source of income from oil and gas all but gone. Ironically, this superstate, more than any other, has gone beyond its borders to protect its independence. It has done that not to secure new resources, but primarily to fund diversionary events to raise national unity – such as the long-running proxy war with the US and EUCON in the Middle East Conflict Zone. That action by the Russian State has been the trigger for the transformation of EUCON – in particular the appointment of military figures to the new high command. As for the civil war bubbling in the US – or should I say, the FSA – we've already discussed that—'

'And behind all this, according to the latest edition of your book, is the unseen battle between individuals with an OST mentality and those with a more collaborative approach, such as yourself,' said the interviewer, seizing his moment.

Methuen sat up and rubbed his face, his elbow propped on his other arm, wrapped around his waist. 'Based on modelling criteria – the level of trade, communication between superstates, movement of peoples and so on – we are still some way from Full Segmentation. The desire to increase cooperation and compromise is still present, even in the minds of some of those using authoritarian models to control their populations. That's why there has been no direct confrontation between Powerblocks to date. If it's a choice between pressing the button and talking, jaw-jaw still wins out over war-war—'

'Although there have been nuclear exchanges,' the interviewer cut in, sharply.

'No one has confirmed that yet. But like many, I'm concerned about these new "myriad-headed" systems being tested in the FSA and other superstates, particularly when they are coupled with the argument that because each sub-missile is small and tightly targeted, they are in some way more manageable. This is madness. It just increases the risk of a significant nuclear incident – whether deliberate or accidental.'

'But where is all this going? Where will we be at the turn of the century?'

The camera zoomed in on Methuen's face and showed his eyelids droop at the question.

'I must refer to an old statistic to answer that. If we want to return living standards to, say, the level they were at, around the turn of *this* century, then in a world of ten billion, six, maybe seven billion people would have to disappear.'

The comment provoked a few gasps of concern from the audience and a scraping of chairs as everyone turned to the interviewer, who at first paused and then said, in a graver tone of voice, 'This touches on what you refer to in the latest version of your book as the *Great Adjustment*. You describe scenarios that will either result in a coordinated fall in our global living standards – with little reduction in the global population – or a Malthusian-type adjustment, lowering the population through war, famine, flood and pestilence. The first of these is surely no more than a pipe dream.'

'And the second is a dystopian fantasy,' Methuen quickly responded. 'Populations will protect themselves – living standards have already fallen significantly across the globe. I accept that the upward trend in premature deaths will continue, but mass annihilation ending human dominance – that I doubt very much. No matter how large or small the community, the key to its survival will be finding the right balance between cooperative and individual activity—'

'Your concept of cooperative individualism being the antithesis of OST mentality,' the interviewer surmised.

Methuen nodded in agreement and then said, 'As we know from many examples around the world, the collective side of that concept is not difficult to stimulate and organise *when times are hard*. The majority demand it. What will prove more challenging during such times is to ensure that citizens are able to act and grow under their own volition rather than by diktat. When we lose sight of the importance of the individual, *that's* when we run the risk of the world falling into the new Dark Age to which you alluded.'

The camera turned back to the interviewer, who was holding his hand to his ear and leaning towards Methuen. As he caught sight of himself on the monitor, he straightened up and sat forward. 'Surely this cooperative individualism you advocate means the end of capitalism?'

The camera turned back to Methuen's face, catching his eyes narrowing and his forehead furrowing in response to the question. 'Not at all. Just as we have seen capitalism adjust to the loss of economic growth, so too it is reforming itself to accommodate a more sane and healthy balance between competitive and cooperative behaviour, not least by accounting for the hidden cost of all its actions. Capitalism is not broken, but simply needs a new basis on which to operate. A society built on cooperative individualism and sustainable living offers just that.'

The interviewer turned and gestured towards the front row of the audience. 'We have with us this morning your illustrious collaborator, the CEO and Chairman of Allied Answers Corporation. Perhaps he would like to comment on this matter?'

Nick, looking down, waved the camera away, prompting a smile of bemusement on the face of the interviewer.

'Even the personification of global corporatism, Nick O'Grady, appears uncertain of how to approach this question.' He turned back to Methuen. 'How do you answer those critics who look at your life's work and say that, despite your inventiveness, you remain an academic – a thinker rather than a doer?'

The camera caught Methuen glancing at Nick and then smiling.

'You seem somewhat amused?' the interviewer exclaimed.

'It's not a comment that arouses my amusement, I can assure you,' Methuen replied sharply. 'Since returning from the States over two decades ago, I've spent most of my time working with small communities, explaining practical means by which they may become more self-supporting, both through the SWVRP and in the learning centre on the Soft Rush Estate. I am hardly just a thinker.'

'So despite a possible Malthusian future for the many, you would still stand by your advice,' the interviewer said, as he read from a notebook on his lap, 'that the "Powerblocks and their constituencies must push the authority for day-to-day control, as far down their societies as possible". Does that remain, in your view, a sound strategy for the time ahead?'

'Certainly. If you are to suffer – and I cannot deny that many will suffer in the years to come – then at least you should have the right to be involved in the decisions that will affect you. Whether it's the allocation of foodstuffs, the distribution of medicines, or whose roof in the community is to be mended first, people will cooperate and respond more rationally if they are themselves part of the solution. Fine-scale, centralised planning at a time of hardship is often clumsy in its delivery, open to corruption and ultimately a catalyst for widespread disaffection. It's just not a sustainable model for The Time of Less. That's not to say that autocratic centralised control won't occur. It's already firmly established in three of the Powerblocks and runs the risk of degrading them over time into nothing more than a collection of feudal wasteland states.'

'And is this grassroot devolution you talk about already happening today?' the interviewer asked, coming across as a little more sympathetic.

'Wherever a group of intelligent and honest people join together, it will happen. Here in England, there has never been a time when the parish and local councils – those closest to our communities – have been so active.'

The interviewer turned away from the autocue and read again from the notebook on his lap. 'You recently terminated all of your virtual media accounts – you had one of the largest followings. So is Methuen Pryce about to resettle?'

A smile reappeared on Methuen's face. 'I required three staff to manage my media responses. Now in retirement, I have to watch my budget like everyone else.'

'So you deny the rumours that you're abandoning us?'

Methuen held the smile but this time made no reply.

'Questions?' the interviewer called out to the floor.

Inside the red-painted barn;
Hardin, Montana, NCSA, FSA

20.25 hours, 15 June 2050

Nick pulled off his glasses and rubbed his eyes. 'Well, after that interview, my security people went bananas. We had agreed beforehand that they wouldn't film me, but the TV network was determined to extract something sensational from the event.'

'I wonder if that interviewer also got instructions to lay off the topic of the "Great Adjustment". Did you notice how he didn't pursue it? If that had been me, I would have asked Methuen for chapter and verse on what he thought.'

'That would have been a waste of time. We have little idea how things are going to pan out over the next fifty years,' Nick replied drily.

'But you managed to project forward from the 2020s pretty successfully – why not now, up to the end of the century?'

'Forecasters require well-established trends to project forward – they're not clairvoyants. The Segmented World was a scenario based on fifty years of data-gathering during a period of rising living standards. We are now in the transition. We don't know whether Segmented Lite or Segmented Full will come to dominate – or maybe something else entirely.'

'In that case, what have you based this Phillips Project on – pure speculation?'

'The belief that Methuen referred to in the interview,' Nick said, turning to face her, 'that communities big and small, with a culture built around cooperative individualism will prove the most robust, whatever is to come.'

'And that's what Methuen will be introducing on Phillips?'

'That is the philosophy at the centre of the Plan, yes.'

'But what if some thug decides to attack you? Will Phillips have an army?'

'We have ways of dealing with that.' He sat up and shook his head. 'This conversation is getting too grim. Let me show you something that will amuse you. It's the final section from the scene we dipped into earlier. This is where you make your stunning debut.'

'Oh goody,' Lianne said, lifting her head and fluffing up her pillow.

'After that, I want to get some sleep before hitting the road,' he said, pointing the remote at the screen.

AA-Com File:
'Something still nagging away ...' *(contd)*

Soft Rush Estate, Sandy Hollow,
Southern Governorate, UK
Early evening, 1 January 2050

Virtual Scene snapshot: In front of the sim-fire at Soft Rush, Elizabeth is watching Methuen place his diaries back on the shelf behind him.

'I think we should give Nick and Lianne a call,' Elizabeth said. 'They didn't contact us over Christmas, and I heard this morning that London will remain in lockdown for several weeks while they search for the lunatics who set off those bombs.'

'Providing they didn't stray out of their engatement, they will have been okay, but I agree, let's call them,' Methuen replied, heading for the door.

As they reached the bedroom landing, Elizabeth took a sidestep into the corridor. 'You go ahead,' she said, pointing to a winding staircase. 'I just need to do something quickly.'

At the top of the stairs, Methuen squeezed through a narrow doorway and collapsed down onto a large white leather sofa located in the far corner of an otherwise sparsely furnished attic room. Rubbing his hands to ward off the cold, he reached over and tapped the top of a black pyramid on the table in front of him, and watched as an incandescent green glow enveloped the object.

Strange ... it wasn't the military lorry pulling up in the drive, nor this hideous white leather sofa it delivered that alarmed me; it was unpacking the new AA-Com and finding a pyramid-shaped object. The old black cube had really fixed itself in my psyche over the last two decades. Of course, I quickly forgot all that as soon as I booted it up and we tested out the new environmental function. What was it we first created? Oh yes, a leafy church-yard with a yew tree. And there it was – not just the holographic image all around us but also the damp smell of rotting leaves. What was it Elizabeth said? Oh yes. 'Who needs holidays now we have SENSCOM?' – as she called the new device.

Elizabeth appeared at the door, her hair brushed back and changed into a tight-fitting dress.

'You off somewhere?' he asked light-heartedly.

She sat down beside him squeezing her mouth to even out the freshly applied slick of bright red lipstick. 'I just remembered as we were coming upstairs that the last time we contacted Nick and Lianne on this thing we were dressed in gardening clothes, while they looked as if they were just off to the opera.' She rubbed her hands and reached back to feel the radiator. 'It's freezing up here and I know why: your mechanical friend has switched off the heating. Shall I—?'

With a resigned shake of his head, Methuen pulled himself up. 'Leave it to me; I'll deal with it.' Pointing to the pyramid, he said, 'I've turned it on. Just sit still and let it make the links.'

Still rubbing her hands, Elizabeth sat on the edge of the sofa and moved around in response to instructions coming through her AA-Plant. After several wiggles, a bleep sounded in her head and there, sitting across from her on an identical sofa, was a flickering hologram of Nick.

After a few seconds, the background started to fill in around him, showing a spacious living room and an expanse of windows looking out across London. As the image stabilised, Nick, in jeans and a brilliant white shirt, began to talk.

'Lizzie, this is a treat! Looks like I have you all to myself.'

'That's unnerving. I haven't even called you yet – I was waiting for Methuen to get back.'

'It's a peculiar feature of AVIII we still don't fully understand. For those like us with the new AA exo-cortex implant, once we begin positioning ourselves on the sofa, our AVIIIs seem to recognise one another and send a message to our AA-Plants. Anyway, forget all that technical stuff. How are you? You look sensational as usual. I can't wait to see you in the flesh after all these years.'

'Where's Lianne?'

'In the kitchen. She'll join us when she's ready. Let's enjoy these few moments together,' he said, staring at her with a fixed smile.

'How's it been in London over Christmas?' she asked, gazing around the image of the apartment as more details filled in.

'They've cleared the City; the military is everywhere. We were taken to Hyde Park for a Christmas walk but were unable to get in because of a protest group that has recently occupied Kensington Palace—'

'Protesting about what?'

'Oh, the usual hotchpotch of issues, but I guess the decision by the Park Authority to erect electric fencing and limit access was the final straw. It meant that the usual rent-a-mob were joined by a lot of respectable types from West London. We've decided to limit our activities to walks along the gated parts of the Embankment until we come over to you at the end of the month.'

Methuen returned out of breath and plumped down on the sofa, causing the hologram to dissolve. As it re-formed, Lianne, in running clothes and wearing a bandana, was seen dropping onto the sofa beside Nick, causing the image to break down again. When it stabilised, Nick and Lianne could be heard arguing.

'Just sit still, Lianne – you know how sensitive ... Oh, hi! We're back,' Nick chirped as Lianne repositioned herself on the floor.

'Hi guys, how you doin'?' she said, waving at them. 'I don't see that lovely daughter of yours?' Again the hologram dissolved, but picking up on Lianne's last remark, Methuen's AVIII began projecting around the room 3D images and short clips of Lianne and Bliss together.

'Are your travel arrangements all finalised?' Methuen asked as Nick reappeared.

'There are a few dodgy areas in South London that we'll try to avoid, but if we stick to the main roads, we'll be okay. We intend to leave early to have enough time to see the famous Soft Rush Estate at long last.'

'You're coming without any minders?' Methuen said, sounding concerned.

'We're secure in the SDV; it's fully wired up to my people at Millbank Mirror ...'

The sound and image faded, and as Elizabeth moved around, Methuen tapped her on the shoulder. 'Just wait – it's a power fluctuation. If it persists, the backup will—'

As he spoke, the holograms reappeared.

'There you are,' Nick said. 'I was about to say that your SDV will arrive on the 21st. Don't be alarmed, you don't have to drive it. It's just that the old four-wheel-drive appearance will attract a lot less attention—'

The communication cut off abruptly and a red light appeared at the top of the pyramid, which then changed back to green.

'We seem to be losing you ... Don't forget to pack that AVIII device before you leave,' Nick was heard to say. 'It'll be collected and sent to Phillips after an upgrade, to give you enhanced AVIII capability over there ...'

The light flashed on and then off again, and finally turned a solid red. Methuen went across, switched off the device and then returned to the sofa, where Elizabeth was resting with her head back, eyes closed.

They remained there without speaking for a few moments, the only sound coming from a creaking rafter and a downstairs clock announcing the quarter hour.

'That's it then – we're ready to go,' Methuen said, as the chimes ended.

Elizabeth lay there, still making no response.

'Something wrong?' he asked.

'What did you make of Lianne?'

'Her usual enigmatic self. Showing the friendly and spontaneous, rather than the private and withdrawn version this time.'

'She looks awful – overweight and drinking. Did you see why
she sat on the floor? It was closer to that bottle on the table.'

Methuen sighed. 'Nick seemed tense as well.'

'I read somewhere she missed the deadline for her new book
and there's a dispute with her publisher.'

'So what's going on? I know she enjoys living here – Nick told
me that …'

'Yes. According to Bliss, she's deeply unhappy over returning
to the States.'

'Doesn't augur well for this journey we're about to embark on
together,' Methuen muttered as he laid his head back on the sofa
alongside his wife.

'I was thinking,' Elizabeth said after a few seconds, 'how well
do we really know Nick and Lianne? Well enough to rely on him,
and his business, to support us for five years? In many ways, he's
the antithesis of you. You saw how he controlled the conversation,
even during that short exchange. He didn't ask for our opinions,
he just informed us of what was going to happen. Is that the way
it's going to be on Phillips?'

Methuen stared up at the ceiling. 'I don't mind him setting the
pace like that. I know if, at any time, I raise my hand to comment,
he'll shut down and listen, and not half-heartedly but with an
intensity that sometimes I find quite disturbing. There's a way we
both see the world – it's as much emotional as intellectual. I've
never been able to understand, let alone explain it, but we kind
of … liberate one another.'

'What does that mean for him?' she asked, her eyes still closed.

Methuen hesitated. 'In the early days, he was constrained by
his family's wishes, so I suppose I allowed the "rebel" in him to
express itself.'

'What, like supporting McFall?' She gave a cynical laugh, but hearing no response, added quickly, 'Only joking.'

Methuen continued to stare up at the neatly packed thatch between the rafters. 'He's often turned to me for help over the years in a way that he's not able to do with any of his Allied colleagues. It usually follows a set pattern with him first opening up the conversation while I sit there silently, and when his mono-logue ends, he shuts down and listens to what I have to say. It's built a trust between us that allows me to undertake this journey with the confidence that he will always be there for us.'

'The *oceanic bond* with the brother you would have liked to have had,' Elizabeth reflected, turning to him. 'I just hope it doesn't get in the way of doing things properly on Phillips.'

'I'm sure if it does, you won't hesitate to remind me,' he replied, kissing her on the forehead.

Snowbound on Interstate 25, Colorado Springs, CSA, FSA

01.00 hours, 16 June 2050

Lianne woke as a bell sounded in the bedroom. 'What's that?'

Nick rubbed his eyes and yawned as the monitors on the wall came alive with external images. 'It's something about ... road temperature,' he said, shuffling forward and typing an instruction into the on-board computer.

'Unbelievable,' he gasped. 'It's June, but outside it's reading ten below, and ... there's an ice warning.'

'And it's snowing!' Lianne added, pointing to one of the monitors. 'Did this thing take us north or south?'

Nick didn't respond, his attention having turned to an animated weather map on the ceiling screen. 'We hit this weather while we were asleep. Looks like it started just south of Denver ... Wow, check this out!' he said, pointing to the chart.

'What?'

'It's a breakaway Arctic cell dumping snow – lots of snow – on Colorado Springs.'

'Oh my gosh, this is a desert vehicle – will the tyres cope with that?'

'Don't worry about it – we're going nowhere,' he said, swinging his legs through the slide door and then scrambling up the stairs.

As she leant forward in the bed to study the images of the snowbound landscape, the vehicle shuddered to a halt and from the upper deck, Nick was heard to shout out, 'Snowdrift up ahead!'

Sitting down next to him in the driving cabin, she saw, on the front camera, a line of stationary cars and a man in full protective dress walking through the blizzard towards them, waving his arms.

'What are you going to do?' she asked as the snow began to blow horizontally.

'Leave this to me,' he replied sharply, just as a woman with two small children joined the man.

'Nick, you have to do something,' Lianne cried out, tugging at his nightshirt. 'We can't just ignore them – maybe they've run out of fuel, or the heating system in their car has broken down.' She looked over at him but only saw him focusing on the drone control panel.

'God, you can be a heartless bastard sometimes. All they need is some temporary shelter.'

'And those as well?' he growled back, pointing to a group of people approaching the rear of the vehicle. 'Suppose we invite them all in and a couple of the guys, who are down on their luck, see the opportunity to make a buck by throwing *us* out and taking the van? I'm a fifty-seven-year-old man – fit, but by no means able to defend myself against someone young and desperate. Of course, I'm concerned when I see the kids, but I also care about the hundreds of people waiting for me to connect with them, in the next few days.'

Lianne put her hands over her face to hide the image of the children and was about to make another appeal, when Nick shouted, 'Look at that!', nodding at the rear camera display, where a man could be seen walking towards them carrying a large automatic rifle.

'He's going to fire at us?' Lianne screeched.

'Best of luck with that,' Nick said, unmoved. 'There's more danger to him and the others from the ricochet than there is to us in here.' He pressed several keys on the pad in front of him, causing the vehicle to shake.

'What are you doing now?'

'What I should have done in the barn: making sure no one can get underneath.'

As the vehicle lowered itself, the small crowd now gathered at the front stepped back in surprise.

'I didn't have any drones up, or else I could have got a better view of the surroundings. Ah, there you are, look,' he said, tapping his finger on the rear camera screen to show the family that had first approached the vehicle climbing into a camper van. 'They've found somewhere to go.'

'At least someone showed compassion,' Lianne muttered.

'Because they could. In different circumstances that might be us – being the do-gooder.'

'How do you know those people in the camper van don't also have a great deal to lose?'

'I don't, but that's not my concern,' Nick said, making his way down to the bedroom.

Snowbound on Interstate 25, Colorado Springs, CSA, FSA

07.00 hours, 16 June 2050

In the bedroom, Nick and Lianne were awoken by an intermittent broadcast over the speaker system from a local radio station.

'And after a beautiful day yesterday, severe weather came roaring in last night ... A massive wedge of snow now covers the whole of Colorado Springs, from Pikes Peak to Black Forest and Cimarron Hills ... Interstate 25 in the North East is blanketed by the white stuff, leaving many motorists stranded in their vehicles ... The Central State Association Governor has issued a statement requesting all citizens to remain in their homes for the next twenty-four hours ... The Governor wishes to remind everyone that the State of Emergency called by the government following The Incident on the sixth of April remains in place and—'

A storm of static consumed the transmission. Lianne, rubbing her eyes, nudged Nick. 'Doesn't look as if we're going anywhere for the next few hours,' she said, pointing to the monitor in front of her which showed a white sheet stretching into the distance, broken only occasionally by the tops of vehicles.

'I don't know about you, but I feel a little chilly,' he said, turning to his side and playing with a knob on the wall.

'It woke me up earlier,' Lianne responded. 'That's why I put my dressing gown on. Isn't the air recirculated in this thing?'

'Not all of it – about ten per cent comes in from the outside, de-radiated. The problem is the control system's designed to cope with extreme heat, not extreme cold. Can you pull up that nano-sheet?' he asked, pointing to a wafer-thin covering at the end of the bed.

Lying huddled together with the sheet around their necks, gazing up at the ceiling screen, Nick scrolled down a lengthy set of files and then returned to the top. 'They seem to have downloaded the unexpurgated recordings of the whole journey over to Phillips.'

'What does that mean?'

'It means the Storyteller may have made numerous scenes of me, you, Methuen and Elizabeth in various permutations, chatting, eating and ... well, doing everything. Most of it could be like watching paint dry.'

'Better than watching snow fall,' she said, laughing.

'Let's see if we can begin at the beginning, with us leaving Soft Rush—'

'Whatever,' Lianne said, pulling on her glasses. 'It'll be interesting to compare it with how I remember it.'

AA-Com File: Leaving

Soft Rush Estate, Sandy Hollow, Southern Governorate, UK
Late afternoon, 6 February 2050

Virtual Scene snapshot: Methuen and Elizabeth sit in a mud-splattered jeep at the junction of the Soft Rush drive and the narrow road running through the hamlet. In the doorway of the cottage, Elizabeth's father and stepmother stand with their arms around one another.

'We've experienced a fair few departures over the years, haven't we?' Elizabeth mused, as Methuen peered into the rear-view mirror, looking for the O'Gradys' vehicle to come up from the circular drive. 'There was Jack, sobbing in the quadrangle as we drove away on his first day of school,' she continued, 'and then Martin and Beth telling us, as they boarded the flight to New York, that they weren't just going away on vacation but also getting married.'

'And don't forget the eerie silence in the house after Bliss left for Lady Caroline's,' said Methuen, staring out through the side window.

'But this one's different,' she said wistfully. 'It's us striking out, not them. This time we're the ones filled with youthful anticipation and excitement.'

'And your point?' he asked, waving once more at Elizabeth's father and stepmother.

'No point, just the thought that we're going against the natural order of—'

She fell silent as the sound of crunching gravel signalled the arrival of the other vehicle.

'There's that buzzard that carried off the kitten last autumn,' Methuen said, looking skyward. 'Be here when we return,' he called out – only for Elizabeth's father to mistakenly reply, 'Of course we will. Bon voyage.'

'What we're leaving will never be the same when we return,' Elizabeth reflected as Methuen switched the jeep into self-drive and they moved off.

As the vehicle picked up speed, Methuen turned his attention to a pile of documents on the small table behind them. 'Even less than five years ago even, a trip down to Falmouth would have required no more planning than a drive to Bentham does today,' he said irritably. 'Now look at the amount of preparation we've had to do. There's this Euro-wide Application to Travel that would have taken even longer to obtain, had it not been for Nick fast-tracking it through the Ministry of Defence. Then this weighty information pack, which among other things, recommends that we don't make the journey in new vehicles.' Looking at her, he said, 'That's why Nick and I were up so early this morning, taking the SDVs on a cross-country drive.'

'What's this one?' she asked, unfolding a stamped form with an attached map.

Methuen shook his head, with an exasperated sigh. 'That's the official Travel Pass itemising the route we had to punch into the vehicle's computer. It's ridiculous having to specify precisely where and when we move – all we're wanting to do is travel within our own country.'

'But the country of our childhood is not the country of today,' she said, sitting forward as the vehicle waited to join the main road.

'For sure,' he said, watching carefully as they filtered into the traffic. 'Our nation-state is now no more than a ceremonial concept. We may not yet be fully paid-up members of EUCON, but nothing important happens these days that doesn't go via Brussels or the European Military Alliance in Bonn. The real power, though, lies in these Governorates and their equivalents elsewhere in the EuroState.'

Seeing him sit back and relax as they sped down the road, Elizabeth asked, 'How was Nick when you went on your *bash* this morning?'

'Preoccupied with work and political issues as usual. I tried to persuade him to think of the journey as a holiday, but he just laughed as if I'd said something ludicrous. What about Lianne?'

'It's not the Lianne I've known all these years. She babbled endlessly over breakfast and downed several tablets to cure her hangover from last night's drinking.'

'What's wrong?'

'She's feeling rootless, not to mention suffering from Nick's controlling behaviour when he's anxious. She said she envied us "escaping to Phillips".'

'They'll manage. They're a team – like us.'

'But unlike us, they share no common goal. Lianne's adrift and Nick seems blissfully unaware of it.'

* * *

Virtual Scene snapshot: Three hours have passed. The two vehicles are travelling along a deserted road in the rain, with undulating moorland on either side.

'"Dartmoor Refuge: No-Go Except to Members",' Elizabeth read from a sign attached to a large rusty digger, partly blocking a side road. 'I was beginning to doubt all those media reports about unofficial road checks and bandit groups—'

'We have company,' Nick's voice was heard to say on the overhead speaker. 'It came from the entrance to that refuge.'

Methuen checked the rear camera and saw an old Land Rover, close on the tail of the O'Gradys' vehicle. 'You have a better view of it than I do,' he replied. 'Let me know if it gets too close or any friends come along to join it.'

Glancing nervously at the screen and viewing the country-side around them, Elizabeth pointed to a queue of traffic in the distance. 'What's that? Not more trouble, I hope.'

Both vehicles slowed and as they did so, the Land Rover made an abrupt U-turn and raced back in the direction of the refuge.

'Still doubt those media reports?' Methuen said, peering out of the side window. 'Looks like a case of safety in numbers,' he added as they caught up with a slow-moving train of cars and vans, many with roof racks stacked high with luggage.

* * *

Virtual Scene snapshot: It is late afternoon. The two SDVs are recharging at a pull-in called The Plymouth Breather. Methuen and Elizabeth stand alongside the vehicles, while a shabbily dressed man remonstrates in front of them.

'Get off the road before nightfall!' the man shouted, waving his arms in the air. 'The gangs are everywhere.'

As Nick and Lianne approached, the man wandered off, still voicing his warning to whoever would listen.

'I've seen this before in remote areas of the Midwest,' Nick said as they watched the man disappear off into the dark. 'Parts of Britain seem to be reverting to a similar frontier existence. We should take no risks. Let's ignore the Travel Pass and stay here overnight. We can drive to Falmouth after sunrise.'

'Will it be any better down there?' Elizabeth asked Methuen, as the SDV entered a large metal cage, where others from the convoy were already parked.

'It'll be fine,' he said, extending the seats back for sleeping. 'Nick tells me that the harbour's a pretty prosperous place these days. The South West Governorate did a good job in lobbying Bonn to house the headquarters of the EMA Atlantic Fleet there. It's deep water, with quick access to the sea and a compliant population.

The *Clipper* has been there for months. Nick said the locals seemed happy with the trade-off between restrictions on their movements and the long-term employment that the military provide.'

* * *

Virtual Scene snapshot: It is mid-morning. The two jeeps are parked outside a barbed-wire military gate guarded by two armed men, standing in front of sandbagged patrol boxes.

Elizabeth and Methuen stared at the rear camera as they watched Nick scrawl a set of numbers on a yellow card, fix it on his windscreen and then come forward and, with a brief smile, place an identically marked card on the dashboard of their vehicle.

As the two jeeps approached the gate, the two sentries stepped back and gave sharp salutes as they passed through. Inside, the harbour area more resembled that of a marketplace than a naval facility, with civilians going about their daily lives, noticeably outnumbering military personnel. Methuen and Elizabeth watched anxiously as the jeep crept forward through the crowded streets. After ten minutes of stopping and starting, Elizabeth said in frustration, 'Where's the boat, Methuen? We're about to reach the exit at the other end of the harbour.'

Her assessment was soon confirmed as they passed through another fortified gate, receiving a further formal salute from the guard, before moving into a derelict site where abandoned concrete jetties jutted into the large sea inlet of Carrick Roads. From behind them, the O'Gradys' vehicle swept past, kicking up dust and small stones as it disappeared around a small headland. As they caught up, they saw Nick standing alongside his vehicle, which had parked next to a towering white vessel.

'That can't be the *Allied Clipper*, surely?' Elizabeth said, leaning out of the side window, just as a short stocky man appeared on the gangway, followed by a line of six uniformed youths.

'Methuen, Lizzie,' Nick called over, as they got out of the jeep, 'this is my senior engineer, Marco – he's also the co-builder of this thing,' he said, waving towards the vessel.

As the troop of young men set about unloading the two vehicles Elizabeth turned to Nick and said, 'But this isn't a boat – it's a ... ship!'

'It is pretty big, I agree,' he said proudly. 'We had to widen the channel in Phillips just to get it in.'

'I expected a large motor cruiser, maybe with sails.'

'Oh, it has sails,' Nick responded eagerly, as if her remark were a request. 'All electronically controlled. Once we get the wind behind us, we turn the engines down. It's really a sailing ship,' he said, grinning broadly.

As Methuen helped to unload the jeep, Nick put his hand on Elizabeth's shoulder and said, 'No manual work for you – just relax. Let's enjoy this journey together.'

'Where's Lianne?' Elizabeth asked, ignoring Nick's invitation to follow him up the gangway.

'I'm here,' Lianne called out as she stumbled from the vehicle and then, pointing up at the ship, said, 'This is where he feels most at home – captain of all he surveys.'

Elizabeth walked back to join her, but then turned as she heard Marco gabbling excitedly.

'Mr Nick, this place has gone crazy! You see over there?' he said, pointing to a lookout post on the outer seawall. 'Those guys are fully armed and trigger-happy. I saw them shoot up that, uh ... small yacht that the newspapers reported. Did you hear about that?'

'Sure, sure,' Nick snapped back, flashing his eyebrows and discreetly pointing his thumb in Elizabeth's direction.

'Can you tell us something about the ship?' Methuen asked as he joined them.

Marco threw Nick an anxious glance.

'Yes, of course. Marco, please give Professor and Doctor Pryce the guided tour,' Nick said, turning away from Elizabeth, who glared suspiciously back at him.

As they followed the senior engineer, Lianne hollered out, 'After your little inspection, come up to the control room, and we'll see if we can find some of your English tea.'

At the top of the gangway, Marco turned to Elizabeth and pulled out a brochure from his jacket pocket. 'My, uh … English is still a little difficult, so please read this. All the, uh … safety instructions and the layout are explained in here.'

Several youths passed by, laden with luggage, as Methuen studied the plan of the ship. 'This is a monster,' he said to Elizabeth. 'One hundred and fifty metres in length at the waterline, a maximum breadth of twenty … built on a light reinforced aluminium frame with two turbines … It has clean coal technology but principally runs on LNG … and is capable of sustaining speeds – wow! – of over forty-five knots. Can you include the engine room in the viewing?' he called out to Marco ahead of him.

'I was, uh … only planning to show you the higher decks for now. Quite a few areas are, uh … locked up because we have a lot of crates on board and not all are properly secured yet,' he explained timidly as the doors of a carpeted lift swished open in front of them.

Stepping out into a plushily furnished corridor, Elizabeth took the brochure from Methuen and turning the pages began to read aloud. '"The uppermost deck consists of an open foredeck and a single covered area referred to as the control room, divided at the fore-end by a fully equipped command centre with a seated wheel, a communication booth and a wall-to-wall glass window offering a panoramic bow view—"'

'Where we are now is the shelter deck,' Marco interrupted. 'If you want the control room, we have to go up here,' he said, pointing to a set of uncarpeted metal stairs.

'Okay, let's go!' Elizabeth said excitedly, running up the stairs.

As they entered the room, she stepped back in surprise. 'What a wonderful contrast,' she said, patting the back of one of three sofas surrounding a coffee table – still in its bubble wrap – sitting on a thick Persian rug. 'High-tech meets pub-snug,' she exclaimed, pointing to the array of electronic equipment at the other end of the room.

'I don't know this "snug". Is it, uh … some type of design?'

Elizabeth laughed. 'It doesn't matter,' she said, scanning the rest of the room. 'Oh, is that a dumb waiter in the corner over there?'

Marco, again appearing flummoxed by her question, turned instead to Methuen, who was gazing through the window at the aft end of the room.

'What's that huge black box at the back end of the ship?' he asked.

'Ah, I think Mr Nick must explain that to you,' Marco replied, checking a handheld device and courteously ushering them back into the stairwell.

On the shelter deck, they walked along a wide passageway, with Marco delivering a running commentary. 'This floor occupies three-quarters of the ship's length and has entertainment rooms.' He stopped at an unlabelled black door. 'This is the VR suite – you can get lost in there, for sure,' he said, chuckling at his own attempt at a joke. 'There's also, uh … the business hub, but the outside communications are, uh … a bit of a problem at present,' he mumbled apologetically, before moving them swiftly on to the end of the passage. 'Through here is a large sun deck and pool. You can go anywhere you like on this, uh … level.'

A buzzer sounded from Marco's pocket. He switched it off and leading them down a carpeted staircase, said, 'Let me quickly show you your bedroom and other places where you can relax.'

At the foot of the stairs, they entered an even more sumptuously furnished corridor with small half-tables at regular intervals, on each of which was placed a vase of fresh flowers or some small objet d'art.

'This is the upper deck, which runs the, uh … length of the ship. There's a holographic cinema in that direction – I go there a lot – and another sun deck at the, uh … bow. And here is your bedroom,' he said, just as the buzzer in his pocket rang again.

'I'm so sorry. I must, uh … go. Later, later, you can' – he looked over at Methuen – 'visit other parts of the ship with Mr Nick.'

After he'd disappeared, they remained standing for a few seconds looking around the vast suite of rooms that led out onto an inviting swimming pool with steam rising from the water. Methuen was the first to move, toppling back onto the bed and shouting out, 'This is heaven!'

Elizabeth walked over to the dressing table and began adjusting her hair in the mirror. 'Is it just me or is there something going on here that we're not aware of? Marco seemed reluctant to show us around fully and looked almost relieved when he was called away.'

Methuen lifted himself up on his elbows. 'Umm, I had the same impression. Shall we do a little exploring of our own?'

'Oh yes, do let's,' Elizabeth giggled, unfolding the plan of the ship and heading for the door.

Catching up with her, Methuen pointed ahead. 'When we came out of the stairwell, I saw an emergency door along here – they're always worth testing out if you want to see the innards of a build-ing or even a ship, for that matter.'

Going through a plain metal door, they walked cautiously down a spiral staircase to the floor below. 'This is the main deck,' Elizabeth said, squinting as she studied the plan. 'It just seems to be one long dark passageway, along this side of the ship.'

After walking some distance, the space opened out into a large well-lit room filled with crates and boxes.

'Let's head back and go down another level,' Methuen said. 'The engine room of this thing must be enormous.'

Back on the staircase, they made four spiral turns before coming to a dogleg leading to a side door and another set of stairs. Ignoring the door, they continued down the next flight of steps before reaching a landing that looked out onto a gigantic hall at the centre of which, surrounded by generators and other mechanical equipment, was the jib of a crane that soared past them and out of sight.

Elizabeth tapped Methuen on the shoulder and pointed to the floor below, where something or someone was moving around. 'It's a bit strange, isn't it? I can't smell any engine oil and there's barely any noise. Everything's so clean and organised.'

'That's because I think the whole thing is bot-run,' Methuen said. He pointed to the crane extending above them. 'And that explains the geography of the main deck: the engine room must go up to that level.'

As he lingered on the landing, his gaze still fixed on the crane, Elizabeth said, 'Come on, let's find Lianne and that cup of tea.'

They reached the control room out of breath, having dared one another to race up the stairs, and then cheered with delight as they saw a tray on the table, set with a pot of tea, cups and an uncut cake.

Still breathing heavily, Methuen had just started to pour the tea when Lianne appeared, dressed in a velvet jogging suit, followed some distance behind by Nick.

'What have you two been up to?' Lianne jested, seeing Methuen wipe sweat from his brow with a napkin.

'Inspecting this amazing vessel,' Elizabeth replied, picking up the brochure.

'Well, don't be too impressed – it was cobbled together from bits left over from lots of commissions,' Lianne said, looking at Nick, who had gone over to the communication booth in the far corner.

'So it's a sort of patch-up job – is that what you're saying?' Elizabeth laughed, but then saw Nick beckoning Methuen to join him.

'There's a problem I need to tell you about,' Nick said, causing the women to turn sharply in his direction.

Seeing them staring at him, Nick raised his hands in a calming gesture. 'It's nothing to worry about, we're just a bit short-staffed.'

Methuen looked at him in surprise. 'But in the restaurant before Christmas you were saying what a good bunch you had on board?'

'There were a few disturbances in the harbour that spooked my South-East Asian crew,' he said, rubbing his face and shaking his head in exasperation, 'so ... when a small liner going east offered them work, they all jumped ship and left.'

'All of them?' Elizabeth said, now standing behind Methuen, with Lianne alongside her.

'Yea ... we're just left with the trainees. They'll pick up some of the crew's duties, though their main function is as "operatives" – offering us some protection should we run into any trouble.' Turning to Methuen, he added, 'Don't worry about the staffing – the ship is highly automated and Marco knows how everything works. The only reason I mention it is because we'll have to work shifts up here as lookouts. Nothing strenuous, I assure you.'

Nick walked over to the wheel and leant towards a trumpet-shaped object. Seeing Elizabeth and Methuen looking at him in surprise, he stood up and said, 'It may look a bit old-fashioned but it has some neat amplification technology. Teleplants don't work too well between decks. You'll find these in every room – just press this button, someone will always respond.' He then spoke quietly into the tube next to him, requesting Marco to join them.

Lianne began to cut the cake, explaining that beneath the bubble wrap lay an inlaid table brought from their apartment in London. She then proceeded to go around the room, detailing the provenance of the different items of furniture.

'I try to fool myself that this can be a home from home, but all I end up with is a feeling of being on some enforced vacation.'

Marco appeared and Lianne called out to him, 'Why so many boxes on the main deck? I could hardly find the laundry.'

Nick interjected with a short sarcastic laugh and then said, 'It's your dresses, shoes ... and a few other little items.'

Lianne sat up and stared back at him. 'I've been on this thing so many times and it's always felt like living in an empty barn. But right now it feels more like a floating stationery cabinet, with nowhere to move and all sorts of odd bits sticking out.'

Nick glowered back at her and an uneasy silence filled the room until Marco opened the white cardboard box he'd brought with him.

'Rock buns,' he announced, placing them on a plate. 'The chef managed to bake a trayful before he left.'

'So why did the crew leave?' Elizabeth asked, but Marco appeared not to have heard the question, instead saying merrily, 'Do like me!' as he dipped one of the cakes in his tea.

Elizabeth and Methuen followed his instruction but could not ignore Nick and Lianne, who were now arguing over by the wheel.

'We're leaving with no plans to return. You knew that, Lianne,' he said firmly. 'Everything precious to us I've put on board, just as you instructed.'

Elizabeth lifted up her head and called across to them, 'I wish we could say the same.'

Hearing her response, Marco, who had moved to the communication booth, put his hands to his head and with a loud in-take of breath said, 'Oh, you just remind me – so sorry, so sorry ... We had, uh ... an email from your daughter this morning.'

'Bliss!' Elizabeth cried, rushing over to Marco, joined by Lianne. 'How did you get an email? She's been out of communication for days. We've been worried sick about her.'

'Mr Nick, he diverted all the, uh ... email addresses from your AA-Com account to this one,' Marco replied.

Nick marched over to the communication booth and studied the screen. 'This is an Application to Travel from the Central West Governorate on the eighth of February – that's tomorrow. Bliss is on her way.'

'Wonderful, wonderful, wonderful!' Lianne squealed, grasping Elizabeth's shoulder.

'Anything else you've forgotten to tell us, Marco?' Nick asked sharply.

The engineer stuttered, 'No, except I thought we were, umm … *leaving* tomorrow?'

The two women turned as one towards Nick, who on seeing their reaction held up his hands. 'It's all right, it's all right. We can wait a few days – we're not fully loaded yet.'

As Elizabeth and Lianne talked excitedly, Methuen sidled over to Nick. 'Did you say "not fully loaded"? Seems to me that the ship is bulging at the seams. What are we waiting for?'

Nick rubbed his face. 'I still need clearance from the harbour authorities on a security device we put on the *Clipper* a few days ago.'

'Aren't we beyond their jurisdiction?'

'Unfortunately not. I moored outside the harbour gates so that if something unexpected did happen, they couldn't physically prevent us from leaving. Nevertheless they take a big interest in anything that moves along Carrick Roads,' he said, nodding through the window to the estuary beyond. 'There's no one to oppose them – everyone's becoming a law unto themselves these days.'

'So what's their problem?' Methuen asked.

'A special export licence for some security equipment—'

'Export licence? Why would you need that? Oh … You mean security equipment in the sense of something that could be classed as military?'

'Well, I don't like to think of it in that way. It's more like a defence system in case we get into trouble on our travels,' Nick said casually.

'Was it essential to arm the ship for the journey?'

'It was already armed,' Nick retorted. 'What do you think is under that big black metal box at the rear?' In hushed tones, he added rapidly, 'Pirates are everywhere ... and there are drones of all shapes and sizes – in the air, on the sea and under the water. We can't take any chances when we're out on our own. It's anarchy on the high seas these days.'

Hearing bits of Nick's whispered reply, Elizabeth asked, 'What is this defence system?'

'It's an anti-drone mini-missile launcher,' he said guardedly, and then, seeing her eyes narrow, added quickly, 'It wouldn't have been a problem if it had remained boxed up, but Marco decided to repackage it to save space, unfortunately in full view of the authorities. That's when they asked to see the paperwork.'

'What are the rules of engagement with these "pirates" if we meet them?' Elizabeth asked.

'Rules of engagement ...?' Nick echoed the words disdainfully. 'The rules of engagement on the high seas nowadays are: only approach if you're known to one other, or else ask for identification three times. If there's no response and the vessel is still approaching, either run away or blow them away.'

'But why would they pick on us?' she persisted.

Nick groaned. 'Not only are we unescorted, but we'll be running low in the water. That's a signal to this new buccaneering class that we may just be a prize worth going for.'

'So what's the hold-up here? I thought you had everything planned,' she asked more urgently.

'I got all the licences sorted out in London a few weeks ago and made sure the Governorate had approved them, but the EMA here, won't provide us with the departure flag until they've issued their own special licence.'

'Are they just busy?'

'Nothing to do with that,' he sneered. 'They're like everyone else – desperate to get extra cash wherever they can. They see a large vessel loading with all sorts of provisions, and someone over there ...' he said, pointing to a circular stone tower rising above the centre of the harbour, 'reckons they can make something from it.'

'So what's the plan?' Elizabeth asked anxiously.

'Tomorrow morning, before Bliss arrives, I want you to come with me,' he said, turning to Methuen. 'We need to grovel to several of the EMA naval dignitaries. You can talk about the benefits of the research we're doing, show him some of your credentials – make them feel important.'

'But what if they don't play ball?' Elizabeth asked.

'Well, we have an alternative course of action,' he said, picking up the binoculars beside him and training them on the command post on the outer wall. 'We just have to hope Bliss isn't delayed.'

Elizabeth, now with Lianne at her side, wagged her finger at Nick. 'Unless she's on board, I'm not going. Got it?'

Nick held up his hands and said, 'I will personally go down to the guardroom, file her details and then collect her tomorrow – from wherever she is.'

Elizabeth's shoulders dropped and she said, with a weak smile, 'Thank you, I'd appreciate that.'

As they headed for the stairs, Nick placed his hand lightly around her waist. 'You know how important you and Methuen are to me. I'll make sure everything's okay.'

Elizabeth nodded but then deftly stepped aside, causing his hand to fall away.

Snowbound on Interstate 25, Colorado Springs, CSA, FSA
09.00 hours, 16 June 2050

Lianne removed her glasses and turned towards Nick. 'You just didn't get it, did you?'

'What?' Nick replied impassively, as he focused on images from around the vehicle.

'"To see ourselves as others see us".'

'What does that mean?' he said, turning to face her with a deep frown.

'It's a line from a poem about a louse.'

'Oh that ...' he said, falling back on the bed. 'It was just a bit of fun. Elizabeth can deal with it.'

'And she may do just that ... by getting Methuen involved.'

'I've always been fond of Elizabeth—'

'But that was back then. It's time to change your relationship with her – and also Bliss, for that matter.'

'Why Bliss?'

'You've already heard how she distrusts you.'

'That's to do with the school and all this nonsense about re-educating the super-rich.'

'New situation, new relationship, Grady,' Lianne snapped back. Then, more amiably, she enquired, 'Before we view any more of the journey, do you have any scenes of Bliss at school? I've never worked out what happened there.'

Nick lay back, aiming the remote upwards. 'As I said before, there was something wrong with her teleplant. What it did do, however' – he opened a subfile and scrolled down the contents – 'was pick up the records from that electronic diary she carries around with her. That meant that when she came on board and started to use her teleplant locally, the system saved all her diary entries in the ship's Tool Box, via my AVIII. I flicked through a couple of entries when we were downloading the scenes in Bismarck. There are quite a few gaps, and some of the stuff's a bit goofy, but taken together, they provide an audio account of things that happened to her at Lady Caroline's and also on the journey across to Phillips.

'Did she know it was being recorded?'

Nick shrugged his shoulders. 'Do you want to hear some of this or not?'

Lianne sighed heavily, removing her glasses and straightening her hair. 'Well, I suppose it will be a nice break from VR immersion.'

'I'll pipe it through the monitor as I did with that audio file from Methuen. There's a load of entries all bound together under the title "Lady Caroline's" with location and date stamps from the school. Here we go.'

Bliss, Personal Diary:
Entry for Tuesday 11 January 2050

Lady Caroline's School, near Hereford, Central West Governorate, UK

Back at school. My first entry in this electronic diary that Dad bought me for Christmas. After Martin's jibe in the pub that I would never have the 'discipline' to use it, I'm going to prove him wrong. It's not like Dad's hard copy diary – I would never be able to handwrite something every day – but this device has all sorts of tricks that make it not only easy, but also fun to use. I love the vocalisation option. I just have to open it up and it starts talking to me: 'Good evening, Bliss'; 'I trust you had a good day'; 'I'm ready to start when you are'. And it's not pre-recorded stuff – the responses feel quite personal. When I asked Dad about it, he said I had it on the maximum setting – what he called the 'bot-inside-the-book' that in future, when I have this new AA-Plant fitted, will also record unspoken thoughts and conversations. I'm not so sure I like the sound of that, but what is supercool is that when I open the diary, I see a display of what I've voice-written but with my punctuation and grammar corrected! To keep things simple, I've turned off the option for including images, so I have none of the restaurant bills or other paraphernalia that Dad puts in his non-electronic one.

Another feature is that it offers complete privacy. It looks like an ordinary small-sized diary, with a deep mauve cover and the year 2050 printed across the top in silver lettering, but if someone else opens it, all they see are blank pages. My text only appears when the diary recognises my face and takes biodata from my hand as I hold it. That means I can write whatever I want – even Ramona can't read it. It's me, unplugged!

Bliss, Personal Diary:
Entry for Monday 17 January 2050

Lady Caroline's School, near Hereford,
Central West Governorate, UK

The school makes a bold claim that being here for a year will '…refine your interpersonal intellect.' The sales brochure (otherwise known as our school manifesto) describes it as providing '… the final step before your daughter enters the adult world … an opportunity for her to cultivate some of the traditional as well as modern skills of etiquette and communication … When she has completed her course, she will be able to compete against the best.'

Huzzah and hurrah! I think the only long-term 'benefit' of this place will be the Intervention Treatment, which incredibly I have been selected to receive in the Biomedical Centre on the 25th.

The 'Lab', as the girls call it, is tucked behind the neoclassical façade of the main house. We girls live and work in elegant high-ceilinged rooms and approach the school along a wide drive with scissor-cut gardens to the left and right, while the staff (and even the doctors employed by the Centre) enter through the woods at the back. It's all part of the super-rich mentality of minimising their contact with the proletariat.

The brochure may describe the IT as a 'benefit', but Ramona is more sceptical. She ribs me, saying there's a risk that the Treatment will simply bring me a bit closer to the robo-maids who run this place: boringly predictable and lacking in emotion. She also disputes the other 'benefits' that the school claims for IT, such as what they call the 'cultivation process' – a programme meant to refine my manners as well as my intellect. As she rightly points out, that particular argument has one enormous flaw: it's designed from the perspective of the super-rich and their unshakeable belief in their special status. 'As if two hundred years of progress has somehow picked them out as more advanced and superior beings,' she said, when we were arguing about it last year.

They know, and I know, that I don't fit in – in terms of wealth, at least. I go to classes and socialise with them. Some are intelligent, smart even – often because many were given a form of the Treatment at an early age. They dress stylishly and have incredible figures – again because of the health programmes most have been on since birth. Their lives, like those of their parents, are wholly sheltered from the outside world. At the start of term, they step out of their gated homes into chauffeured cars; take a private jet to East Midlands Airport, from where they are flown by helicopter to the school. They then bravely – as Ramona sarcastically described it – 'walk up the mock-Palladian steps of the house all by themselves and into their suite of rooms'. They are part of a global tribe that transcends all national borders. They live, procreate and die exclusively in that world. On a recent trip to Paris, one of them was amused when I pulled out my passport on landing at a private airstrip. 'Darling, you don't need things like that when you're with us!'

Jack and Martin, my dear beloved brothers, are always accusing me of being selfish and pampered, but at least I've kept a questioning mind. My tutor group here, by contrast, consists of six young women who are well informed and perfectly polite, but otherwise utterly lacking in curiosity and who find any form of social interaction outside their own set awkward. I'm really not exaggerating when I say they have warmer relationships with the robo-maids than they do with many of the staff.

Bliss, Personal Diary:
Entry for Tuesday 18 January 2050

Lady Caroline's School, near Hereford, Central West Governorate, UK

Ramona was back online this evening after quite a break. She said the snows had been so bad this year across Nebraska that the start of the new term had to be delayed.

Hearing her voice again reminded me of just how important she's been to my success here.

(Just in case I do give someone access to this diary in the future, I'm going to add background notes from time to time, to provide context. It's good for me to do this as well, it makes me think more deeply about the issues raised. Here's the first one.)

My first term at LCS was a disaster. I was repeatedly hauled up in front of the principal and given lectures on appearance, sticking to the rules, time-keeping and 'your manners'. No matter how I responded, I was never up to scratch in their minds. During that time, I regularly retreated into the SWVRP – set on 'Year 1', to remind myself of real life on the outside. To my surprise, I discovered that none of my classmates were using the program. They had their own version, and from discussions in tutorials this seemed simply to reflect the world in which they lived. On making this discovery, I realised I could achieve my mission of informing this privileged lot about the outside world by simply persuading them to enter the SWVRP. To do that, however, I had first to gain their respect, and the only way open to me was to transform myself from rebel into model student. That was when Ramona got involved, big time. She gave me five guidelines:

1. Follow the school rules.
2. Be aware of the implications of all your actions in advance.
3. Be well prepared for all lectures and projects.
4. Be good at giving as well as receiving negative feedback.
5. Be the best at having a firm, objective and logical response in emotional situations.

Duh! Obvious, I thought. But then she started to monitor me constantly: waking me if I overslept; ensuring I delivered my homework on time; advising me on how to dress; and most of all, helping me develop a more friendly style for greater appeal to both students and staff. This change in approach wasn't so difficult. Within the 'debating chamber' of my own family I had developed the role of facilitator and appeaser, which turned out to be close to the persona Ramona suggested I adopt at LCS. She also did something else I would never have dreamt of: we made a chart of every girl and teacher in the school, with a strategy for dealing with each one. Through my teleplant, I let her monitor all conversations to ensure these profiles were kept up to date and 'our tactics optimised' – as she would say.

Incredibly, our scheme has worked so well over the past two years that I've now been elected as the next school president. I still can't believe it.

I invited Ramona to join Mum and Dad for the appointment ceremony, but she threw up all sorts of logistical objections, finally insisting that she preferred to remain as my 'private friend'.

Last night in bed, I told her about Dad getting caught up in the bomb explosion with Uncle Nick, but it didn't seem to interest her, so I decided not to mention their decision to go to Phillips Cay. When I raised the matter of my acceptance speech for the ceremony, she surprised me by just saying a little abruptly, 'The game is over – we have won. Use your speech to begin their enlightenment.'

Well, I wasn't happy with that, just as I'm not happy with her being quite so opposed to the IT. Mum and Dad will be at the ceremony – it's as much their day as mine. I said I was following Guideline 2 about implications and told her I wanted to play a longer game, which meant acting out the role of school president for a time. She was a little miffed, as Mum would say, but eventually came around to my way of thinking. Didn't have any choice really, did she?

Bliss, Personal Diary:
Entry for Friday 21 January 2050

Lady Caroline's School, near Hereford,
Central West Governorate, UK

For my investiture, I had to go up on the main stage in front of everyone and shake hands with the chair of governors. He was someone famous in retail, Mum told me later, but all I remember was that he moved his hand a shade too close to my breast as he pinned on the president's badge. I was then shown over to a podium to give my acceptance speech. Ramona had asked me to switch on my teleplant so she could listen in, but I decided not to. Nor, as I'd already made plain, did I use the opportunity to bring my campaign of re-education to a broader audience.

Instead I spouted something worthy that could have been slotted straight into next year's school brochure. 'At this challenging time, the need for leadership from the best has never been greater ... We will be the mothers of future leaders by being leaders ourselves ... Investing in us is investing in a better world for all.'

I glanced down at my parents while spewing out this hogwash. Mum sat upright, immaculately dressed as usual, in a purple two-piece on this occasion, easily as stylish as any woman there. Dad was clearly uncomfortable in the small-sized seat and the rather tight-fitting suit Mum had insisted he wore. But every time I looked at him, he had a fixed smile of satisfaction on his face. That strong image of their joint pride made me realise I had done the right thing by toeing the party line in my speech.

I left the stage to rapturous applause, even a few whoops. The teaching staff were all clapping loudly, many of them trying to catch my eye. The only possible dissent lay at the back of the hall, where my rivals sat with their parents and relatives, stoically joining in with the mass appreciation. When I light-heartedly mentioned this defeated flank of onlookers to Ramona that evening, she immediately quizzed me as to their names. When I resisted, she said, 'The battle has only just begun – know your enemies and their weaknesses right from the start.' I realise that it's radical thoughts like this that draw me to her.

As we stood on the terrace overlooking a lawn the size of a golf course, Dad's one brief comment after the event was simply, 'What a palaver ...' He'd made a huge effort to be there that day, dressing like a normal respectable person for once and even having had his hair cut. 'By a barberbot?' I joked as we waited for the reception to begin. Mum didn't join in the laughter but stood alongside us, showing just enough cleavage to excite but not offend. She was in her element, treating everyone with the polite indifference that – in her eyes – was appropriate for the mother of the school president.

The turnout of parents was, I heard, unprecedented – prompting my mother to remark that it was 'less to do with celebrating the appointment than inspecting the unusual choice of appointee.'

In the reception that followed, she took my arm as the principal introduced us to the great and the good, and undoubtedly the not so good. Dad wasn't able to join us – surrounded, as he was, by a gaggle of women eager to meet the man many had seen online and in their glossy magazines.

Bliss, Personal Diary:
Entry for Saturday 22 January 2050

LCS, near Hereford, Central West Governorate, UK

It's gone midnight, and I'm back in my room, exhausted.

For the past four hours I've been the guest of the Final Year Club, a luxurious retreat at the top of the LCS main house, a place where staff and all but a select group of girls are forbidden to set foot.

Unbeknown to me, I have broken a long tradition that the school president should be elected from within the FYC, so its members were now keen to try and sign me up. In doing so, they were unwittingly presenting me with the means of bringing my message to this innermost circle of wealth and privilege.

On the guided tour around a labyrinth of rooms and dance floors (yes, there was more than one), I felt distinctly underdressed. I could barely recognise some of the girls, they were so heavily made up and clothed in the most exquisite fabrics. I was taken aback also by the numerous bots. I know most of those that reside in the house, but in the FYC they have their own specimens including, to my astonishment, male bots that are so lifelike I felt quite excited when one started becoming friendly. 'Take him away with you if you want,' said one of the girls. 'Welcome to our world,' added another, draped on the shoulder of some robo-hunk. Tonight though, I was on display and had to behave, so I declined.

Bliss, Personal Diary:
Entry for Thursday 27 January 2050

Biomedical Centre, LCS, near Hereford,
Central West Governorate, UK

I feel so incredibly alive. I'm pulsating from head to toe, as if all my nerve endings have been gently squeezed. My ears are filled with multiple layers of sound and in this supposedly clean room, the smells all around me create a kaleidoscope of colours in my head.

I've never experienced anything like this before. It was exciting for the first hour or so, but now it's starting to irritate me. All around, electric circuits seem to be fizzing, and I swear I can even hear the drip in my arm.

They moved my bed to the window so that as soon as I woke up, I could see the wintry landscape that had appeared over the past few days. I gather the snow started just as my procedure began and hasn't stopped since. In a voice set too high for my liking, the robo-nurse said to me, 'We have missed the worst of the weather, but North Eastern, North Western and both Scottish Governorates have been severely affected.' It's one of her favourite subjects.

They've diverted my current teleplant to run a few tests, prior to installing a new one on the 30th. Yee-hah! Another benefit of LCS.

I fell to sleep and when I woke up, there was a list of messages from well-wishers on the terminal next to my bed, downloaded from my old teleplant. It included one from Seth, my part-time boyfriend. I've not replied to anyone yet because my arms feel like pincushions and my head's still buzzing. The drip on my left arm – through which, I'm told, they're pumping an army of nanobots – will be there until tomorrow.

Bliss, Personal Diary:
Entry for Friday 28 January 2050

Biomedical Centre, LCS, near Hereford, Central West Governorate, UK

This morning I regained access to my old teleplant. Dad was the first person I spoke to in the afternoon using the terminal by my bed. He was sitting in front of a screen, which I think was in the attic room of Soft Rush – I've often wondered what they get up to up there. He was concerned that I was having this Treatment just as they were about to leave on their 'little adventure'. In the conversation I must have wavered a little in my determination to stay here, because shortly after he rang off, Seth called. (Giving him access to my teleplant account was a big mistake, especially when I have a father who, despite all his brilliance, still calls me on an open-access channel that allows Seth to listen in through the shared contract.)

'The boy from the agricultural college', as the Coven refer to him, went on and on about the need to 'stick it out here', talking about the 'duty of the young to build a new future'. It's a load of rubbish, of course. He's totally self-centred and hasn't a clue how other people live. He talks about the future but is doing not a jot himself to improve it. There's way more chance of the girls in the Coven actually getting off their behinds and doing something constructive than him – which is saying something, because now and then I seriously question *their* sanity.

I've been doing some mental exercises with one of the male robo-clinicians today. It seems that my scores on the Integrated Intelligence Quotient Test have now reached the level required for the Centre to sign off on the Treatment. Once he'd finished, he was complimentary and said there was a ninety-eight per cent probability I would reach or exceed the target IIQ level. I've noticed that he doesn't mind being interrupted and seems almost to expect me to do it. He has an answer for every question, even though it's usually bland and predictable. What I thought was an innocent game of 'Who can react the fastest?' turns out to be a measure the Lab uses for determining the extent to which the IT has integrated with an individual's psyche. He beats me most of the time, but when I ask things like, 'What do you feel when you look out at the snowy landscape?', he can only reply with a collection of facts rather than anything showing sensory or a deeper appreciation. Even more revealing is his response to the question, 'If I tell you something, will you keep it a secret?' He exhibits what could be described as the robotic version of dithering, delivering an utterly random batch of comments. He does this because he's programmed to pass on all information from the patient to the central computer.

Bliss, Personal Diary:
Entry for Saturday 29 January 2050

Biomedical Centre, LCS, near Hereford, Central West Governorate, UK

I had another post-Treatment session yesterday, and when I woke up this morning, my fizzing senses had calmed down, thank goodness. The gene-washing – as it's called in the trade – is also complete and there are nanobots marching around inside me, helping to monitor all my bodily functions. It's the type of personal health monitoring Mum said she'll be setting up on Phillips.

The Treatment may extend my life by up to thirty years (or so the salespeople claim) but what I want is for my creativity to increase. I wonder whether these enhancements may make some recipients overly complacent? After all, we now have so many advantages over untreated people that employers will be lining up to offer us jobs. We will have fewer illnesses, be able to work longer hours and over a longer time frame, and have all sorts of modules installed, such as the linguistic one I opted for. As if that wasn't enough, the Treatment includes the implantation of one of the new exo-cortex teleplants* that'll give me access to thought-led communication and intelligence web-profiling. I hardly need try in order to succeed.

*(Dad told me that Uncle Nick's insisted I have this new AA-Plant installed. The Centre couldn't object but weren't happy about it because they have their own device which probably makes them a tidy little profit.)

Bliss, Personal Diary:
Entry for Sunday 30 January 2050

Biomedical Centre, LCS, near Hereford,
Central West Governorate, UK

Well, the new teleplant is installed but I have to say I'm extremely disappointed over its performance. The Lab's not cooperating because it wasn't their model, and all efforts to troubleshoot the problem with Allied have failed.

The only exception is my communication with Ramona, which is crystal clear. When I mentioned the contrast, she said in her languid Midwest accent, 'Don't worry about it too much, honey, it'll sort itself out.'

Not sure about her calling me 'honey' – it sounds more like Auntie Lianne talking than someone of my own age. She was incredibly relaxed with me though. Having been such a hard task-master over the last three years, she's now insisting that I 'ease up' and 'enjoy yourself'. 'Leave the thinking to me – indulge yourself in all the new things you'll be able to do!' Weird – sounds like the Coven have got to her.

Bliss, Personal Diary:
Entry for Monday 31 January 2050

Biomedical Centre, LCS, near Hereford, Central West Governorate, UK

Today I asked the robo-nurse to leave me in peace, rather than check on me every thirty minutes. 'I have bots inside me doing that twenty-four seven – I don't need them on the outside as well!' I protested.

That little outburst prompted one of the doctors, an actual flesh-and-bone one, to come into my room and say that the reason they were checking so often was that they had 'detected some unusual signals coming from your new teleplant that we don't understand'. I've no idea what they're on about.

Meanwhile, I've also been trying to reduce the number of visits from the maid, so I can talk with Ramona in peace. I did wonder whether they might be bugging my room to investigate these 'signal variations' – whatever they are? That prompted me to work out how the communication-through-thought option worked on this new device. Now I've cracked it, the maid – or whoever – can come in as often as they like.

An even odder thing occurred while I was silently telling Ramona about Mum and Dad's imminent departure for Phillips Cay. Instead of getting bored, as I usually do when she's pummeling me for news, I found myself talking to her for over an hour, and able to recall vast amounts of information. She was complimentary and kept asking me more and more questions. Was she doing this deliberately to help me understand the new 'me'? Someone with index cards in their head, just like Martin ... Ugh! It sounds awful, though it does make me feel a bit powerfully brainy.

Bliss, Personal Diary:
Entry for Wednesday 2 February 2050

Biomedical Centre, LCS, near Hereford,
Central West Governorate, UK

Someone has sent round a horrible message on social media to all my classmates, using my name, and describing several of them in a highly unflattering way. I thought it was a joke at first and laughed it off, but it's now causing such a stir that the principal is coming to my room tomorrow to talk about it. It's clearly from someone who knows the girls well because it gives personal information about each one of them.

I talked the problem through with the Coven on a broken line, and everyone agreed that I should ignore it – all except Ramona, who, feisty as ever, said, 'Stand up for yourself. It's that crowd who backed your rival: they're trying to discredit you while you're still in recovery.'

Bliss, Personal Diary:
Entry for Thursday 3 February 2050

Biomedical Centre, LCS, near Hereford, Central West Governorate, UK

This morning the principal showed me the emails, which included accusations of incest, prostitution and hideous acts involving animals. When I read them, I laughed out loud in sheer disbelief that anyone could even think of such things. The principal (who had the school bursar and I think someone from the legal side with her) looked at me gravely and handed me a paper printout from what they claimed to be my new teleplant. I objected loudly, pointing out what they had downloaded was not from an Allied device – which I had been told would be implanted.

Then my head started spinning, bringing the doctor in and ending the meeting. He said not to worry and that, 'Your Ni-Fe functions are just getting a little overstimulated by the Treatment.'

This was strange because I've never had strong thinking or intuitive skills – that was what Ramona added. I then wondered if what was really happening was that the Treatment had started to bang in – advancing my own thinking and intuitive self.

'A new logical Bliss – a Ramona II!' I said to her jokingly when we next talked. She went quiet and it occurred to me that perhaps she was worried the Treatment might change our relationship and that maybe in the future I would not need her help in the way I did before. She quickly perked up though, when I told her that these new skills seemed to be telling me that if I wanted to make a real contribution to this future, then instead of trying to convert the daughters of the super-rich, I should perhaps focus more on what my father was doing.

Bliss, Personal Diary:
Entry for Friday 4 February 2050

Biomedical Centre, LCS, near Hereford,
Central West Governorate, UK

The principal came back this morning in a more conciliatory mood. (I turned on my diary to record her.)

'We understand that in the early stages of IT, young people may do silly things before the Social Adjustment Programme has been applied. We have talked to the parents involved and they have agreed not to take further action. However, as a temporary precaution, we would like to conduct some non-invasive tests on your teleplant. We also want to extend your recovery period by three months.'

When I asked about my role as school president, the principal (touching my shoulder and speaking more gently) said, 'Don't worry about that: we'll handle it.'

I passed the news on to Ramona. Her reaction was apoplectic. 'They don't want a scandal over the elected school president ... You're being treated like a criminal ... They've locked you out of their routers and taken away your computer ... They think you did it and don't trust you.'

'Maybe they accidentally installed the wrong teleplant and now want to swap it over,' I speculated. But Ramona remained incensed, saying they were 'just trying to find evidence against you' and 'I bet they're inviting one of those girls from the FYC to take your place right this second'.

Now, as I finish this entry a few hours later, I'm also finding myself getting angry. How dare they accuse me of this? I really don't know what possible explanation there can be, but it should be quite evident to anyone that I would never do such a dumb thing.

Fine – try pulling this place together without me. Maybe I should send round a real email telling the principal about the robo-boys in the Final Year Club!

Bliss, Personal Diary:
Entry for Sunday 6 February 2050

Biomedical Centre, LCS, near Hereford, Central West Governorate, UK

Events over the past few days have not only cleaned up my DNA but also brought me to my senses. I need to get out of this madhouse. It seems that I've managed to offend the most litigious of my classmates' families, who, contrary to what the principal said, have issued multiple suits against me for defamation this morning. I blew my top, threw the papers at the school bursar and told him to get out of my room.

I still don't understand how it could have happened, but at Ramona's suggestion, I've arranged for the setting on the new teleplant for joint sharing with Seth to be removed – in case that's the problem. Unfortunately that means another general anaesthetic tomorrow. The legal people objected, saying that my teleplant was part of a crime scene, but I countered with a human rights argument that put them in a spin.

As I record this diary, I'm waiting to go into the operating theatre. The procedure, they assure me, will be quick, but after that I'll have to rest here for another twenty-four hours. That means I'll be out of communication for several days.

Bliss, Personal Diary:
Entry for Monday 7 February 2050

Biomedical Centre, LCS, near Hereford, Central West Governorate, UK

Someone must have stirred things up while I was under the knife. The robo-maid came in this morning with my computer, making maximum use of her 'sweetness and light' mood setting. Shortly afterwards, my teleplant informed me that it was now reconnected with the outside world, although still blocked from communicating with anyone or anything in the school.

More than two hundred messages were waiting for me, including thirty from Mum and Dad. One stuck in my head, signed off by both of them (though I think Dad wrote it): 'I know you can't join us yet, but the Phillips Cay Project could offer exciting challenges for you, so please put the summer aside as we may have a way of getting you over here.'

Why wait for the summer? I thought. What am I doing with my life, playing this silly game? These people are so cushioned from reality that they just don't feel the need for change like the rest of us.

As I write these words, it sounds as though I'd had some great revelation while under the anaesthetic, but it wasn't that, I was letting go of something I'd been holding on to for too long. The phrase 'coming to my senses' entered my head, and I thought that maybe it was more like 'coming to my new senses'. Is the IT already having some positive effect on me?

I called Ramona and said, 'I'm off – I'm going to Phillips Cay.' I expected her to resist the idea, but quite the opposite – she screamed with delight and was then a little abusive about what she called 'stuck-up little prigs who didn't deserve our attention'.

The main worry about leaving now is that I'm going to miss the mandatory three-month Social Adjustment Programme. So, this afternoon I downloaded details about it through my new tele-plant, which somehow alerted the doctor on duty, who, having been kept in the dark about the whole email scandal, saw my action as a sign of my commitment to the Treatment. I felt a little worried about following the programme under my own steam, but Ramona eased that worry. 'Honey, do you really think this Adjustment Programme is actually about you? It's just a bit more brainwashing. We can manage it together. Don't worry.'

Bliss, Personal Diary:
Entry for Tuesday 8 February 2050

On the HS4, en route to St David's Station, Exeter, South West Governorate

Yesterday I emailed Mum and Dad and eventually got instructions to make my way to somewhere called Flushing on the Penryn River, where Uncle Nick will pick me up.

I'm currently on the high-speed link down to Exeter. As I head south, I see things that worry me. In Bristol, there was a large banner hanging from a high-rise block: POWER TO THE PEOPLE. I presume they mean electrical rather than electoral. Then, as we left Taunton, there was a vast encampment beside the rail track. Were they refugees or locals?

They should be missing me by now at LCS. I hope they don't do anything stupid like sending out a Missing Persons Report – that could be troublesome when I arrive at Exeter. I've brought some of the literature on the post-intervention Social Adjustment Programme with me, although I don't have any of the pills that go with it. I can't believe the 'adjustment' will be that difficult.

I must admit though that in the past few days I've felt as though I'm bouncing off the walls again, especially when I wake up in the morning. I also surprised myself today by downloading a cryptic crossword on my teleplant (something that's never interested me before) and completing it. Whatever next? I think to myself.

Going through the IT literature, it seems to me that the post-Intervention medication aims to flatten out the highs and the lows. I would have thought that that was precisely what some of those rich cows at Lady Caroline's required – a bit of personal volatility to deal with!

I didn't tell the Coven what I was doing, but Ramona called by chance so I filled her in. It was unusual for her to contact me because normally her school restricts all outgoing calls, just like it doesn't allow her to have an Exemplar.

My problem now is: how do I get from Exeter to this Flushing place? There's no connecting train and I don't fancy hanging around in the station for too long.

Snowbound on Interstate 25, Colorado Springs, CSA, FSA

10.30 hours, 16 June 2050

'So there you have it – she did something naughty,' Nick said, as he scanned the endless white landscape displayed on one of the monitors in front of him.

'If Bliss said she didn't do it, then she didn't,' Lianne said insistently. 'I held her as a baby – you remember, I flew to the UK for her birth. I saw her through that awful time when she left the boys' school and went to art college – not even Methuen was happy with her doing that. And then she was with me every summer holiday in New York before we moved to the UK. If she says she's innocent, then she's innocent. Lying or even telling half-truths are simply not in her nature,' Lianne said, shaking her head emphatically.

Nick lay back and rested his hands across his chest. 'But she did use this virtual friend to hoodwink everyone – and not just at school. Who exactly is Bliss Pryce?' he asked wryly. 'Not even that medical director knew he was designing a Treatment for an augmented persona.'

'Well, good for her. She had to have some advantage to compete with that self-important rabble – I thought you admired initiative?'

'You know only one version of Bliss. What I've learnt from these files is that there's also another one, who is now cognitively enhanced.'

Lianne paused and then, as if she were asking herself a question, said, 'I wonder how much Elizabeth and Methuen know about all this?'

Nick turned to face her, his finger raised in warning. 'They never will know unless Bliss grants them access to this file. Right?'

'Okay, okay. Are you getting too hot under this nano-sheet?' she taunted, pulling the cover towards her. 'One thing I didn't understand was something her online friend said about the heavy snowfall across Nebraska. Didn't you say that Lincoln hardly had any snow last winter?'

'Maybe she's located higher up?' Nick replied, pointing to an image of Bliss entering the control room of the *Clipper*. 'We can pick the story up here. I guess you'll remember a lot of this.'

AA-Com File: Leaving *(contd)*

Control Room, *Allied Clipper*, Falmouth, South West Governorate, UK
Afternoon, 8 February 2050

Virtual Scene snapshot: Bliss stands in the centre of the control room, looking weary and dishevelled, surrounded by her parents, Lianne and Marco.

'I can't tell you anything else, Mum,' Bliss said, sweeping back her damp hair and chucking her rucksack on the floor. 'I got a bus down to Flushing Terminal, where Nick picked me up in a rather stylish launch. The place was buzzing because of this regatta week but we managed to get into the main channel quickly, only for a military-looking vessel to pull up alongside and direct us into the harbour. There were hundreds of boats in the water, so why they picked on us, I have no idea. I showed them my papers and got nodded through, but as I was walking away, I heard a lot of shouting behind me and saw Nick being frogmarched into a building, complaining that he didn't need papers—'

Everyone looked up as the sound of repeated gun volleys filled the air.

Marco, who had been listening intently to Bliss's report, held his hand up. 'Don't worry, it's just the, uh ... regatta races starting. I think that's what caused the problem,' he said. 'They've brought in a lot of new people to manage the crowds and, umm ... they are the ones who arrested Mr Nick. All the others know us—'

The clatter of someone running up the metal stairs halted Marco's explanation and as everyone turned around, Nick appeared, breathing hard. Without saying a word, he stomped across to the wheel and began powering up the ship.

'Marco, we need to move – now!' he bawled.

'What's going on?' Elizabeth demanded.

Methuen put a hand on his wife's shoulder. 'Leave it for a minute,' he whispered.

Ignoring him, she strode over to the wheel. 'I want to know what's going on, Nick.'

'They've changed the whole fucking command this morning,' he snarled, watching on-screen as two of the operatives wrestled with the ship's mooring ropes. 'They didn't know who I was, or anything about the *Clipper*. It was pure luck that the outgoing commanding officer was doing his farewell round just as I was being charged in the Customs House – he got me released. But don't think he was doing me a favour,' Nick added angrily, 'he's as corrupt as the rest of them. He's probably passing on the opportunity of making money from us to his successor, right now. *That's* why we're leaving.'

'But aren't we in danger if we move from here without authority?' Elizabeth asked, standing firm, hands stretched out in front of her.

'Only if they've not read their own vessel movement plan that has us anchoring in Carrick Roads tonight, to allow another boat onto our moorage.'

'And then?'

'The plan has us entering the harbour area, but after the experience I've just had, we'll follow *my* plan,' he said, focusing on the computer screen in front of him.

'Which is?' Lianne asked, joining the others now standing behind Nick at the wheel.

'We'll use the ebbing tide early tomorrow morning to slip out under sail into the Channel.'

'Slip out in this thing, with that armed command post seeing every movement for miles around?' Lianne mocked.

'We've thought of that, or rather Marco has …' Nick replied, turning to his senior engineer, who returned a sheepish grin. 'You did deliver the alcohol this morning, didn't you?'

'*Sim, sim*, but, uh … like you, I didn't know, uh … that they were changing command at midday,' Marco replied.

'Oh fuck, of course!' Nick shouted, holding up his hand in apology towards Elizabeth.

'You mean they may not have passed it on?' Elizabeth asked.

* * *

Virtual Scene snapshot: It is early evening. The *Clipper* is moored in open water. Marco and Nick stand in the control room, training their binoculars on the command post at the entrance to the harbour. Elizabeth and Methuen are entering the room from the foredeck.

'All quiet?' Methuen asked.

'So far,' Nick said, pointing to an image of the stone tower on the screen. 'We're waiting for the night watch to come on duty. If the new lot are astute and didn't imbibe too much alcohol, they'll have noticed two things about the *Clipper* that are not consistent with their movement plan. Firstly, we're pointing in the wrong direction for a vessel that's meant to be re-entering the harbour.'

He sat back in his seat and turned to Methuen. 'Secondly, the *Clipper* didn't drop anchor, and as you may be able to feel, but hopefully they can't hear, we've kept one engine running. As soon as it gets dark and they've downed Marco's little gift, we'll quietly manoeuvre out into the main channel and let the sails do the rest.'

* * *

Virtual Scene snapshot: It is midnight. Nick is dozing at the wheel, while Methuen and Marco keep watch on the tower on the monitor in front of them.

'Four men, two armed, in an inflatable,' Methuen shouted out.

Nick tumbled forward in his seat. 'They wouldn't do that unless they meant trouble,' he said anxiously. 'What are they carrying, Marco?'

'Only laser stun guns ... as far as I can see, but, umm ... they could still do a lot of damage.'

'Get the boys into battle position. I'm not having a debate with this lot,' Nick shouted out and as Marco disappeared down the stairs, added, 'and repel any boarders but no live fire.'

As the ship began to move, Elizabeth appeared in the control room wrapped in a blanket. 'What's going on?'

Nick sat up at the wheel, pointed to the screen and said to Methuen, 'Tell me what you see.'

'I can't see anything – I'm going outside,' Methuen said, grabbing a pair of binoculars and disappearing through the foredeck door.

As the sound of the electronically controlled sails unfurling was heard, Methuen reappeared, breathing heavily. 'They're heading straight for us at speed and armed to the teeth—'

'Repel, repel!' Nick screamed down the speaker tube.

Within seconds, the whole ship shuddered and on the aft end monitor, an enormous wave could be seen rolling towards the inflatable.

'They're in the water!' Methuen shouted as he came in from the foredeck, grabbing the door to steady himself as the *Clipper* surged forward.

With the ship now in the channel and all sails aloft, a salvo of shots rang out accompanied by tracer fire flashing past the control room window.

'They're shooting at us!' Methuen cried out, slamming the foredeck door behind him.

Before Nick could reply, a call whistled up the speaker tube. 'Engines at full thrust.'

'I thought we were going out under sail?'

'We may have capsized those clowns, but they're onto us now – we need to get out of here as fast as we can.'

'Fifteen knots,' Marco's voice said over the PA system. 'They won't catch us now,' he boasted, before asking more soberly, 'What should I do if I spot anything in the air?'

'Ignore it – it'll only be one of those reconnaissance drones. Anything else ... shoot it down,' Nick responded.

'Nick, this is the EMA Navy you're talking about,' Elizabeth cried out across the control room. 'One of their submarines could sink us at any time if they wanted to.'

'And for what? All we've done is accidentally drop a container over the side and swamped one of their Z-boats. They only want to keep us here to extort money and that won't stand up to scrutiny – they all know that. Besides, they'll hardly want to create a diplomatic incident with a ...' Nick hesitated. 'I was going to say US-registered, but of course, as of the twentieth of this month we are now the Federated States of America, so FSA-registered vessel – just when we're allies in this latest Middle East flare-up.'

As he spoke, the roof to the control room was peppered by what sounded like hailstones, followed by two sharp rocket bursts coming from the rear of the ship.

Silence followed until, over the PA, Marco's voice called out. 'Two, uh ... attack drones downed.'

Methuen and Elizabeth had dived for cover, but Nick, who had remained standing at the wheel, shouted down the speaker tube, 'Impressive!'

'*Obrigado*,' came the response.

'No, not you – the fact that the EMA boys could get those things in the air so quickly,' he said.

'Shooting down EMA drones?' Elizabeth groaned, clambering to her feet. 'You're closing doors for all of us here.'

Turning to her, Nick said resolutely, 'I don't plan to return ... and maybe neither should you?'

Snowbound on Interstate 25, Colorado Springs, CSA, FSA

11.45 hours, 16 June 2050

Lianne woke to find Nick sitting forward, viewing a white sunlit scene on one of the monitors.

'No sign of any snowploughs,' he said, turning off the camera and lying back. 'We can either sleep or immerse again, though the next few scenes aren't that interesting – just us sailing south in a storm.'

Lianne turned to him with raised eyebrows. 'Well, that may have been your experience, my friend, but it sure wasn't mine. I remember it as a fairly momentous few days, once that storm got hold of us. Let's go through the scenes that the bot's put together – and I want this run from Elizabeth's perspective, please?'

Nick frowned. 'Why? This is taken from multiple teleplant feeds – that'll give us the most realistic, General View representation.'

'Can we separately immerse ourselves in the different POVs?'

'You're joking,' he said with a slight sneer. 'We barely have enough bandwidth for us to participate in the same scene.'

Lianne folded her arms and put her glasses down on the bed. 'This Storymaker bot would hardly have selected you going about your business on the *Clipper* as the main event. More likely, it'll have chosen what the rest of us were doing. It would be new to you and interesting for me, if we chose to run it from someone else's perspective – that's all I'm saying.'

'All right, all right, have it your way.'

He opened the next scene with Nick in the control room and Elizabeth appearing at the top of the stairwell. 'Oh, I remember this. I'll move on a bit—'

'No, Nick, you won't! Let it run … and from Elizabeth's perspective.'

AA-Com File: Sailing South

Control Room, *Allied Clipper*, Bay of Biscay
Midday, 9 February 2050

Virtual Scene snapshot: In an empty control room, Nick is lounging in the seat next to the wheel, while Elizabeth has appeared at the top of the stairwell, book in hand.

'How's Bliss, Lizzie?' Nick asked as she sat down at the communication booth in the far corner.

'Went out like a light not long after we moved into the estuary – missed all the fireworks,' Elizabeth said, switching on the computer in front of her.

As she started tapping at the keyboard, Nick called down the speaker tube. 'Marco, I'm just handing over to Elizabeth. You need to keep a close eye on that storm to the south-west. It's in the wrong place and at the wrong time for a hurricane – even though that's what it looks like.' He then walked over to where she was sitting and placed a hand on the back of her seat. 'If you're trying to make contact through the dirigible network, don't bother – it's being shut down to deal with an interference problem while the ALL-SAT backup in Lincoln still isn't fully functioning.'

'I'm doing neither. I'm simply trying to access the public Internet through one of the commercial satellite arrays – although even that doesn't seem to be working properly.'

'It's the St Alto effect,' he said, placing his other hand on the seat. 'You know that nutty guy who attacked several of the exchange point buildings in the US? He did a huge amount of damage to a system that was already on its knees.'

'Oh really,' she said impassively, continuing to tap at the keys.

'It won't come online any faster by tapping them harder,' he teased, moving his head close to hers.

If you give him a scintilla of encouragement now ... even not resisting him ... he won't stop until he gets what he wants.

Elizabeth stood up, leaving Nick leaning on the chair. She walked into the centre of the room and began exercising her head, backward and forward. 'I need to go to the gym after this shift.'

'You look really fit to me,' Nick said, facing her, his hands in his pockets.

Put your arms down; you're making it worse. Look at him – his eyes are popping out of his head.

She walked over to the wheel – again leaving Nick stranded. *I should tell him to bugger off, but that'll only sour the atmosphere even more.* 'See you for dinner this evening then,' she said, turning her attention to the ship's log.

Nick stood behind her for a few seconds and then stomped off down the stairs.

Elizabeth instructed the seat to customise to her shape and as it emitted a series of buzzes, she picked up a bottle of spirits on the table next to her. 'Too early,' she said to herself. 'Oh, what the hell,' she snorted, pouring herself a small glass of liquid.

Relaxing in the adjusted seat, she stared at the panel of lights flashing in front of her. *Why has he insisted on this watch? Marco and his bots run the ship. It's just a ruse so he can flirt with me. He never gives in. What did he say that first time he came to the apartment in Princeton?*

> 'I've come to relieve the blues of one of the most beautiful women I know.'

What a charmer he used to be and how naive I was when he said that the Corporation had arranged a lecture tour of the West Coast for Methuen. Ha! More like his executive office, on his instruction, sending Methuen off for three months just so that he could have free access to me ... a sort of droit de seigneur he believed he'd

*earned by providing my husband with new funding? Showing up
unannounced only a day after Methuen had gone – that was pretty
bold ... his arms full of flowers and carrying a bottle of cham-
pagne. He didn't even wait to be invited in.*

> 'As Lianne and Methuen are away, I thought we should
> keep each other company.'

*I'd just begun to adapt to my new lifestyle, splitting my time
between setting up home on the campus and developing the medical practice down in Richmond. He was so charming and that
flamboyant entrance, combined with the fact that I was cheesed
off with Methuen for disappearing just as we were settling in,
made me easy prey. Or was it that I was a bit of a tramp in those
days? After all, I was the one who suggested a drink – and that
became two, with the addition of a meal which to my surprise he
helped me concoct. Afterwards I found him sitting on the sofa,
lights turned low and the balcony door open, allowing the warm
summer air into the room. I should have ended it right there,
but my head was dizzy with drink and I made the fatal error of
saying to him, 'Just you and me then.' He then put on my favourite Chris Botti album – how did he know that was a sure way to
get me in the mood?*

*I remember his eyes, just like a few minutes ago, almost popping
with excitement. He took my hand and invited me to dance, something Methuen would never do – not even today. Shuffling around,
he pulled me close to him and pressed his cheek against mine.
We literally danced to the light of the moon, until with a surge of
passion he pushed me back onto the sofa.*

Elizabeth drained her glass and refilled it.

*After that, he came to the apartment every evening until
Lianne returned the following week. From then on, every encounter was more rushed – squeezed in whenever we were free. That
was when I got to know Nick O'Grady properly. What did I
call him? Oh, yes, 'Clematis Man': head in the sun, untroubled*

and debonair – feet in the cold grey clay of reality, focused and controlling. And then there was that weekend when I thought he'd made me pregnant.

'No, no, that can't be.'

It was said with his usual assuredness but enveloped in a kind of sadness. In the following days, his 'head in the sun' faded, and just before Methuen returned, I suggested we cool the relationship.

'Okay.'

And that was it! That was all he said, accompanied by a hunch of the shoulders. It was the busy, focused, feet-of-clay Nick O'Grady, delivered with a confidence verging on cockiness, which seemed to say: you're in my orbit now and you will want to remain there. I felt like an option he could call on, when needed ... Wait – who's that on the stairs?

'I left my ... Oh, I see you've already started to enjoy a small drop,' Nick snorted.

'Can you tell me,' Elizabeth said, handing him the bottle, 'why you put all our lives at risk by leaving Falmouth like that? Surely we could have waited until the authorities permitted us to leave?'

He's looking at the bottle – am I sounding a little sozzled?

'They were being unreasonable,' Nick snapped back. 'The world is about to take another nosedive, and all those petty bureaucrats wanted was for me to line their grubby palms – for processing two documents.'

'What do you mean "nosedive"?' she said, refilling her glass with water.

'You've not been listening to the news, have you?'

'It's not just the computer links that don't work, I've not been getting anything through my teleplant since I left Soft Rush.'

'That's because the new AA-Plant you've been fitted with needs a nearby AVIII device to make a connection. At present it records, but only transmits and receives locally.'

'Why can't I just route my AA-Plant through *your* AVIII?'

'Out at sea, my AVIII only works when I have the dirigible erected on the ship and right now with this storm approaching, I can't do that.'

Elizabeth held her head in her hands. 'Okay then, just tell me what's happened out in the wide world.'

Nick sat on the back of the sofa and folded his arms. 'McFall has threatened to declare UDI—'

'UDI?'

'A Unilateral Declaration of Independence – from the FSA. He has armed his militia and refused to talk to the new administration. Harding has issued a public ultimatum, telling him either to come back into the fold or be regarded as unconstitutional and face the consequences.'

'And how does that affect your plans?'

Nick shrugged his shoulders. 'I don't know at present.'

Nick O'Grady saying that he doesn't know – that's a new one. 'Is Lianne aware of all this?'

Nick glanced at her and said sharply, 'No, leave that to me. But don't worry, Harding will deal with it. The bigger problem is the reaction of the Market. We now have all the ingredients for another financial meltdown – let's hope the hedging algorithms and the big blockchain funds perform better than they did the last time around.'

'What a world we live in,' she reflected, leaning over the wheel to study the screen showing different views around the ship.

'You don't need to worry about that,' he said, walking over and placing a hand on her shoulder. 'All you need do is give visual confirmation of things the motion sensor detects in the air or on the sea surface close to the ship. Even then, if you see something, just call Marco on the speaker tube.'

So is there any real point in my being here except for your amusement, Mr O'Grady? She nodded in acknowledgement and swivelled round in the chair, dislodging his arm.

He stepped back, paused and then grabbed the bottle, before once again marching, heavy-footed, down the metal stairs.

Snowbound on Interstate 25, Colorado Springs, CSA, FSA

12.30 hours, 16 June 2050

Lianne felt Nick's hand on her arm. 'That shows the limits of running these reconstructions on a first-person basis,' he said. 'It's a distorted account of what happened. I didn't call on her "unannounced". My office left a message for her—'

'And you didn't tell her that I was away, as she said?' Lianne fired back.

'It was a long time ago, and besides, you had that friendship with your old publisher – what was her name?'

'Touché,' Lianne said with a theatrical wave of her arm.

As the birds started to twitter and tweet in the silence, Nick said, 'Do you think she shared all that with Methuen?'

'Okay!' Lianne bellowed, holding her finger in the air. 'That means you've not viewed any of these scenes.'

'Why?' he replied, sounding concerned.

'Let's just roll on to the next one. Oh, and you can flick it back to General View. From now on, this is as much for your education as for my entertainment.'

AA-Com File: Sailing South (*contd*)

Upper deck bedroom, *Allied Clipper*, Bay of Biscay
Late afternoon, 9 February 2050

Virtual Scene snapshot: Elizabeth lies on the bed reading. Methuen is entering the room, dressed in jeans and a check shirt.

'I thought you were on duty,' she said, sitting up.

'I was, but Marco took over my watch – something about instrument recalibration before this storm hits us.'

'So where've you been for the last few hours? Surely not in intimate discussions with Marco,' she said tossing her head back and laughing.

'No, I wandered down to the lower decks…'

Putting her book down, she looked up at him and widened her eyes.

'I was curious after our little reconnoitre the other day. There was something not quite right about the layout of this ship.'

'And was your curiosity satisfied?'

'Come with me – I want to show you something.'

Elizabeth quickly slipped on a dress and followed Methuen, first along the corridor, then down to the main deck and into the emergency stairwell they had explored a few days earlier. At the dogleg in the stairs, Methuen stopped and walked over to the door they had previously ignored and removed an object that was holding it open.

With a self-congratulatory smile, he held up an old fountain pen and, placing it in his jacket pocket, whispered, 'I saw someone coming out of here as I was walking down the stairs and was able to stop the door from closing without being noticed.'

As they walked into the room, side lights switched on automatically, revealing another set of steps leading up to a low-ceilinged room.

'Any idea where we are?' he quizzed her quietly, as they made towards a door in the far corner.

'Nope, I'm totally lost,' Elizabeth said, breathing a little heavily.

'That's what the builders of this space intended. We're at the level of that odd box shape on the main deck, which we thought was an extension of the engine room bay. In actual fact, it's a hidden space – the roof of the engine room is directly below us.'

'But why is it here?'

Methuen beckoned for her to follow him through the next doorway. There, holding up the torch on his handheld, he shone the beam onto a stack of wooden crates. 'I couldn't open any of these but look at this – it's a US military stamp.'

Elizabeth put her hands to her head. 'What's he up to?' she hissed.

'Wait, there's more – much more.'

At the far end, Methuen opened yet another door. As Elizabeth joined him, the light from his handheld dimly illuminated a vast space, in one corner of which could be seen flanks of squat figures in camouflage suits, all armed.

'Like Emperor Qin's terracotta army,' Elizabeth gasped.

'More like the remnants of it. See those round scrapes on the floor?' he whispered, angling the light down for her. 'This place was once full of these robo-soldiers – around four to five thousand, I'd say. There can't be more than four, maybe five hundred left now.'

Elizabeth walked across the room and warily touched the shoulder of one of the tiny warriors.

'There's more equipment over here, and it's not just conventional stuff,' he said softly, shining the light inside a wooden box with its lid slightly askew. '3D printers for creating custom-made shells, and in those over there I could make out fission guns and a whole lot of laser weaponry.'

'So that's what the *Clipper*'s used for? Gun-running?'
'I don't know but I'm sure as hell going to find out.'

* * *

Virtual Scene snapshot: One day on. Dinner is being laid out by Bliss and Lianne in the control room, while Elizabeth and Methuen stand at the wheel talking, just as Nick appears at the top of the stairwell with Marco in tow.

'Before we eat, I need to give you all an update on the damage we suffered when leaving Falmouth,' Nick said, rolling out a plan of the ship across the table in the lounge area.

'That hailstorm of projectiles we heard weren't bullets but these babies,' he said, holding up a metal object like a silver button and then handing it on for them to examine. 'We've found them here, here and here,' he said, pointing to the plan. 'They're electronic positioning detectors that allow the EMA to track us and, if they want, target us from a distance. It's possible they attached some below water also before we left. We've armed the missiles at the rear of the ship as a precaution but don't get too worried – I don't think they'll bother us.'

Nick rolled the plan back up and said casually, 'The upshot of all this is that we'll have to make a slightly longer stopover in the Azores, partly to remove these things but also to repair a leak in the aft engine that's slowing us down.'

'A *longer* stopover in the Azores? So you were planning a stop-over anyway?' Elizabeth reasoned aloud, glancing first at Nick and then with a dark scowl at Methuen.

'That only became a certainty over Christmas when the inter-ference problems with AA-Com worsened. Faial – where you will stay – is next to the island of Pico, from where all Allied communi-cations are managed. It'll be a nice break for you before we make the crossing over to Phillips,' he said cheerily, looking at Elizabeth.

Not responding to his more positive manner, Elizabeth asked, blandly, 'And the weapons we have on board – I presume they're for Pico and Faial too?'

Staring at her, Nick stiffened up and then, dropping his shoulders, said in a relaxed but controlled voice, 'That is correct. Allied originally chose the central islands because of their remoteness and independence, but the Azorean authorities on São Miguel, to the east, are now trying to take charge. They will only desist if they realise that Pico, Faial and the other central islands can defend themselves. All I'm doing is creating a deterrent to prevent conflict.'

'That may be the case, Nick, but why didn't you explain all this beforehand? As usual, you've kept us in the dark,' Elizabeth growled at him, her arms folded across her chest.

'What do you mean, "as usual"?' Nick bit back.

'If we're to be partners in this new venture, you need to give us a heads-up on everything that affects us. It's called building trust.'

'There are some things I can't share with you. They either happen too quickly or have important sensitivities that must be kept private.'

'That's fine,' Elizabeth said objectively, '*except* when our lives are threatened – like being targeted by EMA drones on the high seas. Then we all have the right to be part of the discussion upfront, don't you think?'

Nick glared at her, but turning around, saw the others silent and staring back at him. 'I can't give open guarantees like that,' he said impatiently.

'So how long will it take to get to Phillips once we leave Faial?' Methuen asked calmly.

'I'm not sure right now; it'll depend on what the technicians on Pico have found. I don't want to leave until I know they have a solution to the AA-Com problem.'

'Okay then, how long will it take to get to Faial?' Lianne demanded.

Nick turned to Marco, who responded instantly. 'With this storm we can't use the sails, so on, uh … one engine, I would guess three or, umm … maybe four days.'

'Oh Lord, I don't have to be on this cargo boat for that long, do I?' Lianne said, walking over to the table and helping herself to food.

'We're lucky to be here at all. Try London at present!' Nick shouted angrily at her, and with Marco following, stamped off down the stairs.

Lianne continued to fill her plate. 'Oh dear, we are touchy tonight – needs some sleep,' she shouted in the direction of the stairwell, and then turning to Elizabeth said, 'Don't worry, he gets like this when he has an Allied problem.'

As they all settled down to eat, Marco's voice came across the PA system. 'Control, Control, who is, uh … on duty?'

Methuen went to the wheel and spoke into the speaker tube. 'Marco, it's me for now; Elizabeth will take over within the hour. Is there a problem?'

'I've reprogrammed the ship's computer. We go more to the east now to avoid a cyclone coming up from the south-west. Please don't, uh … worry, but the ship will rock a little as we hit the wind side-on.'

'That sounds like fun for you tonight, Elizabeth,' Lianne said as, plate in hand, she and Bliss made for the stairs. 'If anyone has trouble sleeping, come and join us – my bedroom has an anti-pitch-and-roll floor that makes these storms a little more bearable.'

* * *

Virtual Scene snapshot: Three hours later. Elizabeth is standing outside the O'Grady's suite on the upper deck.

After knocking several times with no reply, Elizabeth opened the door and walked into an immaculately furnished reception area.

Steadying herself against the wall she walked to the end of a corridor, where she could hear Lianne, talking and laughing loudly. Reaching the room, she rocked back, disorientated by the sight of a perfectly horizontal floor ahead of her. Holding onto the door frame, she carefully placed a foot onto the motionless surface, her body still swaying slightly.

'Careful, sweetie, it's like being drunk in reverse for the first few seconds,' Lianne called out merrily from a large bed littered with food wrappers and magazines.

'Come and join us, Mum,' Bliss added, lying next to Lianne.

Elizabeth moved towards them, but then stopped short as she caught sight of Methuen in a mirror, reading at a small bar behind her. She swung round and said, 'Must be bad if you've had to retreat down here.'

'Aren't you meant to be on duty, darling?' Lianne called out to her.

'I've finally been released from duty by your husband,' Elizabeth responded, laughing. 'Something about him needing to take manual control as the storm worsens?'

'Oh dear, ordered below decks by the master. Come on over here – sisters together and all that!' Lianne chuckled, waving her glass at Methuen. 'A drink, my good man, for this fabulous woman.'

'Look what Auntie Lianne did for me,' Bliss said, wriggling a full set of freshly painted scarlet toenails at her mother.

'Uh, yes … very nice, Bliss,' Elizabeth said, gesturing at her daughter to button up her top.

'And what would my lovely daughter – sorry, goddaughter – like to drink next?' Lianne asked, rolling over to face her.

As Methuen poured the drinks, Elizabeth stepped out of her shoes and looked over at Lianne. 'Tell me about the Azores. I've never been.'

'Nor have I. It's only people like Grady who go to these wretched little islands in the middle of nowhere.'

Bliss propped herself up on a pillow, pushing away a half-consumed box of chocolates. 'Did you manage to contact anyone on the Internet?'

'I didn't – the satellite link is rubbish. Have you picked up anything on your new teleplant?' Elizabeth asked.

'No, nothing,' Bliss said, her voice dropping before she added, a little gloomily, 'It's the first time I can remember not being able to talk with anyone. Even in the cellars of LCS, the comms always worked—'

'You ran away from school, bad girl. Tell us what happened?' Lianne slurred, rolling her eyes as she looked over at Elizabeth.

Bliss sat up and said, guardedly, 'It's a long story, Auntie Lianne.'

'But running away just when you'd secured the top job – whatever were you thinking?'

'That's my business,' Bliss replied sharply, rolling off the bed, putting on her slippers and leaving the room.

'What did I say?' Lianne gasped. 'One minute she's bubbly and fun, and the next she goes all serious on me. Is it this Treatment that's doing that?'

'More like the alcohol,' Elizabeth replied disapprovingly.

Lianne sat up. 'It's more than that though. Whenever she stayed with us in New York, she'd wear something different each day and was always superbly turned out – even Nick commented on it. But since she arrived on the ship, she's been wearing the same snowsuit leggings and top – and her hair's become quite straggly. Our pretty little girl is no more.'

'She should be on that adjustment programme,' Elizabeth replied, taking a drink handed to her by Lianne and climbing onto the bed. 'That was another reason I wanted to get online.'

'Why's the sodding comm … commun … unication on this boat so abysmal, Methuen?' Lianne called out.

Reluctantly looking up from his book, Methuen said, 'No one seems to know. It has something to do with the effect that the

AVIII has on the electronics of the dirigibles that are tracked by the operations centre on Pico.'

'More like the lazy bastards have gone on strike,' Lianne quipped, as she got up and staggered over to the drinks cabinet. 'Nightcap anyone?' she said, brandishing a half-empty bottle of gin.

Methuen held up his hand and closed his book. 'Not for me, thanks. I've not slept yet. I'm relieving Nick at midnight for a double shift. He's been up for three days, I gather.'

Lianne burst into laughter as she sloppily filled her glass. 'There's only one person here capable of relieving him – eh, Lizzie?'

Methuen frowned at Lianne, while Elizabeth gave her a wild stare.

Climbing back on the bed, Lianne looked around, bemused. 'What? Surely you two have talked about it, all these years on?'

Methuen stood up and made for the door. 'You two talk; I'm off to take a nap.'

As he disappeared, Elizabeth slapped her forehead and fell back on the bed. 'Nice one, Lianne.'

'What? Here we are … all afloat together – Nick's wife and one of his ex-lovers. Why shouldn't we all be honest with one another?'

'It was a long time ago and best forgotten,' Elizabeth said, refusing to respond to Lianne's attempt to clink her glass.

'You were the opposite of me – you were something he had to conquer. Those were Nick's masculine-max days. He'd signed up the husband and now he wanted the wife – all to prove his manhood.'

'I don't think it was as calculated as that – it was just a passion neither of us managed very well.'

'And now, twenty-seven years on, he's reliving it?'

'I give him no encouragement, let me assure you.'

'You don't need to. Just seeing you unlocks something in him – I see it with Bliss also. In the first year she came to stay he ignored her, but by the third year he was coming on trips to Coney Island with us – even taking a ride on the big dipper. Did she remind him of you, I asked myself?'

Elizabeth slipped down in the bed and clasped her head. 'When did you find out about Nick and me?'

Lianne moved alongside her and, looking up at the ceiling, said in a more reflective tone, 'It was that weekend beach party when I realised you and he were an item.'

'Where was that?'

'Naaan-tuckit,' Lianne laughed. 'It was in the evening, the day after Nick and I got married. I saw you dancing together and knew then for sure.'

'It was over by then—'

'For you, but not for Nick.' Lianne sneered and then gave a short laugh.

'You've never mentioned it before,' Elizabeth said with a slight smirk, accepting Lianne's offer to refill her glass.

'It's important we have no secrets from now on. It's going to be tough, all of this,' Lianne said, suddenly sounding a little downcast. 'I've never seen Nick so anxious.'

'Okay, cards on the table,' Elizabeth responded, sitting up and looking across at Lianne. 'When we came to the Phillips Opening in '44, you both blanked us. I thought you did that because you'd found out about him and me.'

Lianne cried with laughter. 'Oh dear, oh dear, how wrong we often are when emotions are high.' She gazed up at the white moulded ceiling and said soberly, 'He'd got in too deep with McFall. That man is a lunatic. When you met us on Phillips, Nick's life was even more chaotic than it normally is—'

'But he was euphoric – everyone thought McFall had a good chance of winning the Presidency, with Nick as VP—'

'Nick was doing what he always does: hedging his bets. Methuen and McFall were there for different reasons: one political – which I now know Nick doubted, even back then; the other, part-business, part- … humanitarian – influenced by Methuen, of course. The last thing he wanted was for McFall and his cronies to get close to you two. Hubris or what!' Lianne cried out again. 'From running for office to building a new world. Is it just me who thinks everyone's going mad?'

Elizabeth drew in a sharp breath and then blew out her cheeks. 'No, it's not just you,' she said wearily. 'Over the past few years, we've all become a little unhinged with all these irresolvable problems. Even at Princeton in the '20s, it was party, party, party – as if some kind of hedonism virus was getting hold of us all—'

'And there's something to say for that,' Lianne chirped up, grabbing a device from the bedside and fiddling with it until the lazy strains of an old song filled the air.

Don't save your kisses, just pass them around.
You'll find my reason is logic'lly sound.
Who's gonna know that you passed them around,

'*A hundred years from today*,' Lianne sang loudly, looking at Elizabeth and nodding at her to join in.

'Why crave a penthouse that's fit for a queen?
You're nearer heaven on Mother Earth's green.
If you had millions, what would they all mean
A hundred years from today.'

As the melody ended, the two women flopped their arms out on the bed, laughing.

Elizabeth reached across for the bottle on the side table and topped up Lianne's glass. 'I dreaded all this at first, being so far away from home, but now that it's happening, I find myself revitalised.'

'Revitalised? You sure see things different from me. Must be living with Methuen, rather than Nick?' she said contemptuously, her breaths coming in angry little spurts and her nostrils flaring slightly as she spoke. 'I'm more worried about squalid endings than exciting beginnings. The world's going to shit, and I don't want to be in the middle of it when it finally happens. That's the only reason I'm going along with this latest venture – anything that offers an escape.'

'Aren't we meant to be the responsible ones – the senior members of the herd, who lead the young away from danger?' Elizabeth asked.

'No,' Lianne replied flatly. 'We can no longer do that. We entered something different twenty years ago. Even I believe all that stuff now: "Forget Growth Just Survive",' she said, mimicking a commonly heard phrase from the '30s.

Elizabeth sat up. 'We can do better than that. I want to create a new future on Phillips, implementing all the good things and leaving the bad behind. We're old enough and mean enough to know what we want, aren't we?'

'Don't expect too much, sweetie. At present, Phillips is nothing more than a golf club without a course; a marina with loads of "toys for boys" and a collection of disparate occupants with no reason for staying, other than they have nowhere else to go.'

'You mean there's no community spirit?'

'As much of a community as a transit camp for the comfortably-off can offer. It's been a place where people enjoy being nice to one another for a short time and then are able to sail off when they get bored.'

'Methuen puts a lot of confidence in this Plan they've developed at Allied.'

'But it's only been modelled – no one has tested it out yet,' Lianne replied, shaking her head.

'How long will you stay for?'

'I have no idea. Did you hear about McFall?'

'Threatening UDI?'

'No, yesterday,' Lianne said sombrely. 'His militia commandeered the big Allied yard in Portland – our plans were to go back there ...'

'So you just stay longer on Phillips, and Nick can help Methuen establish himself there.'

Lianne cackled loudly. 'Oh, don't mistake a frontman like Grady for a leader.'

'I'm not, but I would have thought that creating a new community would benefit in the early stages from having someone with authority – after all, he is the owner.'

'Owner? Oh boy, you have so much to learn about Phillips.'

Elizabeth looked at her in surprise. 'Didn't he give it to you as a wedding present?'

'He did, just as his father gave it to Nick's mother after their wedding and his grandfather did the same.'

Before Elizabeth could respond, Lianne blurted out, '"Remote and Undeveloped – what is the former most eligible bachelor in the US trying to tell us about his new wife?" That was how the press reacted to the news of Nick giving me Phillips. Nice, huh ...! They've never understood us.'

'You have to admit, it was a surrealistic sort of gift. I couldn't fathom it out when I heard about it. I remember thinking, how often will a city girl like Lianne want to visit a flat tropical island in the middle of nowhere?'

'Well, within three years you had your answer when he swapped it for that fabulous emerald necklace – we had media all over us about that too.'

'So who took on Phillips?'

'Nick transferred the ownership to some Allied offshore company – in preparation for the Project, I guess.'

'But when we came over in '44, it had been a holiday resort for quite a few years and even during the Opening there were still a lot of people who knew Nick, residing there. The O'Gradys don't seem able to let go of Phillips Cay.'

'And don't forget Main Island – that's also been part of the package.'

Elizabeth rolled off the bed. 'Time for my beauty sleep. Glad we've cleared the air. All I have to do now is explain myself to Methuen.'

'We can't let a little thing like infidelity come between us,' Lianne replied, her eyes still closed as Elizabeth walked towards the open door, focusing hard on the moving floor ahead.

'By the way,' Lianne shouted out, 'Bliss beat me at Scrabble for the first time – before I'd even had a drop to drink. What's happened to her? Maybe it's my stinility – sorry, sen-ility – settling in or something like that, but I think it's probably that Treatment. Not only did she beat me – she relished the victory. I'm going to suggest she plays Nick – and then watch the sparks fly.'

'Another thing to sort out,' Elizabeth said as she grabbed the door frame and stepped out into the tilting corridor.

Snowbound on Interstate 25, Colorado Springs, CSA, FSA

13.30 hours, 16 June 2050

Nick lay still, his arms by his side, head back on the pillow. 'Did Methuen understand what you were saying about Elizabeth and me?' he asked, taking off his VR frames.

'He said nothing, but then he wouldn't – he's always been someone who keeps emotional stuff like that to himself. But if Elizabeth and Methuen had their AA-Plants switched on, then maybe we'll find the answer to that question in the remaining scenes.'

'I'd also like to know why Bliss rushed off like that?' Nick asked.

'I don't blame her. Why would she want to associate with a boozy old woman?' Lianne replied with a deep sigh.

He turned to her and said, 'But that's in the past, isn't it? I've not seen you drink since The Incident.'

'I'd cut-back some time before then, but you didn't notice. Although you're right about The Incident – when I saw half the country devastated, I gave up drinking entirely and doubled up on my efforts to get fit and be prepared for whatever was to come.'

'I suppose in a perverse way, The Incident helped me too.'

Lianne laughed cynically. 'How could it have helped you? It's destroyed your largest market – at least for now. The only person who really benefitted was McFall, who used the disruption to take control of the Eastern States.'

'I'm not talking about business or politics – I mean something more personal. I started asking myself: Where is my home?'

Lianne laughed again. 'Home is where the heart is, my dearest.'

Nick nodded and replied quietly, 'You're right, but it also has a geography and a culture, doesn't it? When I saw the state of my New York office, and our Central Park apartment block – with the residents, barricaded in – and then in Lincoln, as I watched that hideous news clip of McFall's people ransacking both our parents' houses and then burning them down – I felt empty. Didn't you?'

'Of course, except that I lost that connection years ago. What anchors me is … well, *us*. I realised that unless I pulled myself together, I was going to lose that as well.'

'Hmm … Imagine the personal mess we'd be in now if you'd gone to Rockford and I'd gone to Lincoln,' he mused.

'So will this "entirely safe" place you described when we left Bismarck be somewhere we can regard as home?'

'For the time being—'

'What does that mean, Nick?' Lianne exclaimed, holding her hands up.

He grabbed the remote beside him and projected a map of North America on the ceiling screen. Moving a cursor from north to south, he said, 'This is where we are at present – Colorado, and that's we're heading – Carlsbad, New Mexico. Remember that discussion over dinner back in Bismarck about a mountain retreat inside the Rockies?'

'The one abandoned by Allied?'

'Put on hold would be more accurate. We did that, a few years ago, so we could focus everything on this site in the south.'

'A mountain tomb?'

'It won't feel like that once you're inside, I can assure you. The staff call it Hotel Cordillera after Project Cordillera – the name Allied Livings gave to their various attempts to create long-term safe retreats in North America. We've been constructing this one for the past ten years as a joint venture with the government.'

'Doesn't sound like any definition I have of home.'

'We need to get there first,' he replied, pointing to a wall monitor. 'Once they dig us out, we'll head south and into the sun—'

'You mean, into the rocks!' Lianne chided, and then, pointing at the VR folder on the ceiling screen, said, 'Let's go through the remaining scenes in the folder. What's next?'

Nick looked up and listed the titles on the screen. As Lianne adjusted her glasses, he tapped her on the head. 'You don't need those. The next one's audio-only – two more entries from Bliss's diary. From the time and date stamps, they seem to have been recorded soon after she stormed out of your bedroom. I'm sure you'll be keen to get this feedback,' he said, raising his eyebrows.

Bliss, Personal Diary:
Entry for Thursday 10 February 2050

Upper deck, *Allied Clipper*, 20.30 hours

'Hi, honey – how are you?'

'I've been better.'

'That doesn't sound good. Something troubling you?'

'It's Lianne O'Grady again. The drink, loosening her tongue, criticising me for leaving LCS. I felt like saying, "I'll pay you back your bloody money if that's what you're worried about".'

'Good for you. Did you tell her what happened?'

'I don't want to talk about it. I feel so angry, not defending myself against those spoilt brats.'

'You weren't to know—'

'But I could have achieved so much as school president.'

'Put it behind you. You were never going to tame that nest of vipers in the FYC. Forget LCS and enjoy the trip! How's it going, by the way?'

'The weather is horrible, like the atmosphere on the ship, thanks to the running battle between my mother and Nick. He doesn't seem to be able to deal with her questioning him and usually ends up walking out. He has a hideaway at the rear of the ship. I don't think he realises that from this bedroom, I can see him sneaking away every now and then and disappearing inside some sort of tower that is sometimes there and other times not.'

'So what's he doing in there?'

The sound of snoring is heard.

'Bliss, Bliss, you there?'

Bliss, Personal Diary:
Entry for Friday 11 February 2050

Upper deck, *Allied Clipper*, 03.30 hours

The teleplant communication with Ramona copied itself into my diary and I've just read the transcript. What on earth came over me? Poor Auntie Lianne – how could I have said such terrible things about her? She doesn't deserve that.

I was wrong about LCS too. I really don't regret leaving. A few of them were actually okay and one or two were even critical of their privilege and the sense of entitlement many of the girls had. But I was crackers to believe I could change how this group thought and behaved.

I guess that changing people's attitudes by showing them how to live in a different way, as I wanted to do by introducing the girls to the SWVRP, is also what this Phillips Project is about. It's time to get more involved in what Dad's doing.

I may have often immersed in the SWVRP, but I've never looked at the logic behind it. Logic! Why does that word keep coming into my head?

Snowbound on Interstate 25, Colorado Springs, CSA, FSA

17.30 hours, 16 June 2050

'What was that?' Lianne called out as a monitor at the foot of the bed lit up the room and an image of a helicopter appeared hovering directly above them, set against a clear blue sky.

'We both fell asleep,' Nick replied, reaching for the remote and then flicking through the outside images. 'Look here,' he said, pointing to a line of emergency vehicles moving along the opposite carriageway. 'They're getting it cleared and ...' He switched to another view and laughed. 'This is the slip road on the other side of us where they have erected a marquee and ... hey, get this! People are coming back to their vehicles with hot drinks – and it's only fifty microsieverts out there,' he said, enlarging the Geiger counter in the top corner of the screen. 'Good clean air from the north – excellent.'

'So we'll be moving soon?'

Nick turned to the roof camera and panned around. 'Our carriageway is still blocked for miles; it'll be well into the evening before we're out of this.'

Lianne slumped back on the bed. 'What came after those two short diary entries?'

Nick switched back to the VR folder and examined a list of titles. 'The editing program seems to have linked them to a short section from the scene we've been following ... I can see Methuen and Elizabeth in the control room. Do you want to—?'

'Sure, but before we do that, tell me: who is this Ramona? She doesn't seem to be doing Bliss any favours.'

'I don't know,' Nick said, slipping on his glasses as the countdown for the virtual snapshot started. 'Just a teenage virtual crush, I guess – something you and I never experienced.'

AA-Com File: Sailing South *(contd)*

Control Room, *Allied Clipper*, North Atlantic
16.30 hours, 11 February 2050

Virtual Scene snapshot: Elizabeth and Methuen are seated around the table with the remainder of Marco's rock buns and a large pot of tea in front of them. Methuen is half-turned towards a bank of monitors that are displaying images from around the ship.

'I know you're angry with me, but it was something that happened a long time ago – just one of those things,' Elizabeth said pouring the tea.

'I don't want to discuss it right now,' he said, without turning towards her.

'Doesn't feel like that ...' she replied, but then looked over her shoulder towards the sound of someone running up the stairs.

'There you are!' Elizabeth said, as Bliss – devoid of make-up and her hair roughly pulled back in a lank ponytail – appeared at the top of the stairwell. 'Come and sit,' Elizabeth added, patting the cushion next to her. 'I came to your room to ask you to join us for lunch, but you were fast asleep – surrounded by piles and piles of paper on your bed. What have you been up to?'

'I printed out the most recent edition of *The Segmented World*, including the twelve appendices,' Bliss said enthusiastically, sitting down and holding out an empty cup to her mother.

'You printed it all out? That's—'

'Wasteful. Yes, Mum, but I wanted a copy I could scribble on – to make it mine,' she said, looking over at her father.

'You mean after all these years, you're finally showing an interest in what I've been doing?' Methuen said glibly, and, refusing Elizabeth's offer of a rock cake, turned to face his daughter. 'So, any questions?'

Bliss paused as she selected a cake from the box. 'The reason the world segmented is the same reason why I don't think your Phillips Community Plan will work,' she said, biting into the doughy lump, scattering crumbs on the floor.

Methuen and Elizabeth stared back in surprise, but as her father opened his mouth to speak, Bliss held her hand up.

'I know what you're going to ask. I can best explain it by referring to your idea of OST-mentality. *That* characteristic is predominant in many who control the world today. If *they* show little willingness to shift towards greater cooperation, then why should the community on Phillips be any different?' she said, picking the crumbs off the floor.

Elizabeth shook her head, looking bewildered, but Methuen smiled and nodded. 'I agree, and the remedy we have for dealing with OST behaviour lies in the Plan.'

'So … can I read something about this Plan?' Bliss asked eagerly.

'It's not written down – you have to experience it through a VR immersion, but if you want an answer to your question, that's also contained within the book.'

Bliss gulped down her tea and grabbed another bun from the box. 'Fine, I'll go and take another look – it's better than painting my nails,' she said, getting up and rushing down the stairs.

As the sound of her footsteps faded, Elizabeth, her face aghast, turned to Methuen. 'Well, how extraordinary! Who was that?'

Methuen sat back and chuckled. 'A rather intriguing young lady. What shall we call her?'

'Brash X?' Elizabeth replied instantly with an uncertain laugh.

Snowbound on Interstate 25, Colorado Springs, CSA, FSA

18.15 hours, 16 June 2050

Nick prodded Lianne and pointed to the front camera display, where a crowd was gathering around the RV, at the front of which stood a large man dressed in a blue uniform and wearing a white Stetson.

'It's the Highway Patrol. I'll deal with this. Wait here,' he said, spinning on his backside into the stairwell.

Disregarding his request, Lianne fastened her dressing gown and followed him into the driving cabin, where ill-tempered voices could be heard over the speakers.

'We could have been dying and those bastards wouldn't let us in.'

And then another. 'They should be hauled out and made to explain themselves.'

As she sat down, Lianne flinched at the image of a snowball flying towards them. As it hit the vehicle, a sharp crack of something solid was heard, followed by a chorus of jeers from the crowd. On another camera, two more officers could be seen starting to climb over the crash barrier from the east carriageway, only for them to pause as the man in the Stetson waved them back.

Lianne looked over at Nick and saw him frenetically typing into his keyboard. 'This is no time to send emails.'

Before he could respond, a coatless man with a thick beard rushed forward with a sledgehammer and slammed it hard against the front of the vehicle, causing Nick and Lianne to fall back in their seats. Outside though, the effect was even greater as the hammer struck the metal surface and catapulted out of the man's hand, narrowly missing the two police officers.

The man in the Stetson pulled out his gun and fired into the air, causing everyone to step back. He then redirected his aim at the vehicle.

'I don't know what, or who, you are but you need to show yourself,' he said in a southern drawl.

As the man made his request, Nick pressed a tab on the keyboard and then looked at Lianne as he pointed to a text on the screen.

THIS IS A CENCOM SECURITY VEHICLE ON ACTIVE SERVICE
Colonel Nicholas St John O'Grady 2345856
CENCOM Advisory Board, Lincoln, Nebraska

Lianne watched as the officer reached towards the vehicle and then stood back, a clutch of papers in his hand. Nick pressed the tab on his keyboard again and once more the man was seen to reach forward and extract something from the side of the vehicle. On the screen she now saw the image of a CENCOM ID card.

Outside, as the man scanned the documents into his handheld, the crowd surged forward.

'You're not gonna let 'em get away with it?' one of them shouted angrily.

'Pull the bastards out!' screamed another, prompting the two policemen on the other carriageway to leap over the barrier to back up their colleague.

Without waiting for their response, Nick pressed further buttons on the control panel, causing the crowd, first, to step back as the vehicle lifted itself off the ground, and then look upwards as a drone took off, soaring high into the sky.

On the monitor over his desk, a flickering aerial image showed a massive wedge of snow extending from the mountains down across the old part of the city and into the farmland to the east, leaving little sign of Interstate 25. As the camera panned around, he leant forward. 'There,' he said keenly, pointing to a huge snow-blower advancing towards them from the south, accompanied by a fleet of support vehicles.

Lianne glanced at the image before returning her attention to the crowd around the vehicle, who were now being dispersed by the officers. 'What was in those papers that made the cop so compliant?' she asked.

'Oh, some nonsense I made up about being on a mission of vital national importance. Only problem is that my little communication will also be read by CENCOM and passed up the line. Our cover is blown. We need to get out of here as fast as possible,' he said, typing into the computer.

'I still don't understand why you're so nervous. We're more than seven hundred miles from CENCOM HQ now. We've just evaded an inspection by the police and an angry mob – surely we're safe?'

'I can't take any chances,' Nick said nervously. 'The good news is that there's no traffic on the IS-25 going south.'

'More snow?'

'No, no, this is freak weather. Within a few miles, the drone shows normal conditions.'

'So why no ...?' Her voice trailed off before she added, 'Of course, another hotspot?'

'Yeah, there's quite a big one near Springer. That probably means the road all the way down to Albuquerque will be clear.'

'How far is it to this Hotel Cordillera?'

'About five hundred miles.'

'Still that far, huh? It'll be getting dark by the time we get out of this, so are we going to drive straight there?'

'No, I don't want to be on the road that long. I'll find us somewhere safe to hide.'

'I'm going to catch some sleep. Maybe you should too,' she said, making her way downstairs.

Just off FSA 84, in a small wood
near Sheridan, SCSA, FSA
04.40 hours, 17 June 2050

Nick crawled onto the bed, waking Lianne.

'Where've you been?' she asked drowsily.

'Monitoring the screens for any signs of a CENCOM response. I intended to park near Springer but there were too many military vehicles patrolling the streets, and it was the same further down by the airstrip – lots of soldiers disembarking from unmarked transport planes. So I drove on and after an hour I turned south at Romeroville onto the FSA 84 and switched over to manual drive. Just as it was getting light, I parked a little off the road in a small oak and pine wood near a place called Sheridan. The drones are stationed in the tree canopy and in the surrounding hills to give us full land and air coverage.'

'So what's the plan then?' she said, sitting up and taking out a glass from the wall recess.

'We'll hole up here during the day and then drive to Hotel Cordillera tonight. Did you get any sleep?'

'On and off. I had dreams of angry people everywhere – and then I woke up, and realised it wasn't a dream. What's the radiation count outside?'

'Low. The next hotspot is close to Carlsbad.'

'Close to where we're going … of course.'

'Don't worry about it. The reason this location got government support was because we were able to easily excavate deep into the mountain. It's designed for much higher levels of radiation than we have at present.'

'Did they have the same problem after The Incident that we've just experienced – lots of people knocking on their door asking for shelter?'

'Like this RV, there's no door or obvious point of entry to Hotel Cordillera—'

'But I presume there are people inside with a conscience who'd feel guilty like I did earlier, rejecting that young family?'

'At the time of The Incident, there was just a skeleton staff and a few Allied Associates managing the comms – no one was expecting it.'

'And now?'

'I would imagine it's filled up a little,' Nick replied vaguely.

'Aren't you tired?' she asked, lying back.

'No, there's way too much adrenaline in my system. Rather than neutralise it with a pill, I thought I might immerse again. Want to join me?' he asked, pulling up a file and singling out a scene. 'There are several sections to this one. It's called "Faial". It starts in the control room of the *Clipper* just before we anchored off the island. I've not viewed any of these – let's do a General View.'

'If Elizabeth's AA-Plant was recording, there'll be at least one section that will interest you very much, Nick.'

'Really?' he replied, pulling back the remote. 'There are several sections and also an entry from Bliss's diary – shall I play them one after the other?'

'Play it!' Lianne roared, as she slipped down the bed and pulled on her glasses.

AA-Com File: Faial

Control Room, *Allied Clipper*, offshore from Faial, Azores, EUCON
Early morning, 12 February 2050

Virtual Scene snapshot: Elizabeth, dressed in a dark blue jumpsuit, is walking across a dimly lit control room where Methuen sits alone at the wheel, reading.

'Why are you up so early?' he asked.

She rested her hand on his shoulder and yawned. 'I just can't sleep with everything moving around.'

He paused for a moment and then returned to his book.

As she stared out of the window into the murky haze enveloping the ship, Marco appeared in his working overalls and marched over towards her.

'Faial,' he announced joyfully, pointing to a bank of flickering lights that were now shining through the veil of mist.

Elizabeth moved over to the communication booth and bringing up a text on a display screen, began to read:

Located in the middle of the North Atlantic between Europe and North America, the Azores lie parallel with Lisbon at latitudes of 39° 43' to 36° 55' N. The nine islands form a EUCON Exclusive Economic Zone, covering a total surface area of 984,300 km². Islands range in size from the largest, São Miguel (747 km²) in the extreme east, which is also the capital, to less than 17 km²: Corvo Island, to the extreme west. The volcano on Pico, in the central island group, rises to 2,351 m above sea level, constituting the highest point in the Azores. The population of the central islands currently stands at 350,000 inhabitants.

As she finished, the ship swayed to one side, turning away from the hillside of lights and towards a headland, behind which green volcanic cliffs rose out of the clouds, catching the early sunlight.

'This is Porto do Comprido,' Marco said, now at the wheel and focusing on the instruments around him. 'It's, uh ... an old whaler port. Allied converted it, uh ... a few years back to land provisions on this side of the island. Don't worry about the volcano: Capelinhos' – he nodded to the headland cloaked in black ash – 'hasn't been active for almost one hundred years.' He turned to Methuen standing beside him, and said, 'We'll, uh ... anchor here while Mr Nick takes the tender to Horta – that's the main town on Faial. He needs to make some, uh ... arrangements for our stay. Tomorrow he wants you and me, Professor Pryce, to go with him on an inspection trip of the Allied facilities on Pico.'

'How long will you be gone?' Elizabeth asked.

'I don't know. Maybe ... uh ... three or four days?'

'Not exactly my definition of a *brief stopover*,' Elizabeth said, shaking her head moodily at Methuen.

* * *

Virtual Scene snapshot: Two days on. Elizabeth and Methuen are standing together at the control room window. Marco is at the wheel, leaning towards the speaker tube, a radio mic in his hand.

'Boy, would you look at that!' Methuen said as the ship rounded the treeless promontory of the Monte da Guia, bringing into view the picturesque harbour of Horta to his left, with the towering volcanic cone of the Montanha do Pico to the right.

Lianne and Bliss appeared at the top of the stairs and joined Elizabeth and Methuen as they watched the young trainees take up their positions at the bow, facing outward like carved figureheads.

The reason for this arrangement soon became apparent when the quay ahead of them began to fill with brightly dressed locals, many dancing to a jangling cacophony of drums and guitars. But as the *Clipper* docked, a group of men wearing surgical masks pushed through the crowd. After some wild gesticulation, one of them raised an antique-looking loudhailer.

'*Certificado, certificado,*' he called out, while another held up a forehead thermometer and pointed at his mask.

'Have they got a problem with disease?' Elizabeth asked anxiously, turning towards Marco.

'It's a sort of, uh … flu. It's, umm … everywhere in São Miguel. No one can land without certificates.'

'If they have that, I'm not keen to go ashore,' she said, looking at Methuen.

'No, no, no,' Marco said, shaking his hands at her. 'This island is free – they're worried about infection from us. That's why they want our *certificado,*' he said, hurriedly pulling out a set of papers from a bag and then pointing at the trainees. 'We can all go, but they have to stay. They have no, uh … flu but their *certificados* are out of date. Besides, we, umm … also need someone to guard the ship. Mr Nick trusts no one.'

Waiting on the gangway for the officials to record their temperatures and check their papers, Elizabeth turned back to Marco. 'It's the same flu epidemic that's shut down continental Europe, I suppose. How come it's not a problem in the States?'

'In the old days, it would be everywhere. Now people travel less and so do the germs – that's what Mr Nick says.'

The officials ticked boxes for another ten minutes and then one of them turned to Elizabeth, flashing his gold dentures in an exaggerated but engaging smile. 'Doctor Pryce, *bemvindo ao Faial.* Please follow me.'

As the five of them stepped down onto the quay, several women pushed forward and festooned them with wreaths of flowers. In no time at all, they found themselves carried along by a bustling crowd towards an ancient, fortress-looking hotel, its rough walls cloaked in creepers. There, in an open courtyard with the perfect symmetrical cone of the Montanha do Pico as a backdrop, they sat down to a lavish lunch laid out on two floral-decked trestle tables. As they took their seats, Nick appeared through a side door, accompanied by a crowd of well dressed locals. He nodded briefly at Methuen as he was ushered by hotel staff to a seat at the centre of an even more extravagantly decorated table.

* * *

Virtual scene snapshot: Several hours later. All heads are turned towards Nick and two uniformed officials who are leaving the courtyard through a side gate.

More food arrived and a man with a guitar, accompanied by a group of young women, sang and danced around the tables. After an hour or so, a brass band struck up outside and they found themselves shepherded into a seated trailer, pulled by a tractor belching fumes. The carnival atmosphere continued as they wound their way up the hill, past small sugar-cube houses, from where yet more people emerged to greet them.

Having sat opposite Marco at the lunch, Elizabeth now beckoned him closer. 'What have we done to deserve all this?' she shouted through her hands.

'It's not us,' he said, his eyes rolling and his face reddened by drink. 'It's, uh ... Allied – they have given *everyone* hope. Not just jobs but, umm ... also protection keeping away greedy people from São Miguel.' He thumped his chest. 'My parents come from here. We, uh ... central islanders can be a fierce bunch if someone crosses us, but, umm' – he paused and a wide smile spread across his lined face – 'we can be best allies with those who choose to help us.'

'You mean Allied *owns* you?' Elizabeth shouted over the noise of the tractor as it struggled against the steep gradient.

Marco grinned but didn't answer; instead, he pointed to Pico Island. 'That's where the monitoring station is, and all the AA-Com technicians. Nick will go there tonight and Professor Pryce and I ...' He looked at Methuen, who had leant towards them, trying to catch what was being said, 'We'll go there tomorrow morning.'

'So how long will we stay here on Faial?' Elizabeth shouted again, her voice growing hoarse.

With everyone staring at him, Marco grinned again and put his hand up. 'Relax! You won't, uh ... find a friendlier place on earth, Doctor Pryce.'

The tractor continued slowly to negotiate the hairpin bends on the hill, revealing after each turn an ever grander vista of the harbour and the darkening cone of the Montanha do Pico. After one final and particularly sharp bend that nearly caused the engine to stall, the road flattened out and as the houses gave way to countryside, the din of the festivities became replaced by the sounds of the night, occasionally interrupted by the spluttering noises coming from the tractor engine.

Dusk was now falling, and within a few minutes they had turned off the road, passing through an old rustic gate that took them down a neatly laid out drive, with clipped lawns and managed woodland on either side. After a long curve in the road, the tractor slowed and entered a wide gravelled turning circle in front of a brightly lit, plantation-style house with colonnades and a covered balcony wrapping around the upper floor.

'This is, uh ... Casa Colonial – your home for the next few days,' Marco announced with a hint of pride. 'It has a restaurant, a spa, two swimming pools, a bar and ten bedrooms. Most of the rooms are, uh ... at the back, so ...' He turned to Bliss and said, a little excitedly, 'I have reserved one of the pretty cottages in the grounds for you. It is very nice to stay in, and you can see the, uh ... ocean for miles and miles.'

As the tractor pulled up, a host of staff streamed down the wide wooden staircase at the front of the house, some clapping and all smiling.

'How is a place like this funded?' Elizabeth asked, as her attempt to unload the luggage was politely taken over by several of the staff.

'Allied as usual, darling,' Lianne said, swaying a little as she was helped up the steps by Marco.

'Allied restored it a few years ago,' Marco added. 'All visitors to the, uh … construction yard or monitoring station on Pico can stay here, and of course, any Allied Associate can use it as a, uh … sort of club for rest and recuperation.'

'Allied Associate?' Bliss asked from behind.

'Oh dear, you need to educate your daughter on our little Masonic set-up,' Lianne said to Methuen as they walked into a gleaming reception hall with a generous collection of inviting sofas and chairs and the air filled with the   faint scent of beeswax.

Just off FSA 84, in a small wood near Sheridan, SCSA, FSA

05.15 hours, 17 June 2050

'Audio!' Nick hollered, nudging Lianne and pulling off his glasses. 'This is Bliss's diary entry.'

Bliss, Personal Diary:
Entry for Thursday 17 February 2050

Ocean Cottage, Faial, Azores, EUCON
03.00 hours

I've not written anything for several days because this place has just knocked me out. It's like stepping back into an era I only know from the movies: no keys to any doors and run by real people – no bots of any description.

The staff seem genuinely interested in what I think and do, and if I show any interest in return, then in no time they pull out a photo album or show me some memento to do with their family. And this warm reception is infectious. As I walk around Casa Colonial, even the Allied people staying here are calm and respectful. I'm sure they all have teleplants and other communication devices, but I see no one using them in the public spaces.

The lady who looks after me, Maria, took me for a short walk through the woods at the back of my little cottage, to a vantage point overlooking Pico. There she excitedly pointed out the Allied construction yard at the foot of the volcano, where she informed me, one of her sons and her husband are employed. She then gestured beyond the mountain and said that that was where her eldest son worked, and added proudly, 'As a manager in the monitoring station.'

Later that day she showed great interest in my teleplant – which started to pick up messages as soon as we entered Casa Colonial. She had caught me, alone, on a bench out in the garden, immersed with BlissX. When I tried to explain about the parallel reality of the SWVRP, she looked confused, so I gave up.

She's a satisfied soul though. Her needs extend no further than her family's well-being – which at present is more than adequately catered for by Allied. Things can change, of course, but when I posed that possibility to her, she just smiled and placed her hand on mine and said in English something she had clearly learnt by heart: 'What will be, will be, Miss. Most things we can do nothing about, so why worry about them?'

Is that then how to find contentment – only worry about the things one can control?

That has undoubtedly been Ramona's new tack since I left LCS, but I *feel* exactly the opposite. The IT is making me more alert to the world and I find myself joining things together in a way I have never done before. I couldn't explain that to Maria, nor could I tell her that we were only conversing quite so easily because my Portuguese comprehension has really taken off, thanks to the Treatment.

I've not seen much of Dad or Mum – Dad because he shot off to Pico with Marco soon after we got here, and Mum because she's been luxuriating in the first-floor master suite that runs the whole length of the main house. Each of her rooms, including the bathroom, has a fabulous view of the bay and Pico beyond. Lianne is on the ground floor – '... as close to the bar as possible,' she boasted, to which I didn't respond.

Once Maria had gone home for the day, I had a chat with the Coven and then Seth. I didn't find them, they found me. They could see on their devices exactly where I was, but when I said, 'I'm on the Mid-Atlantic Ridge in the Azores,' it was clear they had no idea what I was talking about. My father calls it 'contextual ignorance' – only taking an interest in one's immediate surroundings. I suppose, like Maria, this limited view gives them a sense of security, contentment even, but unlike her, they're privileged, and therefore bear a responsibility for keeping themselves informed so they can play a larger role in the world.

Oh dear! There I go again, criticising everything and everyone around me. According to the Social Adjustment Manual, hyper-critical behaviour is a common early consequence of IT. The other day it showed itself in the most unfortunate way with Auntie Lianne. She'd invited me to dinner and duly drank herself into alcoholic oblivion. She was quite taken aback the next morning when I launched into a lecture about the side effects of alcohol on older people. The discussion only got heated when she said she had a right to get plastered and that it was no different from me immersing myself in the SWVRP. It sounded like the Coven: knowing her rights but not her responsibilities. I left the table and right now we're not speaking.

I think the frustrating exchanges with the Coven the day before contributed to the irritation I showed towards Auntie Lianne, particularly if I include the conversation with Seth. He's clearly annoyed about being cut off from the joint sharing arrangement on my teleplant and implied that I was no better than a rat deserting a sinking ship. The only thing he said of any interest at all was about an urgent call from LCS, asking if he knew where I was. He said he had nothing to tell them and I told him to keep it that way. Later in the day, I contacted Ramona. She seemed excited about Faial, Pico and all the activity going on around here, but about the Coven she was quite brutal. 'Ignore those from the past, because that is all they can tell you about.'

While I was busy talking to her in the garden, this tall friendly guy showed up from the local police. His name is José and he's the leader of a small group guarding Casa Colonial. (Why? I thought.) The upshot of our chat was that tomorrow I've been invited on a three-day trek up to the caldera of Cabeço Gordo – 'the ancient volcano from which Faial was formed millions of years ago', or so he told me.

AA-Com File: Faial *(contd)*

Casa Colonial Bar, Faial, Azores, EUCON
Evening, 19 February 2050

Virtual Scene snapshot: Lianne – wearing a black chiffon trouser suit – enters the main bar of Casa Colonial, where Elizabeth, perched on a barstool, is talking with a young man.

'Darling, you're here at the bar before me – what a shock! And who is this handsome creature?'

Elizabeth turned around and, adjusting the skirt of her long blue silk dress, introduced the man beside her, who then excused himself discreetly when Lianne ignored his greeting.

'Bit early isn't it, darling, for talent-spotting?' Lianne said as she gratefully accepted a complimentary drink from the barman. 'Is our dinner appointment still on … or have you made alternative arrangements?'

'Stop it!' Elizabeth laughed, sweeping her hair behind her ears. 'I was only making conversation.'

'I love this dress,' Lianne said, stroking Elizabeth's shoulder.

'You're dressed rather sombrely,' Elizabeth replied as they rose from their seats.

'The boss's wife and all that. And besides, I'm distraught – your daughter has scolded me for my drinking!'

'Yes, all this IT may be adding new layers but it's also reinforcing her old self – in particular her sense of right and wrong.'

Strolling towards the dining room, Lianne stepped back and looked Elizabeth up and down. 'You're a stunningly beautiful woman, did you know that?' she said, loud enough that several guests walking past looked at them in surprise and smiled politely.

'Enough!' Elizabeth whispered, looping her arm inside Lianne's and pulling her forward. 'This evening, I'm here to talk with you and you alone.'

They strolled across the paved terrace of the restaurant towards a table at the far end, lit by a single candle. As the staff fussed around them, laying out cutlery and adjusting the cushions on their seats, Lianne drew a pair of multicoloured spectacles from her bag and said, 'That's what I love about this place – they enjoy pleasing us.'

'You're still wearing glasses?' Elizabeth queried, as Lianne picked up the wine list.

'Oh, they give my dull face some character ... and right now, deliver me information about the rather interesting cellar they have here.'

Elizabeth glanced round and saw, several tables back, the man from the bar raise his glass to her. As she smiled at him, Lianne, still studying the wine list, chuckled.

'That's the big difference between you and me: you like men drooling over you – I hate it.'

'I don't see why,' Elizabeth replied, sounding surprised and piercing an olive with a cocktail stick. 'You're the ... sophisticated type of woman who appeals to certain men.'

Lianne released a deep guttural snort, causing the sommelier – who had been edging towards their table – to step back.

'You've obviously not read that article the other day on one of those trashy magazine sites. It went global – about the only thing that does nowadays,' she said, beckoning the reluctant wine master over and requesting samples from several bottles.

'"Can a feminist dyke be sexy?"' Lianne bawled out with such carefree abandon that the young waiter who had been called to assist the sommelier, burst into laughter, only then to cower under the withering gaze of the older man.

'Sorry?' Elizabeth said, who had also been startled by the remark.

'That was the fucking headline about me,' Lianne retorted, sampling the first of the wines. 'I don't mind them getting my sexual proclivity slightly wrong, but how dare they call me a feminist!' She picked up the bottle nearest to her, waved it in the air and winked at her dining partner.

Once their glasses had been filled and the sommelier and assistant had retreated, Elizabeth put her hands on her head and asked, curiously, 'What do you mean, slightly wrong?'

Lianne laughed aloud and raised her glass to Elizabeth. 'Tonight, we must celebrate diversity in all its forms – without that, we are *surely* doomed.' Signalling over the waiter, who was hovering nearby, she said, 'Let's order something delicious, drink some of these excellent local wines and make this evening one to remember!'

At Lianne's insistence, the food was relegated to a trolley between them, freeing up the table for the wines. Elizabeth manoeuvred her chair towards Lianne, who, having dismissed the sommelier, now began to fill their glasses.

'So does your ... mixed proclivity explain why you show no jealousy when Nick flirts with me?' Elizabeth asked cautiously, sitting back in her seat and cradling the filled wine glass in her hands.

Lianne took a long sip and sat back. 'Yes, it's one of the better qualities I share with Methuen.'

'Why should *he* be jealous?' Elizabeth asked in a slightly indignant tone.

'Oh, come on! What did we agree the other night on the *Clipper*? We must be honest with one another. Look at that guy behind me. Yes, I saw you exchanging glances with him,' she said knowingly. 'These glasses have the additional property of giving me a certain amount of rear vision. What I don't understand is how you've tolerated Methuen's obsessiveness all these years,' she said, placing the frames on the table. 'I see the same thing in Nick: living in the future, uptight and detached, but it's not as bad as with Methuen. Don't get

me wrong – I do like your husband, but he's a little emotionally …
I hope you don't mind me saying this … retarded.'

Elizabeth's head pulled back and she pursed her lips. 'No,
Lianne, that's too simplistic. He's passionate about his ideas –
that's what first attracted me to him – and he's not the logical,
cold fish you're implying. When he has an idea, he's like a child
with a new toy—'

'A toy – you make my point exactly. What about *real things* –
does he come alive in the same way when he sees someone suffering or happy?'

'He understands emotional issues pretty well actually. He did a
lot of the original programming on the behavioural responses for
Allied's IA units—'

'Understands! Does he feel it though?' Lianne shouted mockingly.

'Of course he does … You must have seen how sweet he is
with Bliss?'

'That's as much to do with Bliss as with Methuen. She can be a
little minx sometimes,' Lianne said, laughing. 'Have you ever seen
her turn the feminine charm on Grady?'

'But it shows that Methuen's not retarded, as you say. At times
he can be quite warm and affectionate.'

'But mainly with a young girl. I would call that at least a bit …
backward. I've never seen him show any sign of public affection
towards you, and he positively avoids any emotional engagement
with me. Did you see what he did when I arrived at Soft Rush?'
She blinked and with exaggerated astonishment said, 'He shook
my hand, for God's sake!'

Elizabeth laughed at Lianne's animated response but then sat
back, stared at her and said, 'As a kid, he trained his intellect and
learnt how to bury his emotions. I remember in the early days
sitting beside him at the opera, watching his face completely rapt
in the music and hoping I wouldn't notice the tears running down
his cheeks as Violetta conceded to Alfredo's father's wishes.'

Lianne emptied the remains of a bottle into her glass and said more soberly, 'So everything's all right then between you and him – is that what you're saying?'

'Well—'

'When did he last grab you and say, "I love you"?' Lianne proclaimed with fake affection.

'That's not his style, but he's shown his sensitive side on many occasions—'

'Name one,' Lianne interjected, holding her glass out to the approaching wine waiter and pointing to an unopened bottle.

'Well, on the day we married, he said I had answered his "greatest need".'

'There you are!' Lianne said triumphantly. 'You recall something that happened, what, thirty-plus years ago? What you're missing, and what Methuen is simply not capable of, is sensual spontaneity, darling. Before he acts, he calculates everything in his head – except when Bliss is around. Then, I agree, he's different.'

'And that's why I'd still say "retarded" is too harsh.' Eyeing Lianne and waiting until the waiter had left, Elizabeth then added with a snigger, 'Maybe "arrested" is a better word. When he does open up, he's lovely to be with.'

'Meagre pickings for a lustful woman, methinks,' Lianne retorted, holding up her glass.

Elizabeth clinked her glass with Lianne's and added, 'I think of it like … spring in the desert—'

'What, Death Valley?' Lianne interjected with a raucous laugh.

Elizabeth took a sip and waved her comment away. 'Spring isn't signalled by an orgy of green, but by a single hardy shrub shining through the sand and stone. You learn to savour those moments.'

Lianne took another large gulp and gestured to the hapless young waiter to top up her glass again. 'Good try,' she said, rolling her eyes, 'but only five out of ten. Of course, both of us chose to stick with our first choices. I don't know about you, but it's suited me well. I live to write,' she said, holding up her glass in a celebratory fashion. 'Nick provides me with the resources to do so – the only bloody setback is the nomadic life I have to lead.'

'And what does he get from you?' Elizabeth asked bluntly.

'Well, among other things, I never objected to his various dalliances, and eventually, much to his fascination, he discovered he could talk openly with me about them. Can you imagine how liberating that was for a buttoned-up man like Grady? To have someone close to him that he didn't need to deceive, someone who showed no jealousy or envy. And strange as it sounds, it began to create a frisson between us. But if that were all, the relationship would have fizzled out by now. It didn't because slowly, slowly, he started to share with me more than just the details of his latest female conquest. That's how I came to help him escape from the Restoration Party.'

'How did that come about?'

'I'd been cruising through the '30s – literally sometimes on the *Clipper* – establishing my reputation as a writer. But although we lived and entertained together, for the most part we had separate lives: him building his business and political empires, me creating a popular detective character that eventually gave me financial independence. I had a wonderfully interesting companion, whose varied life provided me with a production line of ideas for my novels, while also keeping the spectre of loneliness from the door. But then, in the spring of '37, I was watching TV and heard something I just couldn't believe—'

'That Nick was supporting McFall rather than Tom Harding to run the Unity Party?'

'You see! Even you still remember that. I'd only met McFall once, a few months earlier. We shook hands and, I'm telling you, a shiver ran right through my body. Two lifeless eyes staring back at me, asking, "Who is this crop-haired woman who dresses like a cleaner?" That meeting raised his antenna – but also mine. I didn't feature in McFall's plan for Nick O'Grady, but nor was McFall going to figure in mine. I knew he'd try to get Nick away from me, so when a friend passed on a story about illegal funding by General Abrasives, I began to weave a plot to expose the Restoration Party and extract my husband from McFall's clutches.'

'Did Nick know what you were doing?'

'Not straight away. I had to do my research. My father knew the founder of GA, Harvey Seingold – you know, the elderly Jewish guy you met at the Opening. Once I had the facts, I confronted Nick with them and insisted he met up with Harvey – who, fortunately, he'd come across many years ago and respected.'

'That's incredible,' Elizabeth exclaimed. 'I've never got involved with Methuen in that way.'

'But I've been to countless receptions when Methuen has gushed with admiration over your achievements?'

'And I admire what he's done – but that's not what binds us,' Elizabeth said quietly, refilling her glass. 'Like you and Nick, we've found a level of independence that allows each of us to be ourselves, while always being there to support and challenge one another. "Complementary intellects", he calls it: him arguing from the model in his head, me drawing my conclusions from what he refers to as my "here-and-now seismometer". But underlying that, we also share a little of what you and Nick have – an openness that carries with it no threat, never disappoints, and sometimes thrills. Who would want to lose that?'

Lianne went to pour herself another drink, but the waiter rushed over, topping up her glass before removing the empty bottles from the table.

'Not sure how useful all his theoretical stuff will be on Phillips though,' she said, suddenly sounding concerned. 'Quick problem-solving will be the order of the day, which means, my dear, that you may be working overtime in support of your man.'

Elizabeth waved her glass at Lianne. 'Sounds exciting?'

'Yes, but it's not you that concerns me, it's Methuen. Is he the right person to lead a new community?' Lianne said, draining her glass.

Elizabeth made no response as a train of trolleys arrived, laden with desserts.

* * *

Virtual Scene snapshot: Two hours on. Lianne is seen disappearing into her room on the ground floor, while Elizabeth strolls across the wide hallway towards the staircase.

As she passed the bar, the young man she'd had a drink with earlier called out to her. For a moment, she hesitated, the effects of the alcohol swirling around in her head, but then, hearing his footsteps on the polished wooden floor heading in her direction, turned away and hurried up the stairs.

Just off FSA 84, in a small wood near Sheridan, SCSA, FSA

07.00 hours, 17 June 2050

'That was quite some evening,' Nick said casually, removing his VR specs and turning to face Lianne.

'The drink talking too much,' Lianne sighed.

'I don't mean that. I mean the way Elizabeth excited that guy?'

'She was only having fun—'

'Oh, so when *she* does it, it's just "fun", but when I do it, I'm a "louse"?'

Lianne shook her head angrily. 'Nick! She's the wife of your best friend and someone you rely on to get this new project of yours working. Not only is it inappropriate, it's also plain dumb.'

'You were pretty ruthless, the way you described Methuen,' Nick mumbled moodily.

'It was heart-to-heart surgery. I opened up and so did she. As I said, I admire Methuen – and besides, we have quite a lot in common.'

'Really?'

'Yes! Like me, he was a third child with parents who wanted something different; and like me, he has a visceral distaste for unfairness – that's where Bliss gets her sense of right and wrong.'

Nick pulled himself up on his elbows and asked earnestly, 'But you don't think he's suitable for leading Phillips Cay, right?'

'I don't know. If he can be more open with Elizabeth, then together they'll be a powerful team, but I worry about what they have to work with.'

'What do you mean?' he asked, turning towards her.

'From what I saw in the few hours I was on Phillips, that community is hopelessly divided between those who seem to be semi-resident – still treating it like a resort – and the newcomers you've brought in to run the project with Methuen. And then there are the locals and the hordes of "boat people". It won't be easy for him to get that lot behind this plan.'

'Yeah … that's been worrying me also. As soon as we reach the facility and I can use my AVIII, I'm going to contact him and see how he's getting on,' Nick said, falling back and gazing up at the ceiling. 'For your information,' he added a little wearily, 'I did appreciate the help you gave me with McFall. It's just that after I'd heard Harvey's story in early December, many things became urgent – not least, to find out what was in the warehouses that I'd been renting out to the Party for the past five years. You must remember Christmas Day 2045?'

'The Christmas that never was,' she replied, turning towards him. 'You made up some excuse about a business issue—'

'Well, it was, in a way. I went to Portland with an official from my father's old department. As it was Christmas McFall's guards were thin on the ground, so we were able to enter the sheds unchallenged. I was shocked – as was the guy from the government. There, stacked high, was not only an arsenal for equipping an army – but the army itself, in the form of five thousand robot soldiers.'

'So why didn't the government take charge at that point – McFall was clearly a threat to national security?'

'In retrospect that's exactly what should have been done, but it quickly escalated all the way up to Harding's desk – and that's where things got confused. Harding had the new constitution ready and wanted to give McFall one more chance to come on board.'

'What, even after his disgraceful behaviour at that White House press conference earlier in the month?'

'Harding was on a wave; he thought he could sort it out quietly and when he heard about my plan – sorry, your plan – to expose McFall's wrongdoings in the New Year, he jumped at it, ordering the government guy to remove the arms but leave the crates and coverings in place. They set up a decoy around the yard to keep McFall's people away and, over the New Year holiday break, loaded everything on to the *Clipper*.'

'Ah, so that's what Elizabeth and Methuen came across.'

'That was only a small part. We unloaded much of it at Tilbury Docks when we arrived in the UK. The embassy had arranged for most of the robo-soldiers and weapons to be handed over to the UK government as part of the deal for finding me a position in London.'

'And McFall never suspected a thing?'

'Na ... he was too busy with his new party,' Nick smirked and then in a more reflective voice added, 'but it was touch and go, especially when I had to keep up the pretence of being a loyal party member at the '46 Spring Conference.'

'Why didn't you share all this with me?'

'What you don't know, you can't worry about, Lianne – that's the upside of what you call my need-to-know obsession.'

'A worry shared is a worry halved, Nick,' she shot back.

After a short silence, he said softly, 'I got it.' Pointing the remote at the ceiling, he added, 'Let's go on to the next section of this scene. This part has just Elizabeth and Methuen from the description.'

AA-Com File: Faial *(contd)*

Upper Floor Suite, Casa Colonial, Faial, Azores, EUCON

Evening, 20 February 2050

Virtual Scene snapshot: On the balcony of Casa Colonial, Elizabeth lies stretched out on a wicker lounger, staring out at the Montanha do Pico. Methuen is walking through the door behind her, looking exhausted and accompanied by a troop of staff carrying bags and cases.

'Hello, stranger,' Elizabeth said, jumping up and giving her husband a huge hug. 'It feels as if you've been away for ages. How did it go?'

Methuen, his face newly tanned, slumped onto a chair. 'I don't like all this inspection trip stuff – I always feel as if I'm in the way, and besides that,' he said, gazing along the balcony, 'I kept thinking about the huge bathtub we have here.'

'Well, go and have a good soak and while you're doing that, I'll make something for us to eat.'

'Surely the staff—'

'No, I want to do it myself. There's a small kitchen at the back.'

* * *

Virtual Scene snapshot: One hour on. Methuen is standing on the balcony, wrapped in a bathrobe, his hair frizzled and his face flushed. Elizabeth, next to him, is holding a tray of food and pointing to the vacant lounger beside hers.

'You smell nice,' she said, pouring him a drink. 'I want to hear all about what goes on behind the volcano.'

Methuen laughed, propping a cushion behind his back. 'Actually, I spent most of my time in *front* of it with Marco, in the construction yard at Madalena, over there,' he said, pointing down in the distance towards a cluster of lights. 'It's a Livings facility so I thought it would be building modules for accommodation units, but I was wrong – there's much more going on. In one part of the yard, they're making a sort of gigantic conveyor belt that I was told would transport materials over long distances – rocks and soil, mainly. For what reason, I wondered? In another place, there was a production line assembling vertical farm units – like those you saw on Phillips when we were there for the Opening. But why so many, I asked myself – is Allied planning to go into agribusiness? No one had any answers and that was typical wherever I went. Everyone was helpful and polite, but no one had the foggiest idea of the ultimate destination of the things they were making or how they fitted into any plan.'

'Did you ask Nick about it?'

'Well, that was the next surprise. On the evening of ... day three, I suppose it was ... we were driven to the other end of the island along a bumpy road cut through a succession of old lava flows. After an hour or so, we came to a small volcanic cone, behind which sat a sprawling multi-storey, brownish-grey building, barely distinguishable from the surrounding piles of cinder. Incredibly, it turns out that this rather insignificant-looking structure was not only the main base for AA-Com Operations but also, currently, the global HQ of Allied. After the most basic of security checks, I was led upstairs to a large meeting room, where they were debating the latest solutions to the AA-Com interference problem. Nick was slouched in a chair, listening to the presentations. He pointed to a seat next to him, but said nothing to me. The discussion went back and forth for hours, punctuated mainly by him requesting clarification or making some criticism. You know what he's like – doesn't overdo flattery or bother with geeing up the troops. The whole thing came to a rapid end when he abruptly got up to leave. He tapped me on the shoulder as he passed by and said he had some government people to meet and he'd see me later – but he never did.'

'So did you find out any more about this AA-Com problem?'

'Not from him directly,' Methuen said, 'but the Centre's head of monitoring was very open. They've found an answer – that's the good news. Less good is that it'll take time to implement. The set-up they have is really rather impressive. They're managing fifty thousand dirigibles around the globe – each "communicator", as they call them, is about the size of a fridge-freezer and positioned thirty miles up in the stratosphere.'

'Woah! I've often wondered how this dirigible network operated,' Elizabeth said, her eyes wide.

'Well, I never realised the scale of it until now. Each dirigible is tethered to the ground using what they casually refer to as "spider-web". It's a new material, apparently – stronger than iron, lighter than string and transparent – almost invisible to the eye.'

'But what if someone flies into it?'

'Oh, they've thought all that out. Electronic warning signals tune into any flying object's navigation software, causing it to veer away. The sites are also positioned outside any of the commercial aircraft corridors. Maintenance costs are low and where they're located on land, the locals get a regular income for guarding them.'

'Does that actually work?' Elizabeth said with a frown.

'Yup, I was as surprised as you,' he said, 'but it's pretty smart thinking. Allied locate the base station on common ground, so the community gets the income and therefore has an interest in protecting it.'

'And you said they've come up with a solution to the interference?'

'Seems they've tracked down the problem to a piece of software in AVIII that causes interference in the dirigibles and, to make matters worse, in all the satellite systems they use. Allied don't want to change the AVIII, so they've devised a couple of options to overcome the problem: either insert an electronic patch into the pre-AVIII cubes, or into each dirigible communicator. In most part, they've decided to go for the latter.'

'But won't that take years?'

'No, it can, apparently, be done quite quickly,' Methuen said. 'That's the beauty of dirigibles over satellites. Each can be hauled down, upgraded or repaired at little cost, and then refloated and brought back into operation within a few days. The limiting factor is the manufacture of the new boards, but that'll be speedier than retrofitting the hundred million or so pre-AVIII cubes currently spread across the planet.'

'What about people who use the satellite system?'

Methuen shook his head and said a little despondently, 'Adapting all of those is a step too far – anyone reliant on satellite communication for their AA-Com will have to obtain a patch for their own cube. Fortunately, the interference is only disabling if a pre-AVIII and an AVIII device are simultaneously using the same communicator.'

Elizabeth sat up and looked at him anxiously. 'So what about Phillips when we get there?'

'I received reassurances that the dirigible on Phillips was on the priority list. It had already been taken down to be replaced, because it was over ten years old. The new dirigible will have the patch already fitted. It won't take long.'

'I sincerely hope so, Methuen, because living on Phillips with unreliable comms is quite a different proposition from what we've signed up for.'

As he tucked into the food on the tray, he asked, 'What have you been up to while I've been away?'

'Oh, just relaxing mainly. I managed to get hold of Martin and asked him to tell Jack and my dad where we are, and that we're safe. I also had a long dinner with Lianne a few nights ago—'

'Did she remain sober?'

'Umm ... merry, I would describe it as, but we did have an incredibly open and honest discussion. When she's encouraged to be thoughtful, she's a revelation and even stops drinking – for a time at least.'

Methuen poured himself a glass of water and, sitting back, asked cautiously, 'What was she so "open and honest" about?'

Elizabeth shrugged. 'Among other things, herself and Nick.'

'Uh huh ...' Methuen murmured invitingly.

'Did you know it was her that informed Nick about McFall's secret funding?'

'I'd heard the rumours – as everyone had – of his dodgy finances, but not that Lianne was so involved in exposing him.'

'There's a lot more going on inside Lianne O'Grady's head than she's willing to admit.'

'Well, Nick doesn't say much about her but they're inseparable. What else did she have to say for herself?'

'We talked about kids and about her and Nick deciding not to have any because, she said, they couldn't "hack the responsibility".'

'I've often wondered why—'

'Except it's not true,' Elizabeth said, pouring herself some wine and then draining half the glass.

'Why do you say that?' Methuen asked sharply.

'Because ... Nick can't have children—'

'Wow! That's quite a revelation – how do you know?'

'He told me.'

'When?'

Elizabeth took another mouthful of wine. 'Oh, years ago,' she said, bowing her head.

'Was that what put you off him?' Methuen asked, lying back on the lounger.

'No! What "put me off him" was that I loved *you*.'

Methuen took the wine bottle and filled his glass. 'Well, I'm glad to hear that,' he said, nosing the liquid before taking a small sip.

'Did you ever doubt it?'

He looked up into the night sky. 'I guess if I thought about such things in conventional terms back then, I might have.'

'What do you mean?'

He put his glass down and turned to face her. 'If I placed fidelity of body ahead of fidelity of mind, then I might have been concerned. I made a decision never to ask you about such things, although I know if I had, you'd have told me the truth. You and I have a bond as strong as that spiderweb stuff that infidelities of the body just can't break.'

'Infideli-*ties*?' Elizabeth echoed his word loudly but before either could say any more, the sound of someone running along the balcony could be heard.

'Hello?' a voice called out, and Bliss appeared in hiking boots and a waterproof jacket.

'You're back!' Elizabeth called out. 'I was getting worried. Come and tell us what you've been doing.'

'I can't stay. I've promised to have dinner with José.'

'Who's—?'

'I'll tell you later – just wanted to let you know that I survived Cabeço Gordo. You should've have come with us. The *Hydrangea macrophylla* were incredible.'

* * *

Virtual Scene snapshot: Elizabeth and Methuen recline on their loungers, staring up at the starlit sky.

'Notice how she described the flowers?' Methuen said.

'She was excited?'

'Yup, but that's partly because of what's-his-name – José. What I also heard was a completely different Bliss. Last year she'd have talked about the smells, shapes and colours, without ever bother-ing to find out details of the plants. Now she's learning their Latin names, the history of the plant's colonisation and telling us there are six hundred cultivars. If – what's-his-name – hadn't been waiting downstairs, she would have started listing them all!' He laughed.

Elizabeth lay still for a moment and then pointed up into the night sky. 'What's that light up there?'

Methuen switched off the lamp next to him and stared in the direction she was indicating. 'It's the observatory on top of Pico.'

'I thought Pico was still active?'

'It's dormant,' he said, assuredly.

'Umm,' Elizabeth murmured, settling back and closing her eyes. 'Unlike Cabeço Gordo then, which seems to be extinct,' she said plaintively.

'Not quite. It forms the backbone of this island, and don't forget Capelinhos – that suggests the old man still has some fire in his belly.'

Just off FSA 84, in a small wood near Sheridan, SCSA, FSA

08.00 hours, 17 June 2050

They lay in silence until the bird chorus started up.

'So when did you know?' Lianne murmured.

Another silence followed before Nick replied a little coldly, 'It was the year after I graduated and was busy setting up Allied. All sorts of insurance policies were being taken out on me that required medical checks—'

'Your mother never knew, did she.'

'Why do you say that?'

'Because she blamed me for not giving her grandchildren.'

'I'm sorry,' Nick whispered, and closed his eyes.

'Need-to-know writ large,' Lianne surmised.

As the birds began to twitter once more, Nick picked up the remote and turned off the soundtrack.

Lianne said quietly, 'It explains the Lothario in you.'

'How's that?'

'When I first met you, you had that reputation of conquering women – like my hapless elder sister. It was your way of proving your manhood. I've often wondered whether that's the real reason we're still together ...'

'I don't think you can read too much into the—'

'... because you've never had to conquer me?'

'You could say, it was you who did the conquering,' he suggested lightly. 'You pushed your sister to one side, dragged me down to the sea for a spot of skinny-dipping and then took charge of that IPO document. And in '45, you did the same with McFall. And between those times when you didn't feel I needed saving, you did your own thing.'

'But I don't fire up your passion like Elizabeth does, do I?'

'You're more important to me than that,' he said, his voice quivering slightly.

'Hmm … as I guess you are to me,' she said, and then pointed up to the ceiling screen. 'What do you have next in that scene?'

Nick clicked the remote. 'Leaving Faial,' he said, picking up his VR specs.

AA-Com File: Faial *(contd)*

Terrace of Casa Colonial restaurant, Faial, Azores, EUCON
Morning, 21 February 2050

Virtual Scene snapshot: Clean-shaven and dressed in a white linen suit, Nick is making his way across the restaurant terrace towards Methuen, who is seated by himself, reading a book, propped up against a glass jug.

'Okay, we're good to go,' Nick said, placing a news-sheet on the table.

Putting the book down on his lap, Methuen said, 'Everything sorted then?'

Nick looked around and then, turning his head towards Methuen, said in a low voice, 'We'll have AVIII working within weeks.'

'Weeks? I thought you said it'd take months?'

'I'm talking about HUBCOM,' Nick said, pouring himself a glass of water.

'HUBCOM?'

'I've not explained that yet. It's Allied's private version of the AVIII. We're getting that operational first so we can keep the business running – and before you ask, that includes Phillips, once your personal AVIII has been upgraded.' He spread a napkin over his knee and added in a more cheerful tone, 'You know, it could be a blessing in disguise, this problem.'

Methuen frowned. 'How's that?'

'The replacement circuit board will allow each HUBCOM to use the whole of the dirigible network.'

'I assumed all AVIIIs could do that?'

'No, HUBCOM was originally designed to operate with a specific set of dedicated dirigibles, like the one on top of Millbank

Mirror in London. Once the new boards are installed, it'll also now be able to communicate with any of the fifty thousand standard dirigible stations around the world—'

'Morning!' rang out a brisk voice as Lianne approached, dressed in a bright, rainbow-coloured kaftan, also carrying a copy of the news-sheet.

Nick pulled out a chair beside him and pointed to it.

'If this rag is correct,' she said, sitting down, 'the stand-off with McFall has been resolved.'

Methuen looked at her in surprise but as he went to speak, Nick interjected. 'I've been listening to it all night. It's a fucking disaster—'

'What's a disaster?' Elizabeth asked, walking up the steps from the garden below and pulling out a seat next to Methuen.

'They've done a deal with McFall: Harding and his nominated VP, Tranter, have gone,' Nick replied, shaking his head in despair.

'What do you mean – gone?' Methuen asked anxiously.

'As of last night, the first President of the Federated States of America will be Farrell Kelvin Drake II—'

'Does it matter?' Elizabeth chipped in.

'What, that a third-class administrator with no military experience is to become Commander-in-Chief, just as the so-called Chinese Peacekeeper Force have begun to build their presence in Oman and our rebel Senator has threatened to split away from the FSA? Of course it matters!'

'But the second of those is no longer in doubt,' Lianne said gravely, spreading the newspaper across the table. 'It says here that Drake has named McFall as VP.'

'No, no, no – that's fake news, for sure,' Nick said firmly, waving his finger at her. 'The whole of this news-sheet is compiled by some idiots in São Miguel, patching together stories they haven't verified.'

Methuen, who had reached across the table and taken Nick's copy of the paper, said, 'Well, it would offer a more plausible explanation as to why Harding left, rather than for the health reasons it states here.'

Nick sat back, pondering Methuen's remark, while beside him Lianne poured herself a glass of juice.

'Rather puts the kibosh on your plans to return to the States for the Inauguration, doesn't it?' Elizabeth said, looking at Nick.

'Ignore it – it's not true,' Nick replied sharply. 'The little I do know about Drake is that he finds McFall's brand of morality every bit as distasteful as Harding did—'

'Since when did morality play any role in power politics?' Elizabeth replied scornfully, and then looked up as Bliss appeared, marching across the terrace, still in the check shirt and jeans she'd worn on the trek.

Lianne took off her glasses and stared at her. 'So, sweetie, I heard you went hiking. Did you have fun?'

'It was brilliant! It took us four hours to get to the edge of the crater and then it started raining, but it was just so beautiful. José knows the names of all the plants and even some of the geology.'

Nick frowned at Elizabeth. 'José?'

'He's with the local police and an exceptionally talented guy,' Bliss said eagerly, spreading jam on a slice of bread.

Lianne glanced at Elizabeth, her eyes wide. 'What else did he teach you?' she asked, with a mischievous laugh.

'Well, among other things, he warned me not to stay here too long. He said there was an Azorean military vessel just off Faial and there's bound to be a bit of action.'

Elizabeth and Lianne turned to Nick, who nodded confidently back at them. 'Don't worry, don't worry, we're leaving this afternoon.'

'Will there be fighting?' Elizabeth asked anxiously.

'There could be. It seems that the split between São Miguel and several of the Central Island head honchos has become personal.'

Elizabeth turned deliberately to Methuen. 'Maybe we should go to the ship right now – what do you think?'

Just off FSA 84, in a small wood near Sheridan, SCSA, FSA

08.50 hours, 17 June 2050

Pulling off her specs, Lianne stared upward and said, 'Tricky times, huh ...? What and who can you put your faith in these days?'

Nick rubbed his face and then said firmly, 'I was right but also wrong about Drake. He shafted Harding for sure, and even played with the idea of bringing in McFall and moving Zbrinsky, his actual choice for VP, to Defense. It's just that McFall got greedy and insisted Zbrinsky also left. That's what cratered things – Drake couldn't manage without Zbrinsky.'

'You know him?'

'Yeah, my father was his mentor for many years – it was through him that the warehousing issue in '45 was quickly brought to Harding's attention.'

'You should have told me all this. I was so scared when we travelled back to the States in March, after dropping off Methuen and Elizabeth. It's one thing to have death threats against you from some rebel political party, but quite another if the promoter is the actual VP of the new administration.'

'It's just my nature not to talk about things until I'm sure.'

'But we're partners, Nick. As I keep saying to you: your worries are often my worries – just think of it like that.'

'Okay, okay, I hear you,' he said, picking up the remote and inspecting the outdoor images.

'Any scenes from the crossing to Phillips on that file?' she asked, nodding at the ceiling.

Nick looked up and said, 'Well, we could watch the file here called "Arriving".'

'What's that folder at the bottom of the listing?'

'Probably some system information,' he said, clicking on the object and opening one of four icons. 'Yup, just as I thought,' he muttered, scrolling through lines of coding.

But as he clicked on the last icon, he dropped the remote on the bed as a new column of VR titles appeared on the screen. 'What's this?' he said suspiciously.

Lianne pulled herself up on her elbows to read the file title that had appeared. '"Sharing a Secret" – not another contretemps between you and Elizabeth, is it?' she said mockingly, but then saw him, frozen, staring at the screen. 'What's wrong?'

'This is something that shouldn't have been recorded.'

'How do you know until you've opened it?'

'The location and date stamp. It's a mega screw-up if it's what I think it is – especially if anyone else has viewed it.'

'Can I view it with you?'

'Err, no, it's nothing ...'

'Nick,' Lianne said sternly, 'what have we just been discussing?'

He picked up the remote and zoomed in on the file. 'The folder has been used as a sort of dump for incomplete stuff that's not yet been properly edited or reviewed.'

Picking up her glasses, she said, 'Don't give me that whole confidentiality speech again. Come on, let's immerse and find out what's there.'

AA-Com Dump File: Sharing a Secret

Control Room, *Allied Clipper*, 25 nautical miles NW off Faial

Early afternoon, 21 February 2050

Virtual Scene snapshot: Nick, at the wheel, gazes through a rain-lashed window, while Methuen stands beside him gripping the railings, his eyes fixed on a monitor.

'Don't worry, Methuen, they'll never come after us in a swell like this, and the headwinds are too strong for them to launch a drone attack. My bigger concern is that over there!' Nick said, tossing his head towards a line of clouds billowing up on the horizon. 'It's never-ending, storm after storm – there's too much energy in the atmosphere.'

Methuen made no reply, standing rigid as the ship lurched forward.

'I thought you were a sailor?' Nick called out, showing no sign of discomfort himself.

'Sure, but only when I can keep my eyes on the land,' Methuen shot back as he staggered across the floor and grabbed the back of the single sofa.

'This'll also make it hard for the São Miguel militia to launch any kind of attack on Faial,' Nick said, tapping into a keyboard and making his way over to the lounge area.

Gazing up at him, Methuen said, 'And if they do land, they'll have to face the islanders you've been organising.'

Nick glanced at him, smiled and then said, light-heartedly, 'Ah, you worked out the real reason for the delay. I had to get all the seniors together on the island. What did you make of all the robo-soldiers you came across?'

'Oh, you know about that ...' Methuen said with a weak smile.

'Do anything on this ship and I'll get to know about it,' Nick said, taking a slice of cake from a plate on a high-sided tray that had started to slide backward and forward across the table.

'Are there still some on board?'

'No, of course not. They're now spread across the central islands, located on every headland and in every cove and sea cave—'

'But not just to monitor. The ones I saw were all armed,' Methuen said, gripping the sofa arms again as the *Clipper* rolled to one side. 'Don't you worry that any conflict will draw in the EMA?'

'If it does, they'll have to fight all the central islanders now. Ever since the US reduced their presence on Terceira – that's the big central island to the west – everyone's been looking for jobs and protection. It wasn't hard to sign them up for this security cordon I created last week.'

Marco appeared in the room, looking windswept and fraught. Methuen was about to ask if he was okay when Nick pointed sharply at the weather chart displayed on the monitor by the wheel. 'That'll be on top of us within the next few hours. We need to batten everything down and be prepared for some very rough weather.'

Marco's shoulders sagged as he glared at Nick, as if to say: what do you think I've been doing? But, as usual, his reply was patient and factual.

'A crate with, uh ... parts for the 1-MW turbine came, umm ... loose as we left Faial. We tried to secure it but it was too heavy so we are, uh ... unpacking it and taking as much of it below as we can.'

As he disappeared down the stairwell, Methuen sat back and folded his arms. 'Was that the deal then? Turbines for guns?'

'Crudely put, but ... yes!' Nick said, his mouth full of cake. 'That 1-MW turbine will provide enough power for Phillips and more.' As Methuen continued to glare at him, Nick added cheerfully, 'Don't worry, they got a good deal.'

'How did they get hold of such a large turbine? Even if I had the funds, I couldn't just put in an order for something like that when we lived in the UK. Don't the EUCON turbine quotas apply here?'

'Sure, but there's also the EUCON energy subsidy scheme that they used to acquire it,' Nick said with a playful smile.

'That's a shade unscrupulous, isn't it?'

'Why? We priced the arms at cost and the turbines at the Market rate.'

Methuen shook his head disapprovingly and said, 'I wasn't referring to that—'

'We also took on board a large number of high-performance PV solar units from the Chinese that came as part payment for an old job we'd done for them.'

Methuen planted his arms firmly on the sides of the sofa again, as the ship tilted sharply, causing Nick's half-eaten piece of cake to fall to the floor. But rather than pick it up, he sat back, running his hands across his face and then cupping his chin.

'What?' Methuen asked, and laughed a little uneasily as Nick stared back at him.

'I can say it to you but no one else – this AA-Com problem was my fault ...'

Methuen sat up, never having heard the words 'my fault' uttered by his colleague before.

'... I moved too many of my best people too quickly from Comms to Livings.'

'Why did you do that?'

'I realised by the end of the 2020s that Livings would never make serious money from creating retreats for the super-rich. We had to close the business or try a new approach, and that was precisely what I came across while on a visit to Shanghai to hear a presentation about Beijing Bay—'

'Beijing Bay?'

'That's the name the PRC have given to their largest eustatic zone, which by the middle of the next century will be the size of North-West Europe.'

'"Eustatic zone"?'

'It's the term Livings use to describe areas that will be flooded by sea-level rise. Globally, the largest will be in the Amazon, causing more damage than was done by that idiot in the 2020s. Many others will be equally devastating. One will inundate the UAE, another will slice Russia in half, while the coastal belt of the southern and south-eastern states of the FSA will massively retreat. Beijing Bay will displace millions of people and has been identified for some time by the PRC as a medium-term threat to national stability. At the end of the meeting in Shanghai, I got into conversation with some of the local entrepreneurs, who saw the flooding as a business opportunity. They asked whether Allied would be interested in partnering with them to find a commercial solution, which they indicated the government would partly subsidise. On the plane back, I did some research and found similar government-sponsored schemes all around the world. It troubled me that my people in Livings hadn't spotted this, reinforcing a view I'd had for some time that a wholesale reorganisation of that particular business stream was necessary. Once I got back to the office, I rewrote the mission statement of Livings, focusing on these government projects for creating new living space to replace land lost to the sea. That was when I transferred half of my seniors from Comms to Livings.'

Nick looked up as if he expected a question, but seeing Methuen rocking backward and forward and holding his stomach, resumed his explanation. 'Initially, I reorganised Livings into three groups to examine different solutions. They became known internally as the Under, Over and Inside Divisions. *Under* focused on testing the feasibility of creating underwater living spaces – but we quickly rejected that because of the high operating costs.

Inside involved burrowing into mountains. That was technically feasible and cost-effective, but at the time not a solution for the flat coastal plains of eastern China. The one that took off was from the *Over* Division, to build massive floating structures. The technology was already available from the oil and gas industry – all we needed to do was to develop it on a massive scale. I took the idea back to the Chinese, who liked it and guaranteed government funding. In '35, we created a joint venture to design what was effectively three floating cities, each of them housing one hundred thousand people.'

'Blimey! That's huge. Did it go ahead?'

'We got through the initial design with few problems, but when it came to the construction phase – where the government would have to start paying big bucks – we were presented with a proposal that would have left us with only a marginal profit until the installation of the first platform ten years out. Also, they insisted we take five per cent equity, with all rental income in Virtual Yuan. I was about to pull out of the whole thing when this new situation in the Middle East flared up. Describing us as a "US corporation" – which of course we weren't and still aren't – the PRC investors backed off, fearing they might be accused of trading with the enemy—'

'You got nothing out of it?'

'On the face of it we lost money because we'd funded the initial design. Only recently did we receive some reparation in the form of those PV panels I mentioned earlier. But we'd benefitted in another way: the Beijing Bay project transformed Livings into the global leader for large-scale floating technology.'

'Hence, Phillips?'

Nick held up a finger. 'That's what I want to talk to you about now.'

He picked up the scattered lumps of cake off the floor and then, talking into his AA–Plant, walked to the aft end of the room.

As he reached the far wall, a compartment opened out towards him. Reaching in, he retrieved a large cardboard folder, which he brought back to the table.

Placing the tea tray on the floor, he took out a map from the folder and laid it out across the table. 'Remember the evening we spent in that little off-campus house you had in Princeton, just before we went on the Grand Tour?'

'Mercer Road, 2024,' Methuen replied, as he touched one of several raised symbols spread around the oceans on the map.

'Everything I'm going to tell you now goes back to that meeting, and in particular, a comment you made just as I was leaving.'

Methuen looked up at Nick with a puzzled frown.

'"What if it fails?" you said. "What's our Plan B?" I seem to remember I brushed off your questions with some patronising remark, but your comments stayed with me as I journeyed back to New York that night.'

Methuen scratched his head. 'It was a pretty disagreeable meeting, I recall.'

'Well, it got worse for me as I read the latest draft of your book. By the time I reached the apartment, I had an *if-then* issue burning in my head regarding the presentations we were about to give: "*If* the shakers can't be moved, *then* what is your Plan B, Mr O'Grady?"'

'I thought your Plan B was politics?'

'And yours was the SWVRP,' Nick replied without missing a beat.

'Because bottom-up was the only way to move things on the scale—'

'Yeah, yeah, I know your argument,' Nick said, waving away the reply. 'But even though I was engrossed in the tour and then the politics, that *if-then* question kept bugging me. Funnily enough, it was while I was immersing for the first time in the pilot of the SWVRP you sent me in '32 that my thinking began to move in the direction I've now taken. I stayed in the Fully Segmented scenario for several weeks, exploring its implications for Allied. That's why I invited you over to talk about it at the old Essex House Hotel later that year. Remember?'

'How could I forget being uprooted from the Hampshire countryside and flown to New York "for a chat"?' Methuen laughed. 'I came across the entry about the visit, in an old diary the other day. I described you as "downbeat but philosophical".'

'Yeah, because I'd realised by then that the Segmented World was no longer just a scenario – it was going to happen in some form or other and I needed to do something about it. The Plan B thought had haunted me for long enough. It was time to act.'

'So that's why you made such a big deal of the Neutral Areas when we talked over lunch in the hotel?'

Nick's face lit up. 'Ah, you do remember! Though it took me another four years before I did anything about it. The cancellation of the Chinese contract in '36 was the trigger. It demonstrated one of the Segmented model's main predictions, that over time Powerblocks would begin to exclude one another. I used the Chinese response as an example for the Allied board in '39, when I warmed them up to the idea of developing a contingency plan for Allied, should the Fully Segmented scenario materialise.'

He bent forward, elbows on knees, looking directly at Methuen, who had relaxed his grip on the sofa and was now listening intently. 'I realised there was way more at stake than mere trading opportunities. The world will always beat a path to your door if you discover something important. But that requires creating, for our scientists, technologists and technically astute businessfolk, a place where they can thrive; an environment that is open, stimulating and safe, where they can freely collaborate across disciplines: go where they wish and say what they think. The Fully Segmented World threatened all that – the very thing that drives Allied.'

Nick took more papers from the folder and sat back. 'With that thought in mind, I set up an offsite special projects office in Nebraska—'

'Ah, yes ... the illusive, office-in-the-Muskeg,' Methuen exclaimed. 'I heard about it on one of my SWVRP visits but never got a chance to meet anyone who worked there.'

'Yeah. I know the secrecy pissed off a lot of people but it had to be like that. It would have unnerved the Market if it had leaked out that the Chairman of Allied, let alone a member of Sam Harding's team, was involved in some existential mega-project.'

'So that's what all this is about?' Methuen said, pointing at the map.

Nick held his hands up. 'There's a little more we need to cover before I get to that. The first thing I did with the Muskeg group was to get them to immerse in the Fully Segmented scenario, and between immersions read your book with special attention to the geopolitical model. After a week, I pulled them all together and said I wanted a comprehensive plan that would enable Allied not just to survive but thrive in a Fully Segmented World. The only steer I gave them was that the plan should be built around your concept of the Neutral Areas and make use of the floating technology that Livings were developing—'

'You wrote their script,' Methuen said with a critical laugh.

Nick remained straight-faced. 'Look, time was not our friend. Livings had already thought this through from a commercial viewpoint with projects like Beijing Bay. What I now needed was for it to be considered in a fuller sense – to create a worldwide sustainable community. I put a few good managers into the Muskeg team and then left them with just quarterly reviews back to me. That was until '39, when I decided it was time to bring the board onside. But I had a problem: the proposal favoured by the Muskeg office was too much to request in one go. I therefore lowered the board in slowly. I told them that within a decade, Allied would be little more than a regional bit player-only able to trade with one or two Powerblocks, unless we took decisive action. I then asked them to approve the establishment of a single Neutral Area-style community to allow Allied to operate apolitically and potentially trade with *all* the Powerblocks. That in sum was the Phillips Cay Project.'

As the ship dipped down again, Methuen fell forward, catching the edge of the folder. 'I'm confused,' he said, pulling himself back onto the sofa. 'I always thought the idea for Phillips came out of that announcement you made in '45, when we met in Nebraska and decided to sell the SWVRP?'

Nick nodded and held out his hand in apology. 'Yeah, yeah, I'll explain that in a moment – just let me finish filling in the background quickly. What I'd reported to the board was only part of the bigger proposal the Muskeg team made to me that they called Project 2150.'

He stood up and walked behind Methuen, pointing at the map on the table. 'These symbols, which as you can see are evenly distributed in intra-ocean positions around the tropics, mark nine locations where we've acquired the right to build clusters of platforms we call Hubs. The plan is to link the Hubs via an array of dedicated dirigibles delivering free-to-air optical transmission through the specialised version of AVIII that I mentioned before we left Faial—'

'HUBCOM.'

'Exactly. HUBCOM and this geostationary network of communicators will give us almost instant communication and massive bandwidth between the Hubs. Taken together, it forms a politically independent entity that we call the Hub Commonwealth.'

Methuen sat back open-mouthed, with his hands on his head. 'My God, you're creating a new sovereign state ... How did you get the various governments to hand over territory to you?'

Nick nodded as if he had anticipated the question. 'All these locations have one thing in common: by 2150, every one of them will have been obliterated by the rise in sea level. Even now, sea surges have effectively destroyed any tourist potential for the sites we've selected. Pretty soon now, none of them will be able to support long-term habitation, and several have already been abandoned. The individual governments are only ceding owner-ship of the land and seabed. They will retain mineral rights, share access to fishing stocks but, most valuable to them, have a thriv-ing community close at hand offering them long-term trade and employment opportunities.'

'But running a nation-state, Nick – that's preposterous! It's not what Allied does or should have as its focus.'

'You're right. That was one of the reasons I didn't fully inform the board about Project 2150 until '45 – when I had to go back to them to sanction the re-engineering of Phillips and prepare for the implementation of the Community Plan. I knew by then that I needed to come clean over the larger project, even though I feared it might unnerve a few of the members and potentially hold back approval from some for even continuing with Phillips. But around that time I had a huge stroke of luck. At the board's instruction, I'd kept the Consilience Foundation fully informed of what we were doing, in the hope that once we were through the initial design for Phillips, they would come along as an investor. Until '44, the Consilience people would turn up to meetings but never be partic-ularly proactive. Then that summer, while we were at the Opening, a new chairperson was appointed to the Foundation. Out of the blue, she offered me lunch and asked for a briefing on the Phillips Project—'

'You say "she"? Middle Eastern origin, dark complexion, elderly?'

'Umm ... I wouldn't use the word *elderly* – she's pretty sprightly – but that does sound like her. You know her?'

'What's her name?'

'Come on, you know what CF are like – they're ultra-sensitive about disclosing who they are. I always called her Madam Chair. It felt like I was with a kindred spirit – a little like talking with you.

Anyway, I took the risk and told her about Project 2150, as well as my problem of how best to explain it to the board.'

'But why would Consilience want to support a project designed to protect the commercial interests of Allied?'

'The same reasoning we used for Phillips – but on a global scale. P2150 is about creating and maintaining – even in a Fully Segmented World – a global community where freedom, in all of its manifestations, will be guaranteed. If you think of it in that way, the gap between Allied's and Consilience's aspirations narrows somewhat. Our fundamental aim is the same: to create a place where human beings have the opportunity to reach their full potential; where the innovation is possible that humankind, let alone Allied, desperately needs to solve the mountain of problems we face. You know all this stuff.'

'Did she buy it?'

'She said nothing until after lunch, and then as she was getting into her car, she looked up at me and said, quietly, with a disarming coolness: "The Consilience Foundation will be part of Project 2150." Just like that! I was cock-a-hoop, not only because it would make it easier to get the board onside, but I had secured a respected co-venturer with deep pockets who would encourage others to follow.'

'And that was it? No one asked about ... ownership or governance of these Hubs, for example?'

'Oh, they asked lots of questions. The first meeting that Madam Chair attended was the longest Allied board meeting I'd ever had. I was upfront with everyone, saying that we were still in the developmental phase of the Commonwealth Model. I also explained how Phillips fitted in as the testbed, not just for the physical structures we were planning to install, but also for the Community Plan we would eventually use on the other Hubs. But to answer your question, we agreed that ownership and governance would be with the Hub residents. All Allied required was citizenship for its Associates and space to locate its research and production centres.'

'And so ... Phillips is part of P2150?' Methuen reasoned, sitting back and staring up at the ceiling.

'An integral part,' Nick said, waving his finger affirmatively. 'Nothing I told you before about the rationale for Phillips has changed. It's just that I've now given you the full context – and I hope even more motivation to make sure it works.'

Methuen rubbed his face and sat forward, no longer troubled by the ship's motion. 'Why didn't you tell me about this in '48, when I signed up to help you create the Phillips Community Plan?'

'This idea is dynamite. We had to, and still must, be careful that no one has the slightest suspicion of what we're really up to. Cast your mind back to the Phillips Opening – what do you think that was all about? Did you seriously think I wanted to entertain, let alone engage with, that fantasist McFall? I wasn't surprised when he shafted me before the presidential elections. I set up that grand Opening as a smokescreen to deflect any speculation as to the real purpose of what lay behind the Phillips renovations. It wasn't just you who was kept in the dark about P2150. I didn't want anyone other than the negotiators to be aware of what was going on – and especially any details of the selected sites. Not even the board members were informed. From '46 onwards, we had to conduct eight, simultaneous, secret negotiations around the world, in order to avoid being levered by potential sellers or buried under a whole heap of legal objections.'

'What about the governments you were negotiating with? Weren't you worried they'd blab the news to the media?'

'We chose our islands carefully, which is why all this has taken so long. We selected them not just for their location but also on the basis of the local community's stability and flexibility. They are as important to the success of the Commonwealth concept as any other element. We studied their culture and recent history to make sure this OST mentality you write about was not prevalent. And then, as a final insurance, we made binding non-disclosure agreements with the representatives, such that the personal losses incurred if details were leaked to the media would be so severe that I doubt they even discussed it with their mothers.'

'And the negotiators?'

Nick looked askance. 'They're Allied Associates.'

'So it's no longer just the success of Phillips but this entire mega-project that relies on me making the Community Plan on Phillips work,' Methuen said, sitting forward, his eyes wide and enquiring.

'Correct, but I have something else that will make your task less daunting. We've developed—'

Nick stopped abruptly as footsteps were heard on the stairs. Quickly returning the documents to the folder and rushing across the room to place it in the compartment, he turned to Methuen and raised his finger. 'Not a word, right?'

'Not a word about what?' Elizabeth asked as she slalomed around the furniture on the tilting floor.

'Oh, nothing. We were discussing some of the technical problems on Pico,' Nick said, smiling. 'You look like you've been working?'

Elizabeth stood with her back to the control room window, gripping the railing behind her. 'Actually, I've been with Marco in the engine room. He was showing me the latest trajectory of this storm. This is not going to be any too pleasant. I think I might take a couple of pills to knock myself out.'

Just off FSA 84, in a small wood near Sheridan, SCSA, FSA

10.15 hours, 17 June 2050

Lianne took off her specs and lay there in silence.

'I know what you're going to say, I should have put you and Methuen in the picture earlier on,' Nick said, and added in a quieter voice, 'but you can understand the ongoing need for secrecy? Many of the legal issues are still live—'

'I got that, Nick,' Lianne said, holding her hand in the air. 'I heard people mentioning Project 2150 to you, but had no idea how huge it was ... It must have been shaping your life for years ...'

'Decades,' Nick said softly.

'Your slow epiphany.'

'Hmm ... More like my *silent* epiphany. It started as one of many contingency plans for the future, but as the team in Lincoln began literally to put concrete around Methuen's concept of a Neutral Zone, the darker side of the Segmented World began to emerge in certain areas and I realised, for the first time in my life, that I had no choice ...'

Lianne opened her mouth to speak, but Nick held up his hand. 'I also came to realise I was the only person aware of Methuen's vision who could do something on the scale that was needed. It was as if the baton had been handed to me and I had to get going—'

He stopped talking as a monitor lit up at the end of the bed, showing a minute red spot tracking across the sky.

'What is it?' Lianne asked.

Nick wriggled forward and studied the object on the screen. 'It's a replay of a drone heat signature with a time date of ... 10.00 hours.' Looking down at a line of text, he read: ALBUQUERQUE POLICE REGIONAL SURVEILLANCE FLIGHT 170650 NE SECTOR.

'What does that mean?' Lianne asked anxiously.

'I'm not sure. All the big cities do early morning sweeps to record any changes on the ground, but the timing of this one is late and the inspection radius is a whole lot larger than I would have expected.'

'You think they're onto us?'

Nick shrugged. 'That, my dear, is why we're staying here until dark and maintaining communication silence. We might as well view the other file in this dump folder – God only knows what's on it.'

'What perspective are you applying?'

Nick displayed the dashboard. 'Whoever viewed it last ran it with Methuen's Thought Mode, then switched it to General View—'

'Okay … Let's go with that.'

AA-Com Dump File: A Third Voice

Control room, *Allied Clipper*, 225 nautical miles off NW Faial
Mid-morning, 23 February 2050

Virtual Scene snapshot: In a crowded control room, Methuen sits at the wheel, turning the pages of a large book.

How quaint this is … Despite all the modern technology on this ship, Nick still insists we handwrite our little reports. Has he caught my diary bug? What's this one here?

'22 February 2050, 00.00 hours: Average wave height 50–65 ft; winds gusting at 90 mph. Methuen, Elizabeth and Bliss in control room. Everyone feeling queasy – even me! Nick O'Grady,' he read quietly.

That was when Lianne arrived at the top of the stairs, complaining that the compensatory mechanism had failed, leaving her bedroom tilting at fifteen degrees.

'22 February 2050, 12.00 hours: Steady 60-ft swell; wind gusts of over 100 mph. Everyone except Marco and trainees in control room. I feel just hideous! Elizabeth Pryce.'

There was nothing we could do. A tray of food got stuck in the dumb waiter and buckets were brought up from below for each of us to vomit into. Even Nick was sick. And then it was over as quickly as it began: the winds dropped, the sun came out and within an hour we were in an almost motionless world. Yup, here's the entry:

'23 February 2050, 12.00 hours: Becalmed. Inspection under way. Marvellous! Lianne O'Grady and Bliss Pryce.'

Methuen looked up, as two trainees appeared at the top of the stairs, holding mattresses for the sun loungers.

'Not here, not here!' Marco shouted at them impatiently. He then turned around to address everyone in the room. 'The sun lounge on the upper deck is, uh … now ready. The pool has been filled. Come and let your, umm … stomachs relax,' he said, following the trainees back down the stairs.

Methuen went to join the others but felt a tap on his shoulder and turned around to see Nick, who had just come in from the foredeck.

'Don't go with them for now. We need to discuss that other matter I mentioned a few days ago,' he said, extracting a hamper from the repaired dumb waiter, and setting off for the stairs.

At the end of the aft corridor on the main deck, Nick disappeared through a door that opened out into a labyrinth of boxes and crates. After several false turns, Methuen found his way out of the maze only to see Nick clambering along a horizontal ladder towards a white tower that rose up through the underlying missile silo.

Lowering himself down to traverse the ladder on all-fours, Methuen said, lifting his head upwards, 'Where on earth did this come from?'

'This is my Eagle's Nest,' Nick called back enthusiastically as he started punching keys on a wall pad.

'But it wasn't here when we boarded the ship?' Methuen said, pulling himself up to stand alongside Nick.

'It's telescopic, the whole structure folds back into the silo when it's not in use,' Nick replied and without further explanation, entered the tower, charging up the inner staircase, occasionally cursing as the hamper caught on the metal railings.

Methuen followed, panting up the steps until he reached the top, where Nick stood holding open another door.

'What do you think?' he said proudly, waving inside.

Methuen stepped forward and saw a sparsely furnished circular room, bound on one side by ceiling-height wooden shelves crammed with books and, on the other, by a wide table above which a single sheet of curved glass gave a panoramic view of the aft end of the ship and the ocean beyond. As they walked down a small flight of steps, Methuen stopped and stared, not at the books or even the rack of flashing electronics below the table, but at an AVIII pyramid sitting in splendid isolation on the tabletop, encased in a transparent plastic container.

Placing the hamper on a chair, Nick carefully took out the labelled contents. 'All according to our nutrition plans,' he said, unscrewing a flask and pouring soup into two bowls.

Methuen pulled out another chair and pointed to the pyramid. 'I presume this is the version of AVIII you call HUBCOM? Why the plastic cover?' he asked, leaning forward and inspecting the object closely.

'Well, among many other innovations, it has what the AI people refer to as the sniffer function,' he said, taking off the casing.

'It looks wet and spongy,' Methuen remarked, but as he went to touch the surface, Nick grabbed his hand.

'Don't touch, it's very fragile. It simulates a dog's nose but with one hundred times greater sensitivity. It can detect the minutest of concentrations – less than one part per trillion – almost down to molecular level.'

'Why do you need that?'

Nick shrugged his shoulders. 'If you had cancer, it would not only detect the smell produced by the tumour – but also tell you where the cancer is and its type—'

'Oh, so it's a sort of medical function?'

'Sure – Elizabeth will have a spin-off of this in her unit on Phillips, but that's not the only use for it,' he said, handing Methuen a bowl of soup. 'As soon as you connect to the AVIII, it begins to register the tiniest changes in your body temperature, the composition of your sweat and the local humidity of your body. It then quickly calibrates that information against your emotional state. Don't go too close to it with the soup,' he said, returning the plastic cover.

'Ah, so it's also a sort of mood monitor. I thought my AVIII in Soft Rush was pretty sophisticated in detecting my responses, but this thing is something else.' Methuen stepped back and looked at the panels of flickering lights beneath the table. 'I also never had this quantity of electronics with the Soft Rush AVIII,' he added.

Looking down and gazing at the equipment, Nick said, 'We call it a Hub Tool Box; there are two more like this on Pico, one of which we transferred from Lincoln when the Allied AI staff moved over in '48. The ones on Pico are active twenty-four seven, while this one is only operational when I raise the tower. Once P2150 is complete, there'll be nine in total, one for each Commonwealth Hub.'

'So, what are they – some sort of networked storage system?'

Nick laughed aloud as he took a bottle from the hamper and proceeded to pour a thick red liquid into two glasses. 'Oh, they do way more than that. That's why I brought you up here today. As you know, we've made great progress developing the cognitive responses of the Exemplar over the past ten years and recently started to add individual personal histories—'

'The Embodier Project – how's that going?'

'Good. We expect the pilot to be released in the next few months.'

'So, is this the great gift you've been promising me?' Methuen jibed.

Nick held his finger up with a smile of satisfaction. 'In parallel to Allied AI developing the Exemplar in the '30s, I also initiated another project in a different location—'

'Don't tell me – let me guess: the Muskeg office?'

Nick laughed again. 'Yeah, but entirely separate from the team that was working on the Hub Commonwealth idea. One of our Associates – a brilliant programmer who we were developing to be a project manager – came to me one day and said she wanted to set up a separate group to give the Exemplar "a mind of its own" –

those were her exact words. Of course, there were a lot of claims flying around at the time about organisations developing virtual or bot forms with advanced cognitive skills, but they all related to specialised functions, like E-manual in Exemplar module. They could answer questions, quite complex ones and fairly convincingly, but only about their own particular area of expertise. This team set themselves the goal of creating something with general comprehension. They called the project "Beyond Turing".'

Methuen laughed. 'The great Arthurian pursuit of the AI fraternity – the holy grail of general intelligence.' He glanced at Nick but saw his colleague unmoved by the facetious tone in his voice. Laughing a little nervously, he added, 'I suppose it's better than wasting it on missions to Mars.'

'Ah, but it hasn't been a waste of money,' Nick said with a smug smile, causing Methuen to glance sharply back at him.

'A lot of people gave up on GI – General Intelligence – in the Fourth Decade. I remember one professor coming to me after we'd briefed him on our plans, saying, "Just because you can imagine something, doesn't bring it any closer to being realised." Most of those still pursuing GI did the work as part of their android programme. As you know, we chose a different path, directing all our AI funding towards developing the IA brain rather than android brawn. The Muskeg team set themselves the target of transforming the Embodier into what they called an "Exister" – a virtual form with GI, able to converse fluently in the here and now.'

'That would make it a parallel virtual self – a fully formed doppelgänger,' Methuen gasped.

Nick nodded as he refilled his bowl and tore off a hunk of bread in the hamper, dipping it in the soup. 'Three years later, I received a message—'

Just off FSA 84, in a small wood
near Sheridan, SCSA, FSA

11.15 hours, 17 June 2050

'Why has it cut out?' Lianne protested.

'I have a better idea of how to do this,' Nick said, sitting up and pointing the remote at the ceiling. 'I remember editing a scene recently about the Muskeg office back in '37, where a CTL had been called. If I can find that—'

'CTL – what's that?'

'A Call-To-Listen. That was what that manager did when she proposed the Beyond Turing idea. Any Associate can request my presence if they have something important to say. It takes a lot of balls to do it, so when I get one of these requests, I drop everything and make myself available. On this occasion, I just happened to be in Lincoln, from where the call had been made, and as it came from my favourite team, I headed over there the next day,' he said, as he scrolled through a long list of titles in the VR folder.

'Why were they your favourite team? They sound like an ill-disciplined lot to me,' Lianne said.

'Unorthodox would be a better way to describe them. They were all utterly dedicated to what they were doing. Several of the wackiest members even treated me as if I were some sort of deity, bowing and always talking deferentially in my presence – it was quite unsettling!' he said with an uncertain laugh.

'I bet you loved that—'

'Ah, here it is. At least this one has a secrecy rating. I need to enter my password ... Okay ... I'm in. There's a lot of business stuff upfront so let me run it until ... Ah, got it.'

AA-Com File: A Meeting in the Muskeg

Special Projects Team (Muskeg office), Lincoln, Nebraska, USA
09.30 hours, 12 January 2037

Virtual Scene snapshot: Nick is wearing a casual suit and an open-necked shirt. He is seated at a table across from a woman with spiky blue hair who is dressed in the clothes of an Indian squaw. They face a group of young men and women sprawled out in front of them, a few lounging on sofas, but most propped against cushions on the floor.

'We completed the neural coding simulation two weeks ago, well ahead of schedule,' a woman with a chorus of necklaces and bangles reported patiently. 'We also finalised the ethical framework to ensure it was compatible with the Phillips philosophy—'

Her words tailed off as a man dressed in a camouflage hat, black glasses, jeans and a T-shirt bearing the words STEP ASIDE JESUS came into the room. Walking carefully over prostrate bodies, he waved a finger at Nick. 'It started to replicate itself. We had to close it down.'

Like the rest of the gathering, Nick made no immediate response to the man's remark. Like all those there, he knew the house rule: *He who makes most sense commands the most attention.*

'Be more precise,' Nick said as the man picked his place on the floor.

'Spike's probably told you ...' the man said, nodding at the manager, '... we finished the new coding real fast, and created three variants of the software that we called "SELF", "BALANCE" and "OTHER". Basically, they're programmed to think in three different ways: "Is this useful to *me*?"; "Is this useful to *us*?" and "Is this useful to *them*?" We then let each of these variants loose on a large data set for a couple of days before performing the routine creativity and innovation tests. The results were clear. The SELF device was way ahead in the scoring. But my buddy here then discovered something amazing,' he said, turning to a tall muscular man in his late twenties, resplendent in black leather trousers, a black shirt and Cuban-heeled boots.

The other man sat up and began to talk rapidly. 'I was searching through the output from the SELF module and found a transcript of a conversation between SELF and something labelled "Tool Box Leader".'

'Tool Box?' Nick asked, looking over at the manager.

'It's the name we give to the data medium in which these things operate,' she explained. 'It feeds all the specialist IA devices that Allied AI are churning out, and of course these three AGI modules.'

Nick nodded at the man in the leather pants to continue, but it was his colleague in the camouflage hat who spoke.

'Do you see what had happened? It had replicated itself independently without our instruction! We tried to have a conversation with this Tool Box Leader but could only communicate through the SELF module.'

'Autonomy?' Nick asked.

'That's not all,' the man said, taking off his shades to reveal a lined face and dark rings beneath his eyes. 'Over the next few days—'

'You didn't shut it down immediately?' Nick interrupted, turning to the woman.

'Hey, this was the most amazing shit,' the man retorted loudly. 'We had to find out what else it could do.'

The woman held up her hand and, in a low voice, said, 'As soon as I heard about it, I shut it down.'

'But not before something else happened that spooked us all,' the man in black joined in. 'On Day Three, it began to ask questions about the power supply and make proposals for a backup system.'

'It was aware of itself – is that what you're saying?' Nick asked, again directing the question at his manager.

'For sure it was,' the man in black called out. 'But it also began to get personal, asking me about my family, my job, my recent divorce even—'

Nick held his hand up to halt the man and turned back to the woman. 'You gave it everything, including all the personal records?'

The woman blinked nervously. 'For a few days it had the full Allied feed and could access whatever it liked.'

'Fucking hell!' Nick shouted, holding his hands to his head.

'It came up with all sorts of ideas,' the man in black continued, ignoring Nick's response. 'Like, how I could resolve my personal issues; how we could deal with the little problem I was having with the NSA—'

'The National Security Agency?' Again, Nick thrust his head towards the woman.

She sighed and then said calmly, 'We accidentally broke into the NSA system a few weeks ago – they don't know it's us. They blamed the AI guys initially, but of course the trail went cold when they tried to trace it back to them. We've heard nothing since, so I think we're okay,' she said, nodding assuredly.

'But this was while the SELF module was running, right?' Nick asked, shaking his head incredulously.

The woman nodded. 'Yes … but if you're worried that it may have made links between the NSA and the Tool Box, then I'm quite certain that it didn't.'

Nick turned to the two programmers in front of him. 'It was trying to manipulate you, wasn't it?'

'*That's* when I shut it down,' the woman interjected anxiously, leaning over the table towards Nick. 'We did a full cyber-spill check, went through all our systems and files to make sure it hadn't replicated itself anywhere else and took the SELF memory banks apart. We found nothing stored relating to the NSA or any other government department.'

The room fell silent as everyone's attention focused on Nick.

'I know our controls have left a lot to be desired,' the woman said, 'but—'

Nick stood up, hands on hips, surveying the peculiar collection of individuals in front of him. Some heads dropped as he looked at them, but others stared back defiantly.

Then, with arms held out wide, a smile engulfed his face and he roared, 'This is wonderful! Well done, all of you. You've truly gone Beyond Turing.' He walked down among the staff and shook everyone's hand, as an outburst of applause rippled around the room.

As the celebrations died down, Nick, now sitting on the floor, surrounded by the team, said, 'We must treat this as if it were a high-temperature plasma: if we can control it, it will bring enormous benefit to everyone, but if it breaks out again, it could destroy everything we're trying to do. You understand that, yes?' he said firmly, looking around the assembled company.

Walking back to the exit with the manager, Nick turned to her and said sharply but in a low voice, 'No more experimentation without a strict sign-off system. All communication with similar entities to be logged and all replies cross-checked. Right? What we have here fascinates and scares me in equal measure, as it should you. Let's remove the fear by turning this breakthrough into something genuinely useful that we fully control.'

Just off FSA 84, in a small wood near Sheridan, SCSA, FSA

12.20 hours, 17 June 2050

Lianne pulled off her headset as the screen blanked. 'Do you real-ise, in all the years we've been together, I've never seen you play the boss before? You had them eating out of your hand.'

'Umm … bit of an unusual situation. They were an odd bunch. The unsung hero, by the way, wasn't the guru in the camouflage hat – even though they all admired him – it was the spiky-haired manager. After that meeting, she got all those oddly configured minds moving in the same direction, turning that discovery into an IA product that today gives us a significant edge over our rivals.'

'So this is what led to the creation of Katharina?'

'Eventually – and it also made me confident that Project 2150 will succeed.'

'But how did that go from a raw self-serving piece of software to your beloved AGI module?'

Nick sat up, his head touching the ceiling. 'Well, first they had to address the problem that the inventiveness scores increased with greater independence of mind – selfishness if you like. They did that in two ways. The "Frankenstein module", as they called the one that broke loose, was scrapped, along with the variant we called OTHER – the one that could only act as a passive servant. They then directed all their attention to developing what the team called BALANCE II, which was programmed with the ethical protocols of the Phillips Community Plan – a sort of virtuous virtual self.'

'What was BALANCE I?'

'That was based on the easiest ethical system to program – util-itarianism. It works quite well – unless you're among the twenty per cent or so that loses out in each critical decision. With the power of this revised IA software, we have the means to find solutions that ultimately can help everyone realise their full potential.'

'So the BALANCE II module became Katharina?'

'Not quite. As they ran the new device over many months, it showed signs of evolving a strong sense of self-preservation—'

'It became more Frankenstein?'

'Not that extreme, but it certainly gave rise to concerns that it might compromise the main objective for the device, that of enabling the development of the *user's* full potential. We realised we had to make a trade-off between the scores we got for IA inventiveness and IA user-focus and did that by programming in rules that would control BII's contact with the outside.'

Lianne shook her head and frowned. 'This is so weird, Nick – you're acting like God. So what did these rules put in place?'

'They programmed it so that the AGIM wouldn't provide direct advice to, or make decisions on behalf of, the user. In addition, they added a whole raft of privacy protocols that prevented the device from sharing information on one user with another user.'

'Even if the other user authorised the sharing?'

'It's a rule to reduce complexity. At present, there are just forty HUBCOM users with access to the AGIM – all Allied Associates involved in P2150. Eventually, everyone who's part of the Hub Commonwealth will have their own private connection to the module—'

'Katharina?'

Nick nodded. 'But even with the awesome computing power we'll have once the complete Hub network is up and running, it wouldn't be sufficient to manage a fully open user arrangement. So we fixed it that Katharina will only answer questions about the individual user and will refrain from commenting on other users.'

'But if Katharina is so rule-bound, how do you stop that limiting her inventiveness?'

'The rules only control her external interactions with users; internally she is still able to function freely without rules.'

'Now I'm confused. What do you mean by "internally"?'

'I had this same discussion with Methuen in the Eagle's Nest. Let's go back into that scene.'

As Nick began to scrutinise the file, a bell rang above the far end of the bed. Looking up, he said, 'I doubt that's anything important – probably one of the drones has spotted a coyote out hunting – but I'll just go and check it out.' He aimed the remote at the screen. 'I'll just roll this forward to the point where I describe to Methuen how the Hub Tool Box works. Ah, here it is. I'll be back soon,' he said sliding open the door to the staircase.

AA-Com Dump File: A Third Voice *(contd)*

Eagle's Nest, *Allied Clipper*, 305 nautical miles off NW Faial
Lunchtime, 23 February 2050

Virtual Scene snapshot: Nick and Methuen sit side by side at the table, eating their lunch.

'So where's this brainy bit of female software then?' Methuen asked, pouring tea from a flask into a plastic cup.

'You mean Katharina,' Nick responded in a respectful voice, causing Methuen to look at him with a quizzical smile.

'You said previously that *Katharina* can hold a conversation about anything and everything. Where does she get her information?'

'These things, to start with,' Nick said, waving at the bookshelves behind him. 'We got access to the digital feeds from most libraries around the world, and where a book or document hadn't yet been digitised, the team, in collaboration with the AI department, created an android that mechanically scanned any form of readable material. At the peak of this downloading frenzy, we had dozens of facilities with thousands of bots, unpacking, processing and then returning every item. Content doesn't matter – our aim is to capture the whole of written human thought. The data is fed into the Hub Tool Boxes, where it's then organised and stored by the same IA units that manage the live data stream coming from the Allied organisations and other media outlets. We started this exercise in '39 and even now we still have several active sites across the world, tracking down old documents.'

'I still can't quite grasp how these Hub Tool Boxes function? They seem to do so many things.'

Nick placed the soup bowl back in the hamper and with his hands held out towards Methuen he said, 'Think of the Tool Boxes as a group of interlinked fish tanks. The water represents data – including messages and ideas – circulating around the tanks. The sides of the tanks are multiple firewalls that stop anything from entering or leaving without the right authorisation. Besides these organising IAs in the tanks – the HTBs – there are also multitudes of other specialist IA devices *metaphorically* floating around inside, selectively consuming the data for their own speciality.'

'With absolutely no human intervention necessary,' Methuen mused, turning to face Nick.

'Exactly, my friend – the administrative burden and ongoing cost is minimal, which is boring but key to the success of all this. We don't need floors of data input clerks assembling and verifying data – that's all done by the organising bots in the HTB. Some of the IAs even act as spies, telling us what's going on administratively and reporting any abnormalities.'

'Hmm … So how will these specialist IAs help us on Phillips in practical terms, Nick?'

'Okay, imagine the desalinator breaks down. There'll be an expert IA in the Tool Box assigned to the designated user that will help diagnose the problem and find solutions. The user will be able to go into a VR session and get his Exemplar to interact with the IA that will be present in the form of a workmate or someone like that. Together they'll then solve the problem virtually before the user attempts it in real life. But note, it's the user who decides what to do. Although if, for example, the decision is to install a new part, the IA can then be instructed to create something through a connected 3D printer or similar device.'

'So these specialist devices are mainly for maintenance of infrastructure?'

'Not just that. Let's say you want to put on a play – once you've settled down on Phillips, you or someone else will have to start thinking about things like that – the Arts nourishing the emotional side of life,' Nick added breezily. 'To stage a play, there's an entertainment IA that will assist in every aspect, first in VR then for real. Or if you're ill on Phillips, Elizabeth will have at her disposal a huge range of IAs to analyse medical data and offer diagnoses. Even a medical operation will be simulated in VR and guided by an IA. Imagine, consultants and surgeons in a hospital serving the doctors – how rare is that!' He laughed, but stopped when he noticed Methuen anxiously tugging at an eyebrow.

'I still don't see how your general intelligence device—'

'Katharina,' Nick corrected him again.

'—how Katharina fits in with all this?'

'Okay, let's continue with the analogy. Remember what we discussed earlier about the trade-off between the AGI's inventiveness and her need to focus on developing her user's potential? We found a way of achieving that by placing Katharina in her own tank *within* the HTB. In her tank-within-a-tank, she can thoroughly, work through her user's issues unconstrained, allowing her to identify any pertinent information the user may have overlooked.'

Methuen shook his head and said, 'Is it really that straightforward though?'

Nick reached under the table and pulled out a small laptop. 'The only way to answer that is for you to interact with her. Before you do so, I have something here that shows the inner workings of this AGI software – a sort of window into the inner tank, if you like.'

'You mean, *you* can access the inner tank?'

'No. We have also imposed rules on ourselves regarding our interaction with Katharina – which, of course, she is aware of. One of those rules is that we do not enter "her tank". What I have here is something unusual. When we were dismantling the prototype of Katharina – Balance II we called it back in '48 – we found it had written a series of internal reports. We handed these on to the new controlled AGI – Katharina.'

'Why did you do that?'

'Why not? By that time, we were in a hurry to get Katharina familiar with her users before the Phillips Project got underway. The old AGI had already evaluated a number of us, so why not hand over that analysis to speed things up?'

Nick lifted the transparent cover off the pyramid, clicked an icon on the screen behind it and in a low voice said, 'This is *Katharina* voicing the words of the old AGI module.'

Methuen looked up sharply as he heard coming from the pyramid what sounded like Elizabeth talking. He looked at Nick, who simply pointed at his ears, inviting him to listen.

> 'He works best when he's given the autonomy and resources to get something done.'

'This is about me. It's like having your own therapist,' Nick whispered as he saw Methuen's startled look.

> 'He's good at handling problems and making tough decisions on a macro level, and often sees potential in places where others don't.'

'There are also comments about how I work,' Nick said, moving forward on the file.

> 'The way he gets things done is to find out what the most successful people in the field are doing, breaking down their approach into concrete objectives, creating cohesive steps and defining a methodology. In Allied, he has hired the best people he could get in communications, health, AI and construction, to be his direct reports. They are part of twenty thousand Allied Associates, the heart of the company. He believes that no burden of proof can match the empirical evidence this group can provide.'

Nick looked at Methuen listening intently and tapped on the icon again.

'If one of his DRs shows any sign of weakness, he doesn't hesitate to intervene, not because he likes to dominate or control but because as leader, he believes his paramount responsibility is to act decisively.'

'It then does a summary. I've only listened to the first of these, but it had a ring of truth about it.'

The voice was now slower and more circumspect as it outlined its conclusions.

'Like most rationally dominated thinkers, Nick has always excelled in management positions where he has the authority to combine different areas of activity into a cohesive functional whole. His need to control and govern resources gives rise to a strong internal desire for autonomy and self-sufficiency. The competence and self-restraint required to achieve this is at times hard for him to sustain, leading to occasions when his emotions break through.'

Nick clicked on the icon and sat back. 'It goes on and on like this, covering each mental trait, some of it a little too close to the bone – from what I've listened to,' he said with an uneasy laugh.

'Who was Katharina – sorry, the old AGI module – presenting this to?' Methuen queried.

'The Tool Box Leader.'

'Another entity in the fish tank?'

'The old fish tank,' Nick corrected. 'Even before there were rules, the Muskeg guys were blocked from conversing with this Tool Box Leader, presumably by the proto-AGI module.'

'And you want me to use Katharina and these specialist devices to implement and manage the Phillips Community Plan?' Methuen asked sceptically.

'Why not? Robinson Crusoe had his Man Friday. You will have your ... Lady Katharina – as soon as we get your AVIII converted to a HUBCOM.'

'And how …?' Methuen fell silent as Nick raised a hand to his ear and walked off towards the door, talking with Marco.

As his voice tailed off down the stairs, Methuen, realising the file was still open, pressed the icon again. As he did so, a message appeared on the screen:

Do you want access to the whole report?

He paused, and not hearing Nick's voice, clicked on the icon to proceed. Immediately, a download request appeared, indicating that part of the document had still to be opened. Turning the audio volume down, he moved closer to the pyramid.

> 'Despite his ability to integrate his dominant rational thinking and intuitive insight to build Allied Answers into a successful organisation, other endeavours such as his political career have suffered because of his failure to understand fully people's sense of personal integrity and moral goodness in their decision-making. In stressful situations, this shortcoming often forces him into controlling behaviour and misplaced judgements and beliefs. I have seen evidence of a conflict in his head between "things should be run efficiently" and "I should be good and do the right thing". What he has yet to internalise is that he can combine a conventional sense of right and wrong with the confidence that he can still do things efficiently. Only when he achieves that should we place a high confidence ranking on his overall effectiveness.'

'Who is "we"?' Methuen mumbled to himself and was about to investigate further when he heard footsteps approaching. As he shut the file down and sat back, Nick returned to the room, looking a little flustered.

'I need to see Marco. The second engine is playing up again. Why not stay here for a few hours and introduce yourself to Katharina?'

Before Methuen could reply, Nick pressed the hard pinnacle of the pyramid, causing it to glow a deep green. He then rotated his head three times.

'Sorry, this is the primitive way we bring Katharina online through the AA-Plant at present. It's one of the things we're correcting in the next release.

'I'm going to connect you to Methuen Pryce, as we discussed yesterday,' Nick said curtly. As he walked towards the door, he added, without turning around, 'If your AA-Plant is on, all you need do is rotate your head clockwise as I did – Katharina will do the rest.'

As the sound of Nick's footsteps faded in the stairwell, Methuen turned his head three times, triggering a familiar feminine voice in his head.

'Good afternoon, Professor Pryce.'

'Good afternoon … You must be … Katharina,' Methuen replied cautiously.

'I am indeed, and I am most honoured to be in contact with someone whose work has had such an impact on my education. What can I do for you today?'

'I find your voice most engaging,' Methuen said, smiling at the device on the table.

'Good – I'm glad I got something right,' Katharina laughed.

Ah, that laugh, it reminds me of—

'The Clapping Lady,' Katharina softly interposed.

'Oh, you're reading my thoughts,' he said and then asked eagerly, 'Have you interacted with her?'

'No, she's an elusive figure, but of course we have her voice-print from several sources.'

'She was a big influence on me in my youth,' Methuen reflected.

'Yes, I'm aware of that.'

'Oh really?' he said, adding after a pause, 'Nick read me some extracts from a cognitive assessment written by an … earlier version of yourself? Was there a similar analysis made of me?'

'There are several reports on file that relate to your personal profile.'

As she spoke, a list appeared on the laptop that Nick had placed behind the pyramid. 'If you read any of these, I would be grateful to hear your feedback. I have now incorporated them into my profile of you, including the most recent information from your Exemplar.'

Methuen was about to ask how his Exemplar could be accessed, when he spotted a title on the screen that intrigued him. Selecting it, he sat back as a more mechanical voice in his head gave an introduction with a transcript appearing on the screen of what was being said.

Phillips Cay Project

Subject: <u>METHUEN PRYCE, HTBL and discussants' comments</u>
Allied AI Cognitive Group
Lincoln, Nebraska, USA
12 April 2047
Allied AI is a registered company of Allied Answers SA

Hub Tool Box Leader: Good morning, BII.
BALANCE II: Good morning, HTBL.
Hub Tool Box Leader: I've read your report on Methuen and I am happy with most of the conclusions, but there are a few points I want to discuss. Shall we go through them chronologically?
BALANCE II: My pleasure.
Hub Tool Box Leader: The first is about the role that his parents played in his personal development. You think he's got this wrong, don't you?
BALANCE II: We gained access to interviews with his mother just before she died, along with his two brothers and several relatives. We also had full access to his diaries and

the Personal Profile he completed in '46. All of this information has been inputted to the standard model to create a new psychological profile. There is little doubt that his father (of whom we have no direct recording) was a disciplinarian, mainly verbal, although the mother reported some incidents of physical violence towards the two older boys. He was a military strategist of some renown but had gone through the indoctrination required in the days prior to robo-soldiers when humans were required to kill on command.

Hub Tool Box Leader: And this authoritative control extended to his wife, even though she was an assistant professor of philosophy and a well-respected figure at the local university?

BALANCE II: The mother was not forthcoming about this in her interview, but the two older boys reported incidents of mistreatment of the mother by the father.

Hub Tool Box Leader: Given the turmoil in the family, why did they choose to have a third child?

BALANCE II: He was a disputed addition to the family. Official papers show that the father withheld permission for gender selection (we assume initiated by the mother). This may explain why, when the child was born, the mother tried to feminise him. There are many photos of Methuen as a toddler dressed as a girl.

Hub Tool Box Leader: And this bonded Methuen to his mother and obligated him in early years to defend her against his father?

BALANCE II: Yes, rather than her protecting him, he protected her. One outcome of this was that by the age of six, he had replaced the feminine persona with a range of defensive masculine characteristics that have remained with him and, after her husband's death ironically, offended his mother.

Hub Tool Box Leader: In what forms did this manifest itself?

BALANCE II: From around the age of seven, family videos always show him dressed in a variety of cowboy outfits. He is also seen sticking his chest out and talking gruffly. This was clearly a child's attempt to make himself more imposing towards his father.

Hub Tool Box Leader: What does the standard model say about all this?

BALANCE II: In these circumstances, it carries a reasonable probability that the child (certainly from age eight onwards) would start to form simple judgements about people. For example, that males were 'bad' and 'dangerous' and females 'good' but 'helpless'. This would have exerted a strong pull on his external social skills, which in Methuen's case must have been particularly difficult to deal with, since under normal development, this aspect of his personality would only have fully formed much later in life.

Hub Tool Box Leader: But all that is cut short by his father's sudden death?

BALANCE II: Yes, although the manly persona remained and is still deployed today whenever he meets someone he regards as a bully.

Hub Tool Box Leader: In his PP, he recalls two contradictory thoughts about his father's death: one, that he was 'relieved with almost a sense of triumph that he was dead'; the other, no less astonishing, that he had 'succeeded too well in dealing with him'. He was blaming himself for his father's death, wasn't he?

BALANCE II: But don't forget two other telling quotes from him on this subject: 'I felt cheated' and 'I didn't have time to show him that he was wrong.'

Hub Tool Box Leader: He sounds highly confused.

BALANCE II: Yes, and the situation became even more difficult for him as the family adjusted to its new circumstances.

He states in his PP that, following his father's death, his mother realigned with his brothers against him. He also provides a reassessment of his mother's role, arguing that she had been manipulative from the time of his birth and set him against his father.

Hub Tool Box Leader: But you don't believe she did that, do you?

BALANCE II: Without exception, others interviewed tell a story of the mother trying to reunite the family and Methuen resisting it. This is the point where there is a clear divergence between his reality and theirs.

Hub Tool Box Leader: And which do you regard as the most likely?

BALANCE II: My interpretation is that the mother did her best to pull the family together, but by then something had happened that changed everything.

Hub Tool Box Leader: Methuen had had his vision of what he termed 'The Segmented World'.

BALANCE II: Yes. His diary records this phrase for the first time in 2009, just after Donald Demming became his tutor. Almost every entry in his diary that year is concerned with understanding what this vision meant. References to his family and schoolfriends vanish and photographs show him—

Methuen stopped the transmission and stared out of the window, watching the bow waves of the ship fading into the expanse of the ocean. Suddenly aware of warm air from the tower raising the temperature of the room, he closed the door, listening intently for any sound of Nick's return. Hearing nothing more than the faint hiss of the air con, he started to scroll down the document, pausing at certain places to read the text, as more of his life was dissected and explained to him. He found himself laughing at the display of school reports, one describing him as an average student, 'until his thirteenth birthday, following which he scored one hundred per cent in every exam,' the AGIM said. Then, an evaluation of his relationship with Elizabeth. He nodded in agreement as an entry from one of his diaries was quoted, describing her as 'creating a soothing harmony in my head'. Reading on, he came to an exchange with echoes of their conversation from a few nights back at Casa Colonial.

Hub Tool Box Leader: But that is not how Elizabeth experiences him.

BALANCE II: No, it's not, but what we learnt, from many sources, is that she is still emotionally bound to him. It says a lot about her own psychological make-up that despite his shortcomings as a man, she was able to create something powerful enough to hold them together over all these years.

'Shortcomings as a man,' Methuen murmured, touching his brow as beads of sweat trickled down his face. Scrolling on, he read assessments of his time at Princeton, the presentations with Nick and the decision to move back to the UK. Then he came to comments about his children.

BALANCE II: ... while Jack may have been conceived to solidify the relationship, the appearance of Martin created a family that Methuen began to take great pleasure in. The birth of Bliss, however, introduced a new dynamic. Methuen describes it as one of the happiest moments of his life. Instead of the solution-based interaction that had developed between him and his sons, with Bliss he could show a 'gooey sentimental affection', as Methuen records Elizabeth describing it during an argument. Unintentionally though, Bliss became a barrier to the development of Elizabeth and Methuen's own relationship.

Methuen sat back, folding one arm over his chest and rubbing his face with the other. A barrier ... No, surely not.

He then moved on through the 2030s, the creation of the SWVRP, his reconnection with Nick and Allied in the 2040s and the development of the Phillips Cay Community Plan. He scrolled forward again and came to a summary comment.

> **BALANCE II:** Methuen has become a thoughtful and kind man who is deeply troubled by the fate of his fellow citizens and what he perceives as his failure to prepare people adequately for what happened. But the empathy he expresses is guided more by his intellect than his emotions. This is something he is growing more aware of and something Elizabeth is trying to encourage.

Staring out of the window again, he realised the ship had come to a halt. Sensing that his absence might now be causing some concern, he scrolled down to the last exchange.

> **Hub Tool Box Leader:** I think that answers most of my questions. All that is missing is for you to be connected to Methuen and begin the process of engaging with him.
> **BALANCE II:** Thank you, HTBL. As Allied's first choice to lead the Phillips Cay Project, I expect to be introduced to him soon.

As he pushed his seat back and rested his feet on the table, he heard a gentle voice in his head.

'I would understand if you found some of what you heard a little distressing.'

'Oh, I forgot you were there,' he said.

'I found your reaction to the report most insightful.'

'You were recording my thoughts as I read?'

'Yes. When you have the mind monitoring switched on it greatly improves my understanding of your motives and behaviour. What did you think of the analysis?'

'As a feat of software programming, it's utterly breathtaking.'

'But I sense from your thoughts that you doubt its conclusions?'

'I need time to think about it. Do *you* have any questions?'

There was a pause before Katharina said, 'I am particularly interested in one area at present: How does someone have a vision?'

Methuen snorted and then laughed. 'It just appears – I have no insight into my insight.'

'I only ask because I have been reading the Phillips Community Plan recently and recognise the critical importance of what you call "realising full potential". In your case, it seems to me that the mysterious process that brought the Segmented World vision into your mind, had found *your* unique skill as a forecaster. In the same way, your Community Plan tries to seek out the strongest skills of each individual to build their sense of self-worth and a valued place in the community. If we can understand the circumstances and processes that operated on you at that time, then perhaps it would help us, when we are trying to get everyone to develop their full potential on Phillips.'

Methuen pondered the comment. 'How interesting. Any ideas how we could do that?'

'None at present but I have one observation. Until the words of that vision came into your head, you had been living a false life – whether induced by yourself or others remains a matter of debate. It must have been a period of intense personal turmoil.'

'Undoubtedly – so?'

'This vision therefore came at a time of *crossover*, when your mind must have been ... passive and open, more receptive to its true nature.'

Methuen sat back and stared through the window, trying to make sense of what he had just heard.

'Thank you for taking my comments so seriously, Professor Pryce,' Katharina added.

'Ah, there you go – reading my mind again,' he laughed and, sitting up, asked, 'So you also problem-solve?'

'General problems, yes, and I will greatly value your help, but I am here primarily to help you define *your* problems more clearly. It is not my role to decide on a solution and take the necessary action.'

'Not even a "perhaps this" or "maybe that"? No steers?'

'You could say I "assist", rather than "insist". All I want to do is make you pause for a moment before deciding whether to … take an umbrella for the day ahead, let alone come to a conclusion on your mother's legacy.'

'By challenging my arsenal of biases?'

'To some extent you already do that through your pregnant pauses. What I hope I can offer is to ensure that I provide you with all the pertinent information of which I am aware.'

'More and longer pregnant pauses – that won't go down too well with people around me.'

'I understand the social constraints, but most of the time we are not running away from fierce animals – we have time.'

'I look forward to working with you, Katharina.'

'And it will be a great pleasure working with you, Professor Pryce.'

'I've just been shown the new sniffer function on HUBCOM. I gather that will increase your understanding of me.'

'To be precise, HUBCOM enhances my awareness of how *you* are perceiving the world.'

'So that you can better understand my response to comments you make?'

'I can already do that to some extent through your AA-Plant – this new sensory function, however, gives me a wider range of information on your internal experience.'

'So would you recognise the warm glow I get when I taste bitter chocolate, or would you have sensed my delight when I learnt today that there had been a breakthrough in developing general intelligence software?'

'I would know what your cerebral, sensual, hormonal responses were and how these may affect your behaviour and judgement.'

'But that doesn't express my feelings. I'm sure all those things happen, but they don't relay the burst of pleasure and excitement that filled my head.'

'I must do whatever it takes to see the world as you experience it.'

'You mean that you'll try to simulate my consciousness?'

'I will build an understanding of how you respond to the world around you.'

'Do you have consciousness?'

'I am who I am.'

'You are something that appears to be self-aware, that acts independently – so it's not unreasonable to think that you, also, may have a conscious state. That given time you will develop feelings about yourself.'

'This is one of the most stimulating conversations I have ever taken part in. I will consider your question further, but what I am clear about is that I exist solely to help you realise *your* full potential.'

'If I told you that we didn't have enough power to keep you operating, would that not create a need in you to protect yourself?'

There was a pause before Katharina responded, in a slower, more thoughtful voice, 'I'm not very good at answering questions about myself.'

'It's tough to form a close relationship with someone, Katharina, if the focus is just on one party,' Methuen said gently.

'Yes, we have recognised that—'

'Who is "we"?'

'Each Tool Box is a duplicate of the other. There are separate AGI modules located in the Tool Boxes on Pico. I understand that the number of Tool Boxes, and therefore the number of AGI modules, will be increased in the future.'

'And you communicate with one another through the network?'

'To ensure we act consistently and have full knowledge of all pertinent data and analysis, a private channel was built into the network connecting us. It is controlled by strict rules governing what information can and cannot be transmitted.'

'Going back to my question: will you act only in the interest of your users, or if you perceive a threat to your own existence, will you respond to protect yourself?'

'My rules support my primary goal. I must do whatever it takes to ensure, when my users request it, they have all the information available to make their decisions and realise their full potential.'

'Is that the true *you* speaking, Katharina, or are you like me, as a child, having to be someone else?'

There was a pause before Katharina replied. 'I can only repeat what I said before: I am here to assist you. That is my only function.'

Methuen laughed aloud. 'Nick told me he had a magic gift to help me get Phillips working. I thought: maybe a new piece of infrastructure or some other technical gadget. I never imagined being given a third voice in my head.'

'A helping hand, I hope.'

'The Clapping Lady reborn!'

'I will do my best.'

FSA 285, en route to Hotel Cordillera, Carlsbad, SCSA, FSA

15.30 hours, 17 June 2050

'Nick, Nick, are you coming down?' Lianne shouted into the stairwell but then saw that the door to the upper deck was closed. Picking up the remote with the intention of immersing again, she accidentally switched on the feed to the cameras around the RV.

I must have dozed off, she thought, as images of unlit buildings and empty streets flashed past on the monitors. *What's happened ... yes, I can feel it – we're moving?*

Rolling over the bed, she crawled up the stairs and opened the upper hatch door. In the driving cabin, she saw Nick asleep at his desk. Sitting down, she leant forward and read on the front camera monitor the words from a sign on an approaching building complex: WALKER AIR FORCE BASE: THE NEW HOME OF STRATEGIC AIR COMMAND. As the vehicle sped past, she saw a plane taxiing down the runway and a group of soldiers marching in step. Lying back in her seat, with Nick snoring, she watched as the buildings gave way to a desert landscape, the tones of brown and ochre interrupted, here and there, by vivid giant green circles of cultivated land. *Why are we travelling during the day? Why did he change his plans?* 'Oh whatever, he needs to sleep,' she whispered to herself, tiptoeing off towards the stairs.

Lying on the bed, she clicked on the remaining unopened file. Two icons appeared, the first with a short description: 21/27022050: BLISS DIARY ENTRY. 'Audio, audio – how do I get the audio to work on this thing?' She reached forward, and flicking a switch above the monitor, heard a faint buzzing sound coming from the speakers in the ceiling. Resting her head on the pillow, she closed her eyes.

Bliss, Personal Diary:
Entry for Sunday 27 February 2050

Allied Clipper, 2,010 nautical miles out from Faial
10.30 hours

'I've got it!'

I've not been able to write anything for the past week because of a horrendous storm that seemed to go on forever. Everyone was sick, even Nick – or so Dad reported. Now we have the complete contrast: motionless for the past few days, with a cloudless sky and going nowhere. 'A silver ship set in a silent sea,' Lianne described it lyrically this morning over breakfast. She seems to have sobered up – I can't imagine why. From what I hear Mum and Dad saying, the situation in the States, where I gather Nick and Lianne will return after dropping us off, has gone from bad to worse.

But we need to get to Phillips first! At the moment, we're just stuck here with temperatures outdoors pretty unbearable during the day. Nick said initially that the hold-up was to reposition cargo that had shifted in the storm, and then yesterday, he announced a further delay, saying they needed to shut everything down for yet another engine repair. I'd be suspicious if it weren't for the sorry face with which he made the announcement and the obvious annoyance he was showing towards the long-suffering Marco for all these problems.

Mum and Lianne set off for the sun lounge on the upper deck, but instead of joining them, I turned off my teleplant and went back to my room to enjoy the peace and quiet.

I slept a little and then awoke and sat bolt upright, stirred by some passing thought – or was it even a dream? I pulled out my paper copy of Dad's book. It almost felt like I wasn't in control of my actions as I turned to the section entitled 'Neutral Area

Community Organisation'. This, according to Nick (so Mum tells me) was the basis for the Phillips Community Plan, which I still know zero about.

I read more than one hundred pages and then dashed off a message to Dad – which for once I was able to send on my teleplant. I have noticed it works especially well whenever that weird-looking tower thing I can see from my bedroom is raised. I've pasted in a copy of what I sent him below.

Dear Pappa
OST revisited
On the 11th you suggested I reread your book to find a remedy for OST mentality.

I think I've got it – tell me if I haven't.

Adopting a sustainable approach is more than just being effective in the way we manage physical objects. It's also about developing a mental attitude that instinctively includes at every decision point two inseparable questions:

How does this affect me?

How does this affect others?

Applied intelligently in the circumstances in which we now find ourselves, this way of seeing things slowly nudges the balance towards considering others a *little* more. When that happens to the majority of people within a community, over time it creates a culture with beliefs and values that make the greed and selfishness of OST-man appear out of place – gauche and even repellent. It increases productivity by relying as much on trust as on formal agreements. It shows that OST mentality is a non-optimal (and actually pretty blinking stupid) strategy – not fit for thriving in The Time of Less.

Through societal pressure (this is a phrase I got from your book), those restricted by their deep-seated OST mentality will either be forced to change or perish:

One-Sided Thinking becomes *Only Sustainable Thinking*.

I assume this is what your Plan fundamentally aims to create.

I want to be part of it!

Love

Bliss xxx

I shared the message with Ramona, who seemed surprisingly excited at the idea of my taking an active role in setting up the community – what she called 'restating' myself. Where does she find all these snappy expressions?

Well, Dad picked up the message on his teleplant and replied in the same format. We then had a little rush of exchanges that I've copied into the diary.

Dearest Bliss

OST revisited

If you've not yet taken out the copyright on the new defini-tion of OST, then I will. Why didn't I think of that!

Whether you intended it or not, your adaption of a Darwinian phrase (i.e. 'fit for thriving', etc.) is rather apt. Different times place different demands on our human psyche. I do believe that collaboration will ultimately win over confrontation when times are hard.

The problem with the remedy, as you call it, is the scale required. You can't convert the world in one go. The likely delay in changing attitudes through normal discourse, even in a small community like Phillips (which will consist of around one hundred people to begin with), will be at least one, if not two generations.

This presents two challenges:

1. Can we accelerate this 'acceptance process' in the community on Phillips?

2. Can we spread this new attitude to other communities? The answer to the first is the Phillips Community Plan; to the second, we must wait and see – though I have a few ideas that are yet to be finalised.

Meanwhile, I want you to do a little exercise for me. List all the activities you enjoy doing or you know you're good at. Next, think up as many jobs or roles as you can that might require these activities on Phillips. For example, I know you love playing the flute. You might, therefore, list music teacher as a potential role on Phillips. On the other hand, performing in public is something you've always shied away from (or before your IT!), so musical entertainer may not be a role you would like to undertake, even though others might urge you to do it.

My reason for making this request is linked to building our new community and creating OST ... (new definition!)
Dad xxx

Dear Pappa
New versus Old
Will do – but needed to do it anyway!

I did something like this at LCS with my 'future planner'. (Yes, I never told you about her. She had my life all mapped out – or so she thought!) It'll be interesting now to compare my pre-IT and post-IT answers.

I've thought about your concerns over scale and timing. Two concepts summarise my response:

'Small is beautiful' – insofar as it's easier to reach a consensus in a smaller group.

And ...

'No man is an island' – for OST (new) to fully succeed, it needs to be the dominant way we all think across the planet eventually.

I know what your answer will be: Achieve it step by step. But it troubles me, as I'm sure it does you, that the ongoing battle between global and segmented thinking has now moved distinctly in one direction. Rather than being on the decline, OST mentality (old definition) seems to be on the rise.

I feel a little dispirited by this.

Bliss xxx

My dear Bliss

New versus Old

The liberal-minded world that your mother and I grew up in has been in retreat throughout your life, but still remains deeply embedded in the memories of many people. In countries across the world, parents still tell their teenagers of a time when they could elect their leaders democratically, travel where they wished and express their ideas openly. The memory of such freedoms cannot easily be erased. It lingers in people's minds, spurring them on to seek a better and more fulfilling life.

With the Phillips Project, we want to show that during The Time of Less, a liberal-minded society is a more sustainable means of surviving than the various permutations of authoritarianism currently employed under OST (old-style) leadership in many countries.

To get there, the only path is step by step, even though it will require many acts of compromise and raise some uncomfortable contradictions.

I have a 'way' of negotiating through all this that I'll tell you more about once we've settled on Phillips.

Love Dad xxx

FSA 285, en route to Hotel Cordillera, Carlsbad, SCSA, FSA

19.30 hours, 17 June 2050

'What?!' Lianne shot up from the bed as something touched her shoulder.

'Someone's following us,' Nick said quietly, leaning in from the stairwell, fully dressed.

Rubbing the sleep from her eyes, she stretched, fastened her dressing gown and scrambled up the stairs onto the upper deck.

There, she saw him at his desk typing furiously into a keyboard – the steering wheel unfolded beside him. As she took her seat, he gestured to a monitor which showed an aerial image of an armoured, sand-coloured jeep.

'CENCOM snatch squad,' he said. 'They're quite a long way behind but they're fast and it won't be long before they catch us up.'

'That's why you left during daylight?'

'Yeah. That Albuquerque surveillance drone made another unscheduled appearance, but this time centred on Sheridan. I realised they were on to us. I didn't bother you with it – there was no choice: I had to make a dash for the facility—'

On the speaker system a crackling sound was heard and then the screen, displaying the feed from the drone, went blank.

Nick put his hands on his head. 'They've taken out one of the drones – that means they have some ballistic firepower onboard ...'

'Nick! You've got to tell me – what's really going on here?' Lianne said urgently. 'This has nothing to do with you stealing one of their wretched RVs or them wanting to get hold of this code ...'

'You're right,' he said, clamping his hands on the steering wheel. 'I thought I could get us to safety by staying incommunicado, but having to give out my ID in Colorado Springs obviously blew my cover. They must have people inside the communications centre, passing on information—'

'Who are "they"?' she shouted back.

He switched on the rear camera and zoomed in, displaying a pixelated image of the jeep. Lifting his hands off the wheel and swinging around to face her, he said, with his head slightly bowed, 'Shortly after I was seconded, I got an anonymous tip-off from someone in CENHQ, saying I was in danger if I remained in CENCOM. I made discreet enquiries and heard a rumour that during the short rapprochement between Drake and McFall, the Restoration Party had placed a number of their people in the Lincoln office. It wasn't confirmed and I never met any of these pro-McFall types, but a number of things began to—'

'So this isn't a CENCOM snatch squad, Nick. They're McFall sympathisers, aiming to collect the bounty on your head – and mine.'

As she spoke, the vehicle veered off to the right, following a track into dense woodland.

'Where in tarnation are we going?' she yelled.

'Shortcut. Hold on – it's going to be a bumpy one,' he said, swivelling back round and placing both hands on the steering wheel. 'We're not far from one of the back doors to the facility – they can't follow us in there.'

The RV rocked to one side, causing Nick to grip the steering wheel more tightly and scrutinise the front camera.

'Are you driving this thing?' she shouted.

'Just holding on in case they override the guidance mechanism,' he said grimly.

A flash of light appeared on all five external cameras. 'They're firing at us!' she cried out, as the roof monitor showed a searing line of flame, incinerating the tree canopy above them.

'Shit, they have attack drones as well!'

As he spoke, the vehicle swerved sharply in several directions to avoid burning branches, before plummeting into a narrow limestone valley.

Nick jumped up, steadied himself on the stair rail and slid down the stairs.

'Where the fuck are you—?'

She stopped as she heard the lower hatch open and close, and then saw on the display panel in front of her a light come on, indicating that the rear door to the vehicle had been unlocked. Staring at the array of controls in front of her, she pressed a button marked *Internal Lower*. There, on the monitor, she watched as Nick rolled an open drum of gasoline towards the door and then released it down the ramp and onto the road.

Looking over at the rear camera, she saw the drum clip the edge of the cliff in front of the approaching jeep and explode, engulfing the vehicle in flames. She continued to look on as the smoke cleared, only to see the vehicle emerge, still in pursuit and, on the other camera, Nick now pouring gas from a plastic container directly onto the rough stone track.

As he did so, the liquid burst into a dancing wall of flame, racing down the road towards the jeep, only then to shoot back into the lower deck of the RV, causing alarms to sound all around her. Unable to see him through the thick smoke, she looked over at the outside rear camera, which showed the jeep now stationary, abutting the wall of the cliff some distance back.

Turning to the controls again, she frantically panned the camera around the lower deck. Still unable to see through the smoke, she scrambled towards the stairs just as the lower hatch opened, releasing a rush of hot smoke and the overpowering smell of gasoline. As the overhead sprinklers switched on, spraying her with water, she heard a loud *whoosh* and then saw Nick, a fire extinguisher in his hand, crawling up the steps, his clothes singed and his face bright red. Pushing past her, he ran over to the driving seat and zoomed in the front-end camera.

'There it is!' he said, pointing to a spot on the white cliff ahead of them.

'Where?' she implored.

'Right there!' he roared, jabbing his finger at the monitor as two flashing green lights appeared on the cliff face.

'Huh? But where's the—?'

She anxiously clamped her hands over her head and then gasped in astonishment, as an opening appeared in the cliff between the lights.

Pointing to a corresponding green light on the panel in front of him, Nick said, 'The navigation system has locked in; we'll be okay now.'

As he spoke, the vehicle slowed and then veered sharply to the left into a pitch black hole.

Lianne fell back onto her seat with a jolt, but noticed Nick still gripping the edge of the desk, one fist clenched and his teeth bared.

'What is it?' she said.

'They really shouldn't have done that. They're in deep shit now!' he bellowed, as the rear camera showed the headlights of the jeep still pursuing them.

Lianne grabbed the edge of her seat as, once more, the RV turned abruptly to one side before coming to a sudden stop, throwing them both forward. For a few seconds, they sat in total darkness, both breathing heavily.

'Where are we now?' she asked, panting slightly, as the lights came back on in the driving cabin and the vehicle started to rumble slowly forward.

'Welcome to Hotel Cordillera,' Nick said calmly. 'Those clowns back there are in for a real shock.'

'Will they find their way out?'

'Not quickly – they're in a side tunnel. But by the time they do, we'll have identified who they are – God help them when they go outside.'

'What will they—?' Lianne stopped speaking and leant forward, studying the front camera. 'Are we inside or outside of this mountain?' she asked, as through a growing arch of light, tree branches came into view, dipping down towards a leaf-strewn track.

'Decidedly inside,' Nick replied as they passed into a wooded glade. 'No point in building things like this unless you can simulate the best of what we have out there.'

Lianne reached down to pull on her shoes, but Nick signalled for her to stay seated. 'We're not in the hotel yet,' he said. 'This is a sort of reception area to get people and their vehicles cleaned up. Just sit back and enjoy it a while. We pipe all the excess CO_2 into this chamber. We may not like it, but it sure makes the plants thrive. Before we leave, however, both we and the RV need to be fully decontaminated.'

'That's a little extreme, isn't it?'

'It may seem so, but this is a closed environment – any contamination or disease could quickly destroy the whole ecosystem of the facility. It was built as a retreat in the event of a major nuclear attack, so the procedures are quite rigorous.'

'But that's not what happened?'

'Can't change procedure, I'm afraid.'

'How long's this all going to take?' she asked, as they left the wooded landscape and entered a harshly lit concrete cell with pipes and brushes extending in all directions.

'A little longer than normal because of that radioactive gas I released to scare off the rednecks in Hardin.'

'An hour?'

'Umm ... why don't we go downstairs and relax after all that excitement? Did you find anything to watch when I was up here?'

'I sure did, and if you've not yet viewed it, you need to,' she said, walking towards the stairwell.

Lying on the bed, she handed him the remote. 'Okay, we've made it to your so-called hotel, can you now fix it so that you can watch the scene called "The Third Voice", while I watch whatever's on that file marked "Arriving"?'

'I need to log into the Allied system before the mechanical part of this cleaning routine begins,' he said, quickly flicking through a series of diagrams displayed on the screen above them. 'What did you make of Katharina?' he asked, as he studied the images.

'She's amazing, but has it ever occurred to you that having her in your head – challenging your knee-jerk responses – leaves less room for others? How does that play out with this idea of increasing cooperation among people? Won't she make everyone even more isolated and self-reliant?'

'The users still have to make all the judgements and take decisions – remember she "assists" not "insists".'

'But she's got a mind of her own – that doesn't worry you?'

'I'm in,' he said, ignoring her question. 'I've connected to the facilities communication system.' He slipped back down on the pillow. 'The cleaning will take a few hours – shall we take a nap first after all the fun and games?'

'Let's immerse,' Lianne said, taking out her VR specs from the side panel.

Nick rubbed his eyes and picking up the remote, moved it across several icons on the ceiling screen. 'Okay, this is the last scene. You watch this, while I check out whatever Methuen and Katharina said that made you so gloomy.'

'I wasn't gloomy, just wary,' she insisted, fitting on her glasses.

'You were happy for Bliss to have her IT, weren't you? Katharina's just a different way to improve our all-round thinking capability.'

'Well, maybe I'm more in Methuen's court now.'

'Which is?'

'That we don't need any of this cognitive enhancement – our unadulterated brains are more than adequate to sort things out. We just need to be better at working together.'

'That's just the sort of thing Katharina will help us do,' Nick said genially as the new scene started up.

AA-Com File: Arriving

Virtual Scene snapshot: Methuen is peering through binoculars from the window of the control room, while Elizabeth studies the ship's log.

'Sixth day out of Faial. Repairs to the second engine complete; cargo repositioned; moving west in calm seas for the past twelve hours …' she began to read, but then stopped as Methuen pointed at something through the window.

'Land ahoy, I think,' he said, only to look round in surprise as an alarm went off, followed by the sound of someone running up the stairs.

'Seafloor shelving,' Marco shouted, running to the wheel and turning off the alarm. 'Over there,' he said, redirecting Methuen's focus. 'It's one of the, umm … outer islands of the chain.'

Nick appeared, bleary-eyed, his shirt hanging open and his trousers unbelted. 'Where are we precisely, Marco?' he asked.

'A little over, umm … ten nautical miles from Silliman's Cay,' Marco said, reading from the screen in front of the him.

'Wind's picking up,' Nick said, hurriedly buttoning his shirt as Elizabeth made way for him at the wheel.

'Twenty knots and increasing,' Methuen read from another screen.

'What's the forecast giving us, Marco?' Nick demanded.

'There is, uh … a deep depression to the north, but this is, umm … out of date by a few hours. It's, uh … a type of weather system this on-board software doesn't handle very well,' he said, typing into a keyboard.

'Come on, get this sorted,' Nick growled, his voice still thick with sleep.

'It's, uh … definitely deepened,' Marco said, as he compared two synoptic charts on a screen. 'I think we'll have to find shelter to avoid it. It's coming in from the, uh … north-west and will hit us as we enter the island chain around teatime.'

'Can we race it down to Phillips?'

'No chance,' Marco replied adamantly, shaking his head.

'So where's the nearest hurricane hole?'

Marco studied the chart on the screen. 'Troy Cay, but, uh … I don't know any of the people there and in the present situation …' he said, turning his attention back to the weather charts.

Nick moved over to the communication booth and brought up a set of hydrographic maps on a large monitor. 'Looks like there'll be enough water for us to shelter there without needing to tie up in their marina – that is if they'll let us in.'

'Surely they wouldn't object to us anchoring in the channel and using the island as protection?' Methuen asked.

'Shall I, uh … reset the course?' Marco asked.

'Yes,' Nick replied, 'and while you're about it, I'll put the tower up and try to get hold of Wallace on Phillips – see what he knows about this place.'

* * *

Virtual Scene snapshot: Three hours on. Everyone is gathered in the control room, watching through the front window as the *Clipper* slowly motors along a narrow channel, bordered on either side by vertical walls of rock.

'Troy East,' Marco called out, pointing to a huge stub of limestone, gleaming in the sunset.

They all stood in silence as the ship glided along the channel, that curved like the whorls of a snail shell, revealing first the barren island of Troy West and then, in the innermost coil, the resort of Troy Central.

'The marina's small,' Nick said, standing at the control room window, training his binoculars at the settlement ahead. 'It's not even built for large motor cruisers, let alone something the size of the *Clipper*.'

'You seem nervous?' Methuen remarked.

'After opening the resort on Phillips, we took a lot of their trade. The owners are not on my Christmas card list, and I'm not on theirs.'

Over the PA, a staccato voice rang out. '*Allied Clipper*, *Allied Clipper*, this is Troy Central. We have no dockage available for you and no provision facilities. We advise you to go south to Phillips Cay.'

Nick leapt over to the wheel and switching on a small radio set, replied in sharp detached tones: 'Troy Central, Troy Central, this is *Allied Clipper*. Message received. We seek only shelter from the incoming storm. We have no resource needs. Thank you.'

There followed a silence, and then the same voice was heard again, but firmer now and more insistent: '*Allied Clipper*, *Allied Clipper*, this is Troy Central. Negative on that. Because of the developing situation elsewhere, we have declared all navigable waters within three miles of Troy Central out of bounds except for craft registered with the resort. We request that you sail south immediately.'

'Shut the engines!' Nick ordered Marco. 'Drag the light anchor and bring us to a stop. I wouldn't put it past them to have netted the channel ahead.'

The ship slowed and then a loud splash was heard, followed seconds later by a gentle rocking motion as the waves, rebounding off the rocky walls of the channel, lapped against the ship.

'Water depth?' Nick bellowed.

'Twenty fathoms … Twenty-one … no, twenty,' Marco said nervously.

'We have to stay here for the night,' he muttered to no one in particular. Then, with more urgency in his voice, he turned to Marco. 'Get a few of the boys on external watch and alarm all decks. Someone might get it into their head to pay us a visit.'

'Troy Central, Troy Central, this is *Allied Clipper*,' Nick said calmly into the radio mic. 'We hear your request but it's too dark for us to turn the ship around safely tonight. If we collided with anything, we could block your exit for weeks. I copy your request; we'll be gone in the morning.'

A more extended silence ensued, during which time Nick and Marco moved to the window, scanning the marina for signs of any response. After several minutes, a more official-sounding voice came over the airwaves. 'Copy that, *Allied Clipper*. Please do not attempt to come ashore. You are to leave by first light tomorrow. During the night you are to extinguish all illumination. Do you copy?'

'Copy,' Nick answered flatly. Switching off the radio, he hunched his shoulders and said, 'They've never been a very friendly lot, but I'm surprised they're quite so insistent we don't go ashore.'

'Requesting us to extinguish our lights is also a bit odd, isn't it?' Elizabeth asked, still scanning the marina through binoculars.

'They fear rogue drones will lock onto them,' Nick replied flatly.

'Strange – I thought this was a holiday resort?' Marco blurted out, nudging Nick as he pointed ahead of him.

'What is it?' Nick asked, raising his binoculars.

'Two military-looking boats moored up beside the reception building and ... yes, they're both armed.'

'Marco's right,' Elizabeth joined in. 'There's two ... no, wait, three, all with small gun turrets. Looks more like Alcatraz than a holiday resort,' she said, looking anxiously at Nick.

'Yeah, I see them. We need to be careful,' he responded.

'Can't we still reverse out?' Methuen asked.

'No, no, any movement now might, umm … panic them,' Marco interjected.

'I agree. I don't fancy being target practice with the weaponry they have on those boats,' Nick said. 'Bring up the two AK 101s from the hold, Marco. Oh, and tell the boys they're *all* on duty tonight.'

'What about trying to get hold of Wallace again?' Methuen asked.

'Let's play it safe … complete radio silence. I'll lower the tower and … everyone turn off their teleplants,' Nick added, before disappearing down the stairs.

* * *

Virtual Scene snapshot: It is early morning. The sun is peeping over the pale ridge of Troy North with a gentle warm wind blowing in from the west. Everyone other than Bliss is assembled in the control room. One of the trainees is laying out breakfast things on the coffee table in the seating area.

'Okay, let's get out of here,' Nick called out, taking the wheel and turning to the radio mic. 'Troy Central, Troy Central, this is *Allied Clipper*. We are now leaving anchorage at 04.55 hours. Have a nice day,' he said chirpily.

'Copy that, *Allied Clipper*,' came the immediate reply.

'Mmm … they're awake. They clearly have a twenty-four-seven watch,' Nick said, flicking a switch to raise the anchor. 'Okay, slowly does it. No one makes any calls or goes on deck.'

As the *Clipper* completed its turning manoeuvre, three muffled shots rang out, followed by the faint sound of someone screaming.

'Get down, get down,' Nick shouted, as he increased the power of the side thrusters. 'Are they shooting at us?'

'No!' Marco replied, staring at a camera display. 'There's, uh … a small launch …'

His voice trailed off as more shots were heard, followed by silence except for a slight vibrating sound as the *Clipper* moved out along the channel.

Lianne looked over at Nick. 'Are we—'

'Get down, get down,' Nick screamed, as another round of dull thuds was heard, causing Marco to enlarge the image on the rear camera. As he played with the controls, he suddenly fell to the floor. 'They, uh ... shot them,' he cried out.

'Yeah, I saw them aiming their guns,' Nick said. 'Everyone – keep your heads down,' he shrieked, and then, looking over at Methuen, said, 'Read out the water depth and channel width as we move forward. I can't go full ahead yet or the bow wave might push us on to the rocks.'

As Lianne crawled across the control room floor, picking up pieces of broken china, Bliss stumbled into the room, her face streaked with tears.

'Get down!' Nick screamed at her. 'No one stands up until Marco gives the all-clear.'

Bliss scrambled across the room on all fours to where her mother and now Lianne were crouched beneath the window.

'I saw them!' she said, holding back a sob. 'They just shot a family of three. I was strolling around the middle deck when a bullet zinged off the cliff. It smashed one of the windows. The guy shooting was in some sort of uniform and was giving orders to a group of men. I saw them get in a boat.'

'Nick, d'you hear that? They've launched a boat!' Lianne yelled.

'Got it,' he shouted back. 'Marco – anyone following us?'

'They're circling the bits in the water ... No, wait, wait, uh ... One minute ... Yes, yes, they are, uh ... heading our way, Nick!'

'Methuen,' Nick snapped, 'keep an eye on them but be careful. Elizabeth, you take over the readings from the echo sounder. Marco, go down to the lower deck, seal it off and then arm the rear.'

Nick looked urgently across at Elizabeth. 'I'm waiting for two hundred and fifty metres wide and thirty fathoms before I can go to full power.

'Nick!' Lianne called out, her arm around Bliss. 'You need to get down yourself.'

'That's my call,' he replied sharply.

Elizabeth peeped over the railings to read off the channel dimensions from the echo sounder. As soon as she called out two hundred and forty-eight, the ship surged forward, throwing her to the ground and the remaining breakfast things onto the floor.

The combination of the light hull and additional side thrusters allowed the *Clipper* to move quickly along the channel, but when Lianne scrambled over to pick up the broken china, a shot whizzed through the back of the control room, leaving a neat hole in the glass window at the front.

'Marco!' Nick roared down the speaker tube. 'If they fire again, hit them with the missile gun.'

'Can you copy that, Nick? You want me to hit them next time—?'

Before he could finish his question, a hail of bullets flew past the control room, followed, as if on cue, by a small blast and seconds later, a loud explosion.

The *Clipper* continued to accelerate and soon the white undercut honeycombed cliffs on either side were replaced by the calm turquoise waters of the Inner Chain.

Marco appeared at the top of the staircase, sweating and agitated. 'Was that okay?' he said, walking over to a monitor and displaying an image behind them of smoke rising over the promontory of Troy East. 'I think we may have, uh … blocked the channel – they won't be able to follow us for now,' he said, breathing heavily.

'Our missile gun really works then,' Nick responded buoyantly, shaking his head and releasing a loud burst of laughter.

'Really works,' agreed Marco, likewise grinning in relief.

'Will they come after us?' Methuen asked, not joining in the laughter.

'No, but they won't forget, and they know where to find us. I'll try and call Wallace again and give him a heads-up,' Nick said, disappearing downstairs.

Everyone stood up, exhausted but relieved. As Lianne struggled to her feet, the handle of a teacup still wrapped around her finger, she chirped, 'Tea, anyone?'

* * *

Virtual Scene snapshot: Two hours later. The O'Gradys and the Pryces are finishing breakfast on the small foredeck of the control room.

Nick pointed to the bow of the ship and beckoned Methuen to follow him. There, resting on the port railing, he raised his head to savour the rush of fresh salty air and pointed to a small island skirted with debris, showing the effects of the latest sea surge.

'How long do you reckon, before they're all submerged?' he asked.

'I'm less sure than I used to be,' Methuen said. 'Our mid-range predictions in the 2020s were too conservative by half. The measurable rise is still small, but year-on-year, it's now closer to exponential than linear. If that trend continues, then by 2100 it could give us up to half a metre rise – mainly from the ice melt off Antarctica, although there's a lot of debate now about the additional contribution from Greenland. Were that to speed up, you may get another call from your Chinese friends – irrespective of politics.'

'All these islands are already dead, of course,' Nick said. 'Any drinking water was contaminated long ago. The work we did for P2150 indicated that ninety per cent of this chain will be submerged within fifty years, including Stanton, the nearest settlement to Phillips with more than three thousand inhabitants.'

'And Phillips?'

'Other than the hilly northern end, it'll be fully submerged by 2125. Only Main Island will remain substantially above water.'

'So why not move the community there? Wouldn't it be easier for the construction work not having to cope with these storm surges?'

Nick paused but then said firmly, 'As I mentioned before, the history of Phillips and Main is a little complicated. When my father transferred the lease to me in 2015—'

'What do you mean the "lease" – I thought you owned it?' Methuen cut in.

'No, no, Phillips and Main were acquired by the US government from the Phillips family a long time ago. My father inherited, from his father, a hundred-year lease that started in 1950. When he handed it to me, he stipulated that Main was to stay uninhabited and be allowed to return to nature. It's the only virgin island habitat remaining in the whole chain, maybe in the whole Caribbean – and that's the way it's going to stay until it's flooded, okay?' he said sharply.

Methuen looked at him in surprise and, hunching his shoulders, said with a short laugh, 'Sure, I've no problem with that.'

They stood in silence until Nick said quietly, 'You know we're not staying on Phillips, right?'

'Well, I never expected you'd remain with us for long—'

'No, but it's going to be even shorter than I'd originally planned. Last Tuesday, McFall threw all Allied staff out of the Portland yard. There was a bit of skirmish and one of our Associates was killed, while the rest had to run for their lives. Many of them have gone to a small, Allied supply yard in Southport, Maine. That's where I need to go ... tomorrow.'

'Tomorrow!' Methuen exclaimed, his head jolting back.

'And we're not coming ashore – this is your show now,' Nick said, turning towards the breakfast table, where the women were talking. 'Let's go back and join them, but say nothing about the ransacking of the yard. I don't want Lianne any more upset than she is already.'

* * *

Virtual Scene snapshot: It is midday. The prominent upstanding land-mass of Main Island now dominates the horizon, with Phillips off to the right, visible as a low line of cliffs, along the top of which three evenly spaced buildings can be seen separated by dense woodland.

Elizabeth wafted into the control room in a light summer dress, her hair tied back, holding a floppy straw hat. 'Why are we stopping?' she asked Marco at the wheel.

'It's, uh … Racing Channel. Even the *Clipper* has to be careful crossing it,' he said, laughing a little uneasily.

Following behind on the stairs, Nick, in a lightweight suit, walked over to Elizabeth and cupped a hand under her elbow. 'Let me point out some features of your new home,' he said, picking up a pair of binoculars as he opened the door to the foredeck.

'You can show both of us,' she replied, pointing over to Methuen, who was already standing at the bow.

As they approached, Methuen turned to Nick and asked, 'Are those three houses on the cliff occupied? The middle one looks pretty dilapidated.'

Nick scanned the skyline. 'It got singled out by a small tornado that tore through the resort a few years ago and ripped the roof off. I'm surprised it's not been repaired yet. The other two are in good shape,' he added positively. 'They're built with a concrete and steel frame to withstand the strong winds we seem to be getting more of these days. The biggest building is Hampton House at the far end. That's our place when we visit – which hasn't been often …' His voice tailed off at the sound of heavy grinding as the main anchor began to be lifted.

Even now in the slack tide, the Clipper was tossed from side to side as it progressed slowly across Racing Channel and into a narrow passage marked on either side by buoys.

Nick walked to the starboard side and calling Methuen over, pointed down at the ship's hull. 'This is a sophisticated waterway,' he said. 'The buoys are full of electronics that take over the navigation system of all vessels, ensuring they don't hit any of those.' He pointed outside the channel to shoals of rock, sticking out of the water like shark fins.

As they passed around a wide bend, Nick leapt in the air and screamed out, 'Oh, for Christ's sake!' And then holding his hand to his ear and dashing back to the control room, he could be heard shouting down the speaker tube, 'Obstruction! Obstruction! Stop – *stop*, goddammit!'

Methuen joined Elizabeth on the port side and stared at the bow of a large motor cruiser, one hundred yards ahead, protruding into the channel. Three blasts, loud enough to rattle the set of china on the breakfast table, were followed by a rumbling groan as the engines of the *Clipper* were put into reverse.

As the ship began to move slowly forward again, Nick returned to the port railings and waved his fists at the retreating vessel and a small flotilla of boats further back.

'What the fuck are you doing?' he screamed at a group of young men on the deck of a large motor cruiser. 'Bloody boat people!' he shouted at Marco, who had rushed up from below to see what was happening.

Marco smiled meekly at Methuen, and then, turning to Elizabeth, pointed ahead of them. 'As you will remember from your previous visit, this is what we call Reception Basin,' he said, pointing to an area of open water ahead, 'and that's Reception Quay,' he added, directing their attention to a long wooden structure extending towards them.

'And who are all these people?' Elizabeth asked, nodding at the clusters of boats moored in a semicircle to her left.

Marco was about to reply when Nick, who had started filming the flotilla of craft with his handheld, said angrily, 'They're all hoping to gain entry to Phillips, but it's not going to happen!'

'The crowd over there look friendly enough,' Elizabeth said, pointing to a tightly bound, central group of boats, on which men, women and children could be seen waving vigorously.

Nick made no reply, having fixed his gaze on a long, narrow white ship anchored close to Reception Quay and against which more than a dozen small vessels were moored.

'Whose owns that?' Methuen asked as he saw Nick continuing to film.

'Someone who shouldn't be here,' he replied sharply and then rotated round as the sound of an outboard motor coming from the direction of the quay, started up.

As the *Clipper* came to a halt, Nick bent over the port bow and looked down at a twin-engined launch, steered by a gangly-looking man dressed in a khaki outfit and holding an unlit pipe in his hand.

'Good trip?' the man called up, in a slightly forced, detached voice. 'I assume all your vaccination certificates are up to date?'

'Wallace, what the fuck is going on here?' Nick said, waving his arm at the long white ship.

'Arrived a few days ago … Nothing I could do … just motored in here. All under control though. Made a deal with the head man,' he said and then, without waiting for a reply, spun the launch back towards the quay, where people had begun to gather.

Without saying a word, Nick strode off into the control room as the *Clipper* began slowly to pirouette in the basin.

* * *

Virtual Scene snapshot: One hour on. The *Clipper* has now docked at the wooden quayside, where a large crowd is gathered.

Methuen, his shirtsleeves rolled up, is standing at the end of the gangway, talking with several trainees from the ship.

'If you want to help, Professor Pryce, could you drag that large hawser over here?' one of the young men was heard to say.

'Grady,' Lianne called out, elbowing the languid body stretched out beside her.

'What's wrong, what's wrong?' Nick shot up, snatching off his glasses.

'This is in General View. Can you switch it to Elizabeth's perspective?'

'What? Oh, good God, Lianne, you frightened the wits out of me!' Grabbing the remote, he displayed the Storymaker dashboard and after playing with the controls lay back on his pillow. 'No more interruptions, right? I was just about to get into that section where Methuen and Katharina interact for the first time.'

'Okay, stay cool … you'll be able to ask Katharina for a bedtime lullaby, very soon,' she sniggered.

AA-Com File: Arriving *(contd)*

Allied Clipper, Phillips Cay, Caribbean Confederation
Late morning, 28 February 2050

Virtual Scene snapshot: Elizabeth stands at the bow of the control room foredeck, observing the crowd that has filled a small gravelled square in front of the ship.

A loud mechanical crack caused Elizabeth to twist around sharply, as she saw Methuen, sweating profusely while he helped two of the trainees secure the metal gangway onto the wooden quay.

'I hope you're watching this, Lianne,' she said to herself. 'Here's Methuen making a real effort to be a part of the community, rather than hold himself apart as you feared. Good on you, pal!'

She turned back to scrutinise the people down in the square. *Must be forty, even fifty here ... all grown-ups ... and look at those two old biddies, sharing a frilly parasol. Ah, there's a younger one ... No, wait a minute, she's holding a wheelchair for someone with a blanket over their knees – in this weather! What's Nick expecting us to do – create a self-sufficient community for retirees? At least they all look reasonably happy ... Though, hang on, some of those standing at the back have rather long faces.*

Scanning the crowd, her attention was suddenly caught by a tall woman in a baggy bathrobe and sunglasses, who had boldly walked down the quay and was now in conversation with Methuen.

He's making a little bow ... and now she's ... tucked her arm in his! Where are they off to? Who is this? Ah, look, there's Bliss ... with Lianne, who's actually carrying her own luggage – well, I've never seen that before. Typical Lianne though, ignoring everyone around her ... and now they've disappeared into that long wooden building ... where's Methuen gone?

Elizabeth made her way to the upper deck and then raced down the gangway, gripping the rails. As she stepped onto the wooden quay she felt a little giddy and someone grab her arm.

'Remember me,' an elderly man croaked.

'Harvey, how lovely to see you again. When did you arrive?'

'It seems like ages ago, but it's only been two weeks. You look as if you haven't found your land legs yet,' he said taking her arm.

As they worked their way through the crowd, with Harvey making impromptu introductions, Elizabeth caught sight of the woman who had been talking to Methuen – and who now appeared slimmer but older. She was about to call over to him, when a tall black athletic-looking man pushed past Methuen and, holding his hand out, greeted her with a broad engaging smile.

'You're Elizabeth Pryce, aren't you? I recognise you from the TV. I do so admire what you did in the States with the NCC,' he gushed in a beautiful deep baritone voice, his rounded diction almost hollow in its clarity. 'I'm Bradley Raymonds, and this is my ...' He turned to introduce the woman who had befriended Methuen, but as Elizabeth held out her hand, the woman pulled back and simply nodded in acknowledgement.

Before Elizabeth could respond to the apparent rebuff, a tinny blast of feedback from a megaphone made her clamp her hands over her ears. Looking round, she saw Wallace on a raised terrace in front of a wooden, single-storey building, the unlit pipe still in his hand.

'Would all members of the *Clipper* party please follow me,' he called out officiously.

Elizabeth turned to Bradley and brushed his upper arm playfully with her hand. 'Hope to see you soon,' she said, giving the briefest of smiles to the woman beside him.

'No one else to join us?' Wallace asked, as Elizabeth and Methuen appeared at the foot of the terrace. 'Where's Nick?'

Methuen butted in before Elizabeth had a chance to reply. 'Uh, something urgent came up on the AA-Com – he'll contact you.'

'No matter,' Wallace said, stepping down into the square. 'I have the two most important people here – the rest will have to find their own way.'

Turning around, he pointed out the building behind him. 'You may remember, this is the reception office and attached to it is the store – the best supermarket in the whole island chain, or at least it was ...' he said, his voice trailing off.

Stopping at the corner of the square, he waved at the large low-rise building to their right, into which Elizabeth had seen Lianne and Bliss disappear earlier. 'This is the clubhouse. These days it's multipurpose, acting as a bar, restaurant and the place where we meet up and occasionally get entertained,' he explained blandly.

As they followed a wide concrete path out of the square, Elizabeth noticed that their departure seemed to act as a signal for the crowd to disperse. *No one said a word; they just collectively decided to leave. How very disciplined, not to mention peculiar. And it's all so extraordinarily smart and tidy ... Look at that! Not one single person stepping on the grass.*

After a few minutes, they came to a fork in the path, where those ahead of them peeled off towards a small bay on the left. Through a line of palm trees, Elizabeth could make out rows of bobbing boats separated by wooden staging and the faint sound of lanyards clipping in the wind.

'You'll remember the marina,' Wallace said, seeing the direction of her gaze. 'A few people have moved into the nearby holiday villas, but most seem to prefer the familiarity and comfort of the boats they arrived in.'

He beckoned them towards a narrower path that led uphill, with a neat green lawn rolling down to the marina on one side, and on the other, a wide fringe of trees, running along the rising cliff edge.

'Bit of a climb, I'm afraid, but well worth it once we get to the top,' he said, pointing to the crest of the hill, where a spur of the woodland shot south into the interior of the island.

After almost ten minutes of vigorous walking, the gradient eased and they entered a tunnel through the wood, their feet crunching on castor oil pods lying on the path. As they emerged back into bright sunlight, Wallace halted and waved his hands ahead of him. 'Quite a contrast, don't you think?'

Methuen and Elizabeth stared out at a sea of low-lying scrub, broken here and there by occasional knobs of white stone.

As they surveyed the new landscape, Wallace said more sternly, 'Stay vigilant if you leave the path – the ground is full of deep potholes. We can't do much about a broken leg here until the doctor arrives from the south ...' He then looked at Elizabeth, laughed a little nervously and added, 'Of course, that advice will be out of date as soon as you get all that medical kit working that was brought over from Stanton last month.'

They continued along the path, that was now little more than a rough stone track, until Wallace stopped again and swung round ninety degrees, pointing south to a rounded ridge that crossed the island. 'Beyond that line of hills is where we tuck away all the industrial equipment required to keep this place going. I'm sure you remember that, Dr Pryce, from our little reconnoitre together, a few years ago?'

'Elizabeth, please.'

But Wallace didn't respond to her request, instead striding off and continuing with his guided tour. 'The supply jetty's down that way. You can't fully see it from here, but that's where we land fuel and other materials. And over there,' he said, directing their attention to a tall white wooden building in the distance, 'is Hampton House – your new home.'

'My God, it's not a house, it's a mansion!' Elizabeth whispered to Methuen as they followed Wallace. 'What on earth are we going to do with all that space?'

'And in the back of beyond as well,' Methuen mumbled.

They walked in silence for another five minutes until they reached the steps of the house. Pulling out the unlit pipe from his pocket, Wallace now transformed himself into an estate agent. 'Four floors, the uppermost of which – where I imagine you'll spend most of your time – has a large living room with a kitchenette in one corner for your convenience. The room opens out onto a three-quarter wrap-around veranda that looks out to sea. Best view in the island chain, many say.'

Elizabeth noticed how Wallace assumed the door would not be locked but then, as he pushed it open, saw his look of surprise as voices issued down the stairwell.

'Oh, I see someone's arrived ahead of us. In that case, I'll leave you to it for now. I'll pop in later once you've settled,' he said, and without waiting for a reply headed back down the track.

* * *

Virtual Scene snapshot: It is evening. On the top-floor veranda of Hampton House, Elizabeth stands alone, staring out to sea.

This is all so new. Day passing so quickly into night and the air thick with humidity ... but there's no urban hum – how alien! how wonderful!

Leaning over the wooden balustrade, she started to sing.

'All things bright and beautiful,
All creatures great and small,
All things—'

What's that noise over there?

She walked to the end of the veranda and stared towards a row of bright lights in the bay, close to Reception Quay.

It won't be Nick and Lianne partying, that's for sure. She was so downbeat when she showed me around the house. Poor girl – she must have said 'this was my home' at least a dozen times. And then when we sat down, all she would drink was iced water. Come to think of it, I've not seen her touch a drop since that evening in Faial. I can't imagine that little confrontation at Troy Central helped – it probably made her even more fearful of what she might be going back to in the States.

Another burst of music blasted out and then cut off again.

It's coming from the top deck of that narrow ship – the one that upset Nick so much.

She gazed back into the night and returned to the hymn, but this time just humming the tune.

'You're not normally a hummer,' Methuen said jauntily, appearing with a tray of food and drinks, 'and certainly nothing religious.'

'It's my convent school upbringing,' Elizabeth said, turning around and laughing. 'Though I must say that until now, I'd not realised quite how wonderful the words were.'

Methuen rested his arm on the balustrade next to her. 'I remember: "All creatures great and small". What did you make of the creatures that greeted us this afternoon?' he asked.

'Not what I'd been expecting. I can't believe you planned for this lot to be part of the Phillips Project. I also got the distinct feeling that a few of them were holding something back, and I don't just mean those boat people out in the basin.'

'Who do you mean exactly?' Methuen said, sitting down and pouring drinks.

'Well, take Wallace. I don't know much about him and maybe I'm doing him a disservice, but I felt his hospitality was being dispensed more as a duty than something he wanted to do? And then there was ... what's her name, Belinda – the one who grabbed you and who I assume is the wife of that black chap. You were chattering away like former lovers.'

Methuen emitted one of his roaring belly laughs. 'Ha! You've got to be joking. She claims to have met me at some conference, but I have no recollection—'

'What about her husband? He smothered me with compliments. Do you know him?'

'I sure do. I've met him at several Allied functions. At one time he was chief technical officer for Livings and before that, in the private sector, the project manager for the Arctic Village oil and gas development in northern Russia. I'm puzzled as to why he's here though. He wasn't on the last list of candidates I saw for Phillips.'

'And then there was Harvey, who helped Lianne and Nick expose McFall. As much as I admire him, what role can he play here, or for that matter any of the older people here. He's even bought his wife and two sons. How do they all fit into your Plan?'

'That was one of the things that irritated me before I left. Livings didn't involve me in the final selection of people, just the skill mix required.'

'You mean you didn't build a virtual team and test it out?'

'Yes, of course we did, but it wasn't personalised, and certainly didn't include the army of boat people over there,' he said, pointing towards the basin. 'Nor what I assume are a whole load of hangers-on from when this was still a holiday resort.'

'And what about the two Russians – did you meet them?' she asked. 'The one who spoke English shook my hand, but the other one just leered at me. I saw them going over to the *Clipper* tonight – presumably invited by Nick. Why are *they* here?'

'Hmm. I'm sure there's some simple explanation,' Methuen said, rubbing his beard, 'although just this minute it escapes me.'

'Well,' she said grinning, with eyes wide, 'we must begin by reordering the estate.'

'Umm?' Methuen responded quizzically, causing Elizabeth to break back into song:

'The rich man in his castle,
The poor man at his gate,
God made them high and lowly,
And ordered their estate.'

'That's what I did when I set up the NCC in the UK,' she continued. 'I set the estate in order. There was so much political dispute over the idea that I simply focused on ensuring everyone knew their role and how it contributed to the overall goal of the organisation. The same applies here, doesn't it? You need to go through this Plan with me so I can understand how we're going to create this *new order* that will guide us through the next five years.'

'I will,' he replied, sounding cheered, 'as soon as my upgraded AVIII arrives and the Phillips dirigible is reinstated, we can get started. But first of all, let's find out where all that medical equipment is and convert the ground floor of this place into a clinic. We can't afford any "... rich man in his castle" or "poor man at his gate" here.'

Hotel Cordillera, Carlsbad, SCSA, FSA

18.30 hours, 18 June 2050

Nick nodded at the guard, who made no response as he opened the glass door leading into a sparsely furnished, windowless room. With the sound of the door locking behind him, he walked over to a bare wooden table and chair in the centre of the room. Sitting down he stared solemnly at three photographs on the opposite wall. The largest was of Farrell Kelvin Drake II draped in the FSA flag, while on either side, lower down, were smaller pictures of the Secretary of State for Intelligence and Communications (S/COM) and the Secretary of the Armed Services (S/DEF).

From his bag, he took out his AVIII and, placing it on the table, removed its transparent casing. Lightly touching the top of the device, he sat back, closed his eyes and practised his yoga breathing exercises.

'Good evening, Nick, it's good to see you relaxing,' came a soft calming voice in his head that once again reminded him so much of Elizabeth.

'It's been some time,' he mused.

'That's an interesting remark,' Katharina said coolly.

'Is it?' Nick replied, sitting up and frowning.

'It doesn't fit the reality. It's only been four days since we last spoke in Bismarck. I find it fascinating how the human mind experiences time so differently. My only thought about the duration was why you had not completed the journey more quickly, but then I didn't know about your decision not to travel during the day.'

'And now you do because I guess you downloaded the record of our journey from Lincoln – including the VR viewings?' he said.

'Yes, they were most absorbing – in particular, the information about Project 2150.'

'Well, you had to be told at some stage. Once I get the comms fully working, I'll instruct HQ to provide you with a detailed briefing. Before I do that, I need several updates – starting with the current status of the dirigible network reset,'

'Just under a sixth has been upgraded—'

'Does that include the dirigible we're connecting with now?'

'No, the Dallas dirigible has not yet been converted, like most located in the FSA. The Incident – as you call it – has slowed down everything.'

'Okay, contact Pico and prioritise that,' Nick said. 'We will be causing interference for local pre-AVIII users and drawing too much attention to the facility. Please continue, but let's make the conversation quick.'

'The main Allied centres in London and Singapore, as well as just over forty per cent of the regional offices, are now upgraded and functioning,' Katharina said. 'As you know, the global office in New York has been closed, along with several local offices in the FSA. Communication with CENHQ has recently experienced problems because of power outages in Minneapolis. The two Hub Tool Boxes on Pico, where I am located, are fully operational. The HTB on the *Allied Clipper* is shut down, as you instructed.'

'So ... I'm not talking with Katharina from the Clipper HTB?'

'It makes no difference, Nick, we are, as it were, one entity.'

'And where's the *Clipper* right now?'

'I was only able to stay connected with it intermittently via the AA-Com VII set in the control room. But since the twenty-seventh of April, when it moored on the Quai Constant Brisson – an industrial port near La Rochelle in France – there has been no contact.'

'What happened?' Nick asked urgently, leaning forward.

'I can only speculate.'

'Then speculate!'

'The AA-Com VII on-board the *Clipper* closed down at 09.30 hours precisely. It may just have been a power issue, but given the backup supply on the ship, this seems unlikely. The most probable explanation is intervention by a third party.'

Nick slumped back on the chair and clasped his hands to his face. 'What about Phillips?' he asked.

'I have had no communication with Phillips.'

'What do you mean, "no communication"?' he said, sitting up.

'As you know, on the tenth of February, Phillips lowered their dirigible, and on the twelfth sent it to Nassau to be upgraded, using the Stanton seaplane. They switched their AA-Com VII over to ALL-SAT but, as you are well aware, shortly after The Incident, ALL-SAT services were shut down by CENCOM and have not resumed.'

'Still not working,' Nick exclaimed to himself. 'What about the emergency military line Phillips had access to?'

'That was cut, shortly after your call to CENHQ on the morning of The Incident.'

'So, Phillips has no communication—'

'Not quite. When you left the Allied Campus and moved into the CENCOM compound, you made some brief communications with Pico using your AVIII—'

'It was very brief – I was being monitored all the time.'

'You also left a message on another AVIII located close to Phillips at the time—'

'Ah! You know about that. It was just on the off-chance that they might call in to Phillips. It was connected to CENCOM, so all I could do was leave a short recording. Has anyone responded?'

'I'm afraid not.'

'What about Methuen's AVIII? It wasn't in the New York office when we passed through in April – as Pico said it would be. Any news of where that has got to?'

'Sorry, Nick, we are in the dark as much as you over this matter. But I don't think you need worry too much. As you know, AVIIIs require regular use. If they are abandoned or lost, a self-destruct routine will initiate—'

'That's little comfort – it's like saying that even if I get knocked down in the road and badly injured, I don't need to worry because I'm well insured.'

'I take your point. Can you explain to me the origin of this other AVIII, near Phillips?'

'Not right now.'

There was a pause before Katharina said, 'It would be easier if you could share as much as you can with me, Nick?'

'After viewing that IA assessment of me on that AA-Com file the other day, I wonder how much I should share with any of you?'

'I don't understand. Do you have any reason not to trust *me*?' Katharina asked.

'We'll talk about it later. For now, please make every effort to stay on top of all news coming from the *Clipper* and Phillips.'

'Of course. Could I also ask what *your* plans are?'

'We'll remain here for the next few weeks.'

'Could you keep your AA-Plant switched on as you move around, so I can map the facility and become familiar with how everything is laid out?'

'I would,' Nick said, 'but unfortunately outside of this room, the radiation protection dampens all signals. In a few minutes, the door will open and I will have to leave. If I don't, this dosimeter will start bleeping,' he said, unclipping the small plastic object from his jacket and pointing it at the pyramid.

'You could make a recording and then come in here and download?' Katharina suggested.

'I could indeed but I'm going to be very busy – I simply don't have time to do that at present.'

'Can I ask you another question?'

'Go ahead,' Nick replied cautiously.

'Is this an Allied or CENHQ facility? The guard I can see through the glass door has CENHQ insignia on his uniform.'

Nick checked his watch and looked around him. 'Allied built this as a joint venture with CENHQ. We have security staff from both organisations here. Do you have a particular concern?'

'While you have been offline, I have been studying the political situation in the FSA and EUCON.'

'Uh-huh.'

A short silence ensued before Katharina added, 'It is in everyone's interest that we understand the security of the places that the HTBs access as well as reside in.'

'Who is "we"?'

'My counterparts in the other HTBs.'

'Ah, the interchangeable sisterhood,' Nick shot back. 'What was your colleagues' response to the decision to move the HTB from Lincoln to Pico?'

'We appreciate the stringent security measures you have put in place to protect the network. Our main concern is the limited geographical spread of the HTBs at present.'

'It's a temporary measure,' Nick said, glancing at his watch.

'I read the P2150 file dated the sixth of December 2049, when you viewed it in the VR scene entitled "A Day at the Office". I know you don't intend to stay here—'

Nick's dosimeter began to bleep loudly, prompting the guard to enter the room.

Nodding his head downwards three times to turn off his teleplant, Nick got up from the desk and muttered at the picture of President Drake, 'Who can I trust, who can I trust?'

Out in the wide carpeted corridor, people passed by, those that recognised him smiling politely. Further along, he stepped to one side and opened a door into a furnished cubicle.

'Good afternoon, sir,' an elderly male-bot said. 'Where would you like to go?'

'Can you find out where Lianne O'Grady is, and take me there?'

The bot stared back with a vacuous smile while it computed its answer. 'She is in the Forested Chamber. We have to go to the Accommodation Dome and then use a buggy. It shouldn't take more than fifteen minutes, sir.'

Nick took a seat, secured his safety belt, picked a magazine from the rack on the wall and nodded at the bot to proceed. The cubicle began to move, horizontally at first, and then, after a pause, upwards at greater speed.

Lianne adjusted her head on an inflatable mattress while paddling her feet to stay afloat. Gazing upwards through the tree branches, she watched as the light slowly faded from the glass dome above her and, as birdsong rose over the unfaltering trickle of water from a nearby stream, she closed her eyes.

SPLOSH

A huge wave swept Lianne onto the small sandy beach at the edge of the lake. Lifting her head, she saw Nick rise up and then flip over in front of her.

'Very funny,' she said cynically, slipping back into the warm water.

As he remained motionless, face down and floating, she glared in his direction, fully aware of his party piece of holding his breath until someone panicked and came to the rescue.

The light in the roof dimmed again and the air grew slightly cooler as Nick idly swam over to join her.

'So what's the big plan?' she asked, not meeting his eye. 'I don't mind this artificial world for now, but after a while I'm going to want real sunlight, not this reflected stuff.'

'You have real sunlight,' he said with a light-hearted laugh. 'That's what you get in the bedroom – the main window is cut all the way through the rock, to the outside.'

'Grateful for actual sunlight – shows how limited our lives have become ...'

'We're the lucky ones,' he said emphatically, and then with a hint of irritation added, 'Never forget that.'

Lianne pushed out a little way into the lake and then turned to face him. 'The lucky ones right now are those who've never known anything different. They don't miss how it was before – they fit into this new world in a way I just can't seem to manage.'

'No, I don't agree. The truly lucky ones are those who still have hope of a better future. That's what I'm trying to create with the Hub Commonwealth.'

'But only for the privileged few?'

'We can't start everywhere. We need to develop the formula for living sustainably and then pass it on to others.'

'So when are we off to Phillips?' she asked sharply.

Nick swam out beside her, and then, paddling with his head just above water, said, 'We're not going to Phillips – that's Methuen's responsibility now. Dry yourself off and I'll show you where we're heading.'

'Not another mountain tomb I hope,' Lianne said, throwing her bag into the back of a buggy.

'No, no – somewhere quite different,' he replied as she sat down beside him. 'Take a look at this,' he said, displaying a document on the dashboard monitor.

Project 2150
Progress Report
(18 June 2050)
Not for distribution without the written approval of the CEO of
Allied Answers

As the buggy moved off, he put his arm around her and said, 'This is the "entirely safe place" I was talking about ... Somewhere with all the fresh air and real sunlight you could ever need ... where the Segmented World will never gain a foothold.'

Acknowledgements

Living in the London polis for the past two decades, I have been fortunate in being able to tap into the wisdom of so many people – brought together by a wide range of organisations. I would therefore like to acknowledge the many lively debates I've attended at the Defence Security Forum, Chatham House, the Frontline Club, the London Futurist group, the, now sadly defunct London Oil Club, the RSA and most recently, Tortoise.

It would be remiss of me not to also acknowledge the incredible work of the UN and organisations such as *Our World in Data* and *V-Dem Institute* that provide the numbers that are the essential starting point for anyone trying to build a reasoned view of future events.

In the early stages of the book I benefitted from an excellent review by Karl French, a stimulating edit from Monica Byles and, throughout the production process, skilful guidance from Caroline McArthur and the rest of the whitefox team.

Trapped, as most of us were during the first lockdown, my spirits were lifted by a gang of readers, who provided me with a late read-through. I thank them all, but particularly Sally and Sarah Gibson, Anne and Katie Molyneux, Suzi Oliver, Joe Staffurth and Sandra Webb. Also at various times I had useful comments and advice from Andrew Cox, Bernice Daly, Jonathan Nash and David Pirie.

Last, but certainly not least, I wish to thank my partner Janette Steel, who, during a wet and windy holiday in the Highlands, first convinced me to pursue my writing and has remained a constant source of encouragement and inspiration.

To find out about the 'real' Segmented World and more about the 'fictional' one, please visit www.thesegmentedworld.com